THE LIGHTSTRUCK

Also by Sunya Mara:

The Darkening

THE LIGHTSTRUCK

SUNYA MARA

HODDER &
STOUGHTON

First published in Great Britain in 2023 by Hodder & Stoughton
An Hachette UK company

1

Copyright © Sunya Mara 2023

The right of Sunya Mara to be identified as the Author of the Work has been asserted
by her in accordance with the Copyright, Designs and Patents Act 1988.

A CIP catalogue record for this title is available from the British Library

Hardback ISBN 978 1 529 35550 5
Trade Paperback ISBN 978 1 529 35551 2
eBook ISBN 978 1 529 35552 9

Printed and bound in Great Britain by Clays Ltd, Elcograf S.p.A.

Hodder & Stoughton policy is to use papers that are natural, renewable and recyclable
products and made from wood grown in sustainable forests. The logging and manufacturing
processes are expected to conform to the environmental regulations of the country of origin.

Hodder & Stoughton Ltd
Carmelite House
50 Victoria Embankment
London EC4Y 0DZ

www.hodder.co.uk

To the light,
creator of shadows

The Lightstruck

CHAPTER 1

They say I didn't want to be born. That I stayed in my mother's belly far longer than I was welcome. That Ma was furious, storming about the healer's rooms, commanding them to hasten my departure.

She wasn't callous. She was needed by her people. The Storm was a great torment, a wall of black stormcloud and violet lighting that birthed rampaging beasts and bestowed curses on all whom it touched. Every day it squeezed our kingdom tighter—in Ma's day, it swallowed the farms of the sixth ring inch by inch. In my time, it was halfway through the fifth. Only our ruler, the Regia, had the god-given power to stop the Storm. But he was weak, and my mother believed she could do what he could not.

And she loved me, but what did the needs of one child matter when thousands were suffering? Any mother could protect her own child. But to protect a kingdom? That required a hero.

Ma left me in my father's arms and died trying to save us all. They called her a criminal.

Seventeen years after I was cut out of her, I fought the Regia's son before all our people, in the sands of our great stadium. They saw me weep, they saw me fight, they saw me end the Storm.

Ma would've been proud. I died a hero.

The world of the dead isn't so different from the world above. The palace still gleams cold and indifferent, perched like a crown atop our five-ringed city. The fifth ring is still home to the poor, where buildings crowd together like a mouth full of crooked teeth, where the same old moss still coats our roofs, in a layer of wet, mildly fragrant greenery that's springy underfoot. We even have the ghost of the Storm; but down here it's a wall of white nothingness that encircles the city. It can't be entered; it can't be fought.

There are some things that are different. Up above, there's only one way to enter the city: you're born into it. Here . . .

A crack of distant thunder. Here one comes.

The pale ghost sky opens up, parting like an eye, just wide enough for something small to fall through. A thunderous rumble follows as it—a body, with limbs folded tight—descends to our phantom city. Here comes the newly dead, fresh off of life.

The body falls like a feather on the wind. Gently swinging to and fro.

The slate roof of the watchtower creaks under my weight as I rise to my feet, without taking my eyes off our newest resident. Not until I get a read for where they're falling, where their soul considers home.

The radius of their swinging narrows. Not the fifth ring, then, nor the fourth. Interesting. When I first came here, most folks came from the outermost ring, the fifth. Curses, malnutrition, that sort of thing.

But now folks come from all sorts of places, with all sorts of interesting stories. Why, I met a peculiar fellow just the other day who'd died of heatstroke. No one died of heatstroke when we all lived under the damp shadow of the Storm.

There's no more Storm up there, of course. Not since I ended it. Not since I took within me the god who gave the Storm its power. To save every single living soul up there, all I had to do was sacrifice my own.

I like to think of what Ma would've said. Possibly something noble and stoic, like: *As it should be.*

Our newcomer drops down, down . . . toward the first ring.

A shiver runs up my spine. Not many die up in the first ring, where the palace sits like a flicker of frozen flame.

The newly dead disappears from view, falling somewhere in the palace gardens.

I itch to go directly, but it's not worth getting yelled at for going in without backup.

I fix the direction in my mind, taking measure of the distance so I can report it accurately. From the third's watchtower, it's several hours' walk. Lucky, then, that we don't need to walk.

I take a breath, bracing myself, and sprint toward the roof's edge. I leap and my heart jumps into my throat as I plummet.

I touch the ikondial at my throat and the cloak's black feathers arc around me, guiding my plummeting dive down the side of the watchtower. Sandstone blocks whiz past my nose, faster and faster. I roll to the side, hurtling past a balcony that would've flattened me, and roll again to miss another.

The balcony I want speeds toward me, filling my vision, so close I can see the cracks in the stone—

I pull up. The cloak grows taut as it catches the air and tries to slow my descent. My stomach drops—I've pulled up too late—I twist, getting my legs under me—and land with a thudding impact that rocks through my knees and up my spine.

The crack of my landing reverberates through the balcony, sending shudders up the glass-paned doors. From within, the sounds of bickering fade into startled silence.

I straighten up. The pain in my legs fades away, though I don't doubt they'd be broken in life. Nashira pokes her head out the door, blinking at me with her golden eyes. "You do that once too often."

I shrug her off. "Can't die twice, now, can I?"

"I'd say so, for most people. But you've done one impossible thing—why not two?" Her crooked grin makes me prickly. She's teasing. But I don't like the reminder that all the *doing* is behind me. I'm done. All that's left is—

"Oh," I say, as my thoughts interrupt each other. "There's another one."

The others glance up at me from their various positions around the room. Most wear blood-red uniforms, near identical, save for changes in fashion—extra-thick shoulder pads, black banding around the arms, a few with their family ikons embroidered on their chests. In life, most were Wardana—the city's sworn protectors, armed with ikon-forged weapons, who fought off the beasts that came from the Storm. In death, we're a welcoming committee.

Nashira pumps her fist. "Yes!"

A couple others make unconvincing sounds of excitement. "Have fun," one of them offers.

She turns on them, scowling. "Where's your spirit?"

An orange-haired man glances up from his card game. "If she's going," he says, pointing a card at me, "then what do you need us for?"

"That's not the point," Nashira says. Her eyes gleam with the telltale sign she's working herself up into a good fury.

I sigh, tuning out their argument. He says something about the ghouls, she says something about having each other's backs. I make my way to the balcony's edge and leap.

The thousand-and-one-feather cloak catches me right away. I swoop lower, gliding over third-ring rooftops.

Nashira was the one who welcomed me, who found me when I showed up down here. With her golden cat-slit eyes, dark hair, and slinky, sultry grace, I'd mistaken her for her brother and thrown myself into her arms. My cheeks warm with embarrassment just thinking about it.

When I last saw Izamal Dazera, he was lost in the Storm. I haven't seen him down here, so he could still be alive. I hope so, even though I wish I could see him again.

"Hey!" Nashira calls after me. I glance over my shoulder. She's flying fast in a cloak of her own.

They called her a hero, too. One of the only Wardana to come from the fifth ring, home to the poor and the stormtouched. All the kids at Amma's home idolized her, and we'd all mourned when we heard she'd lost her life.

She laughed herself silly when I told her that she was my hero. That I'd dreamt of wearing blood-red, of flying, of protecting everyone I loved from the Storm. Through gasps, she'd asked, "The girl who ended the Storm looks up to me?"

I don't know. Is that who I am?

I wait till Nashira catches up and tell her, "They fell in the first."

She keeps pace, and we fly low, just a few feet above the stalls of the third-ring market. Sprinkled amongst the crowd are folks who seem a little more faded than they would've looked in life. The colors of their clothes, their skin, their eyes—all of it dimming to gray. The faded ones raise their heads as we pass, and the weight of their gazes makes me fly a little higher.

A twisting alley below is packed with a dozen of them—even fainter than those who still go about their day-to-day business. These are transparent, and they stare openly, eyes wide, mouth agape. These are the ghouls.

My fists clench. I ignore their eyes. There are two ways out of the underworld. Some move forward and pass on. When I came here, I went looking for Amma. I walked my childhood streets until I found the building we lived in: Amma's Home for the Cursed. It had been burned down to its bones up above, but here, it was resurrected. My old friends were inside, but Amma wasn't. They told me she'd come with them. She'd seen that they were safe, tucked in those who needed it. Then, between one breath and the next, she was gone.

Some of us move on. Some of us linger here, eking out what we can from this place that looks so much like home. And some of us try to go back. But there's no going back. Those who try, who can't accept death, they become ghouls. They lurk around, reaching, clawing, siphoning something from the rest of us, until we become like them. They're drawn to the newly dead, like moths to light. Hence, our welcoming committee.

They watch me more than anyone. I have the Great Queen within me—all her wrathful power that once fed the Storm, turned it violent, gave rise to the beasts of cloud and thunder—all that is now in me. It's her they feel. Her power they want.

When I came here, Nashira had to fight them off me. They had grabbed me with blue-pale hands, their eyes blank, their mouths gaping.

On my hands, the darkly iridescent lines of the Queen's mark rise up. I haven't used her power in some time, so it's gathered in me like oil in a clay pot, thick and full and aching to be released.

I touch the ikondial at my throat, urging the cloak faster.

Nashira calls after me. I ignore her—she'll catch up.

The second ring sprawls below: gilded manors with real glass windows, petite gardens with ornamental trees. A white dome of a temple looms up ahead. I glance back as I pass it. At a particular angle, it morphs into a squat black manor. There are many other places like this—places where a building up above was demolished to make way for another. Down here, both old and new exist, superimposed upon each other. To fit it all, the second ring is twice as large as it was above.

Something moves out of the corner of my eye—a massive white serpent. I turn so fast my neck cracks. No. It's the ghouls shambling below, packed so close together that they resemble a pale river.

They clamber up the steps from the second ring to the first, dozens of them, in a fitful stream. Up through the golden gates, through the outer palace. I frown. Who would fall here?

I get closer. They lurch toward the vast palace gardens.

A memory rises, of air thick and honeyed with fragrance, of glimpses of red as I followed a boy through the twists and turns of the hedge wall. My pulse quickens.

The ghouls shamble into the hedge maze.

The hedges run together in dizzying patterns and dozens of dead ends—it's a mash-up of memories of the dead, rather than a perfect depiction of what they were like when I last walked within them.

I don't bother stopping and taking the hedge on foot. I fly straight to the heart of the gardens, to a glassy, still pool shielded by lush trees. It's as I remember.

All that differs is the dark-haired boy, half-submerged, swinging a

Wardana spear. "I don't want to hurt you," he shouts.

His voice—I know that voice.

I twist the dial at my throat, killing the ikonomancy of the cloak. Curses. My heart squeezes as I fall from too high, knees buckling as I land in a crouch.

Half a dozen ghouls have beat me to the water's edge. They turn to me with their pale, filmy eyes, wavering uncertainly between me and the newly dead.

I draw the Queen's power from where it pulses, like a second heart beneath my own. Ribbons of black stormcloud rise and knit themselves across my skin, weaving themselves into a protective barrier, as close to my skin as armor. It's a trick I learnt early on, when Pa and I were experimenting with my new power. *Methodology*, he would bark, *figure it out one step at a time.*

One of the ghouls reaches for me. The wisps of black cloud that make up my armor curl around his fingers. The stormbarrier doesn't deflect his touch; it welcomes his fingers and transforms them into harmless vines, each studded with tiny white flowers.

I push him aside. Others come for me.

I breathe and let the Queen's power pour from me in dark ribbons, in whorls of cloud. They rise into a shifting wall that encircles me and the boy in the pool. Drip by drip, the Queen's power leaches out of me, but I can maintain the wall for some time yet. I turn my back to it and rest my eyes on the boy.

Black, wild hair like a bird's nest. An unyielding jaw. Lips I once knew.

Water laps at my ankles. I wade across without taking my eyes from him.

His features are no longer a boy's. He's sharper around the jaw and cheekbones, as if his adulthood made him come into focus. He's developed a furrow between his brows, and his lips curl down, until he sees me.

Prince Dalca. The Regia's son. His eyes—a summer's sky blue that's too vibrant, making everything else more faded in comparison—they fix on me, shining with wetness.

Ice runs through my veins even as my skin grows hot. I reach for him.

My fingers fist in his collar. Buttery smooth blood-red leather, the ikon embroidery rough. His lips part with a soft sound; his breath puffs against my cheekbone. I can't bring myself to meet his eyes.

Heat rises through me. A crackling, lightning heat.

My fist clenches tighter around his collar. A stormbarrier wraps around me.

"Vesper," Dalca breathes.

His eyes are so bright, gleaming with emotion. His hand encircles my wrist, softly, as if he'd let me choke him.

There's a rushing in my ears. *I can't stand the way he looks at me—I can't stand this crush of feeling, of fury and frustration and—*

I've hated being trapped, being dead—but at least he wasn't here—and now—

Dalca draws in a breath.

I let go, with too much force.

He loses his balance and falls, sending a spray of water into the air.

Dalca was there when I ended the Storm, when I became the vessel of the Great Queen. He held off her counterpart and enemy, the Great King, and gave me the time I needed to bind the Queen. He should be ruling, taking care of our city.

His choices led to Pa's death. He played his part in mine. But I still remember the taste of his lips. I remember him weeping for his mother; I remember him setting his jaw and walking with me into the endless wall of the Storm. I don't know what it is that I feel for him, not anymore. I've hated him. I've cared for him—maybe even something more—but no. I don't know. It's all a jumble in me, a furious, twisting jumble that makes my chest feel too small to hold it in.

But I'm ashamed. I've a job, and this is no welcome. He blinks up at me like a half-drowned puppy. The words *I'm sorry* stick in my throat.

"I deserve that," Dalca says as he picks himself up. "That and more. But we have to move. It isn't safe here."

Move? I blink at his back as he steps between me and the ghouls, his spear at the ready. Oh. He doesn't understand yet what's happened to him.

I unclench my jaw and search for the words, for the usual script. "What's the last thing you remember?"

The water has thoroughly soaked his shirt. Through it, golden lines curl across the skin of his back. A large ikon of some sort. I'd say it's the Regia's mark if I didn't know better. The mark of the Great King—the ikon that once bound the god to his vessel—was corrupted by Dalca's family. Dalca wouldn't dare use it. He'd have no reason to, after we ended the Storm.

The Queen's mark dances across my skin—a living mark, unlike the unmoving golden lines of the Regia's—and it tells me the storm-barrier can hold only so long. I clear my throat. "Dalca. What do you remember?"

"I . . ." A fleeting shadow crosses his eyes, but Dalca shakes it off. "We have to get you safe first. There's too much to say."

You don't understand, I want to say. But the words stick in my throat, mingling with a fury that sits lodged like a burr. I can't stop looking at him. Him being here—it's irritating. Like wasps under my skin. I don't know why. I forgave him. Or at least I thought I did. I thought I'd moved on. Forgotten him.

Dalca's movements are urgent, but he takes a brief moment, his eyes sparkling, full of warmth and emotions I won't name. "After all this time, everything we tried . . . I can't believe you're back."

I drop my gaze to the water, to the rippling reflection of the garden. "I'm not."

Water sloshes as he takes a step forward. "What?"

"It's the other way around." I've given the speech so many times. *I'm afraid you've moved on to the next life. This is that life.* I've found the gentlest words for others. But all that comes is, "You're dead, Dalca."

A long, cold silence falls. He breaks it. "I can't be dead. If I'm dead, then . . . I've failed."

Failed? Surprise makes me glance up and meet his wide, agonized eyes. "Failed at what?"

Dalca doesn't hear me. His gaze is distant, focused somewhere inside. A dozen expressions flicker across his face, and then his shoulders relax. The furrow between his brows disappears, and he gives me a small smile. "Okay."

I let out a slow breath. So many are angry when they learn the truth, when they feel like something's been stolen from them. That's how I was. Angry, and sad, and a thousand other awful, prickly things.

Dalca, though . . . Was that it? Was life such a burden to him that he could put it down so easily? An ache builds in me, somewhere deep. "Dalca . . ."

He opens his mouth, then frowns, tilting his head. "Do you hear that?" He glances over his shoulder. "Cas? Yes, I can hear—"

I follow his gaze, moving closer to see from his angle, but there's no one there.

"No—wait—" His body grows suddenly more vivid, even as his eyes lose focus. The black of his pupils eats away the startling blue.

A creaking groan comes from the direction of the stormbarrier. A ghoul's tried to push through; a spray of pebbles tinkles down, joining the mound of things the others have been transformed into. I've never seen them this desperate.

Dalca whispers, "*Not yet, please*—"

It clicks into place. His vibrancy. The ghouls' persistence. He's not dead, not yet. He's on the verge.

My chest hollows out, as if my breath's been stolen. Dalca's still alive.

"Vesper—" Dalca reaches for me. "There's so much to say— They're trying to bring me back—"

A hot thrum of something—envy? Do I envy him? Of course. But him staying here, trapped like the rest of us . . .

I brush his fingers away with my knuckles. "Then go."

"I don't—" Dalca's hand closes over mine. It's warm but without weight, as if it were made of unspun yarn. His voice trembles, his other hand brushing my shoulder. "Vesper, come with me."

I flinch. "It's too late. I'm dead, Dalca."

The dark of his pupils eat away at the blue as he focuses on me. "You're not dead. Not any more than I am."

A strange, knowing shiver runs through me. "But I am."

"No, Cas—*tell them to wait*—" He raises a hand, pushing away something only he can see, something from the world of the living.

I grip his hand tight, but it's growing more immaterial. "*Dalca. What do you mean, I'm not dead?*"

Dalca's gaze sharpens. "We've been trying—You're still . . . Your body . . . Your heart is still beating."

A veil shatters. An earthquake trembles through my chest, a distant drumbeat growing quicker, louder. My vision grows crisper with each beat, as my heart makes itself known, as it sends blood pulsing throughout me. He's right. How have I not noticed?

"Vesper, please." Dalca's breath is a whisper. His eyes glow blue, his hair deepens to inkiest black, his skin gleams golden, sun-kissed brown—and then his whole body flickers, like a flame in the wind. He presses a kiss to my fingers. "Vesper—they're bringing me back. I can't stay—I wish I could—There's so much I need to—"

He's gone.

CHAPTER 2

Nashira lands, crushing clovers under her boots. Her shoulders are tense, and she has her serious-Wardana-leader expression on. Her mouth moves, and I know she's rattling off commands that I probably should follow, but her voice fades into the fuzz that fills my ears.

"Nashira," I interrupt. "Do you think we could go back?"

She shoots me a look from under furrowed brows. "That kind of thinking will turn you into them."

She gestures at the ghouls breaking through the stormbarrier. The barrier is coming undone in loose threads of stormcloud—I've run out of power.

"But what if . . ." What if my heart is still beating? That drumbeat already feels fainter—I try to focus on it, but how do you make your heart beat?—and Nashira grabs my arm, breaking my concentration. She activates her cloak.

She tugs my arm near out of its socket as we rise into the air. The ghouls swarm the pool below us, their movements slowing down as they register that they've lost their prey.

I touch the ikondial at my throat, and my own cloak activates.

Nashira gives me a long, considering look, but doesn't let me go. "What happened?"

I meet her eyes. She knew Dalca. She was the first fifth-ringer who made it not just into the Wardana, but onto Prince Dalca's three-person team. Izamal was convinced that it was Dalca's fault she died. She never said it was, never showed any grudge toward him or anyone. But I haven't asked her outright.

"It was Dalca," I say.

She sucks in a breath, her golden eyes wide in surprise.

"He wasn't dead, not fully. Just enough to descend for a moment."

Nashira searches me, a question brewing in her eyes.

I tug my arm out of her grip. "I'll meet you later." I let the cloak whisk me away.

"Vesper—" she calls after me.

I pretend I didn't hear.

The watchtower whizzes past, and I angle myself further into the third.

Amma left. But Pa remained.

The Ven looms ahead, a crown-shaped structure in the third, and I drop down to the street several blocks away. Space works strangely down here. From the wide main street, the stronghold of the Wardana is clean and a little worn around the edges, just as it was when I last saw it. But if I entered the Ven from the small door set in a discreet alcove, it would appear smaller, with far fewer walls, as it was some sixty years ago.

One wall is decorated with the faded remains of a fountain. Just under the spout—shaped like a wilting flower—is a small rectangular tile that sticks up from the rest. I twist it, and the hidden ikon embedded in the tile becomes complete.

A small door swings open and I crawl through, into a hallway lit only by thin skylights. Heavy wood doors with iron hinges line the walls, each with an intricate ikonlock. When an ikonomancer is deemed a master of their craft, they earn a place here, a workshop to call their own. And the first thing they all do is design an ikonlock—as much to ensure their privacy as to show off their skill. Pa walked me down this hall wearing a strange sort of giddy smile that I'd never seen on him. He told me he'd spent two months designing his lock so that it'd be impenetrable, and that it'd stain the hands of anyone who tried to pick it. There was a month, he said proudly, where half the mancer apprentices had violently purple fingertips.

I'd died well before I made full Wardana. And only those Wardana who specialized in ikonomancy were allowed entry into this part of the Ven. I still duck my head and pretend I belong the rare times I pass someone. But usually they're too engrossed in their own minds to pay much attention.

Pa is in his workshop. His back is a little less bowed, his shoulders more relaxed. Even the lines on his face seem smoother, though his slightly hollow cheeks still sport a faint shadow of stubble.

We spent most of the early days together. Mourning together. He threw himself into ikonomancy, into the research he should've spent his life doing, rather than living like a fugitive in the fifth ring.

But it became hard to be around him when it became clear how well death suits him.

Pa rises from his desk when he notices me. "Vesper. It's been some time."

It has been. I love my father. But sometimes when I look at him, I see him as he was in the last minutes of his life, in the arena, transformed into glass and beginning to break—

I drop my gaze and tear myself from the memory. To buy myself time, I pretend to find his cluttered workshop fascinating, trailing my fingers along his shelves and peering at the little ikonwork mechanisms that sit in rows. I twist the knob of an ikonlantern that hangs from the ceiling, dimming and brightening the light, until I find my words.

"Someone came today. They were here for just a moment." I tell him about Dalca, about what he said. About my heart, still beating, above.

He listens to it all, chin in hand.

I come to the end, to the reason why I'm here: "Could I . . . go back?"

Pa considers, and a long silence settles between us.

He glances at the work spread out on the table. "Come here."

Three mirrors hang at angles over his desk, each with delicate ikonwork etched into the glass. A fourth one is flat on the tabletop. He pricks his finger, and a drop of blood falls upon the gleaming silver surface.

"Closer," he says. He clears off a stool and drags it beside him.

I perch on it and lean forward. Pa tilts one of the hanging mirrors until I can see.

In the mirror, the drop of blood looks more like a cocoon made of thin threads of red spider silk. I lean closer. The cocoon pulsates, and there's something strange about how it's woven so loosely that I can see through parts of it.

"This place isn't completely real. It's something our minds create, filling in the gaps, so it all makes sense. It's an illusion, though, a mask that shields us from the underlying structure of this place. But ikons are a naming of reality, and they reveal a piece of the truth."

Ikons? Why is he talking about—

I suck in a breath. The cocoon is an ikon. An incredibly complex one, to be in three dimensions. I make out dozens of interlocking threads, shapes that begin as familiar elementary ikons, but twist into dizzying things I've never seen before. And the way that it pulsates—it's moving. Like it's alive.

"I'm calling it a life-ikon," Pa says.

"What does it do?"

"What do you think it does?"

Pa, ever the scholar. I take a stab. "It . . . names you."

He nods. "Your turn."

I prick my finger, and a single drop falls to the mirror, spreading flat. And then . . . threads of blood weave themselves into a shape like a candle flame.

The pattern of the threads is unlike Pa's, and many of the lines wisp into nothingness, like frayed yarn. Intertwined with the red are darkly iridescent lines. The Great Queen.

Where Pa's is fully contained, mine seems fractured. Like it's missing something. I glance at him and venture, "It's . . . incomplete."

"Yes, good." Pa beams, like I'm a perfect student.

I duck my head to hide my smile. My gaze drops to his life-ikon. "And yours is complete. What does that mean?"

He steps away, his back facing me. "Vesper . . . for some time now, I've seen a door."

I look up sharply.

"I know I'm meant to walk through."

To the other place. Where Amma is. I find my voice. "You've stayed . . . for me?" Am I holding Pa back?

He turns, and his eyes are soft. "To be parted from you is nothing I want."

"You should go. I'll be okay."

He shakes his head. "Don't try to take care of me. But you're right.

I think you will be okay. Do you want to return?"

His voice betrays only curiosity.

"I . . ."

"There's nothing you want?"

An ache builds within me.

Pa rests his chin on his knuckles. "For me this was the end. A chance to finish the work I'd begun. For you, perhaps this was a reprieve, a chance for you to heal." He taps his chest, right over his heart. "There's much more ahead of you, if you want it. More to care about. More to love." He doesn't even get embarrassed at saying "love," not like he did when I was small, whenever we spoke of feelings. Maybe the Pa I knew, the Pa of my childhood, has already left me behind.

"I don't know about that," I say, thinking of too-vibrant blue eyes. "I'm done with that."

"There are loves beyond your first, you know."

I roll my eyes. "I didn't love him, Pa."

"Good," he says a little too quickly. "Er, rather—there are just so many other people to choose from, aren't there?"

"Pa."

"You left a life that was not yet done. Really, it had barely gotten started."

The drops of blood on the mirror catch my eye.

"It's not easy," Pa says. "The ghouls are those who never knew themselves. Who were content not to lead their own lives. So tell me, who are you?"

I stare at the droplets, mesmerized. Who am I? What do I want? "I . . . want to see," I whisper, "to know what it's like. I want to stand in the fifth and feel the sun on my skin. I want to walk through the sixth and seventh rings; I want to see what lies beyond. I want things I have no words for. Things I don't know . . ."

Pa leans back. "It sounds like you have questions."

I smile wryly. "A few."

"It's frightening, isn't it? To jump into life without knowing the answers? I don't blame you. I look at your life-ikon, and I can only imagine what it will take to work on it, given what you've already accomplished. Extraordinary people encounter extraordinary obstacles."

My heartbeat quickens, and I meet his eyes. "I'm going to find a way back."

His smile softens into a thoughtful look. "This place is a construct, a structure built upon what we all believe to be true. But I don't see exactly what you do—I don't see the hole in the sky that you say the newly dead fall through. I've been thinking on it, though at first I thought it was a mere quirk of our experiences. But perhaps . . . there's a reason this place built that for you."

And I see. The sky opening like an eye. A body falling.

Where do they fall from?

My feet take me to the edge of the fifth ring, under the shelter of the eerie white stormwall. Amma's home.

From the street, the house is slightly tipsy and moss-eaten, just as it was for most of the years I called it home. But if I made my way to Amma's from the skinny alley behind it, then I'd see it as the prosperous spice shop it was some hundred years ago, before Amma took it over. And if I came at Amma's home from an angle, approaching while keeping it in the very corner of my vision, then it'd be as I last saw it: nothing more than burnt ruins.

What does it look like now? Has someone rebuilt, made a new home of it? Has moss taken it over, have neighborhood children made it into a place of play? Or has it been abandoned, left to decay?

My hand rests on the doorknob. It lingers there, until the metal warms from the heat of my skin. Air comes through gaps in the wooden siding, bringing the scent of cardamom. I breathe it in, but it mingles with other aromas: earthy moss, woodsmoke, and the sickly burnt-sugar smell that once heralded a stormsurge.

I let go. Without Amma . . . this isn't home. I can walk through time all I want, find every angle and every version of this place, but I can never go back home.

Someone laughs from within, sweet and joyful. There's happiness here, even if it isn't mine.

I take that with me, tuck it into my memories as I retrace my path, making for the watchtower. I land on the balcony.

It occurs to me that I don't know if any of the Wardana will miss me. I forget their names, even though it's been weeks. Months, more likely. Maybe even a year. I didn't quite keep track.

The only one I'd miss—footsteps sound, and Nashira walks out onto the balcony.

"So," she says, leaning on the baluster beside me. "You've found a way back."

I tilt my head, looking up at the sky above. "Nashi . . . I never asked you something."

"What?"

"Iz . . . he really looks up to you."

She grins, embarrassed and proud.

"He told me that Dalca loved you. That when you turned him down . . . that's how you ended up here."

She blinks at me slowly. "That's the stupidest thing I've ever heard. Even for Iz."

"Which part?"

Her eyes narrow. "*I* am the reason I'm here. I chose to be a Wardana. I chose to jump, though my cloak was torn. I chose to help Dalca, to save him. I own my choices."

"I know," I say.

Nashira crosses her arms. "It wasn't some tragedy—I told him, he was always reading too many stupid stories—Dalca never loved me. We were friends. He was looking at years of being Regia. He wanted someone to help him rule, someone he could trust. He thought I'd be good for the job. You know, I probably would've been."

I shrug. I don't doubt it.

"Thing is, I couldn't subject myself to a loveless marriage for the sake of duty." She sighs. "I used to think . . . that when Dalca was born, they carved out his heart and left only fear behind. He's too full of terror. For himself, for his family, for his people. Maybe that's what happens to anybody with that kind of responsibility."

I meet her gaze, and she smiles.

"When you see Iz," she says, "tell him that it was all me. And maybe Dalca doesn't know what love is, but I do. I'm going to wait here for the love of my life. And together, we'll go on to the next place."

I smile at the look in her eyes. "Until then?"

She grins. "You're not my only lost little puppy, you know. I've got others to look out for."

"Nashira—"

"Go. Enjoy the world you rescued. But, Vesper . . . Sooner or later, every Wardana learns that nothing ever stays saved."

"The Storm is gone forever, though. I have it within me."

She gives me a strange smile. "Go. Give Iz my love."

She comes with me down to the courtyard of the Ven, where Pa has come to wait, as if he knows.

I run to him and hug him tight. His breath catches. "I'll see you again," I promise.

"Not for a while, though," Pa says, and wipes my cheek.

I touch the ikondial at my throat. The cloak billows out, dust rising as it pressurizes the air.

I fly. Rising faster and faster, higher and higher. The wind cuts at me as if it would hold me down. It freezes my cheeks and whips tears from my eyes.

I look back once. Nashira watches, but it's Pa I look for.

My father has his head tilted up. He's smiling. This is how I'll remember him, for the rest of my life. How many years till we meet again? Decades?

That's optimistic, says a little voice in the back of my mind. *It could be minutes.*

No. It won't be. I want this life, and I'm going to live it.

Even if my heart breaks. Even if I'm leaving behind Pa and the only home I've ever known.

My heart thuds in my chest in a rising rhythm, a drumbeat, quicker and quicker.

A sob wrenches itself from my throat. As I reach the first wisp of sky and the clouds part like an eye.

There's a pinprick of light.

I reach for it and—

CHAPTER 3

I find myself standing in blinding whiteness. I snap my eyes shut.

"Careful, love," comes a rough, whispery voice. "You have to get used to it."

My voice catches in my dry throat. I swallow a few times, and try again. "Why is it so bright?"

"It isn't, really. You've just become accustomed to the dark."

I open my eyes the tiniest slit. A wall of light—and there, in the middle, a bent old woman. My vision blurs with tears, and I blink them away.

She tuts. "The dark never hurts, does it?"

I squint at her. "Who are you?"

She gives me a rather pitying look and leans in.

Her irises are shifting whorls of stormcloud. Shapes dance around her pupils—beasts, vines, rivers—running in dizzying circles.

The Great Queen. I straighten up. "I have to go back."

She breathes a laugh like a cold wind whipping through a forest of creaking, ancient trees. "I've protected you as long as I could."

"Protected me? From what?"

The light grows blinding behind her, outlining her in luminous white gold—so bright she becomes just a suggestion of a person, no more than shadow.

She says, "I'll see you on the other side."

I squeeze my eyes shut. The light sneaks through the infinitesimal gap between my eyelids, all barbs and cutting edges, delivering a thousand pinpricks that drive away the dark.

The light drags me forward, drags me up.

My heartbeat rises.

The dead blood in my veins quickens.

The light surrounds me; the darkness pales to red.

I rise through blood red, warm red, the color of sun through skin, and it presses in on me, squeezing me tight, drawing me higher.

Every inch of me gets folded smaller and smaller, until all of me is squeezed into the tiniest of cages: my body.

My eyes snap open. I'm falling and falling—I jerk up and into myself. My body lifts from the bed I'm lying on, and I fall back onto a soft cushion, willing the world to stop spinning in lopsided circles.

A domed ceiling comes hazily into focus. A mosaic. An expensive one; each tile is no larger than my fingernail. The design is dominated by softly curling waves in black and deep purple. Small somethings break up the pattern—fish, maybe. I blink and my vision clears.

Golden stars with seven points. Like pinpricks against the black clouds of the Storm. I follow the mosaic down, to where ceiling meets wall.

A golden sun rises, with rays like curved swords. The swords pierce the Storm, and below is a long line of sky meeting land. A horizon. A thing from childhood stories—I remember trying to imagine it, to imagine a world where the sky and land weren't kept apart by the Storm. Where the sun owned the entire sky, not just the small disc the Storm permitted.

Horizon. The word feels strange in my mind, stranger still on my tongue. But a desire blooms in my gut, low, yearning, desperate. I want to see it.

My limbs move with that desire, my thighs tensing, my arms pushing me up. My body is so heavy. I grit my teeth and shove up—

Pain blossoms in the back of my head. My scalp stings—I've sat on my hair. I tug my hair from under me. More and more of it pools in my lap, a gleaming river of black, ridiculously long, longer than I've ever had it.

When I died, it hung to my shoulders, perfectly ordinary, a little wild from the humidity of the Storm. I've been resurrected into a body that's lived without me, months and months of life.

A shiver of a thought. I touch my face, but it could be any face with the requisite assortment of eyes, nose, and lips. My hands look like mine, short nail beds and a thin scar along the index finger where I once cut myself peeling shalaj roots. On my right palm is a burn scar in seven lines, perfectly matching the strings of Amma's sitar.

I move my legs and promptly smack them into a glass barrier that surrounds my bed. I prop myself up to take a better look. The glass shimmers, light catching on the hundreds of ikons etched in it. They're far more complex than any I studied, but I make out pieces of a handful—one to clean air, another that has something to do with temperature—and then there's one right above my chest that stands out. It's larger than the rest and surrounded by artistic flourishes—a wisp of cloud, a sun ringed by rays of light, and a pair of dark eyes. But at the center is a simple command: *Open*.

I touch it.

The glass shimmers, iridescence radiating out from the ikon. A sound like the tinkling of bells follows, and the ikons disappear.

My fingertips reach and touch nothing but sparkling dust hanging in the air. I let out a slow breath, and the dust dances, catching in the current. A giddy thrill goes through me—even with all I've seen below, there's nothing quite like ikonomancy.

I inhale. It's a suffocation: my lungs fill with fragrance as thick and sweet as honey, on air heavy with incense smoke.

A heavy thudding comes from far away, filtering through the ringing in my ears. I hadn't realized my ears were ringing, but now that I've noticed, the high, tinny sound fills all the nooks and crannies of my head.

The thudding comes again, and I focus on catching it, but it's as if I'm underwater, as if my ears have forgotten how to listen. The ringing deepens and joins the other sound, and together they sound like clanging. Like immense bells—like those that hang from watchtowers and warn us of impending stormsurges.

But there's no Storm anymore. Is there?

I swing my legs down and hesitate, blinking the dust from my eyes. There's nowhere to step without crushing something.

My toes find a small triangle of floor, and I stand. The world tilts, and I catch myself on the edge of the stone bed. The ringing in my ears grows fainter as a rushing sound—my blood, pumping—drowns everything out.

I breathe through the dizziness until the floor comes back into focus.

Hundreds of faintly glimmering ikonlights encased in globes of glass litter the floor, and amongst them are . . . things. Endless things. I lean and pick up a wooden figurine and turn it over in my hands. It's not unlike a toy I once had, but far more finely carved, of a woman with feet planted and serious eyes. I set it down.

A roll of paper catches my eye. It unfolds to read *You were better than we deserved. May your sleep be easy.*

My breath catches in my throat.

Gently, with my bare feet, I nudge things out of the way, creating a narrow path. I pick things up at random: a gleaming black stone with no writing or message, a child-sized sitar, an ikonlight globe that glows brighter and changes color in my palm. And so many notes. *Thank you for giving us back the sky. Thank you for ending the Storm.*

And pleas:

Please, watch over my family.

Please, we need you.

Please, wake up.

My feet pause before two stuffed dolls with their hands sewn together. One wears a white dress and has long dark hair, the other wears a white and gold uniform, and the stones that serve as his eyes are painted blue.

Dalca. A crush of feeling rises in me. Where is he?

Where am I?

The dolls fall to the floor. The air grows thick and suffocating.

I spin in a circle. It's not a large room, but it's lavishly appointed. A round room—that's unusual. I've only seen people go through the trouble of constructing a circular room for important places, like temples. They've made this . . . for me?

The walls are all soft purples and golds, very pretty colors—all mosaic work, depicting some story I'm sure, but I'm not in the mood to appreciate art—

One of the figures catches my eye. A gray-eyed girl with long black hair. She stands hand in hand with a boy with curling black hair and blue eyes. Behind them is a billow of purple-black swirls, peppered with white specks like diamonds. I move closer, until the specks show themselves to be eyes; serpentine eyes, dozens of them, all watch the girl and the boy. The swirls are made up of multitudes of purple and blue stones, some cut and gleaming, some dark and rough. How much care went into this, into depicting the Storm?

It's so beautiful, rendered so sweetly in a childlike style. The image slips into my mind, into my memories, painting over the horror of the Storm. *It wasn't so bad,* the mosaic says. *It was a storybook adventure.*

The girl and the boy appear on all the walls. They're joined often by two other figures—a thin, pale man with gleaming white hair, and a man with shoulder-length dark hair and golden eyes—but the girl and the prince are always central.

Across the walls is the tale of a girl who went to save her father from a prince . . . who fell in love with the prince. They embrace amongst twining flowers, silhouetted by the golden palace of the first ring. They walk into the Storm, hand in hand.

In the next panel, she stands with arms extended as the Storm wraps around her. The prince kneels at her side, holding an orb of light that's not unlike the sun.

And then, she sleeps. He kneels at her side, weeping glittering stones cut into teardrops.

I turn and the story starts all over again. A heroic story; the four that went into the Storm. They all seem like friends. And the girl and the prince—they seem like something more.

I wonder. Set down in stone, it seems like this story must be the truth. But it's not what I remember.

Where's the girl crying over her father's body? Where's the prince holding his sword to her heart? Where is the moment before her sacrifice, the moment where all power was hers, where she held the thin thread of the prince's life in her hands?

No. This is no truth. Ours was not a love story.

If it were, why would the prince have caged me here, in a beautiful room with no windows and no doors?

Darkly iridescent patterns rise on my skin. The power I gave so much for—the power of a forgotten goddess, the Great Queen—courses under my skin. It grants me awareness. Stone does not change willingly. After raising a stormbarrier so recently, I've got next to nothing of the Queen's power saved.

I run my fingers along the wall, until they catch on a raised edge. A loose tile. I pry it free with my nails. Behind is a crack in the mortar. A little green shows—a little bit of moss.

I close my eyes. This awareness gives me a sense of the moss—something I've never felt in the world of the dead. It already carries a faint thrum of the Queen's power, as if . . . as if it spent a good long time in the Storm.

That tells me two things. One: this room is somewhere in the lands that were once lost to the Storm. That could be anywhere from the outer rim of the fifth ring—which was lost when I was a child—to places I've only ever heard about, places that were lost long before I was born. The farms and orchards of the sixth ring, or perhaps even the great wilds of the seventh.

My chest fills with a giddy warmth.

Two: the moss will answer to me.

I force it to grow, to thicken, to widen the hairsbreadth fissure.

A loud crack splits the air.

I feed it more power. Until the tiles of the mosaic fall, until the moss forces mortar to disintegrate and stones to fall. An orange glow comes through the gaps. One push, and the stone crumbles, leaving a hole big enough for me, if I stoop.

The distant clanging of immense bells grows louder.

The stone dust hangs in the opening. I hold my breath and push through.

My head spins as I straighten up. I lean on the wall as my vision clears.

A sandstone floor. Black stone walls. A hallway that curves. Probably encircling the mosaic room. *A defensible perimeter*, I think in a voice that sounds rather like Nashira's.

A gasp sounds. I don't think it came from me.

I turn. A wide-eyed girl with dark braids, clad in Wardana reds. She stands with arms outstretched, as if frozen. Her gaze lingers on my face and flicks down to my exposed hands, where the dark lines of the Queen's mark are just fading.

I take a step toward her, and she squeaks and backs away, tripping over her feet in her haste. She rights herself and skitters backwards.

"Wait—" I call, but my voice comes like I've a mouth full of yarn and gravel.

I follow her around the curve, into a sea of red. Wardana everywhere, clustered around a massive door set with a complex circular ikonlock. The Wardana closest to the door whoop as the lock clicks open, revealing the room I was just in. A few of them rush inside with a shout of alarm: *"She's gone!"*

Oh. My cheeks heat. There was a door all along. Dalca didn't trap me. With hindsight, I suppose it wasn't entirely reasonable to assume he would. And I've destroyed some poor artisan's handiwork. It might've taken weeks to do that mosaic.

Movement draws my attention. The Wardana at the edge of the crowd have turned to face me. A ripple goes through the crowd as more and more turn away from the open doors. Silence falls, leaving only the clanging of the bells.

So many eyes. I fight the urge to fidget, scanning the crowd for a familiar face.

The girl with braids starts as I lock eyes with her. I beckon her closer.

She tiptoes near in stiff, self-conscious spurts.

I lean in. "Where's Dalca?" My voice comes out a little less gruff, like my throat is remembering how to work.

Her cheeks redden, and she stutters out, "In the in-infirmary."

I frown. "Where's that?"

She abruptly bends double. I blink at the back of her neck, until it dawns on me that she's bowing. "It would be my honor to show you the way."

"Er," I say intelligently, but she's already moving.

The other Wardana back away, clearing a path. One of them drops to his knees and bows his head over clasped hands. His mouth moves as if he's . . . praying?

Another Wardana grabs him by the neck of his jacket and pulls him out of the way.

"Um." I search for something to say to this sea of red. "Thank you, all of you. Carry on," I add, channeling Nashira.

I make my way out the door. *Carry on* echoes through my head. Was protecting my room—my tomb—their entire job?

My guide's braids sway with each step. They're beautiful, woven with small golden rings. My sight narrows and the edges of my vision pulse with gray. My heart's going too fast.

Something's not quite right with my body.

The gleaming black walls blur together, and I focus on breathing, on putting one foot in front of the other. I ignore the rising and falling of my stomach, ignore everything but the Wardana's braids and keeping my feet moving.

One more step, yes, good, left now, then right—I bump into something soft. She yelps. I catch myself on the wall, willing the world to level out.

"Sorry," I murmur to her back.

"It's—it's my honor, Stormender," she squeaks.

Two immense Wardana stand guard in front of a pair of white doors. She murmurs something to them.

I glance behind me. The hallway is packed full. A line of red uniforms snakes through the crowd, for the Wardana have followed.

A faint touch on my arm. My guide, her brown eyes concerned.

I straighten up. "I'm fine."

The two guards push the doors open for me.

I step through into a long white atrium. The air smells of herbs and the metallic tang of blood. Black-robed healers are hard at work; one bends over a heavy pot of something steaming and smelling faintly of vinegar, another consults a book as she draws an ikon onto a bandage, others pluck herbs and poultices from the many glass vials and brass bins that line the walls. Doors lead out, some open to empty rooms, while others are shut.

The doors close behind us, muffling the clanging almost entirely.

Several of the healers glance up and break into loud exclamations. A tall, thin woman glides forward. "None are permitted to enter this ward."

My guide steps forward, her back straight. "Do you know who this is?"

The healer takes me in. Her brows rise.

I smile weakly.

"Yes," my guide says. "She woke up for Prince Dalca."

"That's not exactly true—" I start, but my voice isn't loud enough to carry over the sounds of surprise that erupt from all around. A sick and simmering fury grows in my belly. Why did I ask for Dalca?

The tall healer raises a quelling hand, and silence falls. "Welcome, Stormender. Prince Dalca . . ." She gestures with a flat hand toward a lone door at the far end of the atrium, where a Wardana stands at guard. "He's through there."

CHAPTER 4

The door shuts, and all the sounds of the infirmary are sealed away, leaving a heavy silence between me and the figure on the bed. Dalca slumbers. His dark eyelashes cast shadows on the sharp curve of his cheekbones; his skin is scarred and bruised, imperfections that weren't there in the world of the dead.

My heart thuds in my chest. I've never hated anyone the way I hated Dalca. He was present for so many of the worst moments in my life. Honestly, he caused a few. But . . . I understood him. I understood his desperation to find Pa, to discover a way to save his mother. I understood his fear of becoming Regia via the corrupted mark, having the Great King take over his body and leaving him imprisoned inside. I even understood the way he broke, when his mother leapt to her death, when I ended the curse that made him happy and he snapped under the blowback of all his fears returning, when he realized he would have to step into the shoes that drove his mother to her death. Him turning on me, sentencing me to the Trials, holding a sword to my throat . . . A boy without a family's love, who was brought up by a cruel god to be nothing more than a vessel, a boy who loved his home and was powerless to save it . . . I can understand all that.

Because I understand him, do I need to forgive him? Because he repented in those last moments, because he fought the Great King so I could end the Storm, because I couldn't have done it without him—does that mean I shouldn't hate him?

Every memory of him is like a cut, a pinprick of acid. They gather within me, a whirlwind, spinning faster and faster, in tighter circles, becoming a solid, burning thing that I fear I'll carry always, right between my ribs. It has no name, despite it growing heavy as an anchor. I wish I could call it something—*loathing*, maybe—and dismiss it.

A faint breeze tousles his dark curls. Seeing him in the world of the dead should've prepared me; at least it gave me a heads-up for the way his features have sharpened. But it's as though a gray film's been lifted from my eyes. Everything smarts, too bright and too clear; every detail grows immense, filling my vision.

Scars crisscross his skin. The ones on his face have healed to thin pale lines, but bandages wrap around his chest, concealing whatever wounds he still bears. Precisely drawn ikons dot the bandages. *Only the best for the prince*, says a little voice in the back of my mind. I clench my fists.

I wish this were fury. The heat running through my veins, rising up, pooling in the corners of my eyes as tears that threaten to fall—I wish it were as clean and simple as hate.

"Vesper?"

I startle and scrub my eyes with the back of my hand. The voice came from the far corner of the room, where under a small window is a leather chair with someone curled up in it, silhouetted against the window.

He stands and takes a halting step closer. A thin slant of moonlight molded into a man; white hair and skin, white eyelashes framing pale gray eyes. His hair is a flat white and pulled into a loose braid, with no ikonwork to turn it mirrorlike—his old affectation. He's lost some of the pinched and pointy look he once had, and though he's still on the slender side for a Wardana, he's a little broader about the shoulders.

A smile comes easy to my lips. "Casvian."

"You're here," Casvian Haveli whispers, crossing the room and reaching with a trembling hand. His fingers brush my forearm, and he snatches them back, gray eyes wide and wondering. "You're truly here."

My voice is thick. "Surprise."

He wraps me up in a bony hug. "For Storm's sake," he says thickly, "what took you so long?"

"Catching up on my beauty sleep," I murmur into his neck, patting him on the back. His muscles shift under my touch—he's only in a loose shirt and trousers, no Wardana leathers in sight.

Casvian pulls back, dragging the back of his hand across his eyes and peering down at me. "Fat load of good it did."

I fight a smile. "Should I go back, then? Couple more weeks?"

"No." He tries to force his face into its usual mask of disdain. "It wouldn't help."

A laugh bubbles out of me. "You really missed me."

"Well." Cas shrugs. "It's so very difficult to find a good apprentice these days. Haven't had one for years."

We haven't kept our voices down, but Dalca hasn't stirred. Hasn't moved so much as a finger. "Years," I repeat, suddenly registering Cas's words. "How long has it been?"

Cas recites as if it's always on his mind. "Three years. A thousand days, give or take." His expression falls. "They didn't tell you? When you woke, they should have—It's part of the protocol—"

"I didn't give anyone much of a chance," I say to cut him off. *A thousand days* rumbles around my head. It had felt like a few long months, perhaps a year at most. Three whole years? "I made a Wardana bring me here," I explain.

Cas grows even paler. "You *just* woke up?" He flies into jittery motion, darting for the door.

"Cas—Dalca, is he . . ." I search for my words. "What happened to him?"

Cas hesitates at the door. He presses his lips into a thin line, dropping his gaze to Dalca's sleeping form. "He'll want to tell you himself."

Dalca's so still, his breathing so faint. I don't care, but—I find myself asking, "Will he—he'll wake up, right?"

Cas's gaze softens. "Soon. The healers are keeping him under until the worst is healed."

"I saw him, Cas. In the world of the dead. He told me . . . I didn't know, until then. That my heart was beating—that I could come back."

The Great Queen speaks within me, a wizened old growl in the back of my head: *He did his part in bringing you here. You need not concern yourself with him further.*

Cas keeps his gaze on Dalca, and his expression folds into lines well creased by despair. "There was a moment when we thought he was gone." He presses his lips together. "We need to get you out of here."

Out of here? The room is fairly simple, with little furniture besides the bed and chair. A washbasin stands on a cabinet in the corner. But there aren't a whole lot of luxuries, not what I'd expect for a prince.

Cas opens the door and mutters a curse.

"What?" I ask. I push past him, ignoring his hissed warning of "Wait, Vesper—"

The atrium is packed full of people, despite the shouted orders from the black-robed healers.

A sea of wide, hungry eyes—*Ghouls*, something in me whispers.

But no. I've left that behind.

Some healers and Wardana hold back the crowd, but even their eyes linger upon me. Silence falls.

All is still. As if an unseen force holds them back.

I swallow down the sour fear that rises up my throat and square my shoulders.

Someone gasps—and like a flood, they rush toward me. Hands on my shoulders, my arms, my hands, my hair, touching me—voices, urgent, reverent, all speaking over each other—

Thank you—

Please—

Will you—

Bless us, Stormender—

"Get back!" Cas snaps. He shoves his way in front of me, but they move like water around a rock, reaching under his arms, grasping at me—

The Queen's power roils within me. Her mark rises on my skin, and I hold it there. I don't have much of her power saved. And these aren't ghouls. Nor are they my enemies.

Words of adoration drip from their lips. How can I thank them by using the Queen's power against them?

I brace myself, even as Cas tries to protect me. He curses. "Of all the times to be without a gauntlet—"

The infirmary doors slam open with a bang. A ripple runs through the crowd, from the far side of the corridor.

"Enough!" a voice calls. "Move!"

The crowd parts for what seems like a wave of deep blue.

I rise on my toes to look over Cas's shoulder.

Warriors wearing the blue of shadows at dusk. Some are physically immense, some are slight, but they all carry themselves with a watchful and dangerous air. The cut of their uniforms is not unlike the Wardana's, but with many more belts and pouches slung from their waists and thighs. A faint dusting of sand and dirt coats their clothes and boots, and a healer groans, though she's quickly hushed.

There are at least a half dozen warriors in blue, all looking like they've just returned from some adventure.

"No weapons in the infirmary," an elderly healer scolds.

"An excellent policy," a familiar voice agrees.

My gaze snaps to him as he moves to the front of the pack. Dark hair pulled back at the nape of his neck, warm eyes like molten gold, an expression like a cat after a successfully executed bit of mischief. Izamal Dazera.

When I last saw him he was lost to the Storm. That he's here . . .

The wonder I feel is reflected in his expression.

"So it's true," he breathes. And then something serious snaps over his expression. "We have to get you somewhere safe."

The softness in his eyes disappears as he locks in on Cas beside me. "What are you thinking, bringing her here?"

Cas flushes. "I—" He glances at the others and shuts his mouth with an audible click.

"Let's go." Izamal takes the lead.

Cas glances between me and Dalca behind him. I motion him to come. He gives me a tense look, gaze darting to Izamal, but he relents, pausing only to grab his blood-red Wardana jacket.

Iz offers me his arm.

"How did you find me?" I ask Iz.

He tugs his ear. "The bells. And then I followed the crowd." He glances over his shoulder at one of the other warriors, and as if he issued a command, the others form a barrier, clearing a path out of the infirmary. One shuts the white doors behind us, while two others move ahead, barking orders and clearing the halls.

I glance over my shoulder. Cas keeps pace grimly, and behind him, two other of the blue Wardana watch our backs.

I open my mouth to ask about them, but I can't draw a breath, not with how fast we're walking. I lean on Iz's arm, and my lungs ache with effort to keep the pace.

Down another hall, a woman in black nears, and the blue Wardana let her pass. She falls into step with me. She's familiar—tall, with white-streaked black hair, probably Pa's age.

She gives me a nod when she catches me looking. "Imbas Lahra," she says. "At your service."

I place her. "You're"—I catch my breath—"a knitter."

Her lips quirk. "Amongst other things."

She and her people had been revolutionaries in my parents' time, but when I met them, they kept themselves occupied with smaller ambitions: running safehouses, operating the gray market, and, particularly, spinning moss into cloth. Mosscloth was always in demand, for with the farms and orchards of the sixth gone, there was little else but moss that we could use to make clothes.

Iz cuts in. "The rest of the council will be on their way."

Council? I try to gather my breath to ask, but it takes all I've got to keep pace with Iz. My heart may have kept on beating, but neither my muscles nor my lungs were so considerate.

Cas offers me his arm. I take it gratefully and focus on counting the doors passing by, marking the halls we walk down and the stairs we climb.

"You're going to love the council," he says dryly. "They're all arrogant, and they get nothing done."

I raise an eyebrow. "I've heard some call you arrogant, Cas."

"Perhaps. But I get stuff done."

I don't have enough air in my lungs to laugh. I'm breathing hard by the third flight, and my vision is half gray by the time Iz ushers me through a pair of doors, past a small foyer, and into another set of rooms.

"Here," Cas says at my side, guiding me. "Take a seat."

I fall into a chair, listening to Iz murmur orders to the others.

Cas clears his throat and says quietly, "We need a healer."

Iz hears. His attention snaps to Cas and then me. "Yes, of course."

"I'm fine," I breathe. But no one seems to hear.

I open my eyes a moment later to find a healer's appeared at my side. She clamps a bulky bronze and glass cuff around my wrist. At the clasp is an ikondial with three fourths of a circular ikon etched on it. As she turns the dial, the last piece slots into place and the ikon is completed. The cuff whirrs. A cylinder pops out, rising and falling with my pulse. She leans in, carefully turning my wrist, studying whatever she sees.

"You're all right, love. Just need to get your strength back, that's all."

Get my strength back? I flex my wrist as she takes the cuff away. My blue-green veins are stark, but they're less noticeable when I draw the Queen's power, when the faint lines of her mark appear for a brief second. The reservoir within me is, drop by drop, filling back up with her power. This is the strongest I've ever been.

"How long?" I ask her.

Her eyes are wide as she takes in my arms, but swiftly, a mask of reassuring competence falls over her expression. "Some things can't be rushed. Eat well, take daily walks—as long of a walk as you can manage. Each day you'll find you can do a little more."

She gives me a smile as she leaves.

I draw in a breath and force myself up, getting my first good look around.

Beautiful furniture everywhere—too much to take in—carved divans and armchairs and a half dozen other plush and comfortable places to sit, ornamental tables and wall coverings—everything gilded and gleaming. Wide arches lead into other rooms, the nearest with a table so large several families could eat around it. A fairy story, come to life.

The blue-clad warriors are busy stalking around the room, pulling dustcovers from furniture and who knows what else.

"Here's the food," one says. At the door are people bearing heavy platters. The warriors let them in one by one, checking each dish—for what, I can't say—and slowly the grand table fills up with fragrant food. My stomach growls.

Izamal brings over a platter twice as wide as he is, setting it on the low table before me. Steam rises, carrying the aroma of spices. A pile of half-moons with golden crusts. Small bowls of soup, each a different color. Pieces of cut fruit so beautiful they could be jewels.

Iz holds a small plate, raising an expectant eyebrow. "What'll you eat?"

"I can serve myself," I say.

"Humor me."

My mouth waters. "One of everything."

With a napkin, he picks up one of the flaky golden half-moons and tears a small piece. He pops it in his mouth, chewing seriously, and once he's swallowed, he hands me the remainder.

I blink at him, then at the three fourths of a pastry in my hand. "Do you not want the rest?"

He lowers a spoon filled with pale green soup from his lips. "You're not hungry?"

I glance at Cas, who doesn't seem mystified. Is this some new custom? I suppose I've known stranger things.

I bring the thing to my lips and take a bite. The crust crunches and melts in my mouth. The filling is spiced, with pops of sweetness, but underneath is a bitterness I know well. I grimace, swallowing and hope no one is watching my face. Shalaj. I'd kept a few plants at Amma's to supplement our food rations, because shalaj has two great virtues: it grows with little soil and next to no light. Those are its only virtues. It's mouth-twistingly bitter, with fibrous threads that stick in your teeth, and always smells like it's recently been sneezed on.

Why would anyone choose to eat it? Is there nothing else to eat?

Izamal hands me the soup—minus one spoonful—and the smell of shalaj rises on the steam.

"Is there anything that isn't shalaj?" I ask.

Imbas frowns. "Is it not your favorite?"

My mouth falls open. Is she being funny? "Is it yours? Is it . . . anyone's?"

Her brows furrow deeper, and she flicks her gaze at Cas.

He's pink.

"What?" I ask.

"They asked . . . People wanted to know what you liked. Did you not . . . You grew them, didn't you?"

"Not out of love." I laugh. He looks so nervous—and trust a highringer boy to get it so wrong . . . But no one else laughs.

Cas flinches in on himself, and several of the warriors in blue look furious. Even Izamal scowls at Cas.

"It's fine," I say quickly. "I'm glad to have it."

I grab another pastry off the table and bring it to my lips.

"Wait!" Iz takes the pastry from me and swaps it out for another. Dumbfounded, I let him.

This one has a small piece torn out. "What?"

"That one isn't shalaj."

I glance at Cas. "Shalaj is fine. Or one that you haven't already bitten."

"I didn't bite it, I tore—" Izamal starts.

Imbas laughs, cutting him off. "Forgive him, Vesper. Some foods that we harvest from the wilds seem to have traces of curses within them. Of course, all the food that feeds us in this watchtower has been carefully inspected. Izamal here is merely . . . overcautious."

Iz smiles weakly. "We just got you back."

I grit my teeth. I'm not weak. The Queen's mark rises on my skin. "I can handle curses just fine." I get to my feet. "I want to see the wilds. I want to see everything."

At the far side of the room are diamond-paned glass doors. A balcony. The outside world is gently distorted through the rippled glass. I throw open the doors and step out.

The sound is deafening. Under the clanging bells, under the wailing wind, is a rumble, a crush of something else. A roar. I walk to the balcony's edge.

People. The square is filled with them, cheering, the roar of their voices echoing on stone.

And above them, above the blue-slate rooftops: the horizon.

I hear myself gasp, as if from far away.

The night sky is an endless blanket, punctured by thousandfold pinpricks. And far, far away, the half-moon rises, like a gleaming coin caught mid flip. And there, the line where sky meets land, the view the Storm stole from us—the horizon.

I grip the railing tight. My stomach twists as if my feet are already lifting from the balcony floor, as if I'm already falling. Down is a long way away.

The stars are reflected on the ground—hundreds of tiny luminous dots. The dull roar rises.

"They're here for you."

The dots are people. Hundreds of ikonlanterns cupped in hundreds of hands.

"What do they want from me?"

"Just to see you."

I raise my hand, and sound expands, filling the air, filling my chest up to bursting.

It hits me. I'm alive. And now I know what I came back for.

My people.

CHAPTER 5

Imbas, Izamal, and Cas leave me as the sky lightens, urging me to get some sleep. Izamal's retinue of warriors in blue march out after them, though when I press my ear to the main door, I hear soft shuffling sounds that betray the presence of guards.

I try doors until I find a room with an immense bed. Four people could sleep comfortably in it. Ridiculous for one person. But it's so soft that every time sleep laps at the edges of my mind, the sensation of falling wakes me up.

The third time I snap awake, I give up. The blankets come off the bed with a good tug, and I curl up on the floor.

Sleep takes me. Into a sweet, calming darkness.

My eyes open. I crawl out of the cocoon of blankets. Something has settled within me. My head is calm, and the room stays put when I rise to my feet. My limbs feel, if not strong, then stronger than they did yesterday. And there's something else—a giddy unreality, a foamy, fizzing feeling, rises up through me.

The rooms, though opulent, are simply arranged. Everything is off the main sitting room, except for the bathing room. The only way in there is in the bedroom, through a yellow door painted with flowers.

The door opens, and my feet touch cold stone. A gleaming brass cauldron sits at one end of the room, one large enough to dye several lengths of cloth. A long-necked faucet at its head. I twist the knob and water gushes out.

Astounding. I remember the view from the balcony; this is a tower of some height. To pump water up all that distance . . . It's incredible.

On a ledge beside the cauldron are a dozen faceted little bottles. Oils, fragranced with flowers, release a heady, delirious sort of smell. The scent takes me back to the palace gardens, a place where plants were grown for beauty, not for food. I remember walking through a hedge maze, turning a corner, finding myself face-to-face with Prince Dalca.

His eyes were liquid, molten. I remember him leaning in, his summer's sky–blue eyes filling my vision, his lips following, so very softly—

I tear myself away and stopper the oil. Enough of that.

I slip into the tub and wash away the grime of sleep, the memories of the dead. I wash the absurd length of my hair.

And as I rise, I know somehow that this day will be perfect.

Against one wall of the bedroom is a large, stately wardrobe. I fling open the double doors and freeze.

There are dresses galore. I grew up dressing for protection against the Storm. There's nothing like that here—no thick mosscloth cloak rubbed with slightly rancid wax, no thick shawl to wrap around my head and shoulders. Every scrap of fabric—even the underclothes—is made of a weave so fine that when I raise it to my cheek, it's no rougher than a kiss from the wind. Strangely, most of everything—from the trousers to the jackets to the belts—are shades of violet. Most of what isn't is in colors that would go well with it: soft sand, deep black, pale cream.

A dozen pairs of shoes, but not like any shoes I've known—they're made of a leather so fine that there's not a chance they'd withstand walking outdoors across moss and stone. Each is embroidered and set with gems, each more beautiful than the last—a pink pair embroidered with a pattern of curling vines; a deep violet pair embroidered with dark clouds and golden lightning; a silvery blue pair set with tiny glimmering stones like stars, a flock of long-necked birds rising against a pale gold sun.

I can't believe that all this could be meant for my use. It doesn't make sense that all this even exists, much less that it's for one person.

I reach for an outfit in violet fabric all embroidered with ikons. The jacket reaches past my hips, but otherwise it's not unlike the Wardana uniform. In a small way, it's a shield against the world.

A golden light shines into the sitting room, reaching from the balcony. The glass doors swing open at my touch.

I raise an arm against the red-gold brightness; while I slept, the sun rose and fell once more. I've caught it inching toward the horizon, in the last few moments before it's gone. A roar begins, a rushing sound that seems to come from everywhere.

I squint, letting my eyes adjust. And then I hear myself gasp, as if from far away.

The sky is as wide and colorful as the earth is vast and strange. The globe of the sun hangs lower than I've ever seen—in the time of the Storm, we could only ever see it directly above—and it wears a scarlet halo. Red glints off the rooftops in the distance, and glimmers on the surface of a dark, long river that winds its way from the horizon.

I lean further and make out the gnarled, dark shapes of what can only be trees, and beyond, immense spires of shining black rock, like needles or fingers rising up from the earth.

The roar grows louder. It comes from below. At the base of the tower, the crowd has thinned, but hundreds remain, gathering in the square below, around a grand statue with its back to me. So many people, faces turned up to me—the same way I once tilted my head up to watch the Wardana fly. They cheer and wave, a sea of motion.

A small group stands to the side, separate and still. They're given a wide berth. But they're so few, inconsequential amongst all the others, who revel with such hope and happiness.

A thrill rises through my body. I want to cheer with them. A shadow has lifted, and there's so much of the world to discover. A hunger grows in my belly, a hunger to know more: What are those strange spires? And where does the river lead? How far are we from the city, the inner five rings? How far are we from where the stormwall once stood, from what once felt like the edge of the world?

No wonder they're happy. We have freedom of a kind we've never tasted. To look outside our windows and see only beauty . . . It's out of a dream.

And I can give them more.

The Great Queen whispers, *Do not waste your power.*

This is no waste. Plus, what am I saving it for? There are no ghouls here.

I reach for her power and it rises to the surface of my skin in iridescent lines, and wisps of shadows like stormclouds ring my fingers.

Moss coats the sides of the tower and runs along the balcony's railing. To the touch it's damp and a little springy, and it trembles as it welcomes me. It's a thin and wide presence—one as effervescent as foam—and it's threaded with other life, with hair-thin vines and fingerlike leaves that stand at attention as my awareness passes them by.

I breathe out and pour the Queen's power into it.

Between my fingertips, small violet buds rise and open their petals wide. The change radiates out, and all along the watchtower, the green moss turns purple as flowers rise and take it over.

The crowd's amazement rises in wails, in shouts—and in a small, holy silence.

Look, I tell the Great Queen. She does not answer.

With my people's happiness loud in my ears, I slip back inside and stop dead before the figure waiting for me.

Izamal slinks closer. A cat is on his shoulders. No—not a cat. It has a curved beak, and though its eyes and ears are catlike, it's covered not in fur but dark feathers.

It stares at me.

"Hello," I say to it.

It turns away, shutting its eyes.

"Be nice," Izamal purrs, nuzzling it with his cheek. "She gave you your lovely breakfast."

"I did?" I ask.

Izamal grins and puts a finger to his lips. The catbird slinks down his arm and comes over to inspect my slippers. It has no tail—just a tuft of feathers—and it has something of a hunchback.

I glance at Iz. He pantomimes putting an arm out.

I do. The cat leaps and, midair, it spreads its wings—that wasn't a hump at all—and latches on to my arm with paws tipped in talons.

It looks at me with disdain, as if it's found me to be an inferior perch.

My arm could be made of wood, for all I dare move it. I whisper to Iz, "What now?"

The cat swivels its head to look from me to Iz. Only its head moves; the rest of its body is supernaturally still. A shiver runs down my spine as something in me responds to it. The Queen recognizes one of her own.

"This is a stormbeast," I say.

Izamal nods.

A stormbeast . . . a chimeric creature born of the Storm. They had bodies of swirling cloudsmoke and eyes that glinted with lighting, and were able to change their forms at will. But this creature seems flesh and blood, its form decided, permanent.

"When the Storm ended, many were caught mid-transformation. Some are well blended, others less so."

I let that sink in. "Incredible. Are they all this . . . sweet?"

He smiles. "There are some that are even sweeter. Mancers have been building a classification system. They call her an owlcat. I don't know that they can be so easily understood—there's all sorts, all magnificent." Izamal whistles softly, and the catbird—owlcat—returns to him. Iz brushes its coat; for a second his fingers seem tipped with claws.

He catches me. "Yes. I'm in charge of my curse now." A change ripples through his outstretched hand; nails lengthening into claws, soft downy pelt rising, fingers growing wider. He reverses it quickly. "Not always a pleasant feeling, that."

His hand—his curse—he can *control it?*—I swallow against the dryness in my throat. Of the hundreds of cursed that Amma helped . . . not one of them reversed their curses. Not one. "How?"

"Something to do with being lost in the Storm, maybe. When it ended . . . I was in agony. I was trapped in that body. And I ran to the wilds—I don't know why. To lick my wounds, I suppose. It took a while," he says with an apologetic smile and an air of glossing over something unpleasant. "And then, after a time . . . I felt a little spark. A glimmer of myself."

"A glimmer?"

He taps his temple. "Something in there. And it was like . . . a path unfurled. If I walked it, I could find my way back to myself." He breaks eye contact. "Dalca was there. He . . . helped."

He dips his head, his hair falling in long locks like a shield.

He's revealed a lot of himself to me. And it feels good that he trusts me, that he still sees me as a friend.

"Izamal. When I was gone . . . where I was, Nashira was there too."

He startles.

I go on. "You have to know . . . Nashira doesn't blame Dalca. She doesn't blame anyone. She says . . . her choices are her own."

The owlcat hoots, and I jump.

Izamal exhales, long and low, his shoulders dropping. "I . . . I forgave Dalca. I . . . I'm a different person," he says, and in his eyes is a desperate need for me to believe him. "Not just the curse. But who I was. I've left it all behind."

"All right," I say quietly.

"The past is dead," Izamal says. The words sound worn around the edges; carefully remembered and often spoken.

A snort comes from the door.

Casvian Haveli strides in, dressed more simply than I'm used to—in just a loose white shirt that ties around the wrists and dark trousers. No Wardana reds.

Izamal bristles. "How long have you been here?"

"I'm perfectly permitted to be here." Cas tosses his pale hair over his shoulder. "Vesper, if you'd like me to leave, just let me know."

He leans against the wall, a picture of calm but for the tenseness around his mouth. Izamal glowers openly. I glance between them, grasping for some thread that will help me understand the new undercurrent to their animosity. "Is something wrong?"

"No," Izamal bites out, too quick. "Nothing's wrong."

"Well," Casvian says, "Dalca's still asleep. The wilds are teeming with beasts." He gestures at the owlcat, who snaps at his fingers. Cas snatches his hand back.

Izamal hides his smile in the cat's feathers.

Cas clears his throat. "And . . ."

They hold each other's gaze. "Casvian." A vein in Izamal's jaw jumps.

Cas looks at him coolly. "And Vesper's late to the fine little show you've arranged."

Izamal holds his gaze for a second longer.

I cross my arms. "What?"

"It can wait. A few minutes more. She hasn't eaten."

"I'm not hungry. Iz, tell me what I don't know."

"That would take years." Izamal grins as if he's said something funny. He sighs at my expression and links his arm through mine, guiding me into the long, ornate dining area. "And tell me again that you're not hungry after seeing what the kitchens prepared for you."

He gestures at the table laid with food and moves as if he'll serve me. I grab a plate and hide my surprise at its weight—or lack of it. It's so very thin, made of something smoother than the clay I know, and decorated with delicate engravings. For Storm's sake, this isn't a plate—it deserves to be hung on a wall.

Izamal fills his plate with no such hesitation. I copy him, remembering what he once told me. *Put on your best act. Make them all think you belong, and you will.*

At least he's not asking to try a piece of everything before I eat it. He's calmed down, then, from yesterday.

It isn't until we're sitting that I notice that every last thing—from piping-hot pastries to bright-skinned fruits—has a sliver cut out, as if some mouse with good knife skills has taken to sampling everything. My bun has a neat triangle taken out of it, as does the small square of flatbread.

"When you said your owlcat ate . . ." I say, eyeing it where it perches on his shoulder.

Izamal brushes a crumb from his lapel. "Yes, well. Hila here has a unique gift of being able to sense when food isn't quite . . . edible."

My eyebrows go up.

"Not that anything—There's no—" He glances at Cas, who merely shrugs. "It's that . . . in the wilds, there are things—fruits, roots, all sorts of plants, really—that we didn't know if we could eat."

I recall Imbas saying much the same, but I frown. "The kitchens are cooking with fruits from the wilds."

Izamal nods.

"Fruit . . . that might be inedible," I say slowly. "No one checked it before they cooked it?"

A silence falls. Izamal's mouth opens and shuts.

Cas sighs. "He's skirting around the truth. Truth is—"

"Cas!" Izamal bounds to his feet. "The council—"

Cas gives him the barest glance. "There have been some scuffles, lately, between high ringers and low ringers. And since you are a hero beloved particularly by low ringers, *some* thought the high ringers might target you. Absurd, really. Dazera here is acting in an overabundance of caution."

High ringers and low ringers. I suppose I thought . . . now with the entire world open to us, people would have left all that squabbling behind. I suppose the past isn't so very dead, no matter what Iz thinks.

Izamal glares at Cas, but sits back down. "Cas is right," he says.

"Don't keep secrets from me," I say. "I can handle it."

Iz flinches, and his owlcat spreads its wings wide. He calms it down with a soft crooning. "It's just that . . . you were gone so long. You gave up so much. The least we could do was show you the good, first."

A strange and uneasy warmth fills me. It's like he's talking to me but seeing someone else. Another Vesper.

Cas reaches for a pastry. Instead of eating it, he tears it apart with his fingers.

Izamal looks miserable. "I'm sorry."

I shake off the dark mood that's settled over us. "Let's go. What's this I'm late for?"

Cas brushes the crumbs from his hands and gives me a small smile. "You'll see."

CHAPTER 6

"Are you listening?" Iz laughs at my expression. "Do you even know where we're going?"

I frown. "Downstairs?"

He laughs again. He stops at my door. "Vesper. You are many things, but you are also a vessel. That makes you a Regia. And a Regia needs a Regia's Guard."

I put a smile on my face, the smile he wants. But a pit opens up in my stomach as the doors swing wide. A Regia's Guard . . . Do I need protecting?

From what? Has my life changed so much that I'll never be able to walk around alone, instead of shadowed by hulking warriors?

The question rattles me, but I'm afraid to ask, afraid to put it into words and speak them into air. If the answer is yes, if the answer is this is who I have become . . .

Izamal opens the door and gestures me out.

My new home is at the very top of an ancient watchtower that was repurposed and rebuilt over the years by many, many hands, the most recent being those of the Wardana. They've named it the Queenskeep, Cas tells me, "After, of course, the fact that you were here." His face betrays no indication that he's teasing.

"Is it really?" I ask, my cheeks heating.

"I voted for it," Iz says.

The Queenskeep, Cas continues, sits at the heart of one of the sixth's market towns, where in times long past farmers would bring produce to sell or barter. *Town* seems a bit of an understatement—from what I've seen from my window, it's nearly a quarter the size of the fifth. But the buildings are spread further apart, so I can't quite gauge how many people might live here. Cas tells me that there are three other ancient towns, all also along the river, but only this one has been cleaned up and made fit for habitation. The others, he says, are still overrun with plants, covered in a blanket of moss and creeping, thorny vines.

The tower itself is like nothing I've ever seen. Gleaming black stone is everywhere—it's so well polished that the faint glow from ikonlight sconces casts dozens of glittering reflections. The three of us—Izamal leaves his owlcat behind—step out of my doors onto a wide circular landing, and I pause to take in the details that I missed the first time.

There are two other doors besides mine. My rooms face the south and the horizon, so the door opposite must lead to rooms that face the north and the inner five rings. The last door faces the east—though I can only guess at what the view might be. The farms of the sixth? The landing has no windows, which I suppose makes sense. To the west is a set of stairs leading downward.

Izamal speaks with the soft pride of one introducing a visitor to his home. "This tower is Wardana controlled. Restricted entry. Few can get into the infirmary level—that's three levels below us. And everything above that is ikonlocked and guarded."

I glance again at the door to the east. An intricate ikonlock at waist height covers nearly a third of its surface. It's as complex as Pa's. Maybe more.

"Where do those doors lead?" I ask.

Iz gestures not at the door I indicate, but at the one opposite, the one facing the city. "That one leads to Dalca's rooms."

Something uneasy stirs in me at the thought of Dalca right across the hall. I ignore it. "What about that one, with that ikonlock?" Up close, the lock reveals three layers of rings encircling a central ikon. It gives no clues as to how to solve it.

"That would be mine," Cas says.

"That's an incredible lock," I say. "How does it work?"

His lips quirk. "Try it and tell me."

"You don't want to go in there," Izamal says with a little more emotion than Cas's rooms likely warrant. He clears his throat. "Onward, please."

Two of his Wardana in blue descend the stairs first, then Iz, me, and Cas at the rear. Visions of tumbling down endless stairs—all of that same gleaming black stone—make me take them cautiously, with a hand on the railing. Izamal mentioned the infirmary being three levels below, but we go down at least four flights without seeing anyone, much less the white infirmary doors. The steps are endless. I hate stairs. What kind of Wardana uses stairs?

"Izamal—" I start, and blink at the lack of a thousand-and-one-feather cloak slung around his shoulders. I glance back at Cas, who wears no Wardana leathers at all—he's just strapped his gauntlet over a simple white shirt. No cloak. Have I seen cloaks on any of the Wardana? "Where are your cloaks?"

Izamal touches the hollow of his neck, right where his cloak's ikondial would be. His gaze goes over my shoulder, to Cas. "There's a . . . a shortage. The mancers are working on contraptions. They're calling 'em risers. You'll see—they have one set up that goes from ground floor to the infirmary. But you won't find me in one."

"They're perfectly safe," Cas says. "I worked on the one in this watchtower myself."

"Yes," says Izamal.

A furious shout comes from below, reverberating on the stone walls. Between one blink and the next, Izamal slips into the mold of a guard, his expression serious, and he herds me back up the last flight, to a small landing. I glance at Cas, who has his hand on his gauntlet.

A booming voice, sharply enunciated. "I am on the council. *You have no right to bar my way.*"

A mild voice answers. "Sir, you agreed to wait till the council meets."

"That was before I heard Imbas has already seen her. How can that—"

Iz motions for two of his people to head down. "And find out how he got up here in the first place," he orders.

I peer over the railing, but Izamal tugs me back. "Who's that?"

Izamal winces. "Rosander Tarr. Comes from a long line of land-keepers. Powerful with the merchants and the trades. A council member, as you can hear. You can see why we've hoped to have you meet them all at once. Limits the pain."

Rosander Tarr. I commit the name to memory. What is it he wants from me? I haven't had occasion to meet many people like that, people who are convinced of their place in the world so much so that they can bellow it at others.

His voice fades as he's herded away, and we resume our descent.

The landings grow larger as the tower widens. Here they lead not to doors, but to hallways that branch like spokes on a wheel.

"The council," I repeat. Iz, Cas, Imbas—they've all mentioned it. "What is this council?"

"It's, well, a ruling council. To replace the Regia in matters of governing. With seven seats, so everyone's voices are represented."

Seven seats, instead of all decisions being made by the Regia, who rarely left the first ring. "That's amazing," I say.

Iz grins. "Dalca's idea. Though I'd wager it was inspired by you."

I glance at him to make sure he isn't joking. "Who's on it?"

"Imbas, who you know. Me, as head of the Nosca-Wardana—a specialized bunch of Wardana, you've seen them in the blue uniforms—we go into the wilds, map what's out there . . . And then there's Dalca, who serves as head of the Wardana."

I interrupt. "Not as prince?"

Izamal gives me a laughing look. "That's what he says."

"Who else?"

"There's the mancers—They elected Cas, though he could be a bit more responsible about showing up," Izamal says pointedly.

Cas scowls. "All the shouting gives me a headache."

Izamal bares his teeth in disgust.

Cas bristles. "I am an ikonomancer. My time is better spent on useful endeavors—not *administration*, or what passes for it in your council—sitting in a room and shouting until every idiot at the table agrees on the only sensible course of action, which, in the several times I attended, was the very first thing proposed."

Izamal looks pleased at getting Cas riled up. "You have a point. It is more pleasant when you're not there."

From the spots of red on his cheeks and the sharpness of his glare,

I'd wager my left foot that Cas'll attend the next meeting, just to spite Iz. "Who else?" I ask.

"The landkeepers. That's Rosander. Then there's the trades. And the, uh, priestesses. They've all got representatives." He hesitates. "Thing is, stick with me and Imbas. The others . . . It's just everyone is looking out for their own interests, you know?"

Cas says nothing.

Sitting on the council, dealing with those people, making choices I've no qualifications to make . . . is that my new life?

Our descent ends at a landing guarded by Wardana. They move aside, blood-red and deep blue parting silently, to let us into a corridor. My posture stiffens a degree for every extra guard we pass.

The guards react to Izamal in the way people have always done—like flowers turning toward light. The fire that used to burn hot in him—fueled by rage at losing his sister, of being born cursed, as his father passed his curse along—is now a low, sinuous smolder. His confidence is easier, his beauty a little less weaponized. He returns looks not with smirks but with smiles.

They watch Cas, too. But he stares straight ahead. His face settles into a mask of arrogance, but the pinkness of his ears gives him away. They never watched him like this before, not with admiration. I mostly remember people whispering warnings of his impending arrival and taking great care to get out of his way.

The mosaic wall, in the room I'd awoken in, that depicted the four of us going into the Storm. It was a reminder—a warning—that our lives had become a story. A legend that belonged more to those who told it than to us four.

They watch me, too. I only catch the tail end of their fleeting glances—not a single person sustains eye contact, as if they want to watch me, but can't stand the idea of me seeing them.

Izamal moves a few paces ahead as a Nosca falls in step with him, his head tilted toward her as she speaks. I can't catch what she says, but from her stiff body language, it appears to be some kind of report.

A smell hits me—leather and sweat, sharp metal and bitter oil—that takes me back to the Ven, to the Wardana training rooms. It grows stronger further into the hallway, mingling with other scents, of damp stone and old smoke, of the slightly sweet-smelling wax used to make sticks of mancer's charcoal.

Casvian keeps pace with me and lowers his voice next to my ear. "I know he means a lot to you. But . . . he's changed, all right?"

"We've all changed."

Cas makes an irritated sound. "He loves it, Vesper. He loves being in charge. People looking up to him. The adoration. Every night, he goes and shows off the transformation he can do—that he's conquered his curse—he uses it to charm people into his bed."

His words paint a picture. I hide my smile. "Cas . . . the Storm's gone. Why shouldn't he have fun?"

Cas grows pinker, his lips drawing into a thin line. Is he jealous of Iz? Of the attention? "The Storm may be gone, but—" He stops and sighs. "Just don't trust him so much, all right?"

A flicker of irritation runs through me. "I trust him with my life."

His features arrange themselves into lordly disinterest. "Right. As long as it's your life."

He steps back, but his words stick like a burr. Izamal has a good heart. But do I trust him with my life? I trust Nashira with my life. Or, I suppose, I trusted her with my death. Did I transfer what I felt for her over to Izamal?

I let out a noise of irritation. No. I don't have any reason not to trust

Izamal. I have just as much reason to trust him as I do Cas.

But I don't need to think like this. The Storm is over. There's nothing to fight. Right?

"Right?" Izamal echoes my thoughts.

I jump. When did he return?

"You really haven't been paying attention to me," Iz says laughingly. "Look sharp. We're here."

He stops before a set of wooden double doors, manned by two guards. "Vesper, come meet your Regia's Guard."

I put that same hollow smile back on my face. If they've come to be a Regia's Guard, then let me be a Regia.

The doors open to a large training room with polished metal walls. Ikonlight pendants hang from the ceiling, casting a bright glow upon everyone already gathered.

Cas slinks in and stands against the wall. But no matter the stealthiness of his demeanor, his white hair draws the eye. Imbas inclines her head, all straight-backed confidence and quiet wisdom. A green-eyed woman stands at her side. She shoots me a wink, and I recognize her as one of Imbas's allies.

Izamal joins her side, and two Nosca stand at the door.

And then there are thirteen women who could be my sisters. More than sisters—it's like looking at my reflection in a rippling pond. A thrum goes through them, a vibration that reminds me of plucking at a sitar string.

Iz must read the bewilderment on my face, for he leans in and murmurs, "Dalca went through the Wardana rosters and selected fourteen from his best fighters. One of his picks stepped down to have a child. But these thirteen are here for you, for the honor of being chosen for your Guard."

"All of them?" How can I go anywhere with thirteen people following me?

"You'll pick your seven."

My hands grow clammy, and I wipe them on my dress. I don't want to make this decision. He's asking me to judge them to their faces, and tell half of them that they weren't good enough for me?

Cas meets my gaze. He hesitates only a second before approaching. Izamal tenses as he nears.

When I think of the Regia's Guard, I think of Cas's father, Ragno Haveli. How he glided through the halls of the palace in the Regia's Guard black-and-gold uniform—his status made him untouchable, his competence made him lethal, and his looks—all of Cas's icy paleness, but twice Cas's size—made him impossible to forget.

Intimidating, impressive—and he couldn't have looked less like Dalca's mother, the Regia. This is no tradition of the guards.

I ask them both. "Why do they all look like me?"

Cas steps in after a moment of silence. "That would be Dalca's idea. To give you guards that could be your double, if needed."

Guards that could be my double. It's one thing too far. All the tiny peculiarities of the last day come to mind—things that meant little on their own, but now all together, they paint a picture. Wardana everywhere. Iz and his owlcat testing my food. "You think I'm in that much danger?"

They speak at once: Izamal splutters, "Of course you're not in danger—" as Cas says drolly, "Every Regia is always in danger—"

I cross my arms. "I told you, I can handle it. Is this because of the high ringers?"

They share a terse glance. Izamal speaks first. "Yes. But you don't need to worry, because you're well protected from anything that could happen."

"Dalca saw to that," Cas interjects. "He's been preparing for you to wake, and yes, there are things you need to know." He goes on over Iz's protests. "And when Dalca's healed, when he wakes, he'll tell you everything—"

A voice cuts in. "When he wakes, I'm sure the prince will have much to say." Imbas gives me the tiniest of smiles. Behind her, Izamal relaxes. "But for now . . . these women have waited long for the honor of your attention."

With a hand at my elbow, she steers me toward the women. I side-step her touch. What are they keeping from me? I'm the vessel of the Queen—I can handle it. But I swallow down the prickle of irritation—I don't know if it's self-preservation or some version of the manners Amma instilled in me, but I don't want to argue here.

I take a breath and turn to the women standing, waiting, for me.

One has gray eyes just a tad lighter than mine, set in a heart-shaped face. She smiles, two perfect dimples framing her lips—and that's where our similarities end. I've never been that cute. One looks quite a lot like me, just stretched out—she's taller, with a longer face and longer limbs. Another, who's all curves, stands with her hip cocked, her tip-tilted eyes scanning me from head to toe. She, too, smiles, but I can almost read the self-satisfaction in her thoughts, in whatever way she's measured me and found me wanting.

There are two women who are the least like me—not just because of their facial features or their shorter hair, but because their arms and legs are corded with muscle, their feet set in wide, sure-footed stances—maybe I could look like them if I trained as a Wardana fighter, if I worked at it for years, if I could run up a thousand flights of stairs and not once get winded.

In all these women are the possible lives I might've lived, if I had made different choices.

I come to the end of the line, to a woman who stands a little apart from the rest. A shiver runs down my spine. How did I not notice her first?

She holds herself like a Wardana, confident and in command, and watches me approach. She looks the most like me—and the most unlike me. Everything about me is heightened in her—where I'm too soft, she's sharp; where I'm weak, she's strong. Her eyes are a velvety black that seems to see everything and reveal nothing.

I'm mesmerized by her. She looks like a ruler, like a Regia, like a Queen.

I'd be able to dismiss her as someone just born perfect, but for the smattering of pockmarks across her cheeks. They make her more . . . more something. More real. A bitter ache hollows out my stomach. I know better—Amma taught me better—than to let this slippery sort of envy gain a foothold in my mind.

I offer her a smile and turn to Izamal. I keep my voice low. "How am I supposed to pick?"

Izamal gestures, and one of his Nosca moves forward. She tucks her hands behind her back and calls out a command.

They get into rows of threes, moving into a drill of some sort. They don their gauntlets. These are different from the standard issue, from any I've seen Dalca, Cas, or Iz wear.

The dimpled one wears a gauntlet that goes from wrist to shoulder. When she activates an ikondial, half the mass is transferred into a sword. Swords were rare in the time of the Storm, for if a stormbeast was within the reach of a sword, a Wardana was within reach of claws, stingers, teeth, and likely, their death. She grins, and there's an intelligent sort of slyness to it. "Gamara Tonin, at your service."

I return her smile, though I have a feeling she's as likely to laugh at me as with me.

The two warrior women who look unlike me are Jhuno and Zerin Rin, fraternal twins and brutal fighters.

The one at the end, the one who looks like a queen—she wears two gauntlets that go from fingertip to elbow. She clicks her wrists together, and two circular blades appear, gleaming discs with handles set inside. "Hadria Belvas," she says in a low, velvety voice when she catches my eye, dipping into a shallow bow.

Imbas leans in. "She's not an ideal choice, despite what Dalca thinks. Her mother is a high ringer who leads a group of people unhappy with how things have shaped up since the Storm's end."

"What, they miss the Storm?"

Imbas doesn't laugh.

"They really do?"

"They miss knowing their place in the world," Imbas says. "Fourth- and fifth-ringers now have options. Some of them have power. Dalca likely added her to the list so he wouldn't be accused of showing favoritism to low ringers. But there's no need for you to pick her—this is honor enough."

Imbas slows to a stop before a girl who's easily the worst of the lot. She drops her bladeless staff with a clatter. "This one, I strongly suggest you do pick."

"Her?"

Imbas drops her voice low. "You knew her under another name."

Another name? I stare at her.

She picks up her staff and gives me a wink and a wry smile. There's something in the sheer confidence that appears for a second across her features, before she pulls back on the serene demeanor of a perfect guard. She's an excellent actor—if I judged her on expression and the set of her shoulders, I'd have no doubt she knew her way around a Wardana spear. And yet the evidence of my own eyes shows her dropping it yet again.

An excellent actor . . .

"C—" I cut myself off at Imbas's look. Is this the girl I knew as Carver? An ikonomancer I met in the gray market, who altered faces with ikons—for a price.

"Cardel Maver, at your service." She bows.

"You've changed," I say.

"Thank you," she replies.

Imbas touches my elbow. I step back at her urging, and the potential guards begin another demonstration, splitting into groups of two and sparring.

A couple fighters shine. One has brown hair and wields a scythe—a weapon I've only seen Cas's father use. She moves with such explosive speed that it's like watching a firecracker. Her opponent taps out, and she whoops, beaming so widely that it makes me smile. She leaps, dipping into an extravagant, gallant blow. "I'm Minava Arvanas, but please, call me Mina."

Hadria is silent as she fights her opponent—the only sound from her is the hiss of her circular blades cutting through the air. Her opponent grunts with effort. She blocks Hadria's blows with her staff, but with each parry, she takes a small step backward. Hadria is in control, and she's beautiful to watch, like a dancer.

Hadria's opponent drips sweat. Her lips are twisted in a snarl, but her gaze is strangely distant.

Izamal calls a halt, and Hadria and her opponent break apart, standing side by side, heaving with exertion.

I nod at Hadria, and smile at the other fighter. "What is your name?"

She keeps her head bowed for a long moment, her chest heaving, her hair shadowing her features. She exhales, long and slow. Her eyes fix on me as she rises, her face twisted in a cruel grimace.

My skin prickles in warning. *Danger.* I step back. The Great Queen rises, her mark spreading across my skin.

She lunges toward me, sword in hand, and snarls, "The Great King welcomes you."

The Queen's power is sluggish inside me—I've used too much making the moss bloom—and I fight to pull it out—

A wisp of cloud comes from my hand. Her blade slices across my palm, and the hot sting of blood follows—

I raise the other hand, willing a stormbarrier but knowing I'll be too slow—Izamal shouts, his voice comes from too far away to help—

A clang—a metallic echo.

A curtain of silky black hair stands before me. Hadria. Her circular blades trap the sword, and she tears it from the girl's hand—the girl drives her knee into Hadria's stomach—or rather, where Hadria's stomach was—

Hands grab me and pull me back—

Hadria leaps back and slices with her weapon, but the girl dodges, and the blade cuts through strands of hair instead of her throat.

Izamal lunges—Hadria springs—

Everything stills.

The attacker stands. Hadria's arm is wrapped around her throat, pinning her to Hadria's body.

The girl gasps for air. Her eyes loll in their sockets until they fix, unblinkingly, on me.

She points, her index finger aimed at my heart. Her mouth opens, emits a hollow rasp. She doesn't have the air for words.

For a split second, the light in her eyes brightens—and disappears, like a candle snuffed out.

Her head lolls to the side.

"She's out," Izamal says. "Hadria—let her go."

Hadria drops her with no ceremony. She stands over the girl's unconscious body, chest heaving, eyes sharp and furious. Nosca take over, tying the girl's hands and carrying her away.

I lower my arms, the Queen's mark fading. I pry the hands from my waist—a glance over my shoulder reveals a grim-faced Cas.

Hadria turns to me, bows, then walks back to her place in line.

"I pick her," I say.

The others are frozen still. Mina Arvanas is the closest, with her spear out as if she would've intervened, if Hadria not taken care of it so quickly. She lets out a low, impressed whistle and slaps Hadria on the back. The tiniest smile breaks through Hadria's cool and collected mask, but it's gone the next second.

Cas murmurs in my ear. "It's best we get you away. In case . . ."

In case the attacker awakes? In case there are others? *The Great King welcomes you.*

I scowl. "The attacker—what did she mean?"

Cas shrugs and busies himself with treating the cut on my palm.

Over his head, I meet Iz's gaze. He glances away, at Hadria. "It's a . . . high-ringer squabble," Iz says. "Don't worry about it."

"A high-ringer squabble," I repeat, disbelieving.

"Not here," he murmurs. "Please. Let me take care of this." There's earnestness in his golden eyes, and fear too. The others are watching. I've stepped into a role that I don't understand, that I'm not sure I know how to play. But I trust Izamal.

I unclench my jaw. A horrible feeling turns my stomach. "Iz."

Iz smiles. "Don't worry."

He turns away, but not before I see what's in his eyes.

A deep and terrible sorrow.

CHAPTER 7

Everyone tells me lies.

The first is innocent. "You look beautiful," the seven members of my guard say when I step out into the sitting room, wearing the silvery gown the city's finest tailors made for me.

Each of them dons an identical dress, save for Jhuno and Zerin. We've already gone through a few sets of more ordinary clothing—each made with five copies, so no matter what I wear, I can be sure someone will be ready to take my place. This particular dress is for a festival to celebrate my awakening. The thought of it turns my blood cold.

I've put on a smile for most of these two long days since meeting my guard, but it falls when I step up to the polished mirror. The mirror tells me the truth: I don't look good in it. Hadria does. The thick cloth curls along her body in a way that makes me think of the arches of a temple—austere, holy, beautiful.

I look like a melting candle. All the embroidered flourishes at my chest and hips pucker and wilt with little to support them.

"Beautiful," Gamara says again, flashing her dimples.

"Absolutely," agrees Ozra Tull, who had to dye her red hair black for the job and still seems to mourn it.

"Fits you better than it does me," says Mina, and at least that inches toward the truth. The seams strain around her shoulders, but the cloth droops hollowly everywhere else. I'd still say I have her beat, but she's angling for second place.

Jhuno and Zerin laugh, until Gamara asks the tailor to make copies for them as well.

The tailor glances at me. I shrug. "Yes, of course."

"We're not meant to be your doubles," Jhuno says, gesturing at her height.

I smile. "You both have every right to feel just as pretty as I do."

They look less than pleased.

Only Hadria doesn't speak. She merely tugs the dress off when the tailor finishes.

"Just needs a tweak or two," says Carver, as she pinches and plucks her dress, resettling it around her hips and adjusting her posture, until something clicks—and it looks fantastic.

I scowl at my reflection. Every one of them is better at this. At looking the part, definitely—but they're also all so confident, unworried. Sure of their place.

The giddiness of being back, being alive—it's faded into a cold realization that I'm just playing a role. And if I don't play it well . . . if they see me as I am . . . will they still feel that all of it was worth it? These ornate rooms, the mosaics, the clothes, the guard—how can I deserve this?

The Queen's power, in the form of little wisps of stormcloud, peels out of me, stark and embarrassingly obvious against the pale silver of the gown.

The tailor's face blanches, but his assistant merely tuts. "Think we'd better go in for darker colors, Your Queenship, and a bit more volume, perhaps. We've got a good length of silk made from the nightlock spiders in the hollows a little west of the city. And I'd wager the rumors of them spiders being cursed wouldn't matter much to you, would it?"

She doesn't wait for me to answer, but as she's getting my measurements, she gifts me a small, sisterly smile. "It was the wrong cut for you, love. Worry not."

Gamara sighs as the gowns are packed away. Hila the owlcat trills from its perch atop a high shelf, a sound rather like laughing.

Hadria inches closer, her gaze on the tailor's assistant—I figure she thinks the woman might stab me under the pretense of measuring my waist.

I hide my sigh and plaster on a smile. If this is what it means to be a Regia, if this is how things are supposed to be . . . I can do this.

Imbas comes to visit, bearing news about the council's meeting. She talks for half an hour of unimportant things, until she gets to the point: it's to take place tomorrow night. I listen to her with half an ear—the view out the glass doors to the balcony is far more interesting.

"Vesper . . ." Imbas seems to be working up the courage to say something else when a knock comes at the door.

"Let me answer," Ozra Tull says, rising.

"Imbas," I say, returning my focus to her. "You were saying—"

Imbas's gaze is fixed over my shoulder, at whoever stands in the doorway at my back. The room goes silent.

His voice reaches me first. A soft and halting "Vesper."

Dalca. The room turns, and my guards, Imbas, everything falls away, disappearing under the weight of the miserable fury that quickens my blood.

He leans heavily on a cane. Bandages cover his arms and disappear into his sleeves. Hair-thin scars cross his face in the pattern of a Regia's mark, half-healed but angry-looking.

Dalca breathes, "You're awake."

"So are you." My voice comes out cold.

He hesitates, searching me for some clue, some warmth.

He looks so lost. And I don't know why I can't stand him, why I'm so irritated. I look away and find my words. "I . . . thank you. If you hadn't said what you did, I might not have found the way back."

A flicker of pain in his eyes. "I'm sorry if I forced you to return. It must have been . . . peaceful."

A memory comes unbidden, of how relieved he was to learn he was dead. "No," I say. "I'm glad to be here."

His brows draw together. "You don't know," he says, slowly. "Vesper. There is something I need to tell you."

"Dalca." Imbas appears at his side. "I must borrow him urgently," she says to me.

Without giving me a second to answer, she drags him out the door, shutting it behind them.

Mina clears her throat and leans toward me. "You can hear through the door."

"Mina," Hadria chides.

"Hads, come and stand beside me," Mina says. They neatly block the rest of the room. Feeling a little foolish, I press my ear to the door.

Imbas pitches her voice low. "The council has not agreed."

Dalca, righteous and simmering. "She deserves to know."

A scoff. "You made the council. If you undermine it, why bother with the pretense of distributing power?"

"That—you can't use that against me. Not for this. She must know—"

"She has been asleep for three years. Give her a chance to be a girl. To get used to it all. She never even saw the sixth, Dalca."

A pause. "You're afraid," he says. "Of her."

"Yes."

"Vesper is better than you give her credit for."

"You don't know that. She's been dead, Dalca."

"There's nothing wrong with her."

"You may need that to be true. But that doesn't make it so."

Footsteps sound, uneven and punctuated by the thud of a cane. A knock comes loud and clear through the wood of the door. I jump back and rub my ear, swinging the door open.

Dalca stands on the other side.

His eyes soften. "Vesper."

Over his shoulder, Imbas scowls.

Dalca leans in, one arm going stiffly around me. "Find our city," he whispers into my ear. "Find a way to see it."

The city. I rear back, searching his expression. "Wha—"

"Yes," Dalca interrupts. His gaze flicks over my shoulder. "You'll take good care of her, Hadria, won't you?"

"Of course," Hadria says from right behind me, her voice all silk.

"Dalca," Imbas calls from the landing.

"I must go." He sweeps into a bow. "Vesper. I'm glad you're here, too."

The door shuts. Somewhere in all this is another lie.

Izamal comes in later, hair windswept and cheeks warm, smelling of loamy dirt and rich wood. The owlcat soars down from the rafters to perch on his shoulder, where it plucks a twig from his hair.

"Leave it, Hila," he mutters. "Maybe I liked it there."

"I'm going out," I say.

His lips quirk. "Lovely to see you too."

I move past him. Hadria and Mina are quick on my heels, followed by Jhuno and Zerin. Ozra, Gamara, and Carver stay behind.

"Wait," Iz says. "We'll have a rambler brought. Won't take a moment."

He goes ahead. It takes several moments to descend the stairs. The tower broadens out once we're below the infirmary level, though with the Wardana clearing the way, I barely see anyone else.

The stairs end in a large hall space that smells vaguely sweet, like grain. Hadria and Mina hurry me along—I get a brief impression of high ceilings and heavily fortified doors—we step through an immense archway, and all of a sudden, we're outside.

I take a deep breath of crisp air. The sky is violet; the sun must have just set. It occurs to me that my sleep cycle has gotten strange. I've been awake during the night and asleep during the day. No one's complained, thankfully. In truth, it seems like everyone I've met keeps to a similar nocturnal schedule. For some reason, people have changed their habits. Or perhaps we're all enjoying the novelty of not having to fear the dark.

"There." Hadria ushers me toward a strange cart: a long oval suspended between four wheels, studded with round windows.

Unusual, but not as unusual as the magnificent creatures that pull it. Beasts taller than me, with corkscrewing horns of pale blue-green; long, spindly legs; and a covering of soft blue-black fur that fades to white around their eyes and their hooves. Their soft brown eyes watch me approach, horizontal pupils widening.

The Queen knows them; it is her power that made them. My fingers brush the neck of the one nearest me, and it relaxes, recognizing something familiar in me.

Cas appears at my side. "Magnificent, isn't it?"

Its fur is so soft in one direction, so prickly in opposite. "Yes."

"Took near three months to perfect."

I blink. I don't think we're talking about the same thing. His eyes are trained on the vehicle behind the beasts, his smile soft and proud. I see. "So, this is a rambler."

Cas opens a door in the side and helps me up into it. "Not just any rambler. I designed this one myself," he says as I admire the ikonwork etched into everything. "If need be, we can cut the beasts free, and it'll propel itself for a fair distance."

Hadria joins me and Cas inside, while Mina takes a seat on the driver's bench, right behind the beasts.

"Budge up," Jhuno says, and she and Zerin join Mina, one on each side.

Mina scowls as she's squashed between them. "Fine," she says, "but I'm driving." She takes hold of the straps, and at her urging, the beasts move.

I grab the seat as the rambler lurches, then let go when it settles into a soft swaying motion.

"Where do you want to go?" Hadria asks.

The possibilities steal my breath away. "Everywhere."

"We'll take the long way into the market square, then," Hadria says. She opens a hatch and murmurs the same to Mina.

Round windows the size of plates dot the length of the rambler.

Cas taps one, and I move closer.

The rambler rattles over a bridge, and below glows violet with the reflection of the sky. It sneaks under arching bridges and spidery walkways, all the way to the horizon. "This river . . ." I trail off. Has it always been there?

"It runs from north to south," Cas says, "and separates in two around the inner five rings, like the outline of an eye, with the five rings the iris. It seems, in the sixth's heyday, the farms diverted water from the river through canals."

"How far does it go?" I ask.

"That we don't know." On either side of the riverbank rise buildings with sloping rooftops made of a slate-blue tile.

"The Queenskeep." Cas gestures at a window that shows the view behind us.

What I thought was one watchtower is a set of five. A giant's hand—four tall towers and one squat. The tallest by far—the pointer finger—tapers at its peak, and it alone is covered in flowers. That'll be my rooms at the top, then.

Between the towers should be a view of the inner five rings of the city, but there's only the darkness of the wilds—mottled trees and those odd spires. We must be further from the city than I thought, or at such an angle that the wilds are blocking our view.

I face forward. Rising up over the town's blue-slate rooftops, far in the distance, are tall knobbly spires, like needles in a giant's pincushion. Some curve into immense arches, some just spiral toward the sky, some twine with the gnarled, blackened trees that remain.

The sixth was once farmlands. Orchards, paddies, and fields of grain. "What are those spires?"

Cas answers. "As far as we can tell, that's what happens when lightning strikes the mineral deposits."

"Lightning made those things?"

"Years and years of lightning. They're much taller and stranger in the seventh."

The seventh ring. Longing tugs at me like a thread tied to my navel. The seventh is more a legend than a real place—it was long gone a hundred years before I was born.

My gaze finds the horizon, as the sun dips below. Beyond the sloped blue rooftops, primordial trees raise their branches to the sky, their tall trunks like columns of a strange, solemn palace, light piercing through their leaves in holy slants. A flock of long-tailed birds take to the sky.

"The Storm is really gone, isn't it?"

"Yes," Cas says. "Well and truly."

Mina turns us back toward the towers of the Queenskeep, and we rattle into the town proper, past neat, wide streets bracketed by well-kept two- and three-story buildings.

A good half of the town's buildings still bear moss. Some of them have trimmed it back in tidy squares or patterns. We pass a man on a ladder, trimming the moss on the side of a building into a checkerboard. I swallow down the strange incredulous awe that rises in me. I remember the wonder I felt when I first stepped out of the shadow of the Storm, into the sunlight. This is no less strange.

At Amma's, I spent hours scraping the moss from our windowsills and front door. It would grow back in days. And now people are tending to it as if it's a beloved pet.

Many buildings are near pristine, scrubbed clean and fitted with new doors and shutters. If not for the blue-violet stains that curl like clouds across the stone, there would be little evidence to show for their time in the Storm. Personally, I'd go for one of those. I've had enough of moss.

It's strange. No matter which window I glance out of—perhaps due to the angle or the height of the buildings closest to us—I can't see the city, the inner five rings.

Not even the tallest dome of the palace is visible. If it weren't for Dalca's whispered words, it would be a welcome change—the palace features in so many of my memories, looming over the rest of the city, golden and glittering, haloed in sunlight, unreachable and uncaring.

I'll find a different angle for a better look.

The street curves and lets us out in a central square, illuminated by dozens of twinkling ikonlights. A great statue stands in its very heart; a man sits on the edge of the platform and plucks out a tune on a small stringed instrument, one that looks like a miniature version of Amma's sitar.

Mina knocks on the roof. "We can get out here for a moment, if you'd like."

I hop out before she's finished. Cas and Hadria dog my heels.

Market stalls line the edges of the square, though it looks like the market is closed for the night. A few stragglers remain; one burly shopkeeper finishes loading up his wares in the back of a cart that's led by a peculiar-looking stormbeast.

It's as if two creatures were cut in half and pasted together—the back half is some sort of furred, bushy-tailed giant rodent, the front half is a toothy reptile. Where the halves meet is a clear line where scales become fur. It grins at me.

If it's the Queen's power that made it that way . . . she must have a peculiar sense of humor.

Hoofbeats come from a side street. I circle around the statue, following the sound. Two other beasts are on leads; one has the horns of
an aurochs, but its bovine legs end in chicken's feet.

"There," Cas says from my elbow. "Those are my favorite."

He points partway down a street. Two shaggy frost-blue creatures
with long, many-jointed legs and antlers that look like glass. They scuff
at the floor. A pair of laughing girls brush their coats, while a third,
much younger, child balances on a post, weaving a string of flowers
through the beasts' antlers.

How many kinds of stormbeasts are there? The blue antlered ones
are perfectly peculiar, like they might have stepped out of the pages
of a children's tale. But the reptile-rodent shows its seams, as if it were
caught mid-transformation when the Storm ended.

"They're not afraid at all."

"No," says Cas. "Of course, these beasts have been tamed."

I glance at him. "And those that haven't?"

"That's Dazera's business. He and the Nosca keep those beasts
from leaving the wilds." Cas shrugs. "I'm sure he'll be happy to tell you
more. I've never seen him turn down a chance to brag."

My gaze slips past him, to the statue. We've circled around to the
front, to her face.

She gazes into the distance, a determined furrow to brows set over
mournful large eyes. Her soft lips are curled just a tad downward as if
in focus, and her hands are raised, as if holding something back. Long
hair spills over her shoulders and across the generous curves of her
chest, disappearing into the folds of a dress beautifully sculpted to be
diaphanous. She's a goddess.

But I've never seen her likeness before. It doesn't look like an
old sculpture—there are no moss stains, and none of the worn-away

softness that stone gains with the weathering of time.

Her face. Her features look so familiar—a little like Hadria—and a sharp crack of horror stuns me.

I keep my voice flat, lest it give me away. "Who is that?"

Mina puts her hands on her waist and leans back. "It sure is a feat, isn't it?"

"It's—" Cas's throat works. "It's a depiction—an artist's perspective—"

"It's you," Hadria says.

My stomach sinks, though it's what I feared. A statue of me. But it's not—I'm not her. She looks nothing like me.

It's her they celebrate. Her they love. Not me.

Can I become her?

Cas hasn't stopped talking, though he now wears an irritatingly gracious expression. ". . . You are very pretty, Vesper, and those that don't think so, well—"

I tune him out. He was among those who didn't think so—well, he was three years ago, when everything was terrible but at least it all made sense.

"It's time to move on, isn't it?" Mina says.

The musician at the base of the statue begins again a song he was playing when we entered the square.

Unusual.

The blue beasts haven't moved, and neither have the girls who are still brushing their coats. One glances away quickly when she catches me looking, breaking into a nervous peal of laughter.

A couple strolls arm in arm through the square; she wears a loose, gauzy shawl. A breeze sends it fluttering—revealing the edge of her Wardana gauntlet.

I cross my arms. "What is this?"

"A bad idea," Cas says, running a hand through his hair. "I'm going to kill Dazera."

I jab a finger in his chest. "Why would you do this? Put on a charade, like I'm a child?"

Cas's eyes go sad. "I'm sorry."

"That's not a reason."

Mina steps in. "It was to protect you. To ease you into the world."

I give her a withering look. "Are you my guard? Or my keepers?"

She looks stricken.

I step back. "Let me be."

"Wait—at least, let's take the rambler," Mina calls, but I ignore her. I set out at random, picking one of the many streets that lead out of the square.

I walk on.

Beyond the sanitized area I've been allowed to see, things change dramatically.

Stalls line the alleys, and the way is packed with people.

Cas and Hadria march at my side. Cas flings a cloak of soft brown cloth over my shoulders. "Put your hood up," Cas murmurs.

I ignore him.

"Please," he says.

I sigh and tug it over my ears.

As we go deeper, the stalls disappear, but the people remain. Dozens of them, some hurrying down streets, some walking leisurely, others perched outside their homes.

Two men play a game, moving dark pieces on a white board. One of the men sits on his doorstep; the other sits in a barrel full of pale slime as more oozes from his skin. A stormtouched—bearing the Storm's curse. He uses a long stick to move his pieces.

He's not the only cursed out and about. We pass a group of laughing women sharing cups of sundust tea—one has skin of mottled wood. And maybe we've passed others—not all curses are visible. How many more will overcome their curses, like Izamal?

From an open doorway comes the smell of toasted pastry and spices. I inhale. I bet that's not shalaj.

The crowd thickens. Voices come from somewhere in the crush of people. Shouts and a rising grumble—a fight.

I push my way to the front, dodging elbows and boots.

A weeping woman kneels on the ground, surrounded on all sides. A red-cheeked man, his eyes wide and darting—fear or madness—points at her. "She's one of them!"

"No—please—I'm not," she manages between sobs. "Please—"

Hadria puts an arm in front of me.

A woman steps out from the circle. "Who's her family?"

Hadria is pushed against my side as the crowd jostles. She holds her ground, creating inches of space around me. I stand on my toes. Ripples run through the crowd as people make their way forward; three children—one about eight, the other two around five years old—are thrust into the center.

The red-cheeked man puffs up. "They're all lightstruck!"

The smallest child stares blankly.

"Lightstruck?" I murmur, glancing up at Hadria.

A hand pressed against my back. Cas. "If you've seen enough . . . we must go."

They shoulder their way out, and I follow in their wake. My hood falls back just as we make it out of the crowd.

A three-note whistle rolls over the rooftops, and Hadria's attention snaps to it. She curses and catches Cas's eye. "It's them."

Hadria pulls a small brass ball from a pouch at her waist and tosses it to the ground. A violet flare rises, hissing, high over our heads.

Cas hurries me back toward the market square as a thrum of attention goes through the street.

"Haveli!" A bark from the rooftop. Cas looks up, and I follow his gaze to Izamal, who gestures to a street. "This way."

A half dozen Wardana materialize around us, slipping out from shuttered stalls and jogging up from side streets. A handful wear red leather under nondescript cloaks, but others are in ordinary clothes. I recognize the musician from the market square, but his miniature sitar is nowhere in sight.

Cas makes a turn, and my guard surrounds me. Mina gives me a terse nod as they activate their gauntlets. Shields and spears materialize in a show of ikonomancy, forming a circle around me. Jhuno and Zerin unsling bows from their backs, notching arrows and pointing them at the sky.

The Queen's power rises within me, beating time with my heart, spiking with my panic.

We move. My thoughts fall apart in a blur of sandstone and moss, of gleaming metal and flashes of blue and red leather, of arrows thudding and breaking against stone, of Hadria's hand on my neck, pressing me low, her voice urging me into a run.

An explosion, and a triumphant whoop. Cas rises, silhouetted by a plume of greenish fire. He throws something, and another green flame rises from the stone. Dark shapes stand on the other side of the fire—our pursuers.

A figure moves above him. Someone running on the rooftops.

Jhuno looses an arrow at them, but they knock it away with what looks like a Wardana spear.

"Vesper!" Hadria drags me around the corner. We lose two Wardana—the sitarist and a woman with hair in thick braids—as they hang back, raising spears against our attackers.

My body is jittery, strange. The Queen's power is ready—but what do I do? Who do I use it against? The way the Wardana work together—it's seamless, without a place for me.

Hadria wraps an arm around my middle and half drags, half propels me onto a thin bridge.

A thud sounds—like someone jumping down from a roof—and Hadria spins up, swinging me behind her.

A beautiful man with long red hair and white paint around his eyes. He rises from a crouch, bearing twin swords. With a shout, he leaps.

Hadria parries his attacks. I edge my way back—do I raise a storm-barrier?

A whistle of an arrow. Instinctively, I raise a small puff of a storm-barrier that intercepts the arrow—the arrow comes out the other side as a puff of dandelion fluff.

The arrow came from behind the red-headed man. Three others stand at his back, each with the same white paint around their eyes. What is this? Are these the lightstruck?

Izamal's spear catches one attacker behind her knees and she falls. Cas throws another one of his devices and two attackers go up in green flame. As they flail, Cas shoves them over the bridge's railing, into the river below.

"Enough!" The shout comes from above. A dark figure peels away from a rooftop on the far side of the bridge. Her black hair billows in the wind, unbound in the style of the high ringers. "The Stormender is under my protection. Attack her, and answer to me."

Hadria glances up, and in her moment of distraction, the red-haired man ducks past her, blades raised, face twisted in a snarl as he lunges toward me—

In the blink of an eye, the woman on the rooftop raises a bow and nocks and looses an arrow.

A hollow thud. The man falls to his knees before me, an arrow through his neck. The light leaves his eyes.

My stomach turns.

The woman lowers her bow. A long scar runs from her temple to her jaw. Her eyes are a pale, bewitching blue, the kind of eyes that seem to look right through me.

I find my voice. "Thank you."

"Don't thank me, Stormender." Her voice is low and commanding. "He didn't need to die. His blood is on your hands."

Hadria steps before me, her circular blades at the ready.

"I won't harm you," the woman says. "But remember. There are many who call you a savior. But when you saved them . . . you forsook us."

The rambler pulls up at the mouth of the bridge, Izamal at the wheel. Hadria pushes me into it. "Go!"

"What was that?" My voice shakes with anger and fear. "Who was that?"

Hadria is silent. The rambler rattles on at double speed, bouncing us along. "That was Mother," she says.

I stare at her. "Mother? *Your* mother?"

"Yes." She meets my gaze steadily. No shame, no tension. "We do not see eye to eye at the moment."

I don't understand her. "And you want to be my guard?"

"Yes." She draws words forth, choosing each carefully. "My mother was a Regia's Guard. She wanted the same for me. I wanted to be so for Prince Dalca. But he asked me to be yours, instead."

"So . . . you're my guard out of loyalty to him?"

"Yes."

What has he done to deserve that?

"And now," Hadria continues, "I am loyal to you."

Her dark eyes are fathomless. I look away, back at the window, at the streets of the market town whizzing by.

All this, and I still haven't seen the city.

Izamal wisely keeps his mouth shut as he shadows me back up to my rooms. My guards are all accounted for, but Cas hasn't made it back.

Out my balcony is a perfect view of the horizon, lit by moonlight. Useless to me. I march back through my rooms, out the door, to the landing.

Dalca's rooms face the city. The door has a simple ikonlock.

"Vesper . . ." Izamal says. "He's not there."

The lock clicks open. I march in. I get an impression of bare walls—none of the opulence of my rooms—but my attention is on the windows.

Shutters hang from the walls. I fling them open.

"What?"

The windows have been bricked over. I go from one to the next, but they're all sealed.

I push past Izamal, to Cas's room. Even if his room faces the east—even if I have to stick my head out his windows—I'll get a good look. Why have they hidden all view of the city? What terrible thing has happened? Is it—is it gone? Reduced to rubble? When I ended the Storm . . . did that destroy it all?

The ikonlock on Cas's door stops me dead.

Pa taught me to follow the threads, to see what the lock needs by way of a key. The most common used a pattern as a passphrase—but it was anyone's guess whether it involved something simple like gears being twisted into a particular pattern, or a little trickier, like a tune being played on a set of strings embedded in the lock. Pa showed me one with a spoutlike receptacle that would only unlock if it received pigments mixed to the right color.

Cas's lock is none of those. It has no gears, no buttons, no obvious clue to the key. It doesn't open to my touch, to any number of whispered commands, to any number of shouted curses.

My blood runs hot and fast, the Queen's mark dark against my skin. I fling open the door to my rooms, storming straight through, out to the balcony and leaning over the edge. I need a good look at what's above me. Moss winds all the way up the peak of the tower.

Perfect.

I force the Queen's power into it. I force it to harden, to reshape itself into steps that wind all the way to the top.

I hop out onto the railing, ignoring the drop, ignoring the shouts following me.

I climb. Higher and higher, above the roofline—

And there it is.

The city. It's like a toy figurine, perfect and too precious to play with. Five rings, stacked on top of each other. The rooftops gleam and glimmer, the watchtowers jut upward proud and tall, and the palace glitters so brightly that it burns images into my eyes. All its flaws are imperceptible at this distance.

A long-held tension seeps out of me. The city is whole. It's so bright . . . How can it be so bright at night?

I squint into the brightness. Beams of light radiate from the highest tower of the palace. Thin lines of white-gold light, as bright as the sun. Hundreds of them crisscross over the first and second rings, so dazzling that my vision can't take it, blurring them into a single dome of light.

As I stare, I get the strange feeling of something staring back at me. Of—

A flash of white light.

A soft white orb, expanding.

Warmth, all around. Being held in strong arms, a place I belong. A plan and a path.

Eyes like stars, like blooming balls of fire and dust.

A crackling voice. Embers catching light.

I inhale. A shape materializes, just an arm's length away. A figure made of motes of violet light. I squint at it—do I know—

An arm yanks me back, a hand claps over my eyes. I'm plunged into the dark. A powerful grip draws me backwards, down the moss steps.

Balcony doors bang shut, and the hand falls away. I try to blink away the pale green afterimages, but they won't go. Bright eyes, immense eyes, watching me. Irises of a pattern, like ikons.

I press my palms to my eyes. The cool current inside me wakens, slowly, sluggishly, like water trickling down my spine. The Queen chases away every last trace of that stinging light. Until I'm left with nothing but the memory.

But I know what that was. I've felt his power before, when I met Dalca's mother, the Regia. Her body was weak, dying, consumed by the power of the god within her. She died rather than be his vessel. Tried to take Dalca with her, to spare him the misery. To be free of him.

The Great King is unbound. And he's taken over my city.

CHAPTER 8

The blue of high summer fills my vision. Such a specific blue, one reserved for all that's far and unreachable. A soft rumble penetrates the ringing in my ears: a low, crisp voice. One that knows how to command, how to be heard. It says, "*Vesper.*"

That voice . . . Warm hands touch my cheeks, fingertips rough with calluses.

The blue becomes eyes. Dalca's eyes. "I've got you," he says. "You're safe. Don't let him in."

The Great King has taken over my city. At the slightest push, Dalca's hands fall away, but he remains, both of us kneeling, with our knees almost touching. His presence seems unreal—I take him in inches, the black feather cloak on his shoulders, the trembling of his scar-lined fingers—but I can't focus on anything but the Great King. How did it happen? When? And why did they keep it from me?

Worry furrows Dalca's brows, pulling at the hair-thin scars across his skin. Those lines . . .

"Dalca," I say. "That's is how you died, isn't it—you put on the Regia's mark."

Something flickers in his eyes—shame? But it can't be—I've never known Dalca to feel shame. He gives the smallest nod.

And I remember his voice, what he said when I told him he was dead: *I failed.*

Dalca hasn't lied to me. I drag my gaze from his scars to his eyes. "What happened?"

My voice is drowned in a buzzing that descends upon me. Dalca holds my gaze, even as he's drawn away in small nudges like a leaf in the wind, leaving me to a swarm of furious mouths and grasping hands. I blink, and I lose him.

"Vesper." I search for who spoke—the red of the Wardana, the blue of the Nosca, the violet of my guard, and clothes of no uniform at all—there are too many people.

One voice rises above the rest, and a ripple goes through the crowd as a path is made. "Vesper," Izamal asks. "Are you—are you still yourself?"

"I didn't realize I had other options," I say. I get to my feet, and get a handle on my racing thoughts. My head spins. The reason I've been in the sixth since I woke . . . the reason I could never get a good look at the city . . . it was to hide this from me. I can't think of another explanation.

Izamal hovers, buzzing with irritating energy. "Is that humor?"

I glare at him. He's a liar. Izamal drops his gaze.

A voice shouts, "The healer is here!"

"I'm fine," I say. It's lost in the rising chaos. I missed all the signs. People being out at night and sleeping during the day. Murmurs about the lightstruck. But why didn't they just tell me?

Izamal finds his voice in order to chastise my guard. "Where were you?"

Gamara speaks, with none of her sweetness or dimples in sight. "There was—Prince Dalca had a cloak—we were working on a way around the black clouds—the barrier—whatever it was—but he got there first—"

"Stop." My voice carries. "All of you lied to me. Why?"

Imbas steps forward. "There are good reasons for everything that was done."

I've so admired Imbas, even when I haven't agreed with her. But now fury sparks in me. "Name them."

She's the picture of serenity, without even a single hair out of place. "You have done the impossible. A storm that surrounded the entire world—that stretched as far as the eye could see—it is now contained within you. That is not an easy thing to understand. Forgive us for taking the merest of precautions."

Merest of precautions? I look away from her to get my anger under control, to keep the Queen's mark from appearing on my skin. My gaze lands on Hadria, who stands with Mina and Carver. Her expression is as stony as ever, but her color is high. I'd call it embarrassment, but she meets my eyes steadily.

"You could have talked to me," I say to Imbas. "It's not *easy* for me to understand why you would instead engage in a charade to keep me in the dark. What gives you the right? I ended the Storm. I am the vessel of the Great Queen. I saved our home. And I'll save it once again."

My words hang in the air between us all. They work a change upon the gathered; a wave goes through them, leaving new expressions in its wake. Upon the faces of the Wardana, the healers—even, briefly, on Cas's face—shines the holy reverence reserved for temple idols, for gods. But Imbas wears a pinched, disapproving expression, like a mother scolding a disobedient child.

I clench my fists. A god or a child. Both make me feel the same way—like I'm locked in a shrinking casket.

I stare at the woven hangings on my bedroom wall. Hours have passed, in all likelihood. Judging by the sounds outside, most of them left soon after I disappeared into the bedroom. Some remained, who knock timidly on the door every so often and offer me food.

For a long while, my panicked breathing was my only companion. But now each exhale comes slower and quieter, until they give way to a still and judging silence.

Anger made me brave. But as the fury bleeds out of me, terror sinks in.

The Great King. How can I possibly stop him? How can I do it again? I don't even know what I did—I just walked into the Storm.

My head drops. My hands twist in my hair—this stupid, endless mass of hair—and my head pounds. What an idiotic thing to say. How am I going to do this?

In the dark of my mind, I find her. The Great Queen.

I speak to her. *You know. You saw through my eyes.*

The Queen answers. *My great adversary is unbound.* She doesn't sound surprised, merely pondering.

You knew?

Her voice comes in layers: a rushing river, a thunderclap, a crone's rasp. *You concern yourself with many things, Vesper Vale. The world you left behind. The people you left behind. The minuscule ways in which things have changed. That does not interest me. No. My concern has always been singular.*

I bristle. *Why, then, did you choose me?*

Because you came.

That's it? I don't mean to ask it, but she hears anyway.

If another had come, I would have chosen them.

She means there's nothing special about me, nothing that makes me particularly suited to being her vessel.

My stomach plummets, and my skin grows cold. I pull away from the Queen—I dare not let her hear the briefest whisper of my thoughts. It was all just chance. The luck of fools, as Amma would put it.

I press my palms to my eyes. Any one of my guard—women who've trained for years, real fighters—and in Carver's case, a true genius ikonomancer—any one of them would've been a better choice. If one of them had walked into the Storm instead, we'd all be better off.

But it was me.

The weight of who I must be—the hero I must be—drags me down, like a deep plunge into freezing water, into an endless, crushing dark.

Another knock comes.

"Leave me be," I say through my hair.

A pause. "The council meets in a half hour."

The council. The new leaders of our home. They can help me. Dalca's on the council—I need to know what he tried, what his plan was. Why he failed.

I drag myself up and open my door to a startled Mina. "Let's get ready, then."

Carver paints my face. She lines my eyes with kohl and dabs near-black ocher on my lips. She ties part of my hair up like a crown and lets the rest fall down my shoulder in a thick, intricate braid.

I catch my reflection. The terrified girl is well hidden—I might even be halfway convinced she doesn't exist.

The doors swing open.

A glimpse of Izamal, standing. ". . . She's right. No one can deny what she's done—"

His mouth snaps shut. I square my shoulders and march in. The relative quiet becomes dead silence, as if they've all stopped breathing.

Izamal takes his seat. Imbas and Cas are amongst those already seated.

A hunger fills the air. Expectation. They all want something from me. My throat goes dry, and I swallow. A half dozen gazes drop to my throat.

What am I to say? Hello? I'm back?

What does a hero say?

My throat is dry. "Hello," I say. "I'm Vesper."

The first to respond to my sparkling display of intelligence is a stout, red-headed man with a cheery smile and shrewd eyes. His voice matches the one I heard on the stairs. "Might I humbly welcome you back. I am Rosander Tarr. My father and my father's father were sixth-ring farmers." With a flourish, he presents an intricately woven basket and unfolds the shimmering green cloth to reveal a half dozen heart-shaped fruits. "These are our family specialty, the sugared poma. I put these seeds in my pocket thirty years ago when the Storm forced us to leave our homes in the sixth. I prayed I would be able to plant them again. And you made that possible." He spreads his arms wide. "On behalf of all the landkeepers, I thank you. You have given us the opportunity to regrow and rebuild what was lost."

Cas speaks next. He gestures at the tall, thin man beside him, whose glass-like black hair is cut precisely in the shape of a downturned bowl, so smooth it's impossible to make out individual hairs. "This is

Aysel Marzel, master ikonomancer with a specialization in materials-work, second-in-command of the mancer arm of the Wardana. When I am not present, Aysel represents the mancers."

Aysel tries to bow and wave at the same time. "I've heard so very much—I suppose we all have—I'm so very honored—"

"Yes, yes," Cas says, patting his arm as if he were a pet.

"You know Imbas," Izamal says, I gather more for the others than for me. "And this is Mother Yul."

A wizened old woman, bent-backed and frog-like. She wears the brown garb of the priestesses, who tend to our temples and are otherwise forces of mercy—I grew up watching them give food to the hungry and organize stormshelters for neighborhoods. "A pleasure to meet you," she croaks. "My regards to the Great Queen."

A flash of unease goes through the others at the reminder of what's contained within me.

The last of the council sits beside Imbas. She's a thickset woman with short cropped hair and a burn that runs from her temple past her ear. "Tharmida Sel, speaker for the trades." She gives me a nod, leaning forward in a brusque manner. Her elbow hits the table with a wooden thump—the skin of her arm is not skin, but dark wood threaded with vines. A curse. She wears a chainmail glove that protects her hand and forearm, but judging by her sleeveless vest, she doesn't much care to hide her curse. "I appreciate what you've done, Vesper. But I'd as soon as get to business." She turns to Izamal. "We need more Wardana if my people are to do all the metalwork you've sent us. We need protection if we're to mine the ore from the wilds."

"The Nosca will do what we can—" Izamal begins.

"The Nosca are already scheduled to assist the landkeepers this week," Rosander interrupts in a bellow. "Harvesting what food we can is of utmost importance."

Cas presses fingers to his temples.

"The Wardana may be able to spare some . . ." Izamal says.

Aysel glances at Cas, who gives him a nod. He speaks. "The mancers can spare a few—we're ahead of schedule on the landtreaders—"

Landtreaders. A new word—as new as *ramblers.*

"We'll take 'em," Tharmida Sel says. "And whatever Nosca you can provide."

There's no place for me here.

"Hold on," I say. "What does any of this have to do with fighting the Great King?"

A silence falls. Rosander breaks it. "You have not yet had a chance to see enough. Or you would understand . . ."

"Understand what?"

Another silence. They look at each other, each waiting for someone else to speak first.

"More and more people are getting lightstruck," Cas says, glaring at the others, daring them to stop him. "The light gets them . . . and that's it. They're the same people, they have the same memories—but they get it into their heads that they need to go into the light—that's the King's domain. The first two rings are lost to him. Everyone's afraid. The fear of being lightstruck is bad. But what's worse is fearing someone you love is lightstruck and knowing that there's nothing you can do. No outward signs. Nothing but to wait and see if they'll sabotage your protections—unseal your windows, lure you somewhere in the King's line of sight, keep you out till daylight so you can't make out what's sunlight and what's the King's light . . ."

Izamal sighs. "It's bad. Neighbors accusing neighbors, brothers accusing sisters . . . It's taken a third of my people to just follow up on all the accusations, figure out which had merit and which were just paranoia."

I cross my arms. "So what's the plan? What are we doing?"

"Many are ready to leave," Imbas says. "The landtreaders are our way to another life, free of . . ." She goes silent, but I would wager she was about to say *free of these gods.*

Rosander speaks. "That was before. The Stormender is with us now."

They all look to me.

Rosander leans forward. "My family has tended these fields for generations. When the sixth was lost . . . it was a blow. But you gave it back to us. Will you let them take it away once more?"

"There's no question," I say. "Of course we must fight the Great King."

Izamal and Imbas shift.

"What?" I ask.

Iz answers. "The entire world is open to us now. Why fight for a home that never wanted us?"

That never wanted us? It wasn't our home that did that—it was other people, stupid people, people who can be changed. I grasp for the words that'll help me explain something that feels as obvious, as essential as the heart beating in my chest. "It's home. How can we not fight for it?"

Izamal holds my gaze, but I haven't convinced him. No more than he's convinced me.

The doors bang open.

Four enter, with the bearing and physique of Wardana fighters, but no Wardana uniforms. Perhaps the white painted around their eyes is all the uniform they need. In unison, they step aside.

A woman enters. She sucks all the air out of the room, and all that rattles around my head is that she could snap my neck with her pinky fingers.

"You," I say.

The woman from the rooftop, who killed my attacker. Hadria's mother.

Izamal and Cas move like the wind, stepping in front of me with spears in hand. Hadria's mother looks over their shoulders and raises a hand.

Her four soldiers drop their gauntlets with a clatter.

"Fear not," she says into the silence, holding my gaze. "We are unarmed."

"What do you want?"

"My name is Toran Belvas. I was a Regia's Guard, and a Wardana before that. I taught many of the Wardana I see in this tower." That explains the strength of her build and the muscle straining the silken fabric of her trousers. "But I am also a daughter of the second ring."

Toran smiles, but it's wary. She's getting my measure as I'm getting hers. "They call you the savior. But you didn't save everyone. You didn't save us."

"What do you mean?"

"Those who attacked you—they did so because they wish for the Storm's return."

Anger heats my skin. "Why?"

"The existence we have now . . . When the Great King took over, many had to flee. They lost their homes—"

My voice is a hiss. "For their second-ringer *mansions*? They'd bring the Storm back for that?"

"Did you not end the Storm to save your fifth-ringer homes?"

"No! You don't know—You want my life for your golden doors, your glittering marble? Are you so spoiled that you'd rather have the Storm back—with all the suffering it caused—rather than have to move house?"

Her expression darkens. "It took our families—"

"So you'd rather have the families of low ringers taken?"

"No—"

"For hundreds of years, your people just watched as we suffered. Maybe it's your turn." My blood burns with fury, but it's not until Toran steps back that I notice the Queen's mark dancing on my skin.

"They told me you wouldn't listen," Toran says, chin raised. "They told me you didn't care about us. I told them you were better than that."

Cas starts as if he would say something.

"I was wrong." Toran turns on a heel and makes for the door.

My face burns.

The council disperses with a sigh. Izamal murmurs, "I need a drink."

I need to find Dalca. As far as I can tell, he's the only one who's not committed to the ridiculous plan of leaving our city behind in *landtreaders*, whatever those are.

A few discreet questions later, I find myself in front of the training room where I first met my guard. Hadria and Mina wait at the mouth of the hallway—standing watch close enough to please them, far enough that I can ignore them.

The door is cracked. I hesitate with my hand on the knob and peek inside. The angle is wrong to see them directly, but their reflections dance on the polished metal walls.

Dalca is bent over, hands on his knees, catching his breath.

"I can't go on," Cas says drolly, inspecting his nails. "Stop. I've been beaten."

"Again," Dalca calls. Cas sidesteps as Dalca lunges.

Dalca falls, rolling over onto his back with a grimace. He holds a hand out to Cas. "Help me up."

Cas instead puts a foot on his chest. "If you want to die, I don't see why you bothered waking up."

Dalca grips Cas's leg; his voice is weak but irritated. "Don't be difficult, Cas."

"Difficult? This isn't difficult. What's difficult is having to stitch your idiotic self back together."

If all they're doing is declaring their love, I'd better just go in. I take the smallest step—and Dalca's voice comes.

"I need to regain my strength—she's back, Cas."

"Really. I hadn't noticed."

I hesitate. Are they talking about me?

Dalca pushes Cas's foot, but it only budges an inch. I'm horrified how weak he seems. "Get off me."

"What's this about?" Cas asks. "You trying to get her attention? You think she'll come running if you're the manly muscled prince again?"

"No. I don't want any of that. I want to make amends."

Cas sighs. "You can't fix everything, Dalca."

Dalca makes a vexed sound. "That's such an irritating mindset—"

"And if you keep going like this, ignoring your healers, ignoring me—No, you listen. There'll be nothing—nothing you can do—to fix your body."

Cas removes his foot from Dalca's chest, and Dalca sits up. "Cas. You have to help me. Just hear me out. I'm not a Regia. But I'm still an Illusora. The last one. And maybe it was wrong that my ancestors made themselves lords of this city—I won't argue that. But . . . what I was raised to do—it's all I've got left. I want to do good by our people. And if Vesper's return means we have one last chance at keeping our home . . . I want to be ready."

"It's all you have left?" Cas snarls. "Who do you think will have to organize your funeral?"

Dalca blinks at him. "The stewards?"

Cas huffs. "Yes, fine, true—but it'll be *upon me* to step in when they get it wrong."

"I'm sure any funeral would be all right," Dalca says slowly.

"It's not about the funeral!"

"Then why did you bring it up?"

"You want to fight? Go ahead. Do whatever bullheaded heroics you still can before your body breaks." Cas throws him a spear that Dalca catches without looking. "But consider this: maybe your people don't need a warrior. Not anymore." Cas storms to the door.

I retreat, and my back hits the hallway wall.

From within the room, Dalca calls, "What do they need?"

Cas stops dead when he sees me, his back to Dalca. He holds my gaze. "They need someone to raise them up. To protect not just their bodies, or their houses . . . I don't know, Dalca. But you should take your seat on the council. Without you, it's a waste of time."

Dalca's voice is soft. "Cas . . . I failed to save them from the Great

King. I've failed to be a leader. I wouldn't be of use."

Cas turns to him. "And yet, shockingly, many of them still look to you. They still love you. So don't spit in their faces by giving up on yourself before they have."

Dalca gives Cas a long, considering look. The lines of his face are tense, but his eyes shine. He gives a small nod.

And then Dalca sees me. A shadow crosses his face.

The door shuts, sealing him away. Cas quirks an eyebrow at me. "Spying, are we?"

I move around him. "I need to talk to him."

Cas blocks my way. "It's not a great time."

"When's a good time, then? When the Great King's done taking over the city?"

"That's a bit dramatic," Cas says.

His arm blocks my way; I give it a shove, and he relents, moving gracefully aside.

With a twist of the handle, the door opens.

The room is empty. Dalca's gone.

CHAPTER 9

What Izamal said—*Why fight for a home that never wanted us?*

It rings in my ears. He said it like there's another option. But when I became the Queen's vessel, when I joined with her power, I felt how far the Storm reached. Dalca told me of how he'd flown above the Storm, searching for any boundaries. There were none. There's nothing but our home. Any other settlements or cities would have long since been consumed and destroyed by the Storm or by the progress of time. The sixth was lost only some decade or two ago, and there are still wide sections of it that are uninhabitable.

So why would Izamal say that?

I stop in the middle of the stairwell and turn to my guards.

"What are Iz and Imbas planning?"

They share a look. Gamara answers. "It's no secret. They're leading the landtreader project. To leave the city behind and make another home somewhere out there, in the wilds."

The wilds? The spires of lightning-stricken rock? The gnarled, wicked-looking trees? "That's absurd."

Carver laughs. "Really? If we'd had a chance to just run away from the Storm, don't you think we would've?"

I scowl. She has a point. "But how?"

Carver glances at Hadria and Mina, and shrugs. "You might want to ask them."

I don't want to talk to Imbas. But Iz . . . "Where is he?"

Gamara and Ozra go to find out. In minutes, they return, telling me Izamal's left the watchtower to oversee the landtreaders. That they can leave a message for him, so he'll come to see me when he's back.

I cross my arms. "No need," I say. "I'll go to him."

It takes a great deal of arguing, a modicum of putting on airs ("I'm the vessel of the Queen," I find myself saying, like an absolute arrogant numpty), a threat of going anyway ("How exactly do you intend to keep me here?"), and a shameless show of the Queen's mark rising on my skin, but my guard soothes the Wardana and Nosca and everyone else who for some reason has a stake in my comings and goings.

A rambler is prepared. I get in, followed by Mina, Hadria, Carver, and Ozra—the other three drive, Gamara sandwiched between Jhuno and Zerin—and my blood itches. This is a cage, and again I'll only be shown what others want me to see. The rambler rattles out of the watchtower's courtyard, and with every bump, I grow a little more frustrated. "Enough," I say, swinging the door open. "I'm walking."

Hadria and Mina step out beside me. "Where you go, we go."

Carver follows. "But take this," she says, swinging a nondescript cloak over my clothes.

I take it begrudgingly, giving her a look. Did she pack this cloak, knowing I'd be unreasonable? Some part of me knows I'm being difficult, and that makes the rest of me heat with bullheaded frustration.

"If you please, let me select the safest route," Hadria says, her gaze sweeping across the street and up to the rooftops. She motions, and except for Gamara, who's driving the rambler, the rest of my guard slips away, no doubt watching from the shadows. My skin prickles. Even this is still a cage.

"Fine." I draw the cloak over my hair and wrap it high on my shoulders so it covers my lips and nose. We make our way toward the main market square, our way lit by multicolor ikonlights. I peer up through the gaps between houses, but there's not a single inch of the inner five rings, nor of the King's spiderweb of light. Just the dark sky and occasionally the edge of the wilds. We're at least two hours' walk from the edge of the fifth. If it were flat land with no trees, I'm sure I could see the city. But as it is . . . If I lived in this market town, the rest of the city might as well not exist.

We pass a handful of doors that are marked with an eye in white paint. I nod at them. "What are those?"

"Suspected lightstruck," Hadria states. All facts, no help.

Carver sighs at her. "Some are homes where someone went missing in the middle of the night. Where people are worried they'll return to take others with them. Some are homes where someone maybe acted strangely in front of the wrong person, and got accused."

She steps before me, as if blocking something. I glance over her shoulder. An old woman, face scrunched up in suspicion, peers out of a window at us.

"You can't just . . . tell?" I ask. It wasn't hard to tell who'd been cursed by the Storm. Many curses had some physical aspect, and even the invisible ones led to some pretty obvious changes in behavior. A memory: Dalca's wild smiles—his giddy laughter—I'd never seen him so happy as when he'd been cursed, when the Storm stole all his fears.

The street opens wide, to a bridge. Below, the river winds darkly, reflecting scattered ikonlights like a ribbon of starry sky.

The watchtower rises far up above, the stone studded with golden ikonlights that peek out of the blanket of violet flowers. It's as impressive as the Ven, the original Wardana stronghold in the third ring.

I keep my eyes on the stonework of the bridge as Wardana pass us by. Some of their uniforms seem extra bright and are cut more simply than I remember. Perhaps they're newly made—perhaps the ikonomancers now have access to beasts whose hide can be used.

We join a steady flow of people crossing the bridge. The stone vibrates with their footsteps, and the rustling of their clothes and the murmur of their voices blend together. But there's an excited thrum through it all. Snippets of their conversations rise to my ears.

"—you hear? The Stormender was there, she spoke, I heard it from my cousin, he was there—"

"—the high ringers, but she put them in their place—"

I glance over my shoulder. A young couple, the taller gesturing wildly as he speaks. A weathered woman who taps her cane against the stones for emphasis. Older men, wearing businesslike expressions. It's not everyone. But amongst the talk of the weather and food and little worries, my words spill from strangers' mouths. Has it even been a full hour since I spoke my mind to Toran?

"—it's true, they're spoiled—"

"We have an ally in her—"

"—no pity, as it should be—"

I tune them out and force myself to breathe, slow and even, until the skittering under my skin stills. I don't like it, and I don't know what to make of it. Rationally, I understand why my words now have a power that they didn't before I was the Great Queen's vessel. But it's still me speaking, not the Great Queen. I feel the same inside as I felt then, maybe a little sadder.

I work my way through the sixth. Carver, Mina, and Hadria become nothing more than shadows, a pace behind me.

A red-uniformed Wardana stands at the mouth of a square, chatting with a couple. I pull my shawl tight and skirt past them. The way opens out into a broad square that's packed with market stalls. It's bustling. I pass a man unloading a wheeled cart to refill the goods in his stall. A young woman who shares his red hair wrangles their steed.

The market is full, lit so well by ikonlights that it might as well be day. A handful of people wear the three-layer outfit typical of the low ringers—trousers or a full-length skirt, with a long overdress on top and a shawl wrapped around the shoulders and belted at the waist. A style meant to offer protection against the Storm. I could've counted on one hand the number of bare shoulders I saw on the streets of the fifth ring. Most people have adopted high-ringer styles—thin cloth, bare arms and legs, slim shawls meant more for style than protection. More than one curious look is directed at me in my cloak.

Despite the night, the air is hot. Sweat beads on my forehead. They're all unafraid, freed from fear of the Storm. Only I wander around in a cloak, afraid not of the Storm but of them.

Something smacks into my leg. I twist, look down.

A giggle—a child, gap-toothed, holding a carved-wood toy. She's being chased by a boy with a cloud of hair. They're so young—do they even remember the Storm?

They disappear into the crowd, her laughter lingering behind. Hadria checks me over as Mina laughs. "I don't think those children were assassins, Hads." She gives me a rueful look over Hadria's bowed head.

Hadria pats my knees and straightens. "All clear," she says, showing no indication of having heard Mina.

The sweet smell of ripe fruit draws me away. The stalls are full; there isn't a vast selection, but there's plenty.

A thin woman begs a vendor. Her child stands behind her, gaze fixed on his feet, his hands clenched at his sides.

She shows the man behind the stall a necklace with a large red pendant. The hunger in the shopkeeper's eyes betrays his nonchalant posture. I slip closer.

"That won't get you much," the man drawls. "What use have we for jewels?"

"Please—we weren't able to grab much when the light came. I know what this is worth."

"It's worth half a bag to me."

The bags are filled with rice. Even I know that necklace could buy out his whole stock. But maybe this too has changed.

"Half a bag? We'll starve."

"And what did you care when we were starving?"

"Have pity. It's for my children."

"Have pity? Even the savior doesn't have pity for you."

My stomach turns, something hot and oily rising in my throat. He's so sure of himself, so sure I'm on his side. The cruel twist to his mouth, the way his eyes track the necklace—none of this is right.

I hesitate with my hands on the edges of my hood. I'm deeply aware of the statue behind me, casting its shadow down on the marketplace. What do I say? Where will my words spread?

I take a breath and pull down my hood. "Why don't you give her a fair trade?"

His eyes flick to me.

I wait for the flash of recognition, for fear to enter his eyes. I straighten my shoulders, raise my chin.

He looks me up and down. And snorts. "Stay out of this, girl."

I scowl. Girl? Well, there's proof that the statue looks nothing like me, I guess.

A new voice. "Honey, come here," says the gray-haired woman behind the next stall.

"Fara, you stay out of it too," the man hisses.

The high ringer goes to the gray-haired shopkeeper, who peers at the necklace. "Your necklace can buy everything I have. Do you have anything smaller?"

The woman tears a ring from her finger. "What about this? It was my husband's."

The boy starts. "Ma—"

Fara, the shopkeeper, reaches for it and turns it over. "I can do two bags of rice and one of shalaj. Ilyon there will throw in some greens. I'll settle with him."

The woman does the trade. Her son takes two bags, but his brow darkens and his lower lip trembles.

You have to be better.

I push through the crowd, away from the market. The Queen's power coils in my belly, frustration rising.

Footsteps follow mine down a thin street. Hadria, Mina, and Carver.

"I'm fine," I say. I press my hand into a neatly manicured patch of moss on the wall. My knuckles sink into it, and I breathe in and out, willing the frustration away.

The softness under my hand turns coarse and hot. I glance up.

The moss burns, becoming ash.

I pull myself away. Force the Queen's power under control.

Carver stares at me with cloying concern. "Are you okay—"

Hadria interrupts. "You wanted to see the landtreaders. We're almost there."

She leads us toward the edge of the market town; the spires and blackened trees of the wilds loom taller and taller over the blue-slate rooftops.

The sounds of a gathering reach us first. We turn the corner.

A huge field, carved out of the surrounding wilds, is teeming with activity. Ikonlights hanging from the tallest trees at the edge of the field create pockets of illumination, under which various groups gather. One pocket of illumination reveals a flurry of construction: tree trunks are stripped of their branches and hoisted into place, metal clangs as it's beaten into armored plating, hammers drive iron into wood.

Past them is another pocket: a crowd of people spread across a few rough-hewn tables, most with drink in hand. Someone holds court from a central table—I can't quite make them out from this distance.

"Watch your step," Hadria says.

We skirt around stacks of food in mosscloth sacks—a mound of them labeled *shalaj*—and make our way past a small pile of bolts of fabric. Three wooden chests bear ikons of the sort I've seen around stoves and beside temple fires—ones that stop flames from burning. Inside the chests are stacks of small black discs—some kind of compact fuel. There are piles of stuff, punctuated by spaces that are empty but for the gouges in the dirt where crates once stood.

All that's necessary for the council's absurd plan comes through here and waits to be loaded into the landtreaders.

To one side are stables, from which poke the heads of immense aurochs stormbeasts with skin like scales. Below the stable doors, their feet shine—each is fitted with what appears to be a gleaming metal shoe.

A roar of laughter rises from the crowd. A circle of moss marks the area where they're gathered; it squelches underfoot. Ikonlights are studded in it, like glowing flowers.

A man hops up on the tabletop, a fizzing drink in hand.

Izamal. His blue jacket slung over one shoulder, his hair loose and wild, his grin wide and impish. "And there I was—no longer a man, but a beast—lost to my greatest fears."

He makes it sound like a joke. But his grin falters.

His charm is working on more than just me. Everyone listens to him. Two gray-haired men shoot each other sardonic looks, and yet they pause their card game to listen.

An enraptured crowd of people around our age watch Izamal with stars in their eyes. Some with rather something more—heat rising to their skin, hunger clear in the way they angle their bodies, pressing closer.

He locks gazes with a lanky, pale-haired girl.

"Sometimes, suffering is the teacher we need. Failure is not the end, but a necessary step. Failure teaches us what is worth defeating. If we fail, we know that what we fought is greater than us. A worthy challenge. Every failure teaches us something—and if we keep fighting, we become greater. Great enough to defeat what once defeated us."

She melts. My eyes try to roll out of my head.

He holds out an arm. His fingers widen, nails becoming claws, dark fur covering his skin.

"I was born cursed. I hated it. And for years I ran from it. From myself. I ran until I came to the end. In my darkest hour . . . a thought came. A spark of an idea: my curse is not my fate. This thought freed me. A path rose before me, faint at first, as if it were illuminated by naught but the barest moonlight. I knew then that I had a choice: to take it or to turn my back on it and everything else."

His hand returns to human, but his eyes are shadowed. I can't tell if it's true emotion or a bit of theatrics.

"And now . . . this curse has given me purpose. With it, I can lead the Nosca through the wilds. There are creatures I can speak to, who speak to me. Is that not a blessing? Is finding my purpose not worth the suffering?"

The pale-haired girl takes his hand and kisses his knuckles. He draws her close, and her eyes flutter.

Theatrics, then. But perhaps there's a little truth somewhere in there.

Honestly, I'm impressed. Of the four of us, Izamal seems to have come out the strongest. He seems more real, somehow, like he inhabits his body more deeply than the rest of us. And maybe it's just that he knows what he wants and who he is.

Maybe I've stared at him too long, because he tilts his head as if hearing something at a distance, and his golden eyes scan the crowd until he spots me. With a brief point of his chin, he indicates one end of the stables.

I nod.

"Let me," Hadria says, going ahead. Mina and Carver follow me.

Izamal's voice follows us as he makes his apologies and excuses himself, flirting madly all the while.

The aurochs watch me. There's a path that goes from beside the stables, and Hadria leads us along it, watchful for any sign of trouble.

The path opens up, and I stop dead.

A line of enormous bugs—the kind that roll into a ball when prodded—each the size of a small house. I shudder.

But each step closer reveals that they're not bugs—merely vehicles designed rather like bugs, with jointed plates and welded seams. Ikons are etched in every square foot of metal. The back of one has its armored plates retracted, revealing an interior with bench seating. Bags of food peek out from an open trapdoor in the floor.

I exhale. These must be the landtreaders. Further down the line are skeletons of wood and metal—landtreaders mid-construction, waiting for their innards and their shells. Not all are of the same design; one has several tall, thin windows with slatted metal shutters. Some have scalloped armoring, as if those took inspiration from a different creature.

A moveable city. But even this many can't carry everyone. And what's the end goal? Where do we go? To some bit of land, just far enough away, and then what? We rebuild what it took our ancestors thousands of years to create? The sheer infrastructure of our home, the bones it's grown—its aqueducts and the pipes and ikonomancy that carry and purify water, the roads, the temples, the homes—how would we ever remake that?

The wilds are just beyond. Arches made of glinting black. Long-dead trees, the hollows of their trunks glimmering with crystallized sap. A grove of living trees, pale and weeping with black leaves. Massive blue-black thickets with bulging roots that rise above the soil to strangle piles of pinkish boulders.

Where do they mean to go? How do they look upon this wasteland and see hope?

"Vesper!" Izamal calls.

I turn. He's with a stormbeast as tall as he is, a bearlike creature with an immense rack of antlers.

"Izamal."

"Vesper." His eyes widen in concern, and he glances over my shoulder at my guards. "You shouldn't—"

"You don't get to decide *should* and *shouldn't* for me."

There's so much we haven't said to each other. After I lost him in the Storm—he was half-consumed by his curse, terrified and terrifying—I don't know what happened to him. Remembering it turns my stomach inside out. I've been a coward, not bringing it up. But I'm mad, too.

"What's happened?" I ask. "I wake up, and you're in Imbas's pocket." He flinches, but I keep going. "You keep the truth from me— about the Great King, about the lightstruck, about everything. And you think my food might be poisoned, but you eat it for me." I fix him with a look. "How can you lie to me and yet be willing to die for me?"

He tilts his head, golden eyes glinting in the light. For the first time I notice—instead of cat-slit pupils, he has ordinary human circle pupils. "It's obvious, isn't it? If you look at it from one perspective: I was—I *am*—trying to look out for you."

I cross my arms. "Then why does it feel like you don't trust me?"

"Why wouldn't I?"

"I left you. In the Storm."

"You didn't *leave* me. I'm not your responsibility. I'm not your burden. That fight was mine and mine alone."

"I was your friend."

"You still are." He pats his beast. "Vesper . . . I was angry. So angry. At myself, and other things. At my place in the world. At what was taken from me. And while I was lost in myself . . . you saved us all. And you died for it."

"If it wasn't for you, I wouldn't have ever been in a position to end the Storm."

"Don't give me that."

"What?"

"Everyone—I'm sick of the story of the Storm. People have decided I had some great part in it, but I didn't. I was in the right place at the right time."

So was I. I want to say it, but my throat closes up.

"Out there," he says, gesturing at the wilds, "that's where I'm needed. That's where I found myself. And that's where our future is."

"You've given up on our home."

"Don't you think there's just too much suffering back there? Every stone of our city has known blood."

"Doesn't that make it precious? We honor the sacrifices of those who came before us by protecting it."

"No. We honor their sacrifices by living." Izamal shakes his head. "Vesper . . . the Storm is gone, but you're still trapped."

I rear back as if he slapped me.

"I get it," he says gently. "You became a hero there. You think you know how the story goes. And what if we go out there and step into a new story? One where you're not the hero? Can you bear it?" He pauses. "Yes, we're giving something up. But are you so sure it isn't a story that no longer fits?"

"That's not it at all," I say, and almost believe it.

CHAPTER 10

As the night wears on, I find myself thinking it all over. Maybe Izamal is right. Maybe I'm just playing hero. I don't really know.

My feet begin to wear a path in the plush rugs carpeting my rooms, so I make my way past my guards and stop in front of Cas's door.

I trace the lines of the ikonlock with a fingertip. There must be something, some hint or some bit of familiar ikonwork—some thread that, once pulled, will unravel the lock's secrets.

"Are you caressing my door?" A voice from behind.

I turn. Cas tilts his head.

"Maybe," I say with a shrug.

His fingers brush the lock, then fall still. "Turn around."

I sigh and put my back to the door. Pa had laughed when I finally cracked his ikonlock, but there had also been a flash of uneasy surprise in his eyes. His pride as a father had warred with his pride as a mancer. I can't blame Cas for not wanting to just give away the trick to his lock.

The lock clicks. "Come on up, then."

The door opens straight into a stairwell. It's cold and damp, and I follow him up the spiraling steps until we come out in a place that looks like it once was open to the elements and housed a great bell.

Now there's a strange contraption of mirrors in the heart of the room. Papers are strewn everywhere, piles of books sprout like mushrooms all across the floor, and there are three large maps stuck somehow to one stone wall.

And tucked in a corner, small and lumpy, is a bedroll.

A soft grind of metal as Cas activates a dim blue ikonlantern.

"You sleep here?"

"Out of choice," he snaps, as if that's better.

I say no more. Instead, I turn to the maps. One is of the city, and Cas has marked the edges of the Great King's dominion. He's taken the first and second rings completely and has a quarter of the third ring.

The river is drawn neatly, and it really does look like an eye, with the inner five rings as its iris. The Queenskeep is further than I thought—another city could fit between us and the edge of the fifth's ringwall.

The sound of boiling water surprises me. Cas neatly makes two cups of—

"Sundust?" I can't keep the awe from my voice.

Cas hands a cup of sundust tea to me, his cheeks pink. "Stop making everything a big deal."

I take a sip. "So," I say. "Since I've been gone, Dalca's tried to get himself killed, Izamal's decided to become a man of the wilds . . . And you live here."

He rolls his eyes. "Was there a question? Or just judgment?"

"So what did you do, that everyone hates you?"

"So," he says, mocking my tone, "with zero information, you assumed it must be my fault."

I wince. "Well, Cas, in the time I've known you, you haven't ever tried to have people like you."

He shrugs.

"So why are they like this?"

"Maybe they're all jealous of my good looks," he deadpans.

I get the hint and take a long, slow sip.

The silence stretches into minutes.

"You're cursed," I say. "Stormtouched."

His attention snaps to me. "You can tell?"

"I can see it in you." A flash of a memory: Cas kneeling beside a pool, his reflection reaching out of the water—a warped mirror version of Cas, who was a fighter instead of a mancer, a perfect son instead of . . .

"I thought, in the Storm, when we beat my reflection, that meant I wouldn't be cursed. But . . ." His gaze goes to a shard of mirror on the floor. "It doesn't affect me always, but sometimes it rises. And I have to fight it off yet again."

"It's hurting you now."

Cas picks up the mirror but doesn't answer.

His curse. He wanted to be a perfect son. Or rather, his father's idea of a perfect son. And Ragno Haveli—a brutal, intense, and intimidating man, who once led the Regia's Guard, who burned down Amma's Home for the Cursed and everyone in it, just to get at my father—his idea of perfect was merely a younger version of himself. But Cas prioritized mastering ikonomancy instead of mastering the art of growing biceps larger than his head.

Cas tosses the mirror onto a table. It skids off the edge and hits the floor, shattering. "Izamal goes crowing about how he beat his curse. I suppose one day I'll beat mine." He slumps against the wall, pressing fingers to his temples.

"I could take it away," I say. "I undid Dalca's curse."

Silence falls. Cas fixes me with a long, searching stare. "Are you being funny, Vesper?"

I meet his gaze. "I'm never funny."

His lips twitch. "Then please, by all means."

I sink into the Great Queen's power, and a veil drops over my vision, turning everything to shadows. With the power that she grants me, I reach for Cas, for the curse at his core. It takes the shape of shadows that weave themselves into a dark oval—a mirror. I tug at the wisps of shadows at its edges, urging them apart, coaxing them to not mold themselves so strongly into a curse. It resists me, as if it wants to stay put.

Dalca's came much more easily—but I didn't know what I was doing then.

I shore up my will. I sink deeper into her power. Shadows shape themselves into a mirror at Cas's core, but the tiniest threads of them wisp away and knit themselves into his muscles, into his blood. The shadows are like veins, coming from his curse that beats like a heart.

The curse is trying to become part of him. I snip the tendrils and force my power to a point, and press upon the mirror.

It holds, stubborn—I press harder—it takes far more of the Queen's power than I'd have thought, more than half of what I've saved—

It shatters.

Cas sucks in a breath, holding his chest.

I draw back to myself, tired and aching. It doesn't feel good.

Cas looks at me with wonder. "Just like that."

"It was a little harder than that," I say. The room tilts.

His lips quirk, and I brace for something cutting. "Thank you."

"Thanks for the sundust," I say, getting to my feet. If I'm going to faint, I'd rather do it in my own rooms.

"Vesper—" he calls, as I descend the stairs.

I glance back over my shoulder. He looks young and so very frail. He shakes his head. "Never mind."

Night falls, and I have Hadria ready a rambler. I give her a warning: "Neither Iz nor Imbas—nor anyone on the council—should know where we're going."

"My job is to keep you safe—"

"Then do so. Because my job isn't to sit here in this tower while people suffer."

She crosses her arms, and then pointedly glances at a figure leaning against the wall. Cas. He wears a long, simple cloak, his hair braided and hanging over his shoulder. "I won't tell," he says with a wry look. "Promise."

I frown. "What are you doing here?"

He gestures at his chest. "Trying to extinguish this rather enormous feeling of gratitude."

"You don't owe me."

"Please don't be so noble about it," Cas says, tossing his braid over his shoulder. "It doesn't help. In fact, it would be kinder to be a bit rude, if you could manage."

I find myself wanting to strangle him. "That won't be difficult."

A sudden crack appears in his imperious demeanor: a smile. It's gone in a heartbeat—but the afterimage lingers. I didn't know his face could do that.

I'm disconcerted enough to let him join us, and he puts his head together with Hadria, passing quiet whispers back and forth as she works him into her plan for what she calls a protective perimeter.

Cas settles in on the driver's seat, muttering at the pair of shaggy blue stormbeasts, as Hadria and I slip inside the rambler. The door has barely shut before the wheels begin to turn, and we're on our way.

"I don't think this is wise," Hadria says for the eleventh time.

I study her. "What's the story with you and your mother?"

Her face grows stony. "I thought we had the same perspective on duty. On being a Regia's Guard. It turns out, we don't."

She says nothing more, so I turn my attention to the window, to the rapidly changing scenery.

We're heading in the direction of the city. The river shines, forking around the five rings, and we keep to the western arm. The moss grows thick and wild, and soon we leave the road for a barely there trail. The stormbeasts slow, picking their way with care.

The trees grow dense. Many have kept their leaves, and their branches are weighed down with glistening red-violet fruit. "What's this?"

"This was a poma orchard," Hadria says. She doesn't elaborate.

But I can guess that it was the Storm that turned the thick trunks of these trees into great gnarled hands of bark, turned their green leaves a purplish black, turned the small red fruit into these jewel-like monstrosities.

There are places that are naturally protected from the Great King's line of sight. Much of the sixth's market town is protected by distance, by the bulk of the watchtower, and by the shelter of the wilds.

This place has nothing but the density of the trees and the thickness of the foliage, the pale tendril-like moss that twines around branches and hangs in long curtains.

The trees part naturally, to reveal a clearing of moss-eaten structures—a large building that may have been the home of the orchardkeeper, and several other smaller ones that might have been used for storing the harvest. They're arrayed around a small central courtyard, where a dilapidated fountain has been repurposed: the remnant of a carved kinnari bird has been refitted with a spout and pump for drinking water.

Everything is in poor repair. Stone walls have held up, but everything that was wood has rotted away. Swaths of ikon-reinforced fabric hang between trees, over holes in the roof, over windows. Measures to keep out the weather, I figure.

I glance at the trees. The cloth strung between them has a dull shine—waxed or oiled, to make it durable and waterproof. I used to do the same to my cloaks. But this is thick cloth, tightly woven.

I draw in a breath as understanding sparks. This cloth is all they have to protect them from the Great King's gaze. It must take a great deal of effort to maintain this barrier.

My shoulders inch toward my ears. All it would take is one great gust of wind, or a single frayed thread—and the King's light could reach here. How can anyone relax in a place like this?

The rambler stops before the large building. Hadria throws an arm across my middle. "Let me go in first. I'll get you an audience."

She shuts the rambler door behind her and strides away. The double doors—newly and crudely made from black wood—open at her knock. She disappears inside.

I step out.

"Safer to stay in the rambler," says Cas. He hops down to stand at my side, gauntlet at the ready, scanning our surroundings. "Do you know, Hadria might be rather good at what she does. Dalca always liked her, but it's such an affect to use the chakram as your main weapon."

I press my lips together, but he did say he wanted rude. "An affect, says the man who used ikons to make his hair reflect like a mirror."

"That's different. That was style." He sighs, glancing at the tip of his white braid. "You're right. I should do something with it."

"The chakram—those are her circular blades?"

"She was an ace with them. Played in the Arvegna games—her team won three years in a row—probably the last games we'll ever have."

The Arvegna. The grand stadium in the third ring. Where the Trials were held. Where Pa died.

Hadria returns, saving me from having to respond. She nods at the doors. "Let's go."

I follow on her tail. The doors open to reveal a wide rectangular space—all the interior walls have rotted to nothing—and it's larger than it appears from the outside. A thick carpet of moss blankets the floor, save for where the residents have scraped it away.

New black-wood beams crisscross the roof. Part of it has been rethatched with wood shingles, but waxed canvas cloth is the main source of protection for a good half of the building. Ikonlanterns hang from the walls, from the beams that crisscross the space above our heads. Not heavy-duty ones, but small, twinkling ones—the trinkets of high ringers.

And yet it reminds me of the fifth ring. Of how, in the face of darkness and despair, the hunger for beauty grew keen and sharp enough to draw blood.

We get fewer stares than I'd feared. Most of the high ringers are busy with preparing food—mostly tough and fibrous things, like shalaj, that take a great deal of time and effort to make edible.

Cas walks so close to me he steps on my heel twice. The third time, I stop in my tracks and give him a warning look. He hisses in my ear. "This is a bad idea. I know these people. I *was* these people."

Hadria leads us to the very end of the building, where a figure rises at our approach.

Toran Belvas stands before a table overflowing with scrolls, her hands folded behind her back. She's still, taut as a bowstring. Only her eyes move, tracking us. Her voice has not a glimmer of warmth. "Come to gloat?"

"No," I say. "I came to apologize. I've done you wrong, and I'm sorry for not hearing what you had to say."

The family resemblance between mother and daughter is uncanny—the same dark, mournful eyes, the regal nose bridge, the lips that curl down at serious moments. But Toran is taller, broader, and wears an easy confidence that says she knows her place in the world, and everyone else's too.

"I pray that you mean it." Toran relaxes just a tad. "As I cannot afford to do anything but accept it."

A small, subtle reminder of my power. "I do."

"Then let me show you." Toran gestures me to follow. We walk through the building, high ringers gathering as we near.

Toran catches me looking at a woman—gaunt, stooped—who nonetheless has jewels wrapped around her throat and dripping from her ears and hair.

"They're not fools. Not all fools, anyway. Some had minutes to grab what they could before they ran. Many grabbed sentimental things, things that are now useless in any way save for bolstering their spirits. They look pathetic now, but many of them had mastered the world they knew."

A painting rests against a moss-covered wall. "A privileged world."

"Maybe." She inclines her head. "But that's all they knew. All their mothers and fathers knew, and their ancestors before them."

"And you?"

Toran shrugs. "I'm Wardana. I had occasion to learn. But I was almost a sculptor. If I had been, I'd be just as helpless."

Hadria starts at my side. I glance at her, but she's not looking at either of us, just diligently scanning our surroundings.

Toran leads us out to the courtyard and into one of the smaller stone structures. Inside is a space three times the size of Amma's house, but there are no dividing walls. There are people rubbing wax into coarse cloth. In the corner, drying moss over low embers, are two children. They glance up at us with hungry eyes, dull eyes, no spark left in them.

I've seen those eyes in people huddled on the streets of the fifth ring, shivering in the cold and damp, terrified for their lives. Toran says something. I can't hear. How can people still suffer like this, when the Storm is gone? It's not right. It's not fair.

A clap of thunder—I jump out of my skin. The Storm?

I follow Toran out the doors, into the courtyard. It comes again. This time I place it—it's a mallet against a sheet of metal.

Toran tenses like a spring tightening and launches into action. "Close the shutters! Everyone inside!" she shouts, barking orders left and right. Within seconds, the courtyard is emptied, the buildings are sealed, and those who can fight are gathered around her.

"Some of our people went to forage in the wilds," Toran explains quickly, a question in her eyes. "Will you come?"

Cas speaks. "The alarm—"

Toran gives a sharp nod. "The lightstruck are on their way."

"We'll come," I say over Hadria's objection.

Cas grabs my arm. "Vesper—"

"I'll stay out of the way." Unless I can help. "You and Hadria are trained for this—do what you can to aid them."

Hadria, Cas, and I follow Toran and her warriors through the trees. The orchard thins out—different, slender trees grow here, with mottled gray trunks. They encircle the stone ruins of another orchard-keeper's home—a far more prosperous home, judging by the scale of the ruins. It would be a more comfortable place for the high ringers, but the sparseness of the trees here offers no protection against the King.

Toran gestures—it's some sort of Wardana signal, judging by how Hadria and Cas both react immediately, forcing me into a crouch at the edge of the clearing.

Toran's gaze is locked on the second story of a moss-eaten building within the ruins. A flutter of moss—no, one of her people, wearing clothes that help them blend in. They move their hands in a rapid-fire series of gestures.

Toran curses. "The lightstruck are here. Remember—keep your back to the city at all times." She pauses. "I won't fault you for turning back."

"What will you do?"

"Save as many of my people as we can." She motions at her warriors, who split into three groups and disappear into the ruins.

"Vesper—" Cas starts.

"I need to know what I'm up against. I promise you, no foolish risks."

Toran draws two lengths of ikon-embroidered cloth and gives one to Hadria, who passes it to me. Toran blindfolds herself with the other.

"I have something else—" Cas hands me a curved length of mirrored glass. "For your eyes." A half helm, which covers my forehead to the tip of my nose. My vision blurs for a second—my eyes try to focus on the ikons etched into the glass—and then all becomes clear.

Cas nods. "I only have two." He holds the other to Hadria. It's bulkier than the one he gave me—an earlier prototype, I guess.

"Take it," she tells him, and blindfolds herself.

With the mirrorhelm, I can see fairly clearly. I peek over the edge of the mossy ruins.

Several high ringers—bearing baskets half-full with greens, fruit, mushrooms—cower against the ruins. Those without blindfolds squeeze their eyes shut or train them on the ground.

Through the trees come a dozen or so people—ordinary people—well-fed, clean-faced, and clothed comfortably. They're singing a song, a little off-key, as if they're just out for a day's work. They stop at the edge of the ruins and fall silent.

At their lead is a man with a long curtain of white hair. Ragno Haveli, wearing a kindly smile. Ragno . . . is lightstruck.

Shock parts my lips. "Cas—"

Cas lets out a strangled breath. "Did I forget to mention? He was one of the first to be lightstruck. Always leading the pack, my father."

"Focus now," Hadria hisses to him. "Have feelings later."

"I don't have feelings," Cas says. But he averts his eyes from Ragno.

Light kisses Ragno's hair, bathing him in soft warmth. There's something reddish in the air. What is that?

It could be a trick of the light, but it's so regular. A dusting of red sparks, like a firework suspended in time. I lean in to get a better look—

It's a man. A broad-shouldered figure made of pinpricks of red light. A faint line of that same red light stretches back from his body, through the trees, all the way back to the city. A direct line to the Great King.

The red man tilts his head, as if hearing a familiar tune. His face turns slightly toward us.

Him. The Great Queen recoils, and my heart pounds.

Rendered in red light is a face made in the same mold as Dalca's and his mother's before him. Whoever he is, he shares their blood.

He's a fair bit older than Dalca, and he carries his age in his eyes. He's very symmetrical, with the broad, even features of a storybook hero. And yet my shoulders inch toward my ears and my guard goes up.

He clenches his jaw, and suddenly, I recognize him. Memory whisks me back, to Dalca showing me a line of golden death masks belonging to the Regias of old. Death masks that told the history of Dalca's family, the Illusoras, and through them, the history of our city.

This man is a dead ringer for the ancient Regia Dalcanin—Dalca's namesake. Before Dalcanin, the rule of the city was shared between two vessels, one of the Great King, one of the Great Queen. When he took the throne, he killed every human vessel the Great Queen chose. And he warped the Regia's mark so the Great King could be bound against his will.

Because of him, the Great Queen fled and found shelter in a distant storm. For five hundred years, her power fed that storm, until it became a living embodiment of her power and her despair.

I hold my breath. What is this? How has he returned as a specter of light?

"There are people at the ends of those lines of light?" Cas asks.

"Only in the lines of color. We call them spectrals. There's this one, and another of orange light," Toran whispers. "They are minions of some sort, with a measure of power over the rest of the lightlines."

There's a commotion in the pack of lightstruck. Ragno glances behind him as a sandy-haired man pushes to the front of the crowd, though the other lightstruck hold him back. There are tears in his eyes. "Aravya, my love."

A gasp comes from a gaunt, frail-looking woman, perhaps a decade my senior. She keeps her eyes downturned. "Lin?"

"It's me, I'm here," he sobs.

A young brown-haired woman in a blindfold grabs Aravya. "Don't look!"

"You don't have to look," the sandy-haired man says from behind Ragno, his voice breaking. "I understand. Just know I'm here."

Slowly, shaking, she draws her head up. The brown-haired woman beside her grabs her, tucks her head into the crook of her neck. "Don't look, Aravya, please."

Even across this distance, every one of her sobs reaches my ears, as do the words she gasps in between, over and over: "He's my husband."

My stomach roils with acid. This is nothing like the Storm. The misery and despair in the air is of a different flavor; there is a different set of choices at play. My body is frozen solid—I don't know what to do.

Ragno turns a sorrowful eye to the moss-eaten houses, to the fabric sheets slung between the ruins, to keep out the light. The wind and rain have torn holes in them; through them peeks the city, crowned in light.

"This . . ." His voice is low with sorrow. "Is this right? To live like this? There are children missing their mothers. Do you part from those who love you so easily?"

"Stop." Toran vaults over the ruin and marches forward, between the two groups.

To her left are her high ringers clutching their baskets, to her right are Ragno and the lightstruck.

I tense. She's still blindfolded.

Ragno merely watches her, hands clasped before him. The Dalcanin of red light flickers, as if the red line connecting him to the city was briefly cut. I follow the red line of light back—to Toran's warriors stringing a waxed-cloth barrier between the trees, to cut off the light.

"Have you not entertained this fiction long enough?" Ragno asks. "Is this truly the independence you seek? Are you not yet reliant on the charity of those low ringers who have forsaken you? Will you continue to beg for scraps, rather than return to the hearths and homes of your family, your loved ones, your ancestors?"

Toran takes a step. "Remember, they don't promise a real choice—those aren't your children anymore. He's not your husband, Aravya."

"I am!" the sandy-haired man shouts. "Ask me anything, Aravya. Something only I would know."

"Don't—" Toran starts.

"What would we have named our first child?" Aravya asks, even as her friend holds her tighter.

Her husband smiles. "Ino, after your grandfather."

She pushes free and staggers to her feet, her gaze fixed on her husband. He opens his arms to her—she takes one step before her friend knocks her to the ground, pinning her.

The Great Queen's mark appears upon my skin, wisps of storm-cloud rise like steam from my skin. I make to rise, but a weight pins me down. Hadria—her whole body crushing me. "Do not move," she hisses.

Dalcanin turns toward us, as if he heard. His voice crackles like a woodfire. "All are welcome. Old friends, old foes. The Great King welcomes you all."

He flickers once more. Toran's warriors have deployed three shields that cut the line of red light, and Dalcanin disappears and stays gone. The Great King's line of sight is broken.

Ragno inclines his head. "We will go in peace. Please, remember: you can always come home."

The sandy-haired man takes a step.

His wife claws at her friend until she lets go. She stumbles once, twice, and sprints to him.

Her friend kneels on the ground, weeping.

A small thud. A boy—somewhere in his teens—drops his basket and crosses over to the lightstruck. A handful of others follow.

Toran's taken off her blindfold, and her warriors make as if to fight. She shakes her head. "We don't have the numbers to stop them."

"Then what should we do?"

Her shoulders bow. "Let them go."

As we walk back through the dense poma orchard to the encampment, it's clear that the soul has gone out of the remaining high ringers. Cas keeps his hood up and is silent.

"Less than three hundred left," murmurs one of Toran's warriors, a middle-aged man with serious eyes and hollows around his mouth.

Toran looks at me. "Maybe we are beyond help."

All these people, huddled and fearful . . . What made them run from their extravagant second-ringer homes? What is it that the Great King does with the lightstruck? All I've seen is lightstruck who've come to convince others to . . . to do what? Return to the city? That's not nefarious, especially compared to the beasts and the curses of the Storm. "What does the Great King want?"

Toran answers. "We don't know. He's destroying parts of the city—as far as we can tell, it's at random. The lightstruck . . . they're themselves, but unlike themselves. They become convinced to do things they'd never do. I've seen families destroy their own homes—homes that have stood for hundreds of years. Rather than be lightstruck, people leave."

There must be more to it than that. "Show me. You and I—we'll go into the city. You know how he works, how the lightstruck work. Help me understand. I can't fight until I understand what I'm fighting."

"You'll fight him?" she asks, and in her eyes is doubt: *You're just one girl.*

"You forget," I say. "The Great Queen is on my side."

Her brows furrow, and a little of the film of despair clears from her expression. "Into the city. That's dangerous."

"I'm not interested in courting danger," I say. "We'll watch for the light—the lines of light—and we'll stay far out of the first and second rings."

She looks out over the hall, at her people. "Fine. I need to be with my people tonight. And tomorrow is the festival. There'll be too many eyes on you—we won't be able to slip out. The next night, that's when we'll go. But I have one condition."

I nod. "Tell me."

"Leave Hadria out of it."

Hadria bristles at my side, but I keep my gaze fixed on Toran's. "Done."

CHAPTER 11

I *know these shadows. They are the uncolor of the darkness under my eyelids, the darkness that lives inside me.*

A grayish light shines, peeking through a gap in the shadows. The darkness parts like curtains, and the gray pulls me down.

I fall.

A chair catches me and holds me tight. I forget——have I been sitting here always?

I blink once——and a gnarled old table is before me.

I blink twice——and a woman sits across from me, a sharp chisel in her hands. She's focused on carving whatever it is she holds. Her long hair curls over her shoulder and casts half her face in shadow. Bold, striking features. Still, I know her.

"Ma," I say.

She raises an eyebrow without looking at me. "You can't know," she says, as if responding to a question I've already asked.

"I can't know what?"

"You choose what you want. You'll grow into the life you create for yourself."

I focus on the thing in her hands, the chisel and the wood. Her fingers are flecked with blood, and the wood still seems formless. My own hands seem strange and formless. "What if I choose wrong? What if I choose something I can't handle?"

She hums. "When you were a baby, all you could handle was eating and crying. Should you have stopped there?"

"That's not what—"

"Stop it," she snarls. "When did you learn this fear? What is your life for? Building a little cage of things you can handle? You would be as well served in death. Go out and seek a challenge worth being defeated by."

"And if it defeats me?"

A slow smile breaks over her face. "If you should be so lucky as to be deeply defeated—in that moment, you will know the air that becomes your breath, you will know every single drop of your blood, you will know the nature of that electric thing that drives your mind. You will know what it means to be alive." She leans forward, and the shadows lengthen across her face. "And if you should triumph over it, then go and find something greater to be defeated by."

Her eyes meet mine, and I wonder if it really is Ma before me. Her hands are bloody, chipped all over, as if she's been carving herself all this time.

The shadows release me reluctantly as I wake. Ma's words linger in my mind. It sounds brave, but I won't soon forget that the thing that defeated her was the same thing that ended up killing her.

I've done my sacrificing. I have the Great Queen with me, and I'll triumph. I ache to go with Toran to the city right away and learn what I'm up against—but there's the festival to get through. Though Toran said it would be impossible to slip through the town unnoticed during the festival, I hadn't believed her until I saw how the council grew frenzied with excitement, how the tower buzzed with the work of preparing, how even the sight from my balcony changed, with stalls selling sugared treats and festival clothes, with the market square filling to the brim with people.

There's a persistent knocking in my head. Blearily, I make sense of the stone walls, the plush softness under me, and turn the ikonlight on above my bed.

The knocking continues, and now it comes from the door. "Vesper? We're coming in."

Carver barges in. "We're here to help you get ready."

I blink at her, at the line of my guards following her in. "For what?"

Carver gives me a droll look. "The festivities."

"Already? Isn't that—"

"In two hours."

I blink at my guards. "Is it far?"

Mina answers. "No. A few minutes, perhaps."

My defenses go up. Last time Carver worked her specialized ikonomancy on me . . . "Are you going to change my face?"

"No," says Carver. "We want you as you are, just a little polished."

"Then, why do I need two hours—"

Carver gestures, and Ozra and Gamara tear the blankets from the bed. "If you don't know the answer to that already, you'd better just trust us."

She herds me into the bathing room, where the tub is already filled and fragranced with oil. "Call for me when you're ready."

I tug my sleepdress over my head. My skin pebbles in the cold air, and I step into the tub, slipping under the water.

My knuckles break the surface of the bath; I lower them again. The water distorts my body. If I trust my eyes, my body must be trembling, transmuting, stretching one way and twisting another. If I trust my skin, my body is still as earth, stirred ever so softly by the thrum of my pulse.

My body is no longer mine alone. The Great Queen is a deep presence within me.

I slip into her.

My mind opens. The world around me is cast in soft gray. A heartbeat—I follow it without moving a muscle, just with a strange awareness—and find a figure made of swirling dark smoke. A person. Hadria? The Queen shows me what's in her heart: a mix of steadfast duty and a small kernel of bittersweet hope. Fear, too. Another one of my guards stands beside her, filled with protectiveness, and an undercurrent of mischievous glee. Mina, probably, from the way she watches over Hadria.

There's Jhuno and Zerin, both calm and settled, watchful. Gamara, impatient and curious and determined to prove herself. Ozra, who desires something else, something beyond her work—a family.

The last of my guards. Her hope and joy is boundless. She's happy to be who she is, where she is. She lingers by the door—is this Carver? I never would have guessed there was this kind of joy beneath her cool demeanor. I'm cheered just witnessing it.

The water clings to me as I rise. My skin prickles in the chilly air, and I shiver. In the cold, my body feels my own again.

I ignore the rugs covering the floor and step out onto the stone. A hiss leaves my lips as my feet touch slate, but I like feeling the shock of the cold down to my littlest toes.

My hair sticks to my back and lower, curling against my hips. I'll have to remember to cut it. "I'm done," I call.

Carver enters in a flurry of action. My too-long hair is combed and brushed and tied into an intricate braid, with half left free. A mix of high- and low-ring styles. My eyebrows are plucked, my skin is patted with creams, my eyes are lined in kohl.

She brings a dress. *The* dress—the one the tailor made in multiples. Black threaded with violet, layers of sheer silky charcoal. A walking Storm.

Carver holds a polished mirror up to me.

In the reflection is the woman from my dream. Not quite Ma. Not quite me. I blink, and she blinks.

"Is this how you see me?"

Carver pauses. "Is it different from how you see yourself?"

I stop with *no* on my lips. I don't know. Could I see myself this way?

Carver, Hadria, Mina, and Ozra don identical dresses, their hair done the same way. They've even painted the lines of my sitar-string burn onto their palms.

Jhuno and Zerin are in their black and violet Regia's Guard uniforms, with their gauntlets on full display.

Carver wraps three ikon-inscribed masks with paper and tucks them into her bag. Each will adjust any of my guards' features to mine. She nods.

By the view out the rambler's windows, I'd say there's not a single person in the market town that's not celebrating, not a single inch left undecorated.

The festivities are concentrated in the market square. We take a far more direct route, through a cordoned-off street, and disembark at the edge of the square, stepping out of the rambler behind a newly built platform of sorts. A stage. The sounds of a happy crowd—of chatter and music—fill the air.

A curtain blocks my view of the square—and blocks the people's view of me—but as the fabric shifts in the wind, I catch glimpses of throngs of people, of multicolor ikonlights strung overhead, with larger ikonlanterns nestled at the base of the Stormender statue. I inhale the smell of fried dough, of sweets coated in hard sugar that crackles when bitten, of the spices of sundust and the woody-sweet scents of other drinks.

On this side of the curtain, the council members stand chatting. No sign of Izamal or Cas, but at the far end is a head of dark curls. Dalca. I need a word with him about the city, about what's been hidden from me—about what he's done to stop the King. He catches my eye—I gesture for him to come near—and he turns his back, moving to chat with a Wardana. He saw me, I know he did. Is he avoiding me?

I take a single step before Gamara stands in my way. "It's time," she says, nodding to Rosander, who holds the curtain open for me.

With one last look at his back, I step through.

A crush of sound. A hundred cheers meld into one great roar.

I'm guided to the center of the stage, to a throne—there's no other word for it.

The council follows, then Dalca. He does his best not to be seen as one of them, and also finds a way to stand as far away as possible from me. I sigh and plaster a smile on my face.

It seems the festivities are for all those who wish to look upon me.

A long procession of well-wishers gift me words of thanks. The longer I sit on this throne, the more it chafes that all these decisions are being made for me, that my role has been to sit where I'm told and smile. My blood boils with frustration.

Every person that walks up to me seems to think I'm offering them a kindness in just existing upon this throne. The weight of their tears and praise grows stifling.

Dalca is only fifteen feet away. Under any other circumstances, it would be no distance at all. But with all these people around, with so many who wish to speak with me . . . it's impossible to talk with him.

I sneak glances at him. He's far more gracious in how he receives those who wish to speak to him, so much so that I stop to listen to what he says and follow his lead.

He's in a dark ensemble, looking more part of my guard than the prince. And yet dozens of eyes watch his every move. What makes him a prince? What makes people stand when he walks into a room, what makes people lean to hear his words, what makes them hurry to follow his lead? Is it just the blood in his veins?

What does his blood mean now, when there is no Regia?

If they're silly to follow him—if there's no reason to follow him—is there no reason to follow me?

I ended the Storm. But without Dalca, would I ever have walked into it?

I want to know what I want. I chose to come back to this world, the world of the living. But my choices have had repercussions I never imagined. How did my choices lead me here? How did I end up in the shadow of that ridiculous Stormender statue, with people all around me making decisions for me?

The procession continues, and a familiar face appears before me.

Rosander Tarr, the landkeeper. He bows double and comes forward, clutching my hand in his. "Your support for the sixth is the talk of the town. Won't you join my family for a meal? Dinner with myself and my wife and daughters—and your guards of course—it would be an intimate affair."

Politeness makes me say, "That's very kind."

He murmurs something about finding a time and sweeps away.

Others come and go. In a lull, I turn my attention to the wider hall. People band in groups of those they're most comfortable with. There's one group clothed in priestess brown, but with black shawls draped over their shoulders. A stooped, bent-over woman hobbles toward me. The priestess from the council, Mother Yul.

"Hard seat, isn't it?" she asks.

My lips quirk into a smile of their own accord. "I can't complain."

"Polite of you." She turns her gaze to the partygoers. "You don't want to hear an old woman talk, not on a night like this, not when such a handsome man can't take his eyes off of you."

I raise an eyebrow. She indicates Dalca, who's doing a good job of playing his part. "Quite a few people are watching me, Mother Yul."

"Are they?" She makes a strange crowing sound—a laugh. "I rather think they're staring at themselves, and you happen to be a convenient mirror."

When I don't answer, she nods to herself and toddles off.

The crowd. So many faces look back at me, but she's right. They don't see me at all. They look upon me and see some part of themselves, their inner heroes, their inner gods. I remind them of their hope—though I'd wager they all hope for something a little different.

A commotion draws their attention. Izamal enters the square flanked by Nosca, all looking dashing in their blue uniforms. Izamal's laugh rings out, and in seconds he's surrounded by his adoring fans. A smile comes to my lips. Even if I wanted to get him alone to talk, there's not a chance it'd happen.

Through the crowd, I meet Dalca's eyes. He's alone. He offers me a small, tense smile, and before I can make a move, he joins the circle of dancers, offering his hand to the first girl he meets. I narrow my eyes at him.

Familiar faces move between me and Dalca's obstinate back. The revolutionary knitters. Imbas Lahra embraces several of them before she's called away.

One of them—a woman with a cheeky smile and startling green eyes—catches me looking and salutes me. The gray-bearded man at her side flashes me a smile that reveals a glint of metal—a tooth inscribed with an ikon. Last I saw them, they were all washed-up revolutionaries. Folks who once fought alongside my parents, who had turned to doing small acts of good, like weaving moss into cloth and providing it to those who needed it.

I smooth my expression into a smile and approach them, leaving the dancing behind. Their clothing bears a thick weave that's the signature of mosscloth. A fashion statement, or a political one? "Have you come to court me too?"

Green Eyes smiles back. "We've come to warn you."

I turn to her.

The grizzled man flashes his ikontooth. "Some folks found themselves some power in your absence."

Green Eyes leans in. "Rosander? He's been saying he knew your father. Got himself the support of the merchants with that."

"Leveraged himself a seat on the council," Ikontooth explains.

"Imbas is on the council, too," I say.

Green Eyes grins. "I wasn't sayin' she's above using your name. But she's doing it for the right reasons."

"That's not the point we're making. We're saying . . . now that you're awake, you can speak for yourself, see? The power they've made for themselves in your absence—it's now at risk."

"They'll be trying to control you—or get you out of their way."

"Are you talking about Rosander?" I ask. "Or Imbas?"

"Him, and others too. Note how our dear princeling kept his power. The more he told your story, the better his sounded."

That puts a sour taste in my mouth. "Everyone saw him at the Trial."

"Everyone saw him weeping over you, too."

"Brought a tear to my eye, it did," Ikontooth says.

Dalca, the actor. I frown. "What do you want me to do?"

"Pay a little less attention to the gods. And a little more to the little people."

I cross my arms. Considering I've a god within me, I think it's fair that I pay attention.

"I believe in you, Vesper. Many of us do. Imbas does. That's why I'm warning you. Take charge. You've given them freedom, but they know not what to do with it. They've suffered, these past years. They're willing to lay their freedom at the feet of those who will give them hope. More than hope. A plan. A purpose."

"Is that so bad?"

"As long as whoever is doing the leading is worth following." With that, they melt back into the crowd.

I blink at the space they occupied. I don't like this, this expectation they've dropped on my lap. I can face gods. At least I've got experience in that. But to lead, to govern?

Everything is so frustrating. This dress, the weight of my braids, the stickiness of the color Carver painted on my lips.

The hair on my neck stands, and I catch Dalca staring. He averts his gaze, back to the graceful red-haired girl he's dancing with. The song ends.

Before I can think better, I get up from the throne and cross to him.

A path appears through the crowd; Dalca is surrounded, with no easy way out. Good. He smiles at me, but his eyes dart around, looking for an exit. We'll see what wins: his need to play the part of the heroic prince or his need to get away from me.

"Will you dance with me?" I ask him.

I think he stops breathing. A heartbeat passes, and like a sculpture come to life, he bows and takes my hand. The music starts.

"It's difficult to pin you down long enough to have a conversation," I say.

He gives me a bleak smile. His body is rigid, his hand frozen in mine. "Consider me pinned."

I grit down a rumble of irritation. He doesn't get to find me repulsive. That's my role. "I think . . ."

We spin through the steps of the dance, a low-ringer dance, one I'm surprised he knows. With my hand on his, I feel him compensating to hide a limp. After a pause, he speaks. "Yes?"

"I think you're a coward."

He stumbles ever so slightly, the pleasant, princely mask slipping. "What do you want from me?"

I lower my voice. "Tell me what you did. The mark. The Great King." How it went wrong.

"It's not exactly a story befitting our surroundings," he says quietly.

"I have time. I'll claim all your other dances, if need be."

"Vesper . . ."

"You've never hidden things from me."

His jaw works, and he sighs. He leans in. "I put the mark on. The King sensed it, but he was not drawn inside me. That's how it worked for my mother and my grandfather. Instead, he was angry. The brief connection that was made when the mark was completed . . . he used it to burn me."

He spins me away and draws me back. "That was the first time. I spent weeks healing. We had found a library in the Wardana outpost in the seventh. There were some ancient texts. Cas and I consulted those. A year and a half, we worked on it. And in the end, we made a mark even the illustrious Regia Dalcanin would have wept at."

The steps of the dance pull us apart, and when we draw close, he murmurs in my ear. "The second time we completed the mark . . . the king took pleasure in it. In breaking me."

For a second, his control slips. His weight falls on me as he catches himself with an arm around my shoulders, his limp becoming pronounced. I'm sure it almost looks like an embrace. "I am a coward," Dalca says, his voice restrained. "My life is proof of that. But if you find another way, another mark—I'll do it a third time."

I push him away—I need to see his eyes. "Dalca—"

"Pardon me." He releases me—the song's ended—his face twisting in a smile that's probably convincing from several feet away.

"Dalca," I call again.

But the crowd swallows him whole.

The person speaking to me stops mid-word. "I'm sorry," I say, and slip away.

I make for the curtains behind the throne, passing a Wardana guarding the way. The second the curtain falls behind me, Hadria appears at my side. "What's wrong?"

I shake my head.

"I can take over," a voice says.

I turn and see—me.

My double winks. "It's me, Mina. Relax. I can play you." Her expression flickers, her eyes growing shadowed. Her smile becomes subdued, as if her mind is a thousand years away.

Is that what I look like?

She bows with a little flourish and heads the way I came, back into the fray.

A flash of white hair. Cas, leaning against a rambler. I cross to him. "Ready?"

"Everything you asked for is prepared for tomorrow night," he says. "But you should tell Dalca."

I would rather die. "The more people know, the more dangerous it gets."

"You can't honestly include Dalca in that," Cas says, ever Dalca's faithful pet.

"Dalca—" I stop, not knowing what I mean to say. "I don't want Dalca involved. And all we're doing is the equivalent of walking up to the stormwall. I used to do it all the time."

"It's not the Storm," Cas says.

"I don't want Dalca there." I hold his gaze.

Time stretches long between us, until finally, he shakes his head. "Fine. You know best, Stormender."

I smile, but somehow his subservience makes me more worried. I wanted an equal to argue with. But Cas sees me as something more than that.

I am that, I remind myself. I ended the Storm. I can do this. I can do anything.

This stupid festival didn't defeat me. Dalca didn't defeat me. So on to a greater challenge.

CHAPTER 12

The small globe of light that falls from Cas's ikonlantern is all the illumination the three of us have on the road from the sixth's watchtower to the gates of the fifth. The stormbeasts don't seem to need it; they plod forward with only the scraps of moonlight that filter through the immense trees. The wheels of the rambler roll smoothly, near silently.

Toran is at my side, Cas on the seat opposite. The dark presses in on us, as complete as if the air were made of black velvet. The ancient streetlights that line the road are unlit, and the city's lights are not yet visible.

The dark suggests that the city might not be there. That it's been whisked away into the night.

Cas flicks the ikonlantern off. "Let your eyes adjust," he says to Toran and me.

I blink. At first there's no difference between having my eyes open or shut—but then it appears.

A faint glow in the distance, as if the sun is rising from behind the city. But dawn is far off yet.

My eyes grow comfortable with the dark as we reach the fifth ring. The wall that separates the fifth from the sixth rises fifty feet above our heads. A smooth mass of stone, pale but for veins of black that branch out across it. Scars from years of lightning strikes.

The rambler rolls to a stop before the great black gates that mark the southern road.

The solid wood-and-metal gates are set deep into the wall. They show their age; the gnarled surface is pockmarked, gray peeking through the black wood, but the curling bars of metal are still strong and unyielding.

Cas jumps out and makes for the doors. Three barely noticeable ikondials are inset into the wood and his hand skips from one to the other, twisting and turning them until they slot into place and the ikons are activated. He shoots a speaking look at my cloak, and I tug the hood lower. Toran does the same, but Cas rearranges his cloak so his Wardana gauntlets are prominent.

A small tremor shakes the ground. I tilt my head up to take in the immense height of the gates, to witness them opening. I wait, but they don't move, not an inch.

In the wood of the gates, a line appears, as if someone is drawing the outline of a much smaller door. This door pops open.

Cas pops back in, and the rambler moves through the door—the fit is so tight I hold my breath. Through the gates is a once-lost part of the fifth that I've never seen. On either side are stables for storm-beasts—two other ramblers sit empty near them.

A small gate station stands at the end. A bleary-eyed man pokes his head out, blinking at us and straightening his gray uniform. A gate guard. His sour expression lightens as Cas waves, prominently displaying the reddish black of his Wardana gauntlets.

He gestures us to an empty slot. Toran sees to the beasts as Cas flashes a transit pass at the guard. Cas murmurs something that I don't catch.

"No, sir," the guard answers. "Everythin' as usual. The fifth is as quiet as can be."

"And the third?"

"Oh—well, I wouldn't know—I've been promoted, see, to the fifth. Not that I wouldn't—I've requested to be up on the front lines, of course—but Head Guard knows I have a family—"

"Of course," says Cas easily. "You've done well."

The guard's eyes skim over me and Toran as we slip past after Cas into the fifth. His brows knit together. "Sir—you're not going up to the third?"

"Of course not," Cas says. "That would be foolish."

The guard's face brightens in relief. "Right, yes, of course."

Once he retreats to the gate station, Toran murmurs to Cas, "Please tell me you're not intending to take the main gates all the way up."

"No," Cas says. "This is for effect. Welcome home, Vesper."

Beyond the gate station, the fifth ring beckons. The moonlight kisses every inch of the fifth, and stones I remember being dark gray now look like fresh cream. They might even be made of the same sandstone that they use in the third ring. How funny, if all our buildings are made of the same stuff.

All the moss has been scrubbed from the roads and walls. Some blue-green stains remain, that's all. A handful of people walk the streets—all in cloaks—but the alleyways are empty. I suppose those who once took shelter from the Storm there have now found homes. Maybe in the sixth ring, or maybe in some of the fifth's buildings that were once lost.

Hanging between houses and across alleyways are makeshift shields against the light. Some are made with cloth, others with planks of wood. But all block the higher rings from view.

I tug my hood lower. My shoulders ache under my cloak, heavy with the combined weight of hundreds of interlocking mirrors—my own personal shield against the light. It's not the sort of thing one wears when hoping to go unnoticed, so I'm wearing it inside out. When we get nearer to the third, to the edge of the Great King's domain, I'll turn it back around.

We soon leave the black road, and Cas takes us on a circuitous route through the fifth ring. A yearning builds slow in my gut. I grew up here. I skinned my knee on that step when I was nine. These streets are mapped out in my heart—light or shadow.

At the mouth of a familiar street, I hesitate. If I go further down the street, will I find scorched rubble? Or a rebuilt house, where Amma's once stood?

It doesn't matter. Either way, that's no longer my home. A little voice in the back of my head asks, *Where is your home?*

"Toran," I say. "Tell me what happened."

"There was a flash of light," she begins. "I heard it described as a star falling to the palace. The Regia's Guard were meeting, and they were lightstruck first. We didn't notice."

I listen, keeping one eye on Cas, who takes us into a small courtyard and to a statue so old that time and thousands of hands have reduced its features to nubs and the faintest impression of eyes.

Toran continues. "When the Guard called for others to join them, under the guise of planning for how to repair things, they went."

Cas fiddles with something at the base, and one side of the plinth swings open. We crawl through, into one of the tunnels that lead to the city's underbelly. Cas turns on an ikonlantern and we follow him deeper.

"What happened?"

"Many decision makers—heads of old families, leaders of trade, master ikonomancers—were among those called. I and other Wardana were too, but most of us were at work in the fifth and sixth rings. Some got the message and went, others got it and dismissed it as a power play by Ragno . . ."

Cas's shoulders tense.

"I vaguely remember some boy coming and telling me something, but we'd just tracked this stormbeast—a man-killer—and . . ." She shakes herself. "You don't need to know all that."

She falls silent as we come to a fork in the tunnel. Her lips are pressed tight; pain furrows her brows. I give her a moment.

"Are we headed to the old city?" I ask Cas. The fossilized ruins of an ancient city that ours was built upon—decades of neglect and time turned it into a labyrinth that few could navigate.

Cas shakes his head. "No need."

As we take the fork into a tunnel that slants upward, I wonder—did those ancient city builders dig underground to escape the light?

The tunnel ends in a stone wall; Cas fiddles with the old ikonlock, and a door reveals itself. We push it open, and step out into the fourth ring. The fourth's Pearl Bazaar is bustling. That's different. This deep into the night, it would normally have been empty, with stalls shuttered and goods secreted away.

"In the five rings, they never come out during the day," Cas explains. "Darkness lets them see the lines of light clearly. That's their best protection."

Low, dim ikonlights are the only source of illumination. Without eyes used to the dark, it'd be impossible to see anything.

"And in the sixth?" I ask.

"The high ringers and those out in the wilds keep night hours as a rule. In the Queenskeep there are many who feel safe enough to wake during the day."

I can imagine why some might feel so safe. They can't see the city, so they can pretend that the danger doesn't exist, or that it's too far to hurt them.

As we make our way through the crowds, we're jostled on all sides. My hood slips, and I yank it back in place, wincing as the mirrors catch on my hair.

The faint tinkling from my cloak is masked by the tinkling that comes from many of the stalls. Large round mirrors to hang over doors. Smaller diamond-shaped mirrors no larger than a fingernail. Polished metal for those who can't afford mirrors. And then there are the parasols. Dozens of them in various sizes. I blink at them, wondering.

I don't have to wonder long. A parasol bobs through the crowd, and I understand. Long cloth hangs from the metal rim, shrouding the person carrying it. Only their gloved fingers are visible, parting the cloth just wide enough to see through.

Other stalls carry cuttings of thick fabric as coarse as mosscloth. A woman holds a length of it against her hip, measuring it against her height. A dark-haired man murmurs to a pinched-faced woman, wondering if it'll fit their windows.

There's paste to seal gaps in walls. Tinted eyepieces. Wide hats with cloth sewn to the brims.

A shifty-eyed stall keeper sells amulets with nonsense ikons to protect from the light. No doubt, the same shopkeeper once sold amulets to protect against the Storm. The same false hope, in new packaging.

My fingers brush one, and I fall still.

It's an etching of my face.

The stallkeeper nears. "The Stormender. A good choice. If you wear her image, it's said that she will watch over you."

"I doubt that," I say. I haven't watched over anyone.

"A nonbeliever! She died for us," he hisses. "Show some respect."

Cas's hand finds my elbow, and he grips tight as he makes apologies while steering me away.

"This is ridiculous," I say as we sweep through the fourth.

"Let them love you," he says.

"They need someone to believe in," Toran says. "They need . . . Honestly, we all need hope that there's meaning behind all of this."

I bite back what I want to say. I'm just one girl. It was chance that I was there, that I was given the Great Queen's mark. They might as well put their faith in anyone.

But it's my face on these amulets. It's me that Toran came to. It's on me to make this right.

There are four main roadways between rings—the black we entered on, the red to the west, the white to the east, and the gold to the south, which is the only one that leads all the way to the palace. We take none of them up to the third.

Casvian instead leads us down a crooked alley that seems like a dead end, until we get close enough to see the ikonlocked gate that's hidden by a bend. He opens the gate, and beyond is the stone of the ringwall between the fourth and third rings. Cleverly disguised among the stone is a set of narrow stairs that zigzag up the side. As the gate shuts behind us, Cas presses into my hands a thin oval of mirrored glass set into a length of cloth. He gives another to Toran.

"Like so," he says and wraps his own around his eyes, tying it off behind his head. I can't see even a hint of his eyes through the glass. "I improved upon the last."

I follow suit, tying the soft cloth as tight as I can. Through the glass, the world appears slightly dimmed.

"May I?" Cas asks, hands raised to my face.

I nod.

With a featherlight touch, his fingers run from my cheekbones up to my temples. "Perfect." He lowers his voice. "If something happens . . . If you have to choose between brave and careful, choose careful, won't you?"

"Nothing's going to happen," I say. "I spent a night beside the stormwall, and we're not getting half that close."

"That's lovely and all," Cas mutters. "But this isn't the Storm."

"So I keep hearing."

I flip my cloak right way out while he checks Toran's headgear. She gives him a terse smile for his trouble.

The cloak settles with a rustle of glass on glass. It bothers me that neither of them have mirrorcloaks. Cas called it his prototype, a shield against the light. But wearing it makes me afraid. Like I need the most protection because I'm the most vulnerable.

I close my eyes and find the low thrum of the Great Queen. Her power runs smooth and deep, a river under my skin.

I shake my head to clear it. It doesn't matter. I made a promise to Toran. I spent my life beside the Storm, until I knew its voice as well as my own. I know nothing about the light. And if it's my duty to save the city once more, I need to know what I'm up against.

The climb is long, and my thighs burn. "What happened next, after the meeting?" I ask Toran.

She draws a breath. "All who went were lightstruck. We didn't know. There was one day . . . lightstruck husbands led their wives, daughters led their mothers . . . friends, spouses, children—they were led by those they trusted."

The air brightens the higher we go. And with it comes a warmth that presses down on us, a heated exhale from a monstrous god.

Toran continues. "We heard stories of people leaving doors and windows open, so the light could get in and take their families. In just one day, near half the second-ringers were lost. Those who remained— some left right then, with whatever they could carry. Others stayed, refused to believe, until they, too . . ." She sighs. "The high ringers you met—they're all that's left of the second ring."

I can imagine the lines of light, sweeping, searching. I open my mouth to ask, *What happens to them when the light gets them?* But I can't get the words out, only wheezing gasps for breath. I curse the weakness of my body.

Cas slows to a stop at the top of the stairs.

I lean over, hands on my knees, to catch my breath.

Toran hands me a small container. "Water," she says.

I drink until my heart calms. "None of the thousand-and-one-feather cloaks are left?"

For all his bookish ways, Cas isn't even breathing hard. "There's one left under lock and key. You saw Dalca use it. Those that the light-struck didn't take, they made a mission to destroy. Unless kinnari birds somehow come back from extinction, we've lost our might in the air."

I take one last drink. "Thank you," I say to Toran.

I get a better look at where we are. A twelve-foot wall shields us from the third ring, but also keeps us from getting a good view. Even with the wall, it's as bright as dawn. Even through the goggles.

Cas stands by a ikonlocked door set in the wall, waiting for me to give the command to open it. Instead, I gesture him closer.

"This is what I understand: the light stretches halfway through the third. The domain of the King's power grows at a rate of inches per week. So we could get within several feet of the lines and be perfectly safe."

"Well—" Cas interrupts.

I give him a quelling look and continue. "But it seems that on occasion, the lines of light can stretch further. And there are the people of light."

"The spectrals," Toran offers.

"Right. The spectrals. So we'll take no risks," I say. "We're just getting a good look—the Great Queen might be strong, but we don't want a fight just yet. Not before we understand what the King is doing and what he wants."

The reservoir within me is full to the brim. I exhale and draw the Queen's power to the ready, and her mark rises on my skin.

"Let's go."

CHAPTER 13

The thing that hangs midway through the third ring is not a wall of solid light, not like the Storm was a wall of darkness. It is a spiderweb of light, a cat's cradle. The lines of light come from the tip of the palace and, like spokes in a wheel, shine to the tops of newly built towers that jut up from the wall that separates the first ring from the second.

From there, the lines travel across the second ring's airspace: a lattice of light above the stately homes and beautiful wide streets of the city's wealthiest and, once, most-advantaged citizens. The lightlines meet again at the border of the second and third rings, in another series of towers that didn't exist before I died.

But it's no static cage. Several of the lines move, sweeping from the palace and the towers in tight arcs.

Above the third, the lines grow less organized. A work in progress.

We keep to a narrow alley, protected by the three-story buildings on either side. But it means our view is a narrow sliver of sky. The alley intersects with another; down that way, I catch a glimpse of something at the outer edge of the third ring. A round stone structure, surrounded by wooden scaffolding: a tower, mid-construction.

"What are those towers?" I ask.

"Only the lightstruck know for sure," Cas says, squinting at the second ring. "All we can say is that each tower at the edge of the first ring accepts a single line of light from the palace. Those lines go to the towers of the second ring—but there are far more towers in the second ring than in the first. I'd like to pose some hypotheses."

"Please," I say dryly.

"One, there is something within those towers that redirects the light. Two, there is something within those towers with the ability to split one line of light into multiple."

"Three?"

Cas thinks. "I've only got those two."

"Then," I say, "we should get a better view."

Cas follows my gaze to the unfinished tower. It's thin and already well over four or five stories tall. "It could be dangerous," he begins, "but if it's empty, if we can learn something about them . . ."

Toran tilts her chin up, watching me. Waiting for my decision.

"He's building these towers for a reason," I say. "They're the most visible part of his plan. Yes. We need to see."

"All right," Toran says. "I'm with you. You're the only one willing to help my people, so I'll help you find out all that you want to know." She says it like a reminder, a challenge.

We make for it, keeping to the shadows. Every sound has us freezing still, even the wind whistling through a building, even a bird cooing from somewhere above.

The alley opens out into a wide street; we stop in the mouth and peer around the corner.

A group of young men walk past. Laughing, sharing food amongst themselves. They wear no protection—no parasols, no veiled hats, no visors—and walk without fear. They must be lightstruck, but there's nothing in their appearance that calls them out as anything but ordinary.

They disappear down the street, and I let out a long, slow exhale.

We dart across the street, to the base of the tower.

"I'll go in and check it out," Toran says.

"Wait," I say. I can spare her that risk, at least.

I close my eyes and sink into the Great Queen, into the awareness she grants me, seeking figures made of shadows, seeking fears. Besides the group of young men, there are people scattered through the houses behind us, but there are none in the tower.

"We're good," I say, blinking. "It's empty."

Cas's eyebrows make for his hairline. "If you say so."

A doorless opening lets us in. A spiral stair wraps around the perimeter. I groan at the idea of climbing more stairs, but Toran hops right to it. No wonder Hadria's so fit. It must run in the family.

The first landing is a mess of wood beams and columns holding the higher floors up. The second and third landings are much the same, but when we get to the fourth, it's open to the air.

The third ring spreads out before us.

"They're building something," Cas says.

I follow his gaze deeper into the third, where groups of lightstruck load up strange little carts with piles of stone. They push the cart into the path of a thread of light, and then the cart begins to move.

"Quite a few of the houses of the second have been demolished," Toran says, her gaze fixed higher. "We've not figured out why."

The lightlines sweep across the second and part of the third. Is there a pattern? There's something to the way some of the lightlines move . . . It's like the ikon Pa showed me, the life-ikon in a drop of blood.

On the static lightlines, something moves. I focus.

Like spiders on silken threads, vehicles travel on the light. They're shaped like a pair of cupped hands, with a central post bearing an arc of shimmering gold fabric. Lightstruck onboard direct them with long sticks—somehow, with the sticks, they're able to move the craft from one lightline to the next.

A red beam of light—the red spectral, the Regia Dalcanin—sweeps through the second, interrupting the lightstruck. They move out of its way and resume their work, like a river flowing around a rock.

The spectral is thankfully far away. Near us are only the ordinary white-gold lightlines, bright like sunlight. They crisscross across the third and the second, and there's something about the ones that move . . . a pattern just out of my grasp. What does the Great King want?

Cas's voice comes from somewhere over my shoulder. "Look at this."

Toran and I join him at a raised platform in the middle of the tower. In the center of the platform is a meticulously carved divot. "What is it meant to hold?" I ask.

Cas draws out the shape—like a seven-pointed star—in a little notebook he's pulled from somewhere in his jacket.

I close my eyes. *Do you know what this is?* I ask the Great Queen.

Let me see, she says. *Open yourself.*

It's as though she's kicked over the reservoir within me. Her power pours out of my fingertips, into the cold stone of the platform, and deeper, into the stone and wood of the tower, and down across the street, into the houses and past children huddling under their bedcovers and their parents packing up their belongings, across rooftops, and then—

A flash of pain. A sudden burn. I snap back to myself and slam down a wall on the Queen's power, locking it inside.

The hairs on the back of my neck rise. My palms sweat and my heart taps a quickening beat.

Across the third, right where the Queen's power brushed against *something*, the lightstruck on the ground part for a beam of light. It's much dimmer than the red one, but it's there.

And because of the Queen, it knows I'm here.

"Hide," I hiss. "Now!"

Toran and Cas scramble, disappearing behind half-built walls and thick wooden pillars.

The light draws itself up the side of the tower. It's a deep violet, hard to see against the night and overshadowed by the brighter white-gold lightlines.

I press myself behind a pillar.

A wash of violet light pours in.

Something shifts. Like light catching on dust motes. The dust motes arrange themselves into the shape of a young man. Light thickens on the curls of his hair, on the bridge of his nose, the tips of his eyelashes, the curve of his cheekbones. As if he's lit from above. All that light would touch is illuminated. All that would be shadow is excised.

The light lands heavy on his shoulders, outlining the decoration of a uniform I've seen once before.

It's the uniform Dalca wore for my Trial. He walks forward, tilting his chin up, and the pinpricks of violet light fill in the rest of his face.

Dalca. Younger, as he was when we ended the Storm, the moments before I died.

"Vesper?" he says, in a voice like Dalca's, but with a layer of crackling fire beneath. He scans the landing, glances in my direction, and stands with hands clasped. "I won't look at you, if that's what you wish."

I don't move.

"If I wanted to do something to you, I would have. Didn't you see me? When you stood upon your sixth-ring watchtower, I thought you did."

I frown. I remember an immense pair of eyes—and yes, a figure in bluish light. That was him?

"You don't know how I've waited for you. You were everything I couldn't be, there at the end. You were who our people needed. And I . . ."

I focus on breathing quietly. He's talking as if he's Dalca. I don't understand.

I draw the Great Queen close, and step out to face him.

He turns to me and flickers closer—I didn't see him move—it's as if his beam of light swung closer, bringing him just a foot away.

I can count the specks of light that make up his eyelashes. He reaches, his hand hesitating in the air between us.

"I would beg your forgiveness," he says, "but all I want is to be your equal."

"What are you?"

"He wants you very badly. There's something you should know—something you have to see—" He stops. "You must go. I'll distract him."

He turns his back to me—

An arm wraps around my waist and drags me back, behind the stone platform. Cas hisses. "You idiot." His eyes widen at something over my shoulder and he claps a hand over my mouth.

I follow his gaze over the edge of the platform.

The red beam of light nears and pours through the tower's opening. It forms into a scarlet figure. A dignified, heroic-looking man, with the longish hair and ornamental dress more common to a time a few hundred years in the past. The Regia Dalcanin. "There is neither reason nor precedent for you being here."

Dalca—no, the violet spectral—answers. "I was merely admiring our kingdom. Is that not reason enough?"

Cas gestures for me to make for the stairs. The stairwell is protected, but there's five feet of open space until a wide pillar, and another three feet to the stairs.

On my mark, he mouths and peers over the edge.

I crouch.

He points. *Go.*

I dart to the pillar and glance back. Cas gestures for me to stop and stay.

"You're not worthy of the light," the Regia Dalcanin is saying to the violet spectral. I've missed part of their conversation, but the violet spectral's clenched fists say enough. He's turned them around, so the Regia Dalcanin's scarlet back is to us.

Bent in half, Cas sprints across, his body pressing against mine as we both angle ourselves in the shelter of the pyramid.

I search for Toran. She's across the landing—the platform is between us.

Cas gestures for her to run, and she does, to the platform. Her boot kicks a small pebble that skitters across the floor.

The red spectral turns.

Curses. Time slows.

I call the Queen's power. Curls of stormcloud and darkness. A stormbarrier begins to knit itself—

The Regia Dalcanin snaps his fingers. A thrum hangs in the air, as if all the lines of light were plucked like the strings of a sitar—

My stormbarrier rises, three feet high, then four—

All the nearby beams of white light draw together and slice toward the Regia Dalcanin, and he grows brighter, larger, fuller—

I pour more into the barrier, and it rises ten, twelve, fifteen feet tall, spreading wide.

There's that feeling again—a smarting burn, like hot oil splashed on my skin. He's boring into the stormbarrier—

Something is wrong, the Great Queen hisses in me. *He was never this strong. He was never stronger than I was.*

Like a match held to cloth, the light burns through the barrier, red-hot and then white—

"Run!" I shout.

Cas takes off. Toran is slower to react—her fists are up, like she's expecting a fight—and Cas drags her down the stairs.

I follow them to the next landing. The beam of red light pours through gaps in the stone, flickering as it swings from side to side. The Regia Dalcanin is a dozen feet away—he disappears—he's five feet away—he disappears—he's before me, his kingly face is twisted in fury, his clawlike hand reaching, brushing my arm.

Blisters rise upon my skin as I duck back into the stairwell, darting across the next landing—

The Regia Dalcanin is already there—the violet spectral stands before him, and I run as fast as my legs will take me down the next flight and out the door, into the street.

A hand grabs my arm and drags me into a run. Toran. I grab her wrist tight, and we sprint for it.

Can I transform something? Another barrier?

I raise another stormbarrier—it holds for one second, two, three—

The red light slashes through it as if it were made of paper.

A rock catches my toe, and I stumble—but a hand grips my other arm and pulls me. Cas. They both keep me up and running.

Our shadows stretch longer and longer in front of us as the light behind us brightens. Heat licks at my back, and sweat beads all over my body. Blisters rise on my skin.

What can I do? There must be something—This can't be—

"Vesper!" A shout from above.

I glance up. Black wings spread wide, blotting out the sun. Dalca. Flesh-and-blood Dalca. He dives toward me.

The heat grows at my back. Toran flashes me a grim look. Her hand slips from mine.

Cas's grip tightens around my other wrist.

Dalca's thirty feet away. Ten feet.

Dalca reaches a hand for me. My fingers brush his, once, twice.

He lunges and grabs my wrist, hauling me into the air and swinging me against his chest. We dip low again, and the rise is more labored, slowed by extra weight. Dalca must've grabbed them—I can't see anything but the collar of his uniform and the tense muscles of his neck.

We fly away from the lines of light.

The air grows blinding. Dalca's pulse jumps in his neck, mirroring my heartbeat.

I clutch Dalca's waist as my insides plummet. Falling—we're falling, tumbling to the ground. His arms tighten around me. My knees bang into his, scrape along the stone ground.

We skid to a stop.

I push myself up. Dalca groans under me. The glass of my eyeshield is cracked, and my vision is fractured. Why did we fall?

The feathers of Dalca's cloak are singed—a great section has burned away. I untie the eyeshield and fling it aside. It shatters against the edge of the stairs that lead up into the third. Cas is sprawled a few feet away—Dalca must have dropped him a moment earlier.

Cas scrambles up and grips my chin in his hands, searching my eyes. I try to shake him off, look around him.

"Vesper?" he asks, voice trembling.

"Still me," I say. I push his hand aside. "Toran?"

Dalca staggers to his knees, catching his breath. "I—" He breaks off, hand to his ribs.

Cas's brow furrows as he looks behind me, at the third ring.

"I couldn't—" Dalca breathes. "I couldn't carry all three of you."

Cas looks at Dalca with a strange emotion in his eyes. "You should've left me," he says. "The high ringers . . . they need her."

I fold my fingers into a fist, press them into my thighs. I let go of her hand. I asked her to come. She trusted me and—

Dalca pushes himself up. Flesh-and-blood Dalca, with circles under his eyes and cheeks darkened with stubble. I follow his gaze.

White-gold lines of light stretch to the border of the third and fourth ring. The Great King has expanded his domain.

The entire third is caged. The entire third is lost.

Because of me.

CHAPTER 14

A cry rises, an anguished wail without pause.

A stormbeast—no, it can't be—but can a person make such a sound? Over the rushing in my ears comes an answer, in the unmistakable sound of human weeping. People have begun to understand. Doors bang open around us, as the fourth-ringers come to see, to confirm that it's real.

That the third ring is lost.

Many of them are silent; a bewildered, uncomprehending muteness that says this is too terrible to be true. My skin crawls. Are they watching me? Do they know it's my fault?

An unreal fog clouds my thoughts.

"We need to get out of here," Casvian says. "Dalca—your cloak?"

Dalca tears his gaze away from the crowd. "The cloak? It's done." He holds it out. The last Wardana cloak, made from the feathers of the long-extinct kinnari bird. It's singed and smoking.

"We shouldn't be seen here. Especially you two." Cas frowns. "We have to get you back to the sixth."

No. I can still feel her hand in mine. "Wait—Toran—"

Casvian snaps, "We can't help her now."

I try to find words in the thick gray that clouds my mind. "It was supposed to—no one was supposed to get hurt—"

A pair of blue eyes fills my vision. "Vesper. Can you stand? Or shall I carry you?"

A flicker of irritation cuts through the fog. "I can stand."

I blink until I can see past my thoughts, until I can focus on Dalca's outstretched hand. I reach for it and grip it tight; his skin is hot, his calluses rake across my skin. He hauls me to my feet. I don't let go.

Why did I let go of her hand? "She's—The lightstruck," I say. "She might—We could find her. Maybe she just needs to be pulled out. Maybe the light hasn't taken control yet."

"Vesper." Dalca breathes, so close I can count each of the razor-thin scars that curl across his skin.

I need to let go of his hand. Such long fingers, and the skin of his knuckles is covered in little pale crescents. More scars.

"We all lose, sooner or later," Dalca whispers. "You lost today. That's okay. But if you don't run now, you'll give up all your tomorrows."

I straighten my thumb, and one by one, my other fingers follow suit.

In his eyes is understanding and a pain that mirrors mine. I nod.

The corners of his eyes crinkle in smallest relief.

Cas gestures us after him, into the relative shelter of an alley. We slip through the crowd—Dalca's ruined cloak bundled under Cas's arm—keeping our heads down. It doesn't seem like anyone's paying attention to us, though it's hard to tell with all the veils and parasols. By the tilt of their heads, most folks in the gathering crowd are fixated on the sight above.

"There's a door not far from here," Dalca murmurs. "It lets out in the fifth. If we hurry, we might catch the others."

"The others?" I ask.

"Izamal and the Wardana," Dalca explains. "I came ahead."

My stomach sinks at the thought of facing them.

I follow him through streets of people—some come to gawk at the third, some carrying their belongings and in all likelihood making their way to the sixth. Terror turns the air sour.

A mother hoists a crying child. "Come now, love. Keep your eyes shut."

His cries get muffled against her shoulder. A running man jostles her, and the child screams.

What have I done to all these people?

I barely notice the path we take—just that, at some point, the blistering heat subsides—noting little but the acid churning in my stomach, the horror climbing up my spine, the weight that bends my neck and presses down on my shoulders—

It's powerlessness.

But inside me is the Great Queen. The power that made the Storm the most terrifying threat to our city. How could this have happened?

A voice echoes my thoughts. "What happened?"

I blink and find myself face-to-face with Dalca, in the dark of a tunnel, our way lit only by a small ikonlantern that hangs from Cas's wrist. We've made our way back into the tunnels—I'd kept Dalca's back in sight and put one foot in front of the other.

Dalca repeats the question.

"I don't know," I say. "We were going to stay far away. But they sensed the Queen. The spectrals, I mean. It was so fast . . ."

"But you—with the Great Queen . . ." He trails off, but there's a question in it.

"The King is stronger than he's supposed to be," I say. "That's what she told me."

Another question hangs in the air: *Why?*

None of us voices it. But I catch Dalca glancing at me, his brows furrowed, mulling something over.

We come out in the fifth and are met by the Wardana.

Izamal wraps me up in a hug. "Thank the stars," he murmurs into my hair.

I don't deserve this. He should know what I've done. But when I open my mouth, a mangled sob slips out, and I can't have that. Not here, not in front of anyone.

My guards aren't with the Wardana. "They stayed behind—one is pretending to be you—just in case . . ." He doesn't finish the thought. They're protecting my reputation.

The ride back to the watchtower is silent.

But it echoes through my head: *Why?*

The Queenskeep courtyard is in chaos. Izamal instructs the Nosca to draw attention by making a show of their return, so we four can sneak into the tower. I brace myself and my aching thighs for another long climb. But instead Dalca leads us down a short corridor off to the side of the courtyard, and Wardana quickly block the way behind us.

The corridor leads right to the base of the watchtower. I expect a side entrance—a door of some kind—but we end up before a large bit of machinery that sits right up against the stonework—immense gears and some kind of pulley system hooked up to what looks like a metal birdcage.

A prison of some kind. I stop dead.

Cas walks right in.

"What is this?" I ask.

"You haven't ridden in a riser yet, have you?" Iz asks, following Cas inside. "Don't worry. I was joking earlier. It's safe enough."

"Get in first." Cas waves me in, muttering under his breath. "Of all the times to show caution."

I bite my tongue and step into the cage, my footsteps ringing on the metal floor.

Cas swings the door shut as Dalca twists an ikondial set in a panel between two bars of the cage. A large gear grinds into motion, and the cage rises.

I grab on to the bars. The riser takes us up the side of the watchtower, with a *tick-tick-tick* as the gears click away. The wind joins in with a high-pitched whistle as it slips through the bars.

We rise over the courtyard wall, over the blue-slate rooftops. The market town sprawls as we go ever higher. We climb past the Stormender statue, her face lit by the dim glow of ikonlanterns.

The sky begins to lighten—dawn has come.

At the edge of the town, landtreaders sit like slumbering beasts, all in a line.

How many more people will flee the city in the coming hours and days? Where will they live? Can Izamal's landtreaders take them all? How many more can they build—

No. Why am I thinking about Izamal's plan? I haven't given up on our city. I can't.

The riser slows about three fourths of the way up the tower, as it approaches a stone balcony that juts out toward the horizon. We're not nearly high enough to reach my rooms.

The three of them have been conversing in low tones. They fall quiet as the riser stops. Cas opens the door and we step down onto the balcony. I long for a thousand-and-one-feather cloak. To fly wherever I please—to fly anywhere that's far away.

Would Toran be here, if we had cloaks?

The balcony doors leading into the watchtower have been retrofitted with metal. At Dalca's four-beat knock, they crank open and a head pops out. A dimpled smile. Gamara, my guard. Relief washes across her face, and she smiles at me.

I can't quite bring myself to smile back.

The door pushes the rest of the way, and we slip through.

I recognize this place. A long hallway curves around the perimeter of a circular room. This is where I woke up.

"This is the most secure place in the tower," Iz says.

Another one of my guards sits hunched over, elbows on her knees. Hadria. She has a knife in her hands as she whittles a piece of wood, just like Ma in my dream. I blink—no—she's sharpening her blade.

I stop before her.

"Hadria," I say.

She looks up, surprised, and then smoothly rises to her feet in a graceful, unconscious show of respect, her knife still in hand.

My mouth goes dry. I swallow. "Hadria," I say again, to fill the air between us.

"Is there anything I can do?"

"I have to tell you something," I say.

She tenses.

"Your mother . . . When the third . . . Toran didn't come back."

She holds herself very still. Emotions flicker through her eyes, but the smallest twitch of her eyelashes is all that gives her away.

"She showed me what we're up against. And for that I owe her . . ." I trail off. "I'm sorry."

I hold her gaze until she breaks it. A vein in her jaw works.

Don't look at the knife in her hand, I tell myself.

A body comes between us. A broad back, tanned neck, dark curls.

"Dalca," I say. "What are you doing?"

"Hadria," he says, low and calm.

I snap. "She's not going to hurt me."

Dalca is still as stone. "You won't, Hadria. Will you?"

It's like a tightly coiled spring, suddenly let go. She slams her fist into the wall and strides away, her curtain of silken hair billowing behind her.

I step after her. Dalca grips my arm. "Let her go."

"She needs to know that I'm going to make it right."

A pause. "Are you?"

I glare at him. He's looking not at me but at the knife embedded to its hilt in the stone wall.

"Yes," I say, but it comes out quieter than I'd intended.

He turns to me then, the force of his eyes like all the sky is asking me. "How?"

The only place I can be alone is the circular room where I once slept away years of my life. I sit on the platform I woke up on—a soft bedroll over a stone plinth—and wrap my arms around my knees.

Amongst all the offerings cluttering the floor are small books that depict the story of my life. Some are beautifully bound, others much more cheaply so. The story in most is the same, though the details are different. One goes on at length about how I loved to grow shalaj and how I'm a friend to those that work the land. Another pointedly calls

Imbas Lahra and her revolutionaries friends of Pa's, painting them all as my wise advisors. If I'd listened to Imbas back when Pa was taken by the Wardana, I'd probably still be lying low in a safehouse somewhere, waiting for the Storm to take me.

Several of the other books paint it all as a love story. They end not with my death, but with Dalca calling the citizens of the city to the Arvegna arena, where he tells my story.

When will they add the chapter where I let the third ring fall?

I drop the books. But my story is on the walls, too. I can't get away from it.

How am I going to make this right?

On the wall, a gray-eyed girl with long black hair stands hand in hand with a boy with curling black hair and blue eyes. Behind them is the Storm: a billow of purple-black swirls made of cut and gleaming gemstones, with white stones for the stormbeast's eyes.

I focus on a pair of eyes, breathing deep and slow, until my body settles. I slip into a place between dreams and waking, and I call for her. The Great Queen.

In my dream state, the mosaic clouds shift like rippling water, becoming an immense face.

You said the Great King was stronger than he was supposed to be. What do you mean by that?

She answers, *My great opponent . . . I know him well. He would have had to spend much of his power to maintain those lines of light. He should not have had power to create those creatures, much less to fight me.*

Creatures? You mean the spectrals?

She doesn't answer that.

I bite my cheek, thinking. Another wall catches my eye; the mosaic depicts stormbeasts breaching the stormwall.

I fit my thoughts into words: *But you interacted with the world through the Storm. Your beasts and curses, and the slow encroaching of the stormwall itself . . .*

She speaks. When I was cast out, I was weak. As the King should be. We needed human vessels to interact directly with the world.

But . . . the King has always had a human vessel. The Regia.

In ancient times, the Great King and Queen both had human vessels, chosen from anyone in the kingdom whom they deemed worthy. Those vessels were our ancient rulers—and through them the King and Queen gave us great power, including ikonomancy. But those vessels also inherited the gods' conflicts, and often waged war against each other.

To end those wars, the Regia Dalcanin killed every vessel the Great Queen chose, until she fled to a passing storm. She stayed in it for hundreds of years, made it her vessel, fed it her power.

No human vessel would have given him this power, the Great Queen says.

My mind lingers on the red spectral, on the Regia Dalcanin. He did more than banish the Queen. He wanted control over both the gods. In those days, whomever the King chose as vessel was given his mark instantly—the way the Great Queen's mark appears in darkly iridescent lines on my skin. Dalcanin studied the Great King's mark, and added a layer of ikonomancy that made it a cage for the King, a mark that trapped him in a human body.

Maybe he's had enough of human vessels, I say.

The Great King was trapped for hundreds of years, as Dalcanin's corrupted mark was passed down through Dalca's family. Over the years, he took back power the only way he could: by dominating the mind of his vessel. He got so good at it that modern Regias—like Dalca's mother—were trapped in their own bodies, becoming little more than puppets for the King.

The King would have learnt from you, I say, as an idea dawns. *He saw how much power you had by taking the storm as a vessel. He wouldn't use a storm, but . . .*

The river of the Queen's power runs quicker. *You believe the king has found a new kind of vessel.*

Yes. Something that suits his needs, like the Storm did for the Queen. Dalca tried to use the Regia's mark to trap the King in his body. But it didn't work. It wouldn't, if the Great King already had a vessel.

Perhaps, the Queen allows.

I'm right, I know I am.

But what is it?

CHAPTER 15

With a long, fitful sleep in the mosaic room behind me, I make my way to the council room. Gamara and Mina walk before and after me, the others having already cleared the way. Hadria hasn't returned.

It's still midday, when most people are asleep. The tower is relatively empty, so I'm surprised when the sound of footsteps reaches my ears.

Imbas strides toward me. Mina steps in front of her, but I gesture to let her pass.

Imbas cuts straight to it. "What will you say?"

I blink at her. "The truth."

She shakes her head, her expression kind and condescending. "Is the truth what they need right now?"

"What do you mean?"

She leans closer. "If you make yourself fallible, will they listen to you when you need them?"

"I don't understand what you want me to say."

"Toran went up to the high rings. And then this happened. Cause and effect." She waits a few beats to make sure I understand.

I take a few seconds longer to see if she's joking. "You want me to lie, to say I wasn't there? It's my fault, Imbas."

"What good would that do? If you want to pay penance, do so. But don't seek penance by making it worse for others."

"How can I make it worse?"

"You stand for something. You're a hero."

A hero. She says it so matter-of-factly.

Imbas misreads my expression. "If you don't like it, you have yourself to blame. No one else made you what you are. If you remember, I told you to run, to lie low in a safe house."

"You seriously prefer how things were?"

For a moment, she looks every bit her age, with sadness in every line. "No. But I knew your mother. And she wouldn't want this for you."

It's so unexpected that I can't hide my flinch. I step around her and reach for the doors. What does she know about what Ma would want? Ma could've told me, if she'd waited for me. But even in death, she left me behind.

Ma would've wanted me to be a hero. And if she didn't—well, if she didn't, what Ma wants doesn't matter.

I shove open the doors to the council room.

Anguished faces greet me.

Rosander speaks first. "Imbas—do your people know what happened? We've heard only rumors—"

The ikonomancer with the helmet-hair—Aysel Marzel—gestures. "I've heard it was the high ringers—that they were seduced by the lightstruck."

"Seduced by the lightstruck—how? To do what? That doesn't explain how the third was lost in a single hour," Mother Yul croaks.

Aysel leans in. "We know enough that our priority must be to protect ourselves from the lightstruck. Pull back the Nosca, have them patrol between the fifth and sixth rings."

Tharmida Sel speaks. "No. Our priority must be to increase production. Let the Nosca protect my people. We're on track to have five landtreaders complete this week. With the extra hands, we can have seven done next week."

Mother Yul steeples her fingers. "If what happened is due to the lightstruck gaining some new ability to manipulate, then yes, I agree. We must alter the schedule." Her gaze goes to Imbas. "You've said nothing, Imbas. What do you know?"

The weight of Imbas's gaze lands square on me. My tongue sticks to the roof of my mouth, my words stick in my throat.

I drop my gaze to Izamal, who sits across from me, but his golden eyes are trained on Imbas. No help there.

Cas's and Dalca's seats are empty.

A look comes across Imbas's expression, something knowing and pitying. She clears her throat. "They're saying it was Toran."

Rosander jumps to his feet, bangs his hand on the table. "We should've dealt with her—too lenient—I've been saying—"

"There's to be no violence against the high ringers." I take a breath. "It wasn't Toran alone. If it's anyone's fault . . ."

Rosander breaks the silence. "What are you saying?"

My throat goes dry. *It was me. Blame me. I'm not your hero.*

Izamal stands. "Vesper. Don't blame yourself," he says sharply. And then, to the others: "She thinks she could've handled it better. If she'd made Toran understand."

The tension drains out of the room. Rosander smiles in a way I'm sure he thinks is fatherly. "Don't blame yourself. We've been trying to get through to them for far longer than you've had a chance."

"That's . . ." *Not it.* I'm frozen in my body.

"We'll let our people know that it was a rogue high ringer. An unfortunate circumstance," Imbas says. "But Vesper is right. We shouldn't assign blame. After all, no ordinary person can force the Great King's hand. He was going to take the third with or without Toran. We need to calm our people and prepare them for the journey ahead. Iz, reports from the Nosca-Wardana?"

"The outpost in the seventh should be supplied in another three days."

Speak up, Vesper. Find your voice. Is it truly wrong to tell the truth?

"I was there," I say. "It's my fault. Not Toran's."

A small silence, briefer than the last. Rosander walks around the table and pats my hand. "It's all right. We understand."

"You don't," I say, snatching my hand back.

The expression in his eyes hardens, but his smile moves not at all. "What do you want?"

I force each word out. *"To make it right."*

"We are," Rosander says, and turns to the others. "Imbas, have all the families been assigned to the landtreaders?"

I step aside to avoid his gesturing hands. And find I've stepped away from the head of the table.

Just like that, they're back to negotiating the minutiae of their plan to leave. Their voices melt into one another, a vague roar of sound.

They're all gears in a machine, working smoothly together. They don't need me. Rather, they look at me as if I'm a potential threat.

And I am. Their power is built upon their proximity to Vesper, the Stormender. What do they care for me, the Vesper who makes mistakes? My cheeks grow warm, my palms sweaty. What am I doing here? Why am I pretending my presence matters to them?

Imbas catches my eye. Whatever she sees in my face makes her drop her gaze. I cross the room without looking at any of them, holding my back straight and keeping my gait even until the doors shut behind me, sealing off their chatter.

Mina and Gamara fall into step with me. "They're vile. All of them," I say.

"We can probably take 'em," Mina says. "With Hadria? Easy."

I wonder at Mina's easy assurance that Hadria will come around.

"You can't kill the council," Gamara hisses, eyes wide.

"You want to bet?" Mina grins, then shrugs. "I don't get this whole ruling-by-committee thing, anyway. All we need is one Regia, like always."

"Not always," I say. "There were once two."

"So we leave one of them," she says. "You pick. Who'd rule with you?"

I give her a look. She sure has a way of making assassination sound charming.

From behind us comes a laborious tread. "Stormender." Mother Yul croaks, "I need a word."

Mina and Gamara step to either side of the hall and turn their backs to us.

I put a smile on.

Mother Yul doesn't look impressed. "Did you think they would just listen to you? They all think they know what's best."

"There are things that are morally obvious. No one should have to be convinced of them."

Mother Yul tuts.

I cross my arms. "If you're going to say, 'That's not how the world works,' please don't. I'm tired of feeling naïve."

"You're not." She moves closer. "When they look at you, they see someone who could do what they couldn't. It hurts. So they find reasons to make it hurt less—like saying what you did was a fluke. Or that your job is done, and now it's up to them to rule. They'll come up with a million explanations for why you're no better than them. But you know the truth."

"What?" I ask.

"You're extraordinary. None could do what you did."

She doesn't know. The Queen could've chosen anyone.

Her wizened hand latches on to my arm, and she croaks into my ear, "And that's the problem. People are scared. They're insecure. When people are fearful and destabilized, that's when they seek answers. I should know. That's when they used to come to us, to the temples. And now . . . The light promises answers. You see what's happening, don't you? With the poisonings, people can't trust their food. With the screaming on the streets, paranoia sets in. They can't trust their neighbors. And slowly, slowly, they begin to think: perhaps the light is better than this . . ."

She lets go. I rub my arm, a chill sinking into my skin. "I . . . Mother Yul, I appreciate—"

"Don't let the fear in," she rasps. "They're all looking to you."

Gamara and Mina walk with me to my rooms. The door opens with a fragrant whiff of hot, flaky pastry and the spices of sundust tea.

The rest of my guard finishes clearing the room, and then they gather. Not one of them looks pleased. I face my guard, ignoring the feeling that I'm seeing double.

"Go ahead and eat," I say.

A couple of them shift their weight, but none move toward the table.

Carver comes up to me, her footsteps the only sound in the room. "When you went to the third alone . . . They think you don't trust them," she says, and from the way she keeps her gaze pointed over my shoulder, I'd wager she includes herself in that statement. "They think they've failed as guards."

I owe them an apology. "I . . . It's not that I didn't trust you. It's that I didn't think I'd need a guard. We were just meant to—It's just . . . a lot went wrong."

One of the others speaks. Jhuno, locking eyes with her twin. "We all took a vow. A Regia's Guard serves for life."

Regia, Stormender. I'm collecting titles, and none of them feel all that great.

"I hope you don't regret making that vow," I say.

A smile from Carver. "Not yet."

I open my mouth to say something else, something that could express the warmth and the guilty gratitude filling my chest. But nothing seems adequate. "Shall we eat?" I ask instead.

It breaks the tension, and the air fills with soft chatter as they make their way to the table. I've just taken my seat when the door opens behind me.

The last member of the guard. Hadria.

I stand, and she comes to me. "You're back."

"I know my duty," she says. "I . . . My mother and I don't see eye to eye about lots of things. But we are both Wardana. Which means. We both want the same thing. And she thought you were the way to getting it. And so do I."

I nod. I can understand that.

"And," Hadria says, "my mother is strong. If anyone can beat the light, it's her."

I glance down at my plate—someone's filled it up with pastries. "You're right," I say, and I hope she doesn't hear the guilt in my voice.

I can't just sit here. I grab my plate and make for the door. There's a commotion as the others rise.

"Where are you going?" Carver asks.

"I have to talk to Cas," I say. "I'm taking this as a bribe."

"It's all right," Hadria says. "I'll watch over her."

Curses. I put a smile on my face. "I won't leave the landing without you all," I promise the others over my shoulder.

Hadria dogs my steps as I cross the landing, as I knock on Cas's door. Her silent presence makes me prickle. My back grows stiff and my shoulders inch toward my neck.

The door swings open to darkness.

Cas peers out of the shadows, blinking owlishly.

I hold up the plate. "I bring food. And an idea I want to talk to you about."

He sighs. "I think I need a break from your ideas."

But he lets me in. Something about the life-or-death experience has brought some color back into his cheeks. He looks a little less defeated than before, and he's even got some of his old attitude back. Though I can't say that I missed the attitude.

Hadria follows me up the stairs.

A dim light comes from above. At the top of the steps, I see why: the pinhole contraption is open. A thin beam of light bounces off the mirrors and projects the city on the wall. I put the plate on top of a pile of books that reaches my waist and draw close to the projection.

The web of light is immense. It still goes only so far as the edge of the third, but the towers at the perimeter of the fourth are nearly complete. It's a matter of time before the King comes for the fourth.

Strangely, a thin, dark band snakes through the rings and out of the city. It moves, undulating like a river. I stare at it until I understand: it's a long line of people. Fourth-ringers making their way to the sixth.

They're giving up.

Cas's voice interrupts my thoughts. "So what's your idea?"

I lower my arms from where I've wrapped them around myself and try to sound confident. "I think the Great King has a vessel."

"What?" he says, glancing from me to Hadria.

I glance at Hadria, but her face gives away nothing. There's no reason she can't know. "Like the Queen and the Storm," I say. "Something that amplifies his power. I don't know what—but maybe something that refracts light. It makes sense, right?"

He taps his chin, deep in thought. "The Regia . . . When Dalca's mother passed, that was the only unnatural death of a Regia in recent history—"

"The only—" I start. "How can that be true?"

"They were all watched very carefully. You saw the last Regia. Her attendants and her guards were always there. Not unlike how they watch you." He blinks at Hadria and pauses. "When it seemed her passing was close, they would've put the mark on Dalca, save for a tiny portion. They'd wait to complete the mark at the very instant of the Regia's passing. In some records, it's hinted that they helped the Regia pass at the right moment, so there would be no time at all—a fraction of a second at the most—before the King was bound once more."

"This is the first time he's had a chance to be free," I say.

"Free to find another vessel. Yes, it's possible. But that means . . . putting the Regia's mark on Dalca would never have worked. There's no capturing what's already been caught. Dalca did nothing but draw the King's wrath. I should've seen that."

"We have a chance now. We need to figure out what the vessel is. And where." I turn to the projected image of the city. It's there, somewhere within that maze of light.

I catch Hadria staring at me. I drop my gaze too quickly and cover for it by reaching for the plate piled with food. I offer it to her and Cas.

He takes a pastry absently, but his gaze has turned inward, to some corner of his mind. Hadria shakes her head. I pick one shaped like a crescent moon. It crackles and flakes under my fingertips, and the smell of hot butter and roasted sugar and spices makes my mouth water.

I feel a pair of eyes on me, but Hadria's staring at the reflection of the city.

I bring it to my lips—

A thunderous *crack*.

The door bangs open below. Footsteps thud up the stairs, and Dalca bursts in, frantic, eyes wide, hair nearly standing on end.

"Vesper," he bursts out, "you're in danger."

I stare at him. Then at the room, empty save for Cas, Hadria, and me. Dalca crosses the room and shuts the little pinhole covering. The thin stream of light—and the projection of the city—disappears.

His panicked movements make me nervous. "Have you had a bad dream?" I ask.

"No!"

"I've secured the room," Hadria tells him quietly, but he seems to take no notice.

For something to do, I take a bite of the pastry.

Dalca clutches his chest—briefly the outline of a medallion presses against his shirt—and he whirls on me, slapping the pastry out of my hand. "Spit it out!"

Too shocked to disobey, I open my mouth and let the bite drop onto his palm. "Dalca," I say, "are you all right?"

He puts a hand to his chest, closing his eyes. "That's it." He points at the plate on the floor, still piled high with food. "Don't eat that."

Cas looks from me to Dalca, and then neatly places his unbitten pastry back on the plate.

Shouts come from downstairs. Dalca darts down, and I follow close on his heels.

"Vesper—" Hadria starts.

Izamal meets us at Cas's door, his whole body corded with tension. "Vesper—don't eat anything—have you eaten—any of you, have you eaten anything?"

"No," I say, leaving out Dalca's part in it.

He deflates in relief. "Oh, thank the stars."

"What's happening?"

Iz's gaze flickers to Hadria. "Your guards—there was something in the food."

My heart drops. "Are they okay?"

"The healers are working—we don't know. We don't know how this could've happened—we've checked the kitchens—hold on—" His attention darts away as one of his people steps onto the landing. "Did you round up the attendants? Who brought the food?"

Izamal darts away, and they have a muttered conversation with a few other Nosca.

"We have to get you somewhere safe," Dalca says, scanning the landing as it fills up with Wardana.

"Where?" Hadria asks.

The door to my rooms is wide open. My guards—they can't be hurt. I can't have let them down—

A hand clasps my arm. Hadria searches my face. I nod at her.

"Come with me." Dalca leads us to his door and carefully undoes the ikonlock. The door swings into a set of smaller and much simpler rooms—fitted with a desk and a small training area. Dalca and Hadria sweep through the rooms, one going left, the other going right. Cas locks the door behind us.

I stand still, making sense of it all. No one would mean to poison my guards—they'd mean to poison me. "Who's trying to kill me?"

Dalca answers. "There are two possibilities. One: the high ringers. They learnt what happened to Toran . . . She was always the one who could keep the more aggressive ones in check."

I nod. "And two?"

"Someone in this tower has been lightstruck."

After checking all the doors and windows—or rather the bricked-up areas where there once were windows, as Dalca's rooms face the city— Hadria slips out to discuss with Izamal and check on my guards.

"Don't answer to anyone but me," she warns, and shows me a five-beat knock that she'll do.

The door clicks shut behind her.

"She could be lightstruck," Cas says. "She didn't eat anything."

"That was pure chance," I say. "If she wanted to kill me, she had more than ample opportunity."

"All the same," Dalca says, "best not to rule anyone out." He paces back and forth, combing hands through his hair and making it wilder each time.

That reminds me. "There's something I've been wondering. How did you know?"

He looks up from the maps he's poring over. "Know?"

"About the food. About where I was."

"Izamal told me about the guards and the food."

I frown, replaying the moment. The way Izamal came into the room . . . Izamal didn't sound like he'd already told Dalca about the poison. But there was so much panic . . . I could be wrong. "Well, what about before, in the third?"

"We already talked about this," Dalca says, tapping his fingers on the papers on his desk. "We need to be thinking about how to figure out who's the culprit and how they did it. Or we won't be able to trust any of our food supply."

I don't trust the way he doesn't meet my eyes. But he's right that figuring out who did this is more important. "All right—"

"No, Dalca." Cas cuts me off, wearing a strange expression. "I'd like to know, too. How did you know exactly where Vesper was? Today and yesterday?"

"Cas," Dalca says warningly, his eyes sharp. "Drop it."

"She's right. You didn't know it was poison when you barged in. All you said was *you're in danger*. You thought it was the light. You didn't know about the food. Izamal told you nothing."

Dalca glares at Cas, his jaw clenched.

"Where is it, Dalca?" Cas puts his hands on the desk, looming over Dalca. "When did you do it? You *swore* to me."

Dalca rises to his feet. "If I hadn't, she'd be dead twice over."

"Excuse me," I say. "What?"

Cas breaks from their staring match. "You'd better tell her, Dalca. Or I will."

"Cas," he says quietly.

"Vesper," Cas says through his teeth, glaring at Dalca, "do you know the story of Amon Haider and his oathmark?"

"The children's story?"

"Yes. Knowing it, would you ever—as in, is there even the faintest, infinitesimal chance that you would ever make an oathmark?"

The story of Haider . . . It comes to me in Amma's voice: Amon Haider. A story of him and Oshira, the woman he loved. He swore to protect her, and his love and willpower solidified into a medallion he wore on a chain around his neck—the first oathmark. Every time Oshira was in danger, Amon came. The children's versions make a comedy of it—the villain leads Amon away on some pretext and arranges for Oshira to meet her demise. Amon finds out—and just in the nick of time, gallantly arrives to save her. Until the one time he's coaxed into removing the medallion to bathe in a river. By the time he realizes, it's too late, and Oshira is dead. The oathmark then turns against him— some versions say it has a voice that whispers in his ears, others say it was merely a ringing like that of bells, others still say it was a phantom touch like a hand squeezing his heart—and in all versions, it causes him excruciating pain, until he takes his life so he can follow Oshira into the next world.

I'd thought it a moral tale about not holding on too tightly to things—a children's story, a warning against destroying your own life. There are a couple other stories in the same vein, all with someone well-meaning or besotted making an oathmark. But they're almost all tragedies.

So, no, I wouldn't. But my skin vibrates with strange, cold energy, as if a shadow has fallen over me. I know what Cas is getting at, but I need him to say it. "Cas, oathmarks aren't real. They can't be."

There's a long moment of silence as Cas glares at Dalca.

"Fine." Dalca exhales, deep and slow, then turns to me. "That's what I thought, too. One of the Wardana watchtowers we uncovered in the seventh had a sealed room, an ikonomancer's workshop. No one had been in there for generations upon generations. Much had disintegrated, but some things were intact. Among them . . . There was a book of ancient ikonomancy."

"Forbidden ikonomancy," Cas interjects. "Outlawed and stricken from our libraries. For good reason."

"Perhaps." Dalca gives me a reserved smile. "It turns out an oathmark is just an ancient and complicated ikon."

Cas scoffs. *"Just?"*

"You've made an oathmark," I say blankly, "to me?"

He holds my gaze, and then slowly lets out a long breath. "This oathmark . . . will make sure the Storm never returns."

I pace back and forth, trying to digest this information, but it's like a bad bit of broth that keeps bubbling up my throat. "So, what—you can spy on me?"

"No. That's not it."

"But you know where I am."

"Only when you're in danger."

"How does that work?"

He winces. "It's like . . . a new sense. A distant voice, or pressure. It's not easy to explain. It gets louder, more urgent when danger is present."

"Am I in danger right now?"

"Not exactly. Not in the way you mean—there isn't an active and immediate threat. But there are some who would do you harm—like one of those who live in Toran's encampment—the intent is there, and if you happened upon one of them when you're defenseless, in a circumstance where no one else would witness a crime—then yes. In that sense, you're in danger. Ever since I put it on . . . you've always been in a low degree of danger."

That's unsettling.

He must read my expression. "I'm sorry. I shouldn't have said that. Truth is, I never meant for you to know. It's just my job to keep you safe—"

"What?"

He blinks at me.

"It's not your job to keep me safe. It's not your job to appear when I'm in danger—"

"Would you rather I let you die?"

"I would rather—I would—" My jaw snaps shut. I put some distance between us, and turn my back to him. "I don't need you to do this. I don't want it. I don't want the guilt—what if something does happen to me? Is the oathmark like in the legends?"

Dalca opens his mouth.

"Wait. I don't—that's not the point. I don't like you knowing where I am. I don't want to be tied to you in this way."

"You're not tied to me," Dalca says quietly. "Not at all."

"And anyway, I have a guard."

"They didn't help this time. And . . ."

"And what?"

"One of your guard may be the lightstruck we're looking for."

I have nothing to say to that.

Dalca softens. "I understand. It's not my intention to make you feel . . . spied upon. Or trapped in any way. But I will not see you die if it is within my power to prevent it."

He says it with deep intensity, but I can't read the emotions that darken his eyes. I step closer. "Why?"

Surprise flickers across his eyes. He glances away. "Because you're the vessel of the Queen. And if you died . . . the Storm would return."

"I see," I say, and my voice seems to come from far away. It's a fear I've pushed down. I refuse to think about dying. I won't die. I won't allow the Storm to return. Whatever it takes, I'll make sure of it.

I'm not so shortsighted as to reject his help. As long as one thing is clear: "It's not me you're protecting," I say. "But our people."

"If you let me," Dalca says without meeting my eyes.

I cross my arms. "Do what you will."

CHAPTER 16

Mina Arvanas is dead. She was known for her laugh (always a little too loud), her cheeky wit, and her right uppercut. She'd fought in twenty-seven stormbeast surges, had mastered the spear, the scythe (after her hero, Ragno Haveli), and had lately picked up the bow. As a child, she'd bossed around all the other high-ringer children in her year. They followed her willingly, naturally—all except for Hadria. Hadria, as talkative in her youth as she is now, would not follow. No one explains to me how they became friends—they all start the story and then devolve into *remember when* and *suddenly, one day*—but they did, and Mina became Hadria's self-declared interpreter.

I knew none of this when she was alive. Hadria stands before Mina's body, as still as the statue in the square. Not a single word—not a sound—has left her since we heard about Mina.

She shifts ever so slightly at my approach. I say nothing, and we settle into silence.

Mina is laid out on the infirmary cot. Her dyed-black hair lies in loose curls, and her face is untouched by pain. Her face. Of my guards, she looked most like me, once Carver had her way. But unlike me, Mina's heart has stopped. She's not coming back.

I wish I'd known her. Instead of spending so much time thinking about how she'd serve me—if she was a good enough warrior to guard me, if she was similar-looking enough to play my double. She deserved better.

"Hadria." My voice is blasphemously loud. "The gifts I've been given. The power, the second chance at life. Everything I have. All of it . . . I'll use it all to stop this. No one should die for me."

"She—" A faint rasp. Hadria tries again. "She made her choice. And she died a hero. Don't pity her." Her voice breaks, and she presses her lips into a thin line.

A fury bubbles up in me and stops at my lips when Hadria's shoulders tremble. She turns away.

My hands become fists; my nails bite into my palms. I have no power here. Nothing I have to say, not *I don't pity her* or *I'm sorry*, will make any sort of difference.

The best I can do is leave Hadria alone. The ring of my footsteps feels rude, as does the click of the doorknob. I shut the door behind me and wince at the whirr of the ikonlock engaging.

Izamal looks up at me. His eyes are red-rimmed, and strands of hair escape from the leather cord at the nape of his neck.

"Her family?" I ask.

"Father's long gone. Mother and aunt . . . We'll take care of them."

"Is Hadria . . . ?"

"You'll have my Nosca until she and your guards recover."

"That's not what I'm asking, Iz."

"No." He scrubs a hand over his face. "No, you wouldn't. I'm sorry. I don't know about Hadria. She never lets anyone in. She'll probably show up tomorrow and be fine."

The sharpness in his tone draws my attention. I study him. "You know Hadria well?" I ask, with a little too much emphasis on *know*.

He gives me an annoyed look. "We were trainees together."

There's something he's not saying.

"There's nothing to say," he says as if reading my thoughts. "We were somewhat close as kids, for a little while. Sparring partners, that sort of thing. She didn't seem to notice my being cursed or being from the fifth. But her mother was a Regia's Guard, and that's what she wanted to be, and I wanted to stay Wardana and help fifth-ringers. We chose different paths . . ."

"I'm worried about her," I say. Hadria wouldn't have hurt a hair on Mina's head. And she could've killed me if she wanted to.

If Hadria were lightstruck, would it matter how much she cared for Mina? Do the lightstruck know that they're lightstruck? How can we know so little about it? Ragno Haveli and his people seemed so ordinary when they came to the high-ringer encampment . . . Honestly, Ragno seemed calmer than I've ever seen him.

If only Hadria did want me dead. If anyone deserves to want me gone, it's her. Because of me, she's lost her mother and her best friend in so short a time. "Just . . . if you are close with her in any sense of the word . . . watch over her."

"She might not like that," Iz says.

I'm not asking him to put on an oathmark. "Well, I get that. But she's very alone. And surely you can find it in yourself to be charming enough that she won't mind."

He sighs. "You're overestimating my charms."

We bump into two women, both tall and thin. Iz murmurs in my ear that they're Mina's mother and aunt. They fight their grief to put on polite faces and greet me the way they think I ought to be greeted, with a good deal of bowing and words of gratitude that are sharp as knives.

There's little I can say that would mean anything. I can't fix this. But

I tell them Mina was brave, that she will be missed. And I understand that my presence is a gift and a burden to them—I'm not someone they can grieve with.

I leave them. I can't bring her back, but it's my responsibility to keep this from happening again. Who else will do anything about it? Who else can?

My rooms have been resecured, and my guard stands watch, their number supplemented by the Nosca. Cas sits at the dining table, lording over a mound of paper with a stub of mancer's charcoal, murmuring under his breath all the while. We all settle into an uneasy quiet.

Izamal pops in every so often with reports—on interviews with the kitchen staff, on Wardana sent to the high-ringer encampment, on the logs of all who were permitted into the secure floors of the tower. He also brings quiet reports of more and more people accused of being lightstruck and cast out. Without proof, of course. An alarming number of them left for the relative shelter of the city, where, if they weren't lightstruck already, they'll no doubt end up that way.

Cas takes to diagramming all the possibilities. I peer over his shoulder, listening to his rapid-fire muttering. "Who had the opportunity and who might have had the desire? With the possibility of a lightstruck being among us, anyone might have had the desire?" On the list of possible suspects, Cas has included his name, as well as Dalca's, Izamal's, and Hadria's as possible poisoners.

"Might as well include me, too," I say, half-joking.

Cas frowns. "I can't believe I missed that."

He writes my name down in neat penmanship, humming under his breath. I don't know if I can be lightstruck—when I climbed to the roof and saw those great eyes in the light, it felt like the Queen protected me. But would I know if I were lightstruck? What does it feel like?

The front door bangs open. Dalca strides in, gaze trained upward, and holds a knapsack out to the owlcat. "Hila, would you please?" he asks.

It trills, and only then does he drop the knapsack. "Food," he says. "Checked twice below as well. It's safe."

Gamara distributes flatbreads to everyone.

Dalca's presence sucks the air from the room. Or maybe it's just me—everyone else seems a little more relaxed. But I can just make out the silhouette of his oathmark medallion under his shirt.

My legs move, taking me out to the balcony. A cold breeze kisses my cheeks and wakes me up. The night is full dark, and the ikonlanterns aren't lit. So no one below can see me.

I step out to the balcony's edge. The market square is full, as usual. But there's a different sort of crowd at one corner. Two people are in the center. They grapple and break apart, gesturing like they're shouting, but I can't make out the words.

The doors open with a whisper, and the air warms as someone steps beside me.

A glance reveals dark curls. Dalca.

"Come to save me?" I ask. It comes out more teasing than I'd intended.

He looks down at the crowd. "Are you planning to jump?"

I cross my arms. Misery is making me prickly, but I can't keep quiet. "What would you do if I did? You've got no cloak."

"I'd follow." He shrugs. "I'd figure it out on the way down."

"What confidence."

His eyes flicker through emotions, but his face is still and calm.

I let out a breath, but my chest is still too full of terrible aches. Dalca's made his oathmark to a fool. He must regret it. "You sure you don't want to end your oathmark?"

He doesn't look at me. "No."

If not regret, then . . . "Is it because . . . of guilt, or something? You save my life and the past is forgotten, or something?"

Dalca tenses, just a tad. "No."

"If it were the case, you've saved me twice now. When does it even out?"

He stays silent.

All the fight goes out of me. "You don't need to keep barging through doors. You can stick around."

Dalca turns to me, his eyes searching my face.

"Unless you prefer that," I say.

His jaw works. "I didn't . . . put the oathmark on to impose on you, to force myself into your life. You don't need to make accommodations for me."

So noble. He wants to save my life from a polite distance. "I don't mind."

He starts. The veins in his hands pulse. He's so tense, as if every word from me might be an electric shock.

I drop my gaze. The horizon isn't visible this late at night—the dark sky bleeds into the endless wilds, but I know it's there. "So long as your goal is to keep me alive—sorry, to keep the Queen's vessel alive—then you're free to stick around."

"You *are* the Queen's vessel," he says, as if he didn't hear the second half of what I said.

"I thought the distinction mattered to you."

His hand flexes. "No."

Must be his new favorite word. My fingers sink into the moss coating the railing. How tense he is and how tightly he holds back whatever he might say . . . Perversely, that makes me want to talk. "I don't know what I'm going to do. What seemed like the right thing . . . I don't know. What I do know is that the Storm can't be allowed to return. So whatever your reason for making the oath . . . keep me alive as long as you can."

His eyes darken. "Yes."

I leave him there and retreat to my bedroom. Someone in this tower wants me dead, and I don't even know why. Are they one of Toran's people, out for revenge? Or one of the lightstruck?

I underestimated the light. But the Great King is every bit as powerful and cruel as the Queen. And unlike the Queen and her Storm, we don't have hundreds of years of knowledge and safeguards. We knew the signs of a stormsurge—at first sight, the stormbells would ring, giving us precious minutes to find shelter. People could live a street away from the Storm and still be safe, unless they were particularly unlucky.

And the Wardana knew how to fight it. How many years did it take to find weapons and ikons that would repel stormbeasts? How many decades to develop nets of woven ikons that'd hold back the Storm—if only for minutes at a time?

The stormbeasts—with their cloudsmoke forms and lightning eyes glowing out of the stormwall—seemed much more terrifying than a radiantly glowing web of light. But the light is sinister in a new way. The horrors of the light don't have snapping teeth or shapeshifting bodies that haunt my nightmares—the horror is invisible; it's whatever sneaks along the threads of light and slips into people's minds, stealing them in a way the Storm never did.

Even those cursed by the Storm's touch kept their essential selves. They knew what was happening. They had choice.

If a high ringer is trying to kill me, it's because they fear being lightstruck.

If it's someone who's lightstruck, they don't have a choice.

So it's the lightstruck that I need to understand.

As Vesper, there's little I can do. But as the Queen's vessel . . .

I close my eyes, feeling for the reservoir of the Great Queen's power. The distant noises of the crowd come through the window. The others murmuring in the next room. The silken rustle of my too-fine sheets.

I grab a change of clothes and cross to the bathing room. I turn on the faucets, and with a low clanging from deep below, hot water pours out. The ikonwork and machinery have never failed, and yet I marvel each time they work. What ingenuity, just to bathe. Incredible.

I sink into the water, and then deeper, into her.

The reservoir within me is more empty than full of the Queen's power, but there should be enough. It takes me a moment to get past the chaos in my mind, but I take slow, even breaths until I'm out of my body, in an ever-expanding awareness. I slip past the shadowy figures in the next room—noting only that Cas and Dalca are arguing—and float upward, out of the tower.

There's so much noise.

Shadows painted upon shadows. Buildings and structures are very faintly drawn, but every last person is rendered darkly. A picture made with the darkest ink.

The memory of the burning, sizzling sensation—when my awareness tripped upon a spectral—gives me pause. But they can't get me here—the window doesn't face the city.

I slip through the crowds as little more than a ponderous breeze.

There's nothing obvious to mark any of the crowd or the accused as being lightstruck. No halo of light, no spectral-like shimmer—nothing.

But maybe there are no lightstruck below. Everyone in the market square might be fine.

I turn to the city, and dread sinks my stomach.

Shadows form a long stream down the black road. If I focus hard, I can make out individual people within the stream. People are still making their way to the sixth, but many fifth-ringers are staying. I've heard the stories: fifth-ringers were quick to abandon their homes for the bounty of the sixth, but others, who finally found homes in the fifth after years of insecurity, are loath to give up the dear little they now possess.

I stop before the third ring. Everything is inky shadows, but for the lines of light. It's like someone has laid lines of wax down across fabric before dyeing it. The lines of light reveal nothing; they're pure negative space.

There are no colors in this grayscale vision; I can't tell if any of these lines might be a spectral. I peer through the cage of light. Everyone under it must be lightstruck, but from this distance, they look no different than anyone else.

I stalk the perimeter, circling all the way around to the far side of the third.

How can it be? That even with the Queen's power, the lightstruck appear no different from anyone else?

Lines of light sweep closer, and I back away, into the fourth, then fifth, then past the immense ringwall, into the wilds of the sixth.

I'm on the opposite side of the sixth from the Queenskeep. Where the branches of the river rejoin into one, after parting around the city.

I rise higher. The clay pot within me is nearly drained of the

Queen's power. But something catches my attention. People. Here, in this uninhabited part of the sixth? I draw closer. With them is something that—amidst all the shadows—sparkles like sunlight on a river. A spectral.

It moves toward me—but it can't see me. Can it?

I draw my awareness back, but I'm too slow—a crackle and a stinging, hissing burn—

The spectral wraps its arms around me—and I draw my awareness back like a fleeting ghost, but the spectral has its hooks in me—

I snap back into myself, jolting up out of the tub and sending water splashing over the edge. The cold sends shivers across my skin.

The room has grown dark.

I draw myself up out of the water. The hairs on my neck prickle with warning.

Out of the corner of my eye—a flash of violet—

With the last of the Queen's power, I draw a stormbarrier around myself, one that hugs my skin like armor.

"I must commend you." The violet spectral stands in a dusting of light. He smiles with Dalca's face, and it gives me vertigo. "This is nearly a perfect angle to protect yourself from the other spectrals. The others haven't yet figured out that lightstruck can be convinced to place mirrors in convenient locations."

I step out onto the stone floor. My stormbarrier protects me and conceals my skin to the neck—but without clothes, I feel vulnerable. I back toward the door. My heart thuds in my chest. The spectral is so faint—but if he's here, is there anywhere that we're safe?

He takes a step forward—moving like a beam of light—and I throw up a hand.

"Forgive me," he says. "I didn't mean to alarm you. And you're well protected—bouncing off the mirrors is a fair bit trickier than I made it seem—each surface absorbs a certain amount of light—" He falls silent. "Vesper. I mean you no harm. Didn't I help you, in the third?"

My voice comes out a whisper. "What do you want?"

The door shakes under my hand as someone barrels into it. "Vesper!" Dalca—flesh-and-blood Dalca—bellows from the other side. "Are you okay?"

The spectral waits, hands behind his back. "If you want me to go, I will."

He bangs on the door. Dalca's voice is sharp, terrified, even through the wood. "Vesper. Open the door."

I study the spectral, my mind spinning through dozens of thoughts in a heartbeat. If he could come all the way to this tower, what's another few feet to him? He could've attacked me already, if that was his intent. And . . . he must know about the Great King. About the towers with the empty slots. If he knows about the vessel . . . if I can get him to confirm that a vessel exists—or even what it is—it's worth a try.

"I'm naked, Dalca," I say to the door. "I just stubbed a toe."

The banging stops. The spectral stills when he hears the word *naked* and, in what appears to be politeness, carefully looks up at the ceiling. I check to make sure the stormbarrier armor is in place. It hugs my body, and though I have to keep it thin so it doesn't use too much power, it's a complete shell. There are no gaps. I can sustain it for a few minutes before the reservoir of the Queen's power runs dry.

Silence comes from the other side of the door.

"Dalca, you can tell, can't you?" I don't take my eyes off the spectral. "Am I still in danger?"

There's a long silence from the door, and then comes the muffled sound of a slow exhale. "No . . . It faded . . ."

"Then just give me a minute, all right?"

A pause, and then a faint "I'm sorry." A rustling sound, as if he's moving away.

"Dalca?" I call. "If anything changes, you have my permission to barge in, all right?"

A low, embarrassed laugh. "All right."

The spectral keeps his gaze on the ceiling. "He's obedient."

"Well?" I say to the spectral.

Though my stormbarrier is intact, the spectral keeps his gaze trained modestly away. "I came to apologize. I wronged you. When we were there, in the arena . . . the eyes of thousands upon us . . . I should not have laid my sword at your throat, should not have made you fight. Deep inside I knew it to be so, but I wanted the whole world to burn with me. Everyone left me. My mother, my father, my grandfather. All I knew was the weight of what I must be—and the fear of becoming it. I say this not to have you forgive me, but to tell you . . . I'm thankful that you showed me mercy. And I will never become again the man that hurt you."

A strange wind buffets my insides. "You're a spectral. You're not Dalca."

He sighs and looks down at his translucent hands, examining them.

"It took me a while to come to terms with what I am. When you saved us, when I held back the Great King for that brief moment, to give you a chance . . . I still don't understand how it happened. But that was when I last had a true body. And now . . ."

"And now you serve the Great King."

"I was born from the Great King. That does not mean I must serve only him."

The specks of light that constitute his body flutter in a dance, in a

pattern only he understands. His purpose is just as incomprehensible. I take a step closer. "Are you serving him now, in coming here? To what purpose?"

His gaze meets mine, and in his expression is a dark and molten intensity. "Vesper. You must know what I feel for—that you—" He stops and swallows his words. With an exhale, he tries again. "The Regia Dalcanin—that is, you wouldn't know him, but he's the one of red light—he was hasty in expelling you from the third ring. The Queen brings out the worst in him—even the mention of her sends him into a rage. But I've been speaking to the others. What the Great King is doing . . . If you saw, you would know that he is bringing peace."

I keep my voice neutral, though I feel a flicker as the Queen's power runs thin. I hold on to it with all my will. "Peace? By controlling the minds of all he touches?"

"That's not what he does." He tilts his head. "Is that what you fear?"

I have to find out more. "What does he do?"

"He lets them put down their burdens. For some, yes, their greatest burden was that of choice. Can you truly say that all your choices were good? That they caused no harm?"

Mina's face flashes before my eyes.

He holds my gaze and, in a flicker of light, draws closer. "The Storm was never our only problem. You showed me that. The city you saved was a broken one. Divided, cruel to the weak, poisonous to the powerful. Even here in the sixth, that legacy remains. People divide themselves meaninglessly, based on where they once lived. We need progress, Vesper. Not a return to the old ways."

My pulse quickens. "That's how people are."

"They can be made to be more."

"What does the King want? The towers—what is his goal?" My stormbarrier armor is unraveling, starting at my ankles and wrists. I tuck my hands behind me, but he sees.

"You're coming undone." He gives me a gallant little bow and disappears in a dusting of violet light.

My stormbarrier dissipates, and with it goes the last of the energy holding me standing. My bare knees hit the cold stone floor, but the chill barely registers.

I know where we'll find our answers.

CHAPTER 17

I get dressed so quickly I find myself trying to shove a foot into the arm of my shirt. I get sorted and burst out into the main room.

"I just met a spectral," I say.

Dalca drops what he's holding, and Cas stands with a screech of his chair. My guards fly into action, surrounding me—and with a jolt, I find Hadria among them. Her brows furrow, and she waits for me to continue.

"They can jump on reflections," I say. "So just facing away from the city won't work anymore. We'll want to do something about that. Brick it all up."

Hadria glances at the other guards and crosses past me, into the bedroom and connected bathing room.

Cas nears. "What—why—what did it want?"

I shake my head. "It was strange. It wanted to talk, mostly. It looked like you, Dalca."

Dalca comes sharply alive, his eyes blazing. "Like me?"

"It came . . . It was my fault. I was testing out the Great Queen's powers—I wanted to see if I could tell who was lightstruck . . . It doesn't matter. On the far side of the sixth, I saw a spectral. Got too close. He saw me, followed me."

Dalca starts. "When you say 'he'—"

"In the sixth? Where in the sixth?" Cas shuffles the papers on the desk, throwing some aside as he looks for something.

Hadria returns. Gamara and the twins draw the curtains, as Ozra lights the ikonlanterns.

"Not near here," I say. And then with a glance at Hadria, "Nor the high ringers' encampment."

Dalca shakes his head. "And he looked like . . . me?"

"Violet light," I say. "You as you were three years ago, in the stadium. When you were . . ." I can't say *about to murder me*, especially not with the spectral's apology ringing in my ears. "When you were in your princely outfit. You know the one, the white feather cloak, white-and-gold uniform."

Dalca stills. "Did he hurt you?"

"What? No." I rub the back of my neck. "He wanted to . . . tell me about the Great King."

Cas hoots. "Found it." He waves a rolled-up scroll and flattens it out on the table. "Can you point out where it was?"

I study the map, tracing my route. "There."

Cas marks it with a bit of waxed mancer's charcoal he pulls from his pocket. "Why there?"

"Why?" Dalca echoes, half to himself. "The spires disrupt the line of vision for the spectrals—they can't travel easily in the sixth. And there are no settlements there. No people. If it's not to lure more people back to the city . . ." Dalca sucks in a breath. "That's the old quarry. But those mines were depleted long ago. What can be there?"

"I don't know," I say. "He had people with him."

"Spectrals and lightstruck near the old mine," Dalca muses. "I don't like it. I don't understand it."

"How far is it?" I ask. What if the violet spectral came to distract me from what they were doing?

"A half-night's ride. Less if we take sprinters." Dalca rubs his jaw.

I stifle the urge to dive headlong into a sprinter—whatever that is—and leave right away. "What do we need to do it properly? To see what they're up to—and to defend ourselves if something happens?"

"We need Iz," Dalca says. "No one knows the wilds better."

Cas raises his eyebrows. "You think Imbas'll spare him for a night? With how they're now churning out landtreaders?"

I wince at that. But since the third fell, more and more people are leaving the inner rings for the sixth. Imbas and the council have focused all their energies into the landtreader project.

"We'll convince him," I say. "And, Cas—we'll need mirrorcloaks and whatever else you've been working on."

He glances at Dalca, who nods. Good. Something eases in me now that they're both on board.

"It's important we understand the spectrals," I say. "So let's get what we need." I turn to Hadria. I should offer her a way out. "Hadria—"

"Understood," she says. "We'll be ready by nightfall."

Quiet falls, one threaded with anticipation. In each of their eyes is reflected what I feel: a flicker of hope. That we're on the precipice of understanding something, that there is more to do before we're truly beaten. And that we're each of us committing to doing this together.

Cas gives me a grim smile. This won't be like going up to the third.

We're chased into the wilds by a gentle wind. It bears droplets of soft, sweet rain, like kisses. They fall on my cheeks, on my outstretched palm, on the thousands of black branches that twiningly make the canopy above. Some branches bear leaves of unusual colors: gold interlaces with blue-black interlaces with burgundy.

A raindrop falls on my lip, and I lick it away. It tastes vaguely of things that were once green. There's nothing of the burnt-sugar and copper of the Storm. This is just rain.

I grip the sides of the sprinter as we make a turn. Sprinters turn out to be two-wheeled contraptions designed for the Nosca—open-aired chariots, designed for riders not to sit but to stand. Each has space for two—one to guide the long-legged, antlered stormbeast that pulls us and one to fight off whatever beasts may attack.

And if I thought the ramblers were fast, they're nothing compared to this. The sprinters are designed for speed and only speed—my teeth rattle in my head every time the wheels lurch over a tree root or a rotted branch, and my hands tingle with numbness from how hard I've been gripping the handholds.

Hadria and Gamara are in a sprinter to my right. Dalca drives ours—in what he calls a compromise and I call motivation to learn how to drive. Ozra drives another, with Cas at her side, armed with ikon explosives and a long bow.

Izamal rides an immense stormbeast that's possibly the most uniquely hideous cat I've ever seen. It has a gray, leathery hide and a curved horn right in the middle of its face. And though it's stouter than any cat I've known, it's surprisingly nimble—so much so that it often outpaces the sprinters.

I hadn't expected Izamal to come—I'd expected him to make a fuss about us all focusing on the landtreaders instead—but he took a long look at me and Hadria, and showed up as we were leaving.

The path between the trees widens enough that the sprinter takes on a steadier pace. I relax my hold. We pass orchards where the trees have turned to stone. But their seeds fell to the soil, where they lay dormant and were changed by the cursed power of the Storm, until at last they met sunlight and could sprout. Now those young trees climb over their dead ancestors, winding through them and reaching over their fossils, to the sky.

If I close my eyes and reach out with the Queen's power, I can sense the stormbeasts pulling our sprinter: the glorious thrill of running, vague curiosity about a sweet scent, the faint memory of hunger.

I tilt my head back and catch soft raindrops on my cheeks. Being out of the tower, surrounded by the strange sights and smells, the strange sounds of beasts within the wilds, of the trees creaking, of distant spires snapping and falling—it makes me feel like I really have come back to life. In the shadow of the immense trees, it almost feels like we're just exploring, that there's no Great King.

If there was no Great King, what would you want?

Maybe this. To explore. To chase the horizon—

A sharp spike of fear comes from our stormbeasts. I open my eyes.

We're in a petrified forest of dark trees, each with a gaping split in the trunk that oozes amber resin.

The wilds fall silent.

"The beasts are afraid," I murmur into Dalca's ear. "Something's here."

Three sharp whistles come from up ahead, in the direction I last saw Izamal.

Dalca gathers the reins in one hand, and with the other he pulls his bow from across his back. He whistles the same three notes to alert the others.

"What is it?" I ask.

"A beast," Dalca says. "I need you to drive." He passes the reins to me. They nearly slip through my hands, but I tighten my grip and wrap the leather cords around my wrists.

Dalca strings an arrow. His eyes narrow as he scans the tree line.

Our steeds are close to panic. I send a sense of calm down our connection, and they quiet.

A crack splits the air. Something big thrashes through branches—on our right—

A stormbeast bursts forth. A centipede, each segment of its body as large as a sprinter, with scuttling feet that gouge the ground, the trunks of petrified trees, the branches above us. It turns—and in the light of the sprinter's ikonlantern, I make out not an insect's face, but a cruel beak under large hawk's eyes.

Dalca looses an arrow. It hits the beast in a joint, and in a show of ikonomancy, the arrowhead releases a flurry of sparkles that dazzle the beast. Other arrows whistle through the air, but the beast shakes them all off.

I reach for it with the Queen's power. A sense comes. It's an old beast. One that was a master of its domain within the Storm.

All its segments expand and retract, and the beast begins a strange sideways motion, rolling its head back and forth.

Its beak opens—and Dalca pulls at the reins, sending us in a wide arc and out of the blast range of the centipede-hawk, as it spews forth a fountain of pale yellow liquid. Wherever it falls, the earth sizzles and steams.

A horrible yowling roar comes from behind.

Izamal's horned cat darts past us and tackles the centipede-hawk.

Dalca and the others loose another volley of ikon-enhanced arrows. They set off a series of explosions along the length of the centipede-beast's body.

The stormbeast's pain echoes through my head. The reins fly from my hands, and I reach, catching them with the tips of my fingers. Dalca's tossed against me, and I grip the leather belt at his waist to keep him from flying off.

Izamal leaps from his horned cat onto the centipede, a sword clutched in his hands. He swings, but before his hit lands, the centipede thrashes, throwing him into the air.

He spins, letting out a whistle, and the horned cat pounces, catching Iz as gently as if he were a kitten.

The centipede coils. It begins its dance again.

But the Queen's mark is dark upon my skin, and I taste the beast's fear. I pull on the reins, until the sprinter slows to a stop.

"Vesper!" Dalca shouts.

I hop down onto soft ground. "Let me talk to it," I say.

I close my eyes and reach out with her power. *Creature of the Storm. We mean you no harm. We must cross through your territory, and we seek safe passage.*

It speaks, not in words, but in fleeting images and feeling.

I sort through the strange images. "We've treaded close to its nesting grounds," I say to the others. "Don't move."

We mean you no harm. Let us pass.

Another crush of images and feeling. And, in a voice that speaks of thousands of skittering creatures, it calls me *Mother.*

I send it calm and quiet, and urge it to return to its children.

It lowers its great hawk head and, with a dismissive glance at the others, retreats into the dark of the wilds.

Izamal's horned cat-beast pads up to me. It bares its teeth at me, a grin matched by Izamal, saddled up on its back. "Neatly done. If you ever want to join the Nosca, let me know. Gets the blood flowing, doesn't it?"

My hands shake—the calm of action is wearing off. "How big do these stormbeasts get?"

Iz laughs. "Don't tell me you're scared."

Dalca pulls the sprinter up beside me and gives me a blank look until I hop on beside him.

Iz shoots him an amused glance. "That's a large one. We've seen some larger, but they're rare."

How many more stormbeasts are out there? To know them all . . .

"Ready?" Dalca asks. I nod, and the sprinter rolls on, gaining speed until we're dashing through the trees.

My heart thuds in my chest. It doesn't slow, even as the wilds change. The trees give way to immense spires jutting out of rolling sands. Cas's map called this *the Needles*. Glimmering spires stud the black earth, like so many needles in a pincushion. Some are tall like towers, some are crooked, some are curved like arches—and all are the children of lightning.

At the edge of a sand dune, Dalca calls the sprinters to a stop. The drivers activate ikons that turn the wheels into flat wedges that'll skim across the dunes. I crouch and watch the ikons work. It's the same principle as the Wardana's gauntlets—the mass of the wheels is preserved, just transformed into a new shape.

Dalca's gaze lands on me. He opens his mouth, and my neck heats at the thought that he'll praise me. "The spectrals . . . Their forms . . ."

Oh. "Toran thought they were all past Regias."

"Well," Cas says from a few feet away. "Technically they'd be facsimiles of past Regias. They're not ghosts. They can't be, as Dalca is alive."

"But I was never Regia," Dalca says.

Cas taps his chin. "So why do they take the forms they take?"

"And why is it that one looks like Dalca?" I ask. "He acts a little like you, too." But the spectral apologized, and Dalca never did.

"He's not me," Dalca says gruffly.

"I'm not sure he knows that," I say.

"You're talking like he's a person. He's not," Dalca says. "He's a trick of the light."

"Maybe. But one that might be useful."

From his sprinter, Cas interjects. "We should have names for them. There are a few now."

"The red spectral," Hadria says.

"Call him Red. Or the Regia Dalcanin," I say. "If you're feeling formal."

"And there's the purplish one."

"The Dalca spectral," Iz says.

"Don't call it that," Dalca says.

"What?"

"Not my name." He glances over his shoulder at me.

"What, then?" I ask.

"Violet. Vi for short," Izamal offers, a teasing glint in his eye. "Or Sparkle."

"It's not a pet," Dalca growls. "Don't underestimate it."

Iz nods soberly. "What do you think, Hads?"

She glances at Dalca. "Dazzle," she says.

Izamal laughs. "Dalca and Dazzle—"

He cuts off as Dalca raises a fist, his gaze fixed in the distance.

A dim bluish glow rises through the dark, from beyond a rise. We all get back into the sprinters and make our way as quietly as possible.

We've passed all sorts of spires on our way here. Knobbly ones, like fingers of an ancient hand. Smooth-edged ones, like wax drips. But the ones here are sharp-edged and geometric.

"What are these?" I whisper.

Some are rectangular columns, smooth and pale as salt. Others grow squat, shoulder-height mounds of blue spikes. Most are somewhat translucent, but there are a few of solid black and others that gleam like metal ore.

"The old mine," Dalca murmurs. "The earth must have different elements here. When the Storm's lightning struck the earth here, it made crystals."

The glow comes from behind a dune. We leave the sprinters and creep forward.

A mine like an open pit, with great steps leading down. A spectral, glowing a telltale violet.

"That's Dazzle?" Iz whispers.

The spectral turns to give orders, and we can all take in his features for ourselves. I'm aware of Dalca beside me, the sharp intake of his breath, his hands curling into fists, the breeze ruffling through his hair and pushing his curls out of his too-bright eyes.

I follow the spectral's violet lightline back toward the city. The lightstruck have cleared a path for it. They demolished spires and trees until the spectral had a clear line of sight.

The spectral touches one spire, and the crystal begins to glow the same violet as the spectral. It touches another and another, until a section of the mine is aglow. Like stars, like a constellation.

The spectral stops and tilts his head up to the night sky. My breath catches. What a portrait of longing.

The memory of his voice comes to me. *Can you truly say that all your choices were good?*

As he moves on, the glow within the spires lingers, fading slowly. Some spires only achieve a dim glow and fade quickly; these he ignores. Others glow brilliantly—these he directs a handful of lightstruck people to harvest. They bear a cart half-filled with crystals. The cart propels itself on the violet lightline, back toward the city.

The violet spectral stops before one immense crystal as if startled. He makes a slow circle around it, his phantom hand hovering above the surface, as it drinks up his light.

"This one," he calls, in his voice that's so much like Dalca's, but haunted by the ghost of a crackling fire.

Dalca startles and the sand shifts under him, rippling out in a wave across the dune.

The spectral stills, turning toward us.

A hand touches my shoulder. Hadria. She motions me back from the edge.

"Vesper?" the spectral calls.

Curses. I glance at the others.

Izamal gestures, and the others move.

The lightline shifts toward us.

I scramble to my feet as a violet glow shines on my skin.

"You came to visit," the spectral says. "And you brought me a whole party."

His voice is light, but his eyes dart around us, measuring our ability.

I measure him, too. There's something strange. The violet line of light stretches from him to the palace, but there's a second, far fainter line that goes to the immense crystal behind him.

"Now!" Izamal barks.

Two Nosca shoot arrows that hit two pillars. A fabric that shines like a mirror unfurls, cutting the spectral's lightline off. The same tactic Toran's high ringers used against the red spectral, to force him back to the city.

But the violet spectral only lurches, grimacing in pain. Somehow, the immense crystal is keeping him here. The dim violet light coming from within it is acting like a tether.

I touch my mirrorcloak. I have an idea.

The spectral sees the line of my gaze. "Don't, Vesper. Please."

"Hadria," I call. "Shield me."

She curses as I vault over the dune, but rushes to protect me. I run, swinging the mirrorcloak off my shoulders and turning the mirror-side inward.

A clang of metal on metal—Hadria intercepts a lightstruck.

I throw the mirrorcloak over the crystal, cutting off the violet light. The spectral vanishes.

"What are you doing?" Dalca hisses. For a moment I think he's the spectral—until I see blue eyes and black hair, a scowl fixed on me. He shoves a lightstruck with his shield. She falls—she's not wearing anything that would indicate she's a warrior—and scrambles to her feet, running back in the direction of the city. Other lightstruck join her.

"Cas!" I shout. The violet light from the crystal probes the edges of the cloak, seeking gaps from which to escape.

The spectral's voice comes from the light, a mere whisper. "Vesper, please."

Cas makes his way to me, fending off lightstruck and darting across the crystal-strewn landscape. He sees what I'm doing, and helps pull the cloak shut around the crystal. "Cas," I say, "can you—an ikon, I don't know—melt this around the crystal? To trap the spectral?"

He springs into action without giving me an answer, producing a length of mancer's charcoal and scrawling an ikon on the cloak. The mirrorcloak melts around the crystal, like molten mercury, sealing off all light. All movement stops from within.

In the silence, I find my voice. "Did it work?"

A cool voice answers, "I think not." The spectral appears in a dim beam of light. I follow the violet lightline back toward the city—as they retreated, the lightstruck tore down the fabric shield the Nosca put up, letting the spectral return.

The lightline intensifies, searing a hole into the mirrorcloak. The spectral brightens as the tendril of his power that was in the crystal is returned to him.

Dalca steps in front of me, standing face-to-face with the spectral. "What are you?"

The spectral looks down at him, a little larger than life. It's a peculiar mirror. The Dalca of now—humbled, more thoughtful, slower to anger—and the spectral, an image of Dalca at his strongest, at his noblest, in a ghostly version of the immaculate white-and-gold garb of a Regia's son. The spectral lowers his head, his cheek almost touching Dalca's. "I am you. The best you. The you who was chosen by the Great King."

The spectral moves—a flicker of light, there beside Dalca one second and beside me the next—and he leans close to me. "Vesper. I'm not your enemy."

He leans in closer. And in the inch between his lips and mine, in the second it would've taken to close the gap—

The spectral disappears.

CHAPTER 18

Our return home is a vague blur of spires and dark sand. Dalca and Izamal—with the aid of the collective muscle of the Nosca-Wardana—balance the crystal on a sprinter and haul it back to the tower, up the riser, and into an empty room that Cas—with barked orders at several Wardana—quickly turns into an ikonomancer's workshop.

The neighboring rooms are cleared out—a *defensible perimeter* in case anything were to go wrong—and Cas sets to work.

For a good hour, I watch him as he pokes and prods the crystal, prying the melted mirror from it in small sheets, humming a song under his breath.

I cough.

He screams. Wide-eyed and pink-cheeked, he stares at me. "Have you been here this whole time?"

"Er, yes."

"Go away," he says. "I can't work with you staring at me."

I refrain from pointing out that he did just fine for the last hour. "Will—"

"Yes, when I have something to share, I'll let you know. And no, you can't help me—unless you picked up a specialization in materials ikonwork whilst you were slumbering these past years. No? I rather thought not. Goodbye."

He ushers me out and shuts the door behind me.

"Goodbye," I say to the wood.

Hadria waits in the hall. Has she been there all this time? "I think we'd better get some sleep," I say.

She nods, quick and darting. She's as taut as a bowstring.

Unease twists my stomach. "How are the others?"

"Recovered. Waiting to be cleared by the healers," she says.

It's good news, but— "They're well so soon?"

"The healers think it affected Mina differently. She never could eat certain fruits—they never sat right with her—and maybe that's why." Hadria's voice is quiet, but she's nearly vibrating. She draws a breath and lets it out.

When she doesn't speak, I ask, "Is there something else?"

"Cardel Maver. You called her Carver. She—she's missing."

I stop dead.

Hadria continues. "All signs say . . . she left of her own accord. We got a report of a girl leaving the courtyard at dawn. Doesn't match Carver's description . . . but that was Carver's specialty."

"You're telling me Carver was lightstruck? The poisoner?"

"Yes." She raises a shoulder. "Officially, it has not been proven. Not yet."

My head spins. Carver was the poisoner . . . but, if what Hadria says is true, that Mina was an accident and the others are recovered, then she didn't mean to kill anyone. But then why?

I realize I've said the last out loud when Hadria responds, her gaze fixed far in the distance. "To frighten you. To have you doubt your allies. To isolate you, until you feel too small and too alone to fight back."

I mull that over as we walk. "What happened to your mother . . .
I'm not making the same mistake again, Hadria. Let them know that I
won't order my guard to join me. But if they wish to be at my side when
we face the King . . . I'll welcome them."

Days pass—days where a blanket of unease settles over the watchtower.
The market square grows busier and stays busy—those fleeing the city
gather and stay put, sleeping out in the open until Imbas's people tell
them where to go.

In the distance, several new landtreaders rise up. Their wooden
frames are hammered into place and covered by metal scales.

The second day, my guards appear, as if nothing had happened.
They make an effort to be cheerful, as though by will alone we can move
past Mina and Carver. Neither are mentioned—not even obliquely, not
even in passing—but neither is there talk of finding replacements.

I watch them from my place on the low divan, flipping the pages
of a book of ikonomancy without really reading. I've gotten to know
them a little better.

"This view's a bit tiring, anyhow," Gamara says, leaning against the
doors to the balcony. I've learned her dimples appear even when she
pouts and she doesn't mean half the things she says.

"You must be more grateful, Gamara." Ozra crosses her legs at the
ankles, not a hair out of place. Izamal probably picked her for her close
resemblance—but even if we had the exact same face, it'd be impossible
to mix us up. Not with her graceful posture and absolute inability to
understand when someone's joking.

I rub at my temples, trying to surreptitiously loosen my too-tight braids—Ozra did it for me, taking over for Carver. She took an hour to brush the ridiculous length of my hair, and tied it up in a pair of warrior's braids, even braiding the shorter hairs that fall around my face, and pinned them up.

Jhuno and Zerin have set up at the dining table, working on a new pair of gauntlets. Every so often, something lets off sparks and they burst into laughter.

Hadria sits across from me, spear drawn, silent and watchful. She meets my eyes.

The tension I feel is mirrored in her. Something's missing; something's coming.

The tension follows me as the sun rises and I head to the bedroom. It's with me during the long hours of daylight, in my room with the curtains drawn, and it follows me into my sleep.

I dream of my mother. She appears with her back to me, but I know it's her. Because Ma eluded me in the world of the dead, because she was gone long before I ever showed up, there's no chance I'll ever see her again, no chance she'll turn to me and say she's proud.

She walks away from me, and in this dream I have no feet and no voice, nothing with which to chase her, nothing with which to call her back to me.

The dream ends, and another begins.

A pair of arms hold me safe. A voice—warm, smooth, and honeyed—tells me I'm all right, that I don't need to fight.

His words land like a balm, soothing a part of me I didn't know was wounded. It would be nice if they were true.

The arms release me, and I realize I've pushed them away. I tilt my head up, and meet Dalca's eyes. "You can't keep me safe," I tell him.

His face is troubled, but he smiles. "Let me try."

"I don't think I should."

"Why not?"

"I'm not who you think I am. I'm not a hero. I was in the right place at the right time, that's all."

"You're a hero to me."

"You don't understand," I say, and he doesn't. No one understands. I lean in close. "I don't want to be a hero."

"Oh, Vesper," Dalca says, and I've been looking at him all wrong—I can see the garden through his skin—his eyes are a soft violet, not blue—his body dissolves into a thousand dancing sparks. The spectral whispers as he would to a lover, "You don't have a choice."

I jerk back—

My head hits my pillow. I gasp, blinking the dream away, willing the warmth in my cheeks to disappear. I tear myself from the sheets, barreling through my bedroom and into the washroom, splashing water on my face and getting dressed.

It's not Dalca that bothers me—it's me. It's what I said.

It's so . . . selfish. I don't want to be her. A girl who'd prioritize what she wants. I have to dream of greater things. Of the people I can keep safe. Of the power I wield and what I must do to wield it well.

Jhuno and Zerin follow me as I make my way down the tower, to the room that Cas is holed up in. They stay outside, nodding at the Wardana stationed there as I enter.

"Let me help," I say as the door shuts behind me.

Cas raises his head, his hair flat on one side as if he slept on his desk. "Fine."

Over the next few hours, I slowly charm my way up from sharpening his wax pencils to making notes of the tests he runs on the fragments of crystal.

At the end of the third hour, he exhales, stretching his arms over his head, a dozen little pops coming from his back. "It'll take me a little longer to be absolutely *certain* of how the King uses the crystal for his vessel," he says, "but I think I understand."

"Really?"

"It's not so different from—here, hand me that ikonlantern."

I do. It's a globe of opaque greenish glass with a mechanism inside. Cas gets rid of the glass, and has me take a closer look at the mechanism.

It looks roughly spherical, with hundreds of facets. Light shines from within, through the gaps where each triangular face doesn't quite meet its neighbor. Cas turns the knob on the top of the lantern, and the gaps widen as the facets tilt, until the sphere now looks more like a hundred-pointed star.

"This particular mechanism controls only the amount of light let out. But inside, there's another apparatus . . ."

Cas turns off the light and dismantles the star, showing that its inner surfaces are mirrored. There's a small ignition mechanism inside. "When the lantern's dial is turned, a flint is struck. The spark is channeled through this."

He holds up a glass rod, smaller than one joint of my littlest finger. "This captures and intensifies the light, spreading it over a wider surface. The purity of the crystal matters—that's likely what the spectral was testing for. I think the crystals the spectral was harvesting are similar to this, but on a larger scale—things that can capture and intensify a great amount of light."

"How do we force him out of the crystal?"

"We change its internal structure so it can no longer hold the light."

I nod, brows furrowed. "That's a complex ikon—to change the

angles of the inflections inside—"

Cas sighs. He puts a crystal shard down before me.

I watch carefully, waiting to see what ikon he'll draw, and where.

He smacks it with a hammer. It shatters into dust. "Very complex," he says smugly.

I roll my eyes. He knows as well as I do that it's more complicated than that. "It has to work the first time. Once the King understands what we're doing, he won't give us a second chance."

He looks briefly put out. "Yes, problem is, if we just break it into a few larger pieces, it may still function as a vessel for the King. That's what I need to figure out. If I had a few mancers to run tests . . ."

"I can help."

"Really? You've managed to master materials ikonwork in the last two days?" Cas raises an eyebrow. "No? What a shame."

I glower, which seems to cheer him up.

I sigh. "I'll find you your ikonomancers," I call over my shoulder as I leave.

"They'll be working on the landtreaders, I imagine. Poach them for me, please."

When I open the door, Jhuno and Zerin have been replaced by Hadria and Gamara. I gesture in the vague direction of the riser. "I'm off to the landtreaders."

They share a glance—Hadria stops to murmur something to an unfamiliar Wardana standing guard—and walk with me. A booming voice echoes through the hall—I catch the words *landtreaders* and *whoever has secured a spot*—and we turn the corner and find the source. Rosander Tarr, who stills as if he's been petrified by my gaze.

"Stormender," he says with a bow. There's a shadow in his eyes and his cheeks have lost their ruddiness.

"I'm looking for ikonomancers," I say. "Ones who specialize in materials work."

He's shaking his head before I've finished. "We can't spare anyone. Not so close to when we must leave."

"Leave?"

He gets a shifty look about him, glancing around and taking a step back. "Yes, well. With lightstruck attacking the food stores, we can't delay."

"When was this?"

"I'm terribly sorry," Rosander says, backing away. "I'm late—I'm going with the first group, tonight, see. Have some last bits of packing to do."

Tonight? He's off, walking so fast he's nearly jogging.

"And here I thought they all loved you," Gamara says. "What a peculiar, odious man."

The rest of my guard joins me at the riser and we ride it down to the courtyard. We've taken only a few steps when Izamal rides up on his gray-skinned, horned cat-beast.

He hops down. "Thank the stars—I need to talk to you—"

"I'm looking for ikonomancers—"

"Never mind that," Iz says, dragging me into the stables, his horned beast thumping after us. I nod at my guard, who spread out.

Iz keeps his voice low. "They've held a council meeting. I was delayed—the others'll be back any moment, if they're not already—"

I blink at him. "Council meeting? What council meeting?"

"That's not important—"

"Without me or Cas or Dalca?"

"Yes." He puts his hands on my shoulders. "Listen. Rosander has the others convinced that it's dangerous to have you walking around free. That if the landtreaders move out . . . and you're killed—truly killed, with no heartbeat and no way back, not like last time—then the Storm returns. And everyone will be caught in it."

"That's absurd—"

"Is it possible?" Izamal says, and the seriousness in his eyes chills me.

I look away. I don't know. If my heart stops . . . if I'm truly dead, I wouldn't be a vessel. "Perhaps," I say. "But why not ask me? Why hold a meeting behind my back?"

Iz bites his lip. "They're worried, Vesp. You contain more power in your little finger than they've ever known. And that makes them worry about . . . Well, it's ridiculous, but they're worried that even if you don't die, you could curse everyone who disagrees with you. Curse everyone, period."

"I—I'd never do that. I'd never curse anyone. I *undid* Cas's curse—"

"I know. I told them—even Imbas told them that would be unlike you, but . . ."

They don't trust me. I pinch the skin of my wrist, let the sharp pain ground me. "So what now?"

"Some want to put you—well, it boils down to locking you up. That's why I'm here. You need to take a rambler—take Dalca and Cas and whoever—and hide out for a while. I'll talk some sense into them."

"I can't just wait around, Iz. I can't just hide. You know what Cas is working on? We're close to something—we have a chance at facing the King—"

"Do you really?" Izamal snaps. "Can you truly believe—*for Storm's sake*—"

I fall silent.

He paces, running his hands through his hair. "Going out into the wilds, facing the spectral—that showed me something. You're brave, Vesper, and your quick thinking worked this time. But you have this *thing* propelling you headlong into danger. It's like you're being chased by something inside you. And I know that feeling." He raises a palm, opening his hand. His neatly trimmed nails turn to dark, pointed claws and back again. "I had to deal with mine, and yours . . . You'll have to deal with yours. But until then . . . I can't trust the fate of everyone here . . . to that. To you."

My throat runs dry and my eyes sting. I look over his shoulder. "So you won't join us. You won't fight the Great King."

He's silent for a long moment. "If you decide to go and put your life in danger—if that's what you're telling me—then maybe Rosander has a point."

I snap my mouth shut.

"Vesper . . ."

My blood boils. "You're just running away. What makes you think that there's something better out there?"

Izamal leans in. "What makes you think returning to the past is the only way? Why should the past be the same as the future? Can't we imagine a way of living that's better than what our parents lived?"

My words stick in my throat. My parents, both lost. The hatred Izamal had for his father, the hatred that poisoned him in the Storm. Dalca's mother. The memory of her emaciated body, ravaged by holding the Great King. The memory of her leaping to her death, rather than facing another day under the King's control.

Izamal continues, voice soft, as if he knows he's scored a point. "This city is home, sure. But it was built on pain. On suffering. On someone always suffering the most. That comes with a cost, and we all pay the price of looking away, of agreeing to it. It's a sickness."

"You mean the fifth-ringers then, and the high ringers now?"

"I mean you. The Regia. Don't think I don't see, that I don't empathize. Your burden is more than any one person should bear. And I hate it. I hate that people accept it. That they want to use you while never wanting to be you. I hate that it seems we only know how good we have it if we know someone has it worse."

Shame heats my cheeks. I haven't done a good enough job if this is what he thinks. "Iz . . ."

He sighs, all the fight leaving him. He whistles, and his horned cat-beast nuzzles at his hair. "I'll talk to the council and calm them down. They know they're wrong—they've got enough good in them to hear sense—but I need a moment, and I need you safe."

I can't find my voice. I nod.

Izamal scratches his beast's cheeks. "And, Vesper . . . you have a life here. One that you want. You could join the Nosca. What you did with that stormbeast . . . Out there are beasts you've never imagined, strange and marvelous places, good fights to be had. We have to leave this place behind, but the whole rest of the world is ours."

My vision blurs, but I force my mouth into a smile. "I understand."

He wraps me in a hug. "I'm on your side, Vesp. Always."

I give a gentle push until he lets go. He mounts his beast, glancing over his shoulder just once.

Hadria steps up beside me. "To the landtreaders?"

"No. I need Cas and Dalca . . . And a place where we won't be found. And tell them—we leave tonight."

The house that Hadria found has a view of the market square like none I've seen before. The statue of the Stormender is immense—and even though we're on the second floor, I'm only eye level with her stomach. People gather around her base, no doubt waiting to hear if there's room on a landtreader for them. Mother Yul's people—priestesses in brown garb—walk among them with bags of food.

I let the sheer curtain fall. This house must have been a comfortable one—a rug on the floor, a table and chairs that must've been newly built, seeing as they're made of the black gnarled wood of the storm-touched wilds. They'd even taken care of the moss on the outside of the house, trimmed it neatly into three diamond-shaped patches.

A fairly well-to-do family must have lived here—well-to-do enough to get a spot on the landtreaders.

Movement below catches my eye. Folks in dark cloaks make their meandering way to our front door. I move toward the stairs.

Hadria shakes her head. "Let Gamara check. If all is well, they can come here."

"Careful with that!" Cas's voice comes from below.

I peer down the railing. Dalca meets my eyes, two heavy bags on his shoulders. Cas climbs the stairs after him.

I look away first. Dalca's face reminds me of my dream.

We settle down at the table—Hadria refuses to sit—but Dalca and I take our seats as Cas reaches into his bag. I force myself to ignore Izamal's absence.

Cas presents a crystal shard. "This particular crystal was formed from the unique combination of minerals in that part of the wilds, no doubt due to the presence of the old step mine. Its composition means that it is uniquely suited to hold an immense amount of light and power. Its capabilities—as far as I've been able to test—match what we know of the lightlines."

I reach for the Queen's power within me, just to feel her presence. "This is why the Great King is so strong," I say. "He's using this crystal to capture and amplify his power."

Cas nods.

Dalca steeples his fingers. "So, somewhere up in the city, there is a crystal like this. And that's the Great King's vessel."

"They're also in each tower," I say, remembering the tower in the third. The empty divot was for a crystal. "They use them to redirect the lightlines over each ring."

"How do we know where his vessel is?" Hadria asks. "It could be any one of the towers."

"No, I don't think so," I say. "The towers just redirect the light. We'll find the vessel if we follow the lightlines to their source."

"To the palace." Dalca leans back. His oathmark medallion is briefly outlined as his shirt draws taut over it.

"That's a long way," Hadria says. "Through lightstruck territory."

Dalca leans forward. "And say we get there. What then? We destroy the vessel?"

"Yes," I say. "We destroy it, force the Great King out."

"And then what?"

"The Great King must be convinced to take a human vessel, in the old way, as the Queen has done with me."

"And how will he be convinced?"

"If the vessel is gone—if his power is no longer amplified—the Queen is sure she can force a stalemate. And make the King remember how it used to be."

"Once he's unbound . . . the Regia's mark may work," Dalca says.

"No," I say. "We won't use the Regia's mark."

"The Regia's mark worked for hundreds of years."

"No," I repeat. "The mark is what made the King so angry. The Queen will remind him of the old ways, and he'll choose a vessel. They can be joined like me and the Great Queen. That's the better way."

"Who will he pick?"

"I don't know. It could be anyone."

Cas speaks up. "It could be Dalca."

"Yes," I say. "It could."

"What if he picks some random person?" Cas asks.

"That's fine too. That's how it used to be."

Silence falls, electric and uneasy.

"Unless one of you sees another way?"

"No," Dalca says, standing. "I'm with you."

The five remaining members of my guard follow suit.

I let out a small breath. "We must leave at nightfall. Before the lightstruck can make another move. Before the council can stop us."

Cas glances at Dalca. "That's a few hours from now."

Dalca nods. "We meet at the ramblers."

Night falls. I pace. Dalca has secured a rambler and a Wardana to help drive it. Cas and Dalca converse quietly. My guard is late.

The sound of gravel crunching underfoot. Hadria. She's alone.

My heart plummets. "They didn't want to chance it," I say. "That's okay."

Hadria shakes her head. "That's not it. They tried—we wanted to. But they were waiting for us."

"What do you mean?"

"Once we realized what was happening . . . We used Carver's masks—she left behind four. Gamara was in your rooms, Jhuno in the mancer's workshop, Zerin in the hall, Ozra in Prince Dalca's room. They came all at once—a few Wardana and Nosca, too. They couldn't tell which was you, so they took them all in. I got away."

Dalca asks, "Do we go on?"

Cas scratches his neck. "With just the four of us?"

"If we turn back, that's it," I say. "We give up. Accept that the Great King won."

Cas turns to the direction of the city's inner five rings. "I love my home. And I believe in the plan." He flashes a small smile. "And, to be fair, it only took four of us last time."

Dalca's lips are set in a grim line. "This isn't the Storm."

"I know it isn't," I say. "Hadria, your mother's up in the city somewhere, because of me, and I don't want this to be like last time. If you—any of you—feel it's too dangerous . . ."

"If we do," Dalca says, "what then?"

I bite down what I want to say: *Please come with me. I can't be a hero alone.*

"We don't, though, do we?" Cas says to Dalca, clapping his shoulder.

"No," says Dalca, voice so quiet it could be stolen by the wind. "I'm with you."

Each in turn meets my gaze, and in them all is the same answer.

CHAPTER 19

My body sways with the movement of the covered rambler as we rattle along the road into the fifth ring. A pothole sends my knee knocking against Hadria's, and the metallic crack of armor on armor rings loud in the interior.

Cas designed our new armor, made of interlocking plates of mirrorlike metal for better protection against the light. But it sure is a lot noisier than leather. I shift, and crack my elbow against Hadria's side.

Dalca shoots me a look, but there's really no comfortable way to sit upon a bag of shalaj. The dark interior of the rambler is packed full of lumpy sacks—all food that's too fragile or would take too much space to be worth packing in the landtreaders.

Dalca and Cas perch across from us, Cas consulting a map by the light of a miniature ikonlantern set in the thumb of his glove. None of them have said a word the hour that we've been on the road; all I've had to distract me from my thoughts are the creaking of the wood under us and, from outside, the steady *tip-tip-tap* of the six-legged stormbeast's hoofbeats.

I'm full to the brim of the Great Queen's power, and she's practically licking her lips at the thought of this fight. My heartbeat picks up at the thought of what waits for me up in the palace. I force myself still, my fists resting on my knees. The hair on the back of my neck prickles, and I look up.

Dalca raises his eyebrow, a question in his eyes: *You're good?*

I give him a small nod. *I'm good.*

His gaze falls to the window, but I keep studying him. He's different. Take him out of the world of councils and landtreaders, and he's calmer, more confident, as if he best understands who he is when he's part of a team, facing imminent danger.

If he's this confident when all he has on his side is Wardana armor and Cas's ikon-laced trinkets—if he can be calm, so can I. I have a god on my side. I take a deep breath.

Three knocks come from the front of the car, startling me half out of my skin. Cas turns a dial, and the ikonlantern sputters out. In the dark, I pat around for the wide-brimmed hat by my feet and put it on, pulling the veil down over my face.

The rambler slows; from outside come the low tones of a brief conversation. A creak of gates. The rambler lurches. The floor tilts as the beast goes up the stairs, the wheels rolling up the ramp.

The smell of spices filters through the air as we near the border to the fourth ring and the Pearl Bazaar. The normal sounds of the market are muted—no one is willing to draw the notice of the King. But it's a fine place to disembark, to meld with the crowds and lose any who might be watching us.

The rambler slows.

Dalca flicks the curtain open and slips out first, followed closely by Hadria. Hadria pokes her head back in and gestures for me. I hop down, thankful that my eyes are well-adjusted for the muted light of the Pearl Bazaar. I glance back at our driver—a Wardana wearing the clothes of a farmer, with a pin on his chest marking him as one of

Rosander Tarr's merchants—who begins bargaining in a loud voice, playing his part well.

Near half the stalls are empty, and those that are open are thronged with those desperate to buy what they need. The once-vibrant market is dying.

We blend in with the other patrons. Many wear veiled hats like ours—though the more cautious bear parasols with even wider circumferences and several layers of veils. The braver—or poorer—merely wear cloaks with shawls pulled tight around their faces. Even under the carefully constructed canopies of the Pearl Bazaar, no one is taking chances.

One of the others tugs at my arm. By the width of their shoulders, I'd guess Cas, or maybe Dalca. With all of us wearing veils and dark cloaks to cover our mirrored armor, it's hard to tell who is who.

At least until one of us breaks into a long-legged stride, moving through the bazaar without hesitation, as at home in the chaos of the fourth as anywhere. Not a single glance back; the unconscious tell of a man who trusts that others will follow. That'll be Dalca.

He guides us past the stalls of the bazaar and through crooked alleys, out of the fourth and deeper into the fifth. A path he knows that'll take us to a secret entrance to the old city.

Hadria follows close behind me, taking seriously her duty to protect me. I glance over my shoulder, and behind her is the near-identical figure of Cas.

We make our way to a part of the fifth that was once lost to the Storm, a part of the fifth I don't know at all. There are no ikonlights here—the only illumination comes from the soft moonlight, and the distant glow of the Great King's lightlines.

Dalca leads us into the rubble of what may have been a temple.

Columns are set in a circle, though half are toppled, and the roof is long gone. He kneels on the floor, wiping away a layer of dust from the stonework beneath his feet.

Hadria and Cas make a circuit around the rubble in what seems to be some sort of well-practiced Wardana routine. "All clear," Hadria says.

Dalca scrawls an ikon on the stonework. The slate folds away, and a hole opens in the floor. He hops down. "Clear," he calls. "Come on in."

I go first, swinging my legs over the edge, into pitch-black darkness. I hold my breath and drop. I hit the ground hard, sending a jolt through my ankles. Hands grasp my waist, steadying me, then pulling me out of the way.

A thump as Hadria drops through the opening behind me, rising from a crouch, as graceful as a cat. Cas follows, as Dalca moves away. I can't see what he does, but soon the opening shuts over us, plunging us into darkness. I flip my veil behind my shoulders.

Cas lights an ikonlight.

Crystal flakes in the wall catch the light and reflect it. The tunnel stretches on and on, with no end in sight. I kick a rock, and it skitters away, rolling faster as the path slopes downward.

The angle of our descent grows steeper, until the tunnel opens up into a space large enough for the four of us. A spherical room has been carved out of the stone, and along the wall is a low ledge, perfect to sit upon. A dusty ikonlantern perches on it, and with a twist of its ikondial, it emits a pale light.

We divest ourselves of the hats and cloaks. Dalca drops his pack to the ledge and unlaces it. He keeps his voice quiet. "Food?"

I'm not that hungry, but I nod. He tosses us each a flatbread wrapped in waxed mosscloth.

I turn it over in my hands.

"It's been checked," Dalca says. He takes a bite of his, making a production of swallowing, and then offers it to me.

"I believe you," I say, and take a bite of my own.

After a heartbeat, he retracts his hand.

Dalca murmurs, "We'll have to cross a good part of the old city to make it up into the palace. And we'll have to keep a fairly quick pace to make it there before dawn breaks."

"I've never been down here," Hadria says, wonderingly.

"Let me check your helms," Cas says. "Er, that's all right, Hadria. When you're done eating is fine."

I take bites of the flatbread without really tasting it. My leg jumps up and down. I want to go and be done with it.

Dalca slips on his mirrorhelm—a semi-flexible visor that slides over his eyes. The glass is somewhat transparent in the half-light, enough that Dalca's eyes are visible through it. But Cas has assured us they'll protect us from the lightlines.

"Perfect," Dalca says.

"Yes," Cas mutters. "Unless the light sharpens into a laser and cuts through it, or if one of the lightstruck gets close enough to pull it off your head, or if you trip and crack it—"

Dalca puts a hand on Cas's shoulder and gives him a speaking glance.

Cas sighs deeply, relaxing, his shoulders dropping from where they'd hiked up to his ears. No one's doing a great job of hiding their nervousness, but I can guess what's on Cas's mind. Ragno's somewhere up there.

Hadria lets him check her helm; as soon as he's done, she pulls it back, keeping it perched on the top of her head.

Cas starts. "Keep that on."

She raises an eyebrow at him.

"You're right." Cas's voice drips with derision. "How silly, to wear the one thing that could protect you from ending up like your mother."

Hadria crosses her arms, giving him a withering look. "It's dark."

A furious flush rises on Cas's cheeks, and Hadria's expression grows cold as stone. The air between them crackles; they've found a release valve for their stress.

I step between them. "Okay. She'll put it on at the first sign of light, all right?"

Cas scowls. "Doesn't matter to me. If she wants to be light-struck . . ."

Hadria turns her focus to sorting her pack, folding her cloak and hat inside.

"Hadria, Cas is just looking out for you, all right?"

She shrugs.

I could shake them both. Dalca catches my eye, a small smile on his lips. Understanding passes between us; it'll be our job to keep them focused and calm.

In minutes, we're packed and prepared for the next leg. Dalca takes the lead, and we head deeper into the tunnel. Cas carries the ikonlantern behind us, and my shadow stretches before me. It's as if I'm chasing it, as Dalca chases his. My thighs burn as the tunnel slopes sharply upward.

"There's a light," Dalca says.

A soft glow emanates from ahead. Hadria slips on her helm. Cas clicks off the ikonlantern, and our shadows disappear.

The light intensifies as the tunnel opens up.

Dalca stills, silhouetted in the light. He sucks in a sharp breath. I throw an arm up over my eyes, even though my helm is in place, and step out beside him.

A massive, underground city both rises above us and extends deep into the dark below. A dead city, a corpse shaped like a cocoon, fat in the middle and tapered on both ends. It's supported by enormous pillars of rock that begin far below and rise high above our heads, and some dozen walkways spiderweb out from the ruins and into the purple-red stone that surrounds us, connecting this ghost of a city to ours.

I've been here before, during the day, when a single shaft of dim light fell from above, penetrating the dark. The ground had caved in during a stormbeast attack on the fifth ring, creating an opening that gaped like a wound.

But now dozens—maybe hundreds—of wounds speckle the rock above us. Light punctures the dark in long shafts. One long column of light fades before us as its source is cut off, but another shaft cuts through the dark, illuminating a spindly bridge to our right.

A dance of dappled light plays over the old city and her bridges. The columns of light move in an undecipherable pattern, just like the lightlines above. They, too, are lightlines, just ones diffused by dust and the thick underground air.

Unease curls at the base of my throat. The old city, temple to the dark and forgotten, is not the shelter we were expecting.

"He's breaking the city apart." Dalca's head tilts up, the long line of his throat tensing as he swallows.

"We can still make it through," I say, swallowing my doubt. "There are still fewer lightlines down here than we'll face above."

Dalca frowns. "That may be so. But without thousand-and-one-feather cloaks, we'll have to pick through the maze of the old city while dodging the light. That's no easy task."

"We're not turning back."

Two muttered curses are Hadria and Cas's contributions.

"Cas," Dalca asks, "can our armor withstand it?"

"It'll handle being grazed by the light easily," says Cas. "But it can't withstand prolonged exposure to concentrated lightlines. And the more they're subjected to the Great King's power, the more likely cracks and weak points are to develop. If we walk straight through . . . They'll be useless by the time we make it to the palace."

"Well, we won't walk straight through," I say brightly. "We take cover when we need to. Think of it like the games we used to play as children. Hide-and-shelter, or Wardana and Stormbeasts. That kind."

Cas and Hadria look at me blankly.

"You did play games as children, didn't you? It wasn't all . . . Wardana training?"

Cas tosses his hair. "Obviously. You mean to say this is akin to playing Dominion. We're the red pieces, the King is the white. I see it."

"Oh," Hadria says. "I like Dominion."

Dalca very nearly smiles. He bows his head to hide it, twisting the ikondial on his mirrored gauntlet. The metal of his shoulder-length gauntlet seems to melt, re-forming into a gleaming shield. He looks up, straight into my eyes. "Ready?"

To get to the suspended cocoon of the old city, we have to cross one of the many thin bridges that stretch from the tunnels, across the open air, and into the ruins. Light dances across the one before us, beams sliding across it.

I haven't had nearly enough training with gauntlets, and my shield comes out bulbously misshapen. Hadria's is perfect, and Cas pulls his with a decorative filigree. Well, at least I can make stormbarriers.

We make our way across in a single file. Dalca gestures—a closed fist for stop, hand pointed forward for go. My attention sharpens to a point: in shadows, we run—the light nears and we stop—we wait for the beam to slide across the bridge—shadows fall and we run. In fits and starts we make our way.

A sudden flash of light—a stray beam, quicker and off pattern—swings across. Dalca jumps backwards—right into me. I wrap my arms around his middle, keeping him steady. He's as tense as stone. "Thank you," he says gruffly. "Onward."

We cover the last few feet and make it to the bridge's end. An old boulevard stretches before us, strewn with rubble, beams of light swinging slowly across the path. "This way," Dalca says, making for a tall, long structure with most of its roof remaining. A pile of boulder-sized rubble blocks the door, but Dalca climbs over a toppled stone bust as tall as I am, and swings himself in through a window.

I follow, trying to put my feet where he put his. I can practically feel Hadria's hands hovering, waiting to catch me if I should fall.

My hands grip the windowsill and I drag myself inside.

A long hall, lined with columns. Dalca picks his way through.

"Up here, there'll be a hallway," he murmurs.

He knows this place so well. It is a story that everyone in the city has heard in some form. That when Dalca was a child, his grandfather led him deep into the old city and left him there to find his way out. Dalca has told me a little more. Casually, in passing, as if it didn't matter at all, Dalca told me his grandfather left him with food enough for three days. But it took him six to find his way out.

Dalca also told me what his grandfather said to him before he left: *Only the best will be Regia.*

Does Dalca still want to be the best, by his grandfather's definition?

"I can hear you thinking," Dalca says.

"Your grandfather was cruel."

He glances at me. And suddenly our history hangs between us. His expression flickers and I know surer than I know my own name that he's thinking of how my father killed his grandfather. "Maybe," Dalca says. "But because of his cruelty, I know how to lead you through the old city."

His armor shifts over the planes of his back as he rolls his shoulders. I bite my lip. I shouldn't have spoken. It hurt me to think of a child left down here. But I wasn't thinking about how Dalca might still be hurting, all these years later. How could Dalca take what I said as anything but pity?

We pick our way through the skeletons of ancient buildings, shaped by hands long gone. Crumbling stone arches and half-shattered ceilings provide a patchwork shelter from the lightlines. We carve a zigzag path through the old city, never going too deeply into its interior.

Over and over, we hit what looks to be a dead end, until Dalca points out handholds that'll help us scale a wall, or a small gap behind a boulder that we can just about squeeze through if we take our packs in hand. A thousand secrets this place has, and as far as I know, only Dalca's taken the time to learn them all.

I can't help but compare myself to him, to how much and how well he knows all sorts of things—not just the old city, but how to fight. How to be a hero. Even the way he walks, so alert and aware of everything around him—how long did it take him to learn to be a Wardana?

My arms are still aching from pulling myself over the last wall. Hadria hovers, and Cas keeps looking back at me to make sure I'm fine.

Without the Great Queen, what am I?

CHAPTER 20

Dalca stops in his tracks, holding out a hand to keep us back. I blink, coming out of the muddle of my thoughts, and take in our surroundings. We're on the second floor of a once-ornate structure—flecks of gold paint still ornament some of the walls—and the far wall has long since crumbled. Dalca makes his way to the edge.

The light is strong, casting him in silhouette. I inch closer until I can take in what has him so alarmed.

It's as though an immense hand has dragged a knife through the ruins, leaving a gouge ten paces across. All the buildings in its path have been razed, the rubble cleared. Beams of light sweep along the gouge without pause, giving an impression of a line of marching soldiers. On the other side of the light is a room just like the one we're in, the same details and flourishes—as if a hall was cut in two by the light.

Cas curses under his breath, and I follow his gaze along the row of lightlines, to a point far in the distance.

An unusual beam of light cuts through the dark of the undercity, sharper and brighter than the rest. It glows a deep, lush green, like sunlight filtering through the shifting water of a moss-choked fountain.

A spectral.

"Dalca—"

"I see it," Dalca says.

"That's a new one to add to the list," Cas murmurs, as if taking notes. "Let's call him the emerald spectral, shall we?"

"Who is it?" I ask.

Cas shakes his head. "I can't see from here."

Dalca frowns. "We'll just keep our distance. There must be a way through."

We backtrack down and out of the building and climb through a pile of rubble to enter the next. The going is slow—Dalca has no memory of handholds here—but we follow him silently as he plots a new course that runs roughly parallel to the marching beams.

It becomes an exercise in putting one foot in front of the other, climbing where Dalca tells me to climb, crawling where he says crawl, reminding myself each time that it's wise to follow him, that a good hero leans on the strengths of those around them.

It half works, until my boot sticks between two rocks and the ground rushes up at me. My palms sting with the pain of breaking my fall. Frustration bubbles up in me like hot acid.

It burns hotter as Dalca gently wiggles my boot free. As Hadria offers me a hand and hauls me up.

I brush the grit from my raw, scraped palms and pin Dalca with a look. "Enough of this."

Dalca runs a hand through his hair. What is he waiting for? It's clear there's no easy way through the marching lightlines.

I fold my arms. "We have to make for the gap between the lightlines. One by one."

Dalca meets my gaze. "It's risky. They're unpredictable."

"No." Cas's voice comes from a dozen paces away, where he stands facing the marching beams of light. "There's a pattern to it."

We gather around him. "I don't see it," I admit.

"Look closer," Cas says, eyes alight.

I focus on the several directly before me. Okay. Some beams group closer together; some further. A set of three, then a set of five, then a set of two. In each group, the beams of light move in tandem, with gaps so small nothing but a bird could get through.

But between one group and the next, the gap widens.

Not evenly or consistently. A set of four swings by. The gap between it and the next is wide enough for a person to squeeze sideways. My heart jumps—we sidled through a passage about that size earlier. Except that passage was made out of stone, it wasn't moving, and there was no harm done if we touched the walls on either side. No. A cat might be able to make it through, but not one of us.

The lightlines march on. I count the sets, but no pattern reveals itself. And then it comes—a larger gap, the width of a person standing with arms outstretched. The gap swings past, out of sight.

So we have to time ourselves for a gap that size.

The other problem is that each beam is a different shape—some are rectangular, some are soft columns. It all depends on the opening they fall through. The soft columns don't bother me—they're the same width the whole way around. But the rectangular shafts of light fall like tall knives, with the thin cutting edges facing us. The longer, flat sides run perpendicular to us—so the gap between the beams of light is like a corridor.

A fast-moving corridor that we'll have to run through in a matter of seconds.

Cas glances at me. "You see it now?"

A reliable, predictable pattern? "Um," I say.

"Aim for the big one," Hadria says.

She's not wrong. I scan the lights. The gaps between them all seem horribly short. "Which is the big one?"

"There," says Cas, pointing.

Dalca squints. I'd wager he sees it as well as I do. "Cas, if you see it, count us down. We trust you."

Cas pinks, but nods.

We get as close to the marching beams of light as we dare.

"Hadria, you first," Dalca says.

Cas takes a breath. "All right, the next pattern should be three, then two, and the biggest gap will come before the batch of five, so count with me—"

She leaps before he can begin, darting between two shafts of light, the last strand of her hair making the leap with a split second to spare. That doesn't look so hard.

"Now you, Vesper," Dalca says.

Cas counts me down. "Two, then four—get ready—GO!"

I leap for the gap. My foot slides on rubble the size of teeth—the world tilts as I fall—Hadria grabs me by my belt and whips me out of the light.

Dalca nods at me through the flickering beams. *You're okay.*

Dalca turns. "Cas."

Casvian counts himself down. "And it's coming, three, two—" He starts to leap but hesitates, and the gap swings past.

"That's okay," Dalca says. "Aim for the next gap."

We wait. Cas counts, and the gap nears. His eyes are wide, gaze flicking from the gap to the next, and at *three, two*—I know he won't jump.

Cas tenses before the gap—Dalca gives him a firm push, sending him leaping forward—Cas has no choice but to keep running. He stretches an arm, and I grab it, just as Hadria grabs him by the collar of his jacket, and we pull him out of the light.

Cas doubles over, gasping. "For Storm's sake, this is *nothing* like Dominion."

Hadria pats him on the back.

Dalca catches my eye, radiating urgency. He makes a shooing motion with his hands as he slinks backward, into the shadows.

The rubble gains a soft green tinge. Dalca's helm tilts upwards, as he watches the watery green lightline draw near. The emerald spectral is coming.

I slink back into an alcove, and Hadria covers me with her body. I rise on my toes to see over her shoulder, but all I glimpse is Cas's profile as he watches the spectral approach.

Cas sucks a breath through his teeth.

"What?" I whisper.

Cas pitches his voice low. "It's the Regia Memnon. Dalca's grandfather. Hush."

Everything is tinted green by reflected light, as the spectral glides by in the form of a tall, regal man. The light recedes. Cas doesn't move for a long moment, and when I free myself from Hadria, the spectral is long gone.

On the other side of the marching lights, Dalca steps out of the shadows. His face is determined, his shoulders set.

Cas counts down. "*Three—two—*Wait, something's wrong—"

But Dalca's already jumped. I see what Cas saw—the corridor of light is extra long, and the gap shrinks before our eyes.

Dalca's eyes are narrowed in focus as all his Wardana training comes into play—in one movement, he unslings his pack and tosses it toward us, its momentum carrying him forward—

I lunge for him. Hadria's quicker than me—she grabs on to Dalca's arm and heaves, just as my fingers wrap around his outstretched hand.

We pull.

Dalca's back foot clips the light.

In the space between one heartbeat and the next—

The beams of light still, trembling, and then converge into blisteringly bright lights. A green glow rises as the spectral swings back toward us, just as Dalca and Hadria reach for their gauntlets.

The Queen's mark rises on my skin.

Hadria and Dalca activate ikons, and the mirrored metal of their gauntlets melts and re-forms into faceted shields. Dalca whirls, grabbing my hand and pulling me into a run, his shield held above our heads.

A soft voice comes from behind us. Monotone, with a low layer of crackling embers. "A rat-tat-tat," the emerald spectral sings. "A heavy club and a clever trap will catch us *every last naughty rat.*"

I glance back as the spectral snaps his fingers. Something happens above—shadows scurry across the openings, and several of the beams of light flicker.

Lightstruck descend on ropes that fall from the openings up above. They move with precision, weapons in hand.

I suck in a breath. The lightstruck are like toy soldiers, moving in unison, prepared for violence.

Dalca slows for Hadria and Cas to catch up, and we huddle under a crumbling archway. Hadria's fingers fly across her gauntlet as she lets her shield melt back into it, and with a twist of an ikondial, she pulls something long and curving.

"They'll just pick us off down here," Cas says, reaching in his pack.

I meet Dalca's eyes. "Where's the path to the palace?"

His expression is grim. "Far. Too far. But . . . there's another path. It'll at least take us up cityside."

I don't like the look in his eyes. "Where does it let out?"

"The third." Dalca glances over my shoulder. "Near the Ven."

That's only halfway through the third. We'll have to cross up into the second, and then make our way to the first and into the palace. "We can do it," I say to their apprehensive expressions.

"By 'it,'" Cas asks hopefully, looking up from the ikon-inscribed balls in his palm, "do you mean retreat back to the sixth?"

"No," Hadria and I say at the same time. She gives me a speaking glance before turning her attention back to drawing the last inches of a bow from her gauntlet, and tugs a coiled bowstring from her pack.

I continue: "We go on."

Dalca's lips draw into a thin line. "We've lost the element of surprise."

"We don't need it. We didn't have it when we went into the Storm."

He grits his teeth. I can practically read his thoughts. *This isn't the Storm.*

A shadow passes over us. One of the lightstruck. Time's up.

"We go for the third," I say. "Unless—Cas—"

"No," Cas says. "I'm for it. Let's go on."

Dalca gives me a short nod. "Stay with me."

Hadria tests the draw of her newly strung bow. Her lips curl in satisfaction, and she flicks open the top of the quiver at her waist, drawing an arrow. "Ready."

We run for it, cutting a jagged path through the rubble, as shadows pass above, as beams of light draw near. A lightstruck descends in our path, heaving a spear that Dalca smacks away with his shield.

Hadria looses her arrow, bringing the lightstruck down.

Cas throws one of the little ikon-inscribed balls behind us. A crack of thunder—an explosion—a dust wave hits our backs.

Dalca keeps the shield above us, keeping pace with me, calling directions. "Turning right!"

We skid around a corner, into an alley, and our path comes in sight: it's a straight shot to a skinny bridge that stretches across the chasm, to the mouth of a tunnel.

The lightstruck swarm, blocking the bridge and surrounding us.

Hadria downs three with arrows. Cas readies a handful of ikon explosives—

"No—the bridge will collapse," Dalca barks. "Keep running!" In the blink of an eye, he draws a spear, pivoting and meeting the sword of an immense lightstruck. Hadria clears the way, using her bow as a club.

As I run, I pull the Queen's power around me, raising a stormbarrier, letting it knit into armor like a second skin.

A lightstruck reaches for me, and I fling out my arm. Her fingers turn to wood, and I yank my arm away.

I make it onto the bridge, Cas and Hadria quick on my heels. I glance back.

"Dalca!" Cas calls. "Duck!"

Dalca does, and Cas lobs an explosive over his head.

Dalca sprints onto the bridge. His gaze flicks from my face to something over my shoulder.

A great green beam of light shines down upon the bridge, blocking our path. Caught in it, in motes of light, is a tall man, gaunt of figure and with a face as smooth as a polished stone and just as flat—his eyes and mouth are like gashes, like fractures.

"Dear child," he says in that soft, crackling voice. "Enough foolishness."

"Move," Dalca snarls.

The spectral slinks closer, his face twisting in disgust. "All this wanton mischief is unbecoming of a future Regia."

I glance to my side, where Hadria is quickly re-forming her mirrorshield. Cas has his ready to go. Behind us, a handful of the remaining lightstruck set foot on the bridge.

Dalca's jaw works. "You are not my grandfather."

"How I wish that were so. I told your mother to choose better. But your father's weakness shows in you."

Time slows. Dalca flinches—pain flashing across his face—as his grandfather looks down on him with no love, no pride, nothing but a cruel disdain.

I raise my arms and the stormclouds rise into a barrier that arcs over the bridge, cutting the beam of the emerald spectral's light. The Regia Memnon disappears.

"Now!" I shout. I grab Dalca's arm as Hadria and Cas break into a run.

It's the longest sprint of my life. The stone reverberates with the thudding footfalls of the lightstruck behind us.

The mouth of the tunnel opens.

We dash in, and I draw my stormbarrier back into me.

Cas throws a handful of explosives at the bridge—under the resulting booms comes a loud crack. The stone bridge crumbles.

"Collapse the tunnel behind us!" Dalca barks.

Cas falls to his knees with a stick of mancer's charcoal in hand, drawing a quick ikon as Hadria hovers over him. "Get back!" Cas shouts as he finishes it.

With a groan and a billow of dust, the tunnel caves in behind us, plunging us into the dark.

CHAPTER 21

My heartbeat doesn't slow, not with the sounds of lightstruck clearing the rubble reverberating through the tunnel behind us.

The only illumination comes from the tiny ikonlight in Cas's glove. I follow the bobbing pinprick of light, putting one foot in front of the other. I don't realize it's stopped moving until I walk into Dalca's back. He glances over his shoulder at me, and I put a little space between us.

"Which way?" Cas asks.

"To the right," Dalca murmurs.

Cas's ikonlight just barely illuminates a fork in the tunnel. I follow the others down the rightward path, maneuvering around Cas, who kneels on the ground. He painstakingly sketches three complex ikons that link together like a constellation. He connects the last line, and the ikon activates with a gravelly rasp. Stone rises like liquid from the floor and walls, fusing itself into a solid mass.

A click, and light blooms from a larger ikonlantern in Cas's hand. He inspects the sealed-off entrance. "There won't be an obvious collapse on the other side," he says. "But there'll be a seam where the new stone meets the old. Hopefully they'll run right past it down the other fork. But if they look carefully, they'll find it."

"We're not going to wait for them to find it," Dalca says. "We have to get out of the tunnels as fast as we can."

For some reason, he looks to me.

"I'm ready," I say, hoisting my pack higher.

Dalca nods and we set off at a jog. My thighs burn as the tunnel slopes sharply upward, but I refuse to be the one that slows first.

I don't fool anyone—the stitch in my side has me gasping by the time Dalca calls a halt.

A small door is inset into the wall. Dalca works the lock, and with a soft pop, the door cracks open. A skinny shaft of soft pinkish light worms its way through the gap between door and frame. My gut tightens with alarm—but it's not a spectral. It's the sun rising.

Dalca slips out, shooting a quelling look over his shoulder.

I bite my cheek, thinking. It'll be dangerous to go overground in daylight, when the lightlines can blend in with ordinary sunbeams. Can we do it? I flex my fingers. I expended a good deal of power facing the emerald spectral. And even that was hardly facing him—we ran.

But to spend a day waiting for nightfall—it feels a waste.

The door swings open; Dalca pops his head in. "Let's go."

We come out into a hallway with striated sandstone walls. "This is the Ven," I say with surprise. The scent of sweat and leather is faint but undeniable.

"Very good," Cas says in the same dry tone he used when I was his apprentice.

Dalca hushes us.

I step over discarded spears as we pick our way through the halls and up to the second story walkway that overlooks the central courtyard. The Ven bears marks of being hastily evacuated. But there's no evidence that the lightstruck have come here, to demolish and rebuild in the way they have through the second.

A feeling of safety settles over my shoulders. It's not rational. But this place is thick with the memories of Wardana of the past. Pa would be right at home, scribbling away at some marvel of ikonomancy behind these doors. What would he see in my life-ikon now? Am I getting closer to finishing it? To knowing who I am? Have I faced the extraordinary obstacle that he anticipated?

"Hurry," Dalca murmurs.

I follow him into a reading room. The window opens out onto the roof—a second exit if we need one.

Once the door shuts behind us, he relaxes. "No sign of lightstruck within the Ven."

Cas runs his finger across the table. "No one has been in here." His finger leaves a trail through the layer of dust. Everything is coated in it—a fine sandy dust, likely blown in from all the construction the lightstruck have been doing.

"This seems as good a place as any to get some rest," Dalca says, dropping his pack. "It's safest to stay put till nightfall."

"I'll take first watch," Hadria says.

Dalca nods. "I'll take a look around."

I curl up on the floor. Cas is out within moments. Hadria keeps an eye on the view out the window. I study her profile.

"Yes?" she says without looking at me.

That's what I get for staring. "Hadria . . . we'll find your mother."

"I know," she says. "But what happens after?"

It's the question I've been fearing. The lightstruck are prepared for violence. Can they be cured? I undid Cas's curse, but it took so much out of me . . . I couldn't cure many, and certainly not fast. I can only hope more will overcome their curses on their own, like Izamal. But if not . . . Once we break the Great King's vessel, once the Great Queen reminds him of how it once was . . . maybe whoever the Great King chooses will be able to unstrike the lightstruck.

I say none of it: Hadria's thought of it all.

I roll over onto my back and stare up at the ceiling. Cas murmurs in his sleep. The distant clamor of construction comes muffled through the walls. Hadria lets out a small sigh.

I'm too worked up to sleep.

"I'll take over," I tell Hadria. "Get some sleep."

She studies me, and nods without a word. She props herself up against her pack, and within seconds, her whole body relaxes, her face softening in sleep.

The door clicks. Dalca enters. "No cloaks," he whispers to me. "I didn't expect there would be, but I couldn't help looking, just in case. How the battle would change if we could fight from above . . ."

The bandages that peek out over his collar and wrap around his hands are fresh. He's changed them all, I'd wager. No doubt reinforced them with the numbing and rapid-healing ikons that have Cas and the healers so worked up.

It's not just that. His earlier confidence is gone. His eyes are red-rimmed, his skin a little ghastly. Is it the encounter with his grandfather that has him rattled?

"Dalca, I'll stay up if you want to rest."

He shakes his head. "I'm fine."

Obviously not. Nashira had a similar kind of bullheaded bravado. There was one thing that always worked with her. "Then—if you're not doing anything—I could use a hand."

He straightens immediately. "Of course."

I skirt around Cas and Hadria. "Not here."

We cross the hall, to the study room opposite. I pick it for no other reason but proximity, but Dalca brightens as he glances around the room. "There's a little—" Dalca reaches the table in the center and hoists it up, exposing its underbelly. "Look at this."

There's something carved into the wood. Initials. $E + L$.

"I never figured out who they were," Dalca says. "They left another carving in one of the training rooms."

"You really know every inch of this place, don't you?" It comes out a little softer than I intended.

"This was my home for a long while. I know it about as well as I know the palace. Better, maybe." His hair falls into his eyes. And then slowly, as if offering a secret: "Neither my mother nor my grandfather was Wardana."

"Why did you do it?"

"Become a Wardana?"

I nod. "And . . . not just a Wardana. Why work so hard at it? Why learn every piece of the Ven, of the old city?"

His throat moves as he swallows. "I don't . . ." He rubs at his jaw, and his eyes grow shadowed.

"Never mind," I say. "That's not what I needed help with." I show him my Wardana gauntlet, its mirrored surface catching our reflections. I twist an ikondial, and feel the telltale pressure at my fingertips as a free edge rises. I pull it, letting the mirrorshield form. A breeze brushes my arm as the metal of the gauntlet disappears into the shield. I pull it free.

I hold it up. Dalca blinks at it, face void of all expression. It's roughly shield shaped. Just . . . lumpy.

"Not bad, actually." Dalca lies through his teeth. But some of his confidence returns. "Particularly as you're at a disadvantage. Typically, a smith builds the shield first. The mancers put a lattice of ikons on it that will help it remember its shape before it's melted into the gauntlet. A Wardana studies every tool and weapon well before it's melted into their gauntlet. You probably never saw the shield's true shape, and without that, it can be tough to know at what speed to pull it."

His eyes are alight. Oh, how he loves being good at what he does. I'd roll my eyes if he didn't seem so cheered, if it weren't exactly what I'd hoped would happen. "So," I say, "how do I do it?"

Dalca shows me how, neatly compacting the shield into the gauntlet and pulling it free once more. "The ikon allows not only for matter to change its shape, but controls the level of expansion. You want an even pull."

I try again. The shield has fewer lumps, and Dalca looks a tad less heartbroken. "Better," I say.

"Ah." Dalca's face is blank as he takes in my shield. "It helps if you brace yourself. So you're as still as possible. Why don't you try again?"

I suppose I've got to carry it through. I widen my stance.

Dalca taps my knee. "Wider." His fingers brush my stomach. "Let this be the center of your balance."

I breathe in.

He circles me. "Now straighten your back. And pull."

My fingers brush the cold metal, and I pull it carefully, holding his gaze. He looks away first, and smiles.

In my hand is a perfect shield.

"When I was small," I say, "all I wanted to be was a Wardana."

Dalca doesn't say anything for a long moment. "I don't know if I ever did. If I truly thought about it. Casvian knew he had to be a Wardana, and eventually a Regia's Guard. Because of his father. But he was a small child, with these big spectacles . . . He was so scared. I became a trainee when he did." He scrubs a hand through his hair. "It sounds like I'm saying I wanted to watch out for him. And I did . . . but I'm not so sure it was entirely noble. Perhaps I just didn't want to be alone."

He looks embarrassed at having admitted it.

"But then," I say, "you became the best."

Dalca lets out a sharp bark of laughter. "Hardly that. Izamal and Hadria are far better—and there were dozens of others who were born exceptional. I had to work much harder to measure up. And some instructors hated me. They figured I needed something beaten out of me. I suppose they thought I was proud or high-minded or something, I was never quite sure. And the others thought I didn't need much instructing. As if I'd know everything I needed by virtue of who I was." He walks to the window. "I think it's fair that you know the truth. That I've never quite measured up. Down in the old city . . . It was my job to lead us through. And I failed you."

"What do you want me to say?" I ask.

He turns, brows furrowed.

I go on. "That wasn't an apology. You've never apologized, for anything. The violet spectral—the one that looks like you—he apologized for everything. Isn't that strange?"

Dalca looks stricken. "I . . ."

"Help me understand."

"I . . . I don't want to put it on you. You already bear the burden of living with what I did to you. It would be cruel to add the burden of accepting my apology."

All the fury I once held for him . . . it's cooled enough to see him and what he carries. I don't feel victorious or even happy to see him so crushed by the past, by his mistakes. Because that's what they are. By facing himself, by atoning, by growing, he's turned what might've been legacy-defining acts of cruelty into . . . mistakes. Flaws in himself, in the story of his life, but ones he can grow past.

The mosaic room that I woke up in—and all the little books telling our story—they weren't right. He's not my one great love. But maybe he's not the villain either.

I don't really know when it happened. "Dalca . . . I've forgiven you."

He freezes, lips parted. And turns away abruptly, but not before I catch a glimpse of blue eyes shining with wetness. I draw a breath to say something, I don't know what—

The door creaks open. Hadria steps in, holding out a scroll of paper smaller than my little finger.

"There's a message," she says. "From Iz."

Dalca takes it, and in a gruff voice, asks, "Is Cas awake?"

Hadria follows him out the door. I pause on the threshold—a shiver runs down my spine, like I'm being watched. I turn back.

In the room, beside the window, is a flurry of violet light.

"Vesper," he says, in a voice like crackling embers.

I draw the Queen's power—Dalca and Hadria are in the next room, and the door has swung half-shut—they can't see the spectral—

He raises his hands in an unthreatening gesture. "If you want me gone, just say the word."

My heart pounds. "What do you want?"

"I'm just glad to hear . . . Thank you for saying what you did. That you forgive me."

How long has he been listening? "I didn't forgive you," I say. "I don't know you. Or what you are."

He brightens, and the flurry of violet light expands, making the spectral larger than life-sized. "You—you forgive him? That weakling, that failure who abdicates his responsibility? And not me?"

I have an uncomfortable feeling that it might have been cleverer to lie. "You've apologized," I say. "I appreciate that."

His fists are clenched at his sides. "I'll earn it. Just wait. You *will* forgive me."

I don't have an answer to that.

The light flickers, and his back is turned toward me. "I'll do what I can to keep the other spectrals away. Watch out for the red and the orange. You likely won't have to deal with Grandfather again—he rarely leaves the old city, unless he's called to the palace."

"You're helping me?"

"I told you." His voice is a whisper of dying embers. "I want you to see what I've seen."

"What's that?"

"Vesper?" Dalca—flesh-and-blood Dalca—calls from the other room. The door opens, and he frowns at me from the threshold.

I glance back. The spectral is gone.

"Yes?" I ask. He holds out a rolled-up paper. I cross the hallway, taking it from him and following him into the other room. An owlcat cleans its feathers on the windowsill.

I unfold the note. An incomprehensible string of letters and numbers.

"It's in code," Dalca says, and translates: "This first line says *Treader one moved*—so the first batch of landtreaders are on their way to the outpost. And then . . . *All dark*. Meaning no further attacks from the lightstruck. So Carver truly was the poisoner . . ."

Or the poisoner is with us. I glance at Hadria, who has her back to me. She stares out the gap in the window.

"That's all?" I ask. After how we left . . .

Dalca nods. "There was one last thing: *Be safe*."

My pack makes a poor pillow, but I fall asleep instantly. The Great
Queen waits for me.

Do you know what I hope for?

She shows me another time. The city when it was smaller, when
every ring was home to gardens, before buildings grew tall and
squashed.

This was our brief moment of peace.

At the edge of the first ring stand two figures, deeply in love. Each
a vessel of a god.

*For twenty years, the city grew like it had never grown before. Progress in
everything—how to cultivate the land, the secrets of ikonomancy—everything.*

A crawling, creeping figure rises and stabs one of the vessels.

Misery falls over the city.

*All that progress . . . all that promise . . . The Great King began pulling away
after that. If we can only return to that paradise . . .*

The dream fades. I claw onto it.

There's one thing, I say to the Queen. *Can you do it? Can you remind the
King of what it was like? Can you make sure he chooses a true vessel, like how you've
chosen me?*

We will return, she promises, *to how it once was . . .*

A hand shakes me awake. I blink up at Hadria.

The light from the window is a rusty orange. Sunset has come.

Cas presses a flatbread into my hands, and I eat it mechanically,
tasting nothing. A paradise, the Great Queen had said.

Two vessels . . . but not just any two vessels. Two that were in love.

Dalca kneels by his pack, tugging the drawstring taut. What if the Great King does choose him, once we've destroyed the false vessel? What if he doesn't?

I'm not even sure I know what love is. What it's supposed to be.

Can I only be a good vessel for the Queen if I fall in love with the King's vessel? Things worked well in the old ways, sure, but . . .

"Look at this," Hadria says, cutting through my spiraling thoughts.

I get to my feet and move to the window.

The lightstruck are shepherding carts full of rubble that rattle on, directed by lightlines. Some part of their endless construction. They're clearing out two paths that meet at an angle, ignoring the half-demolished buildings on either side. It makes no sense.

It doesn't have to make sense. The Great King has his plan. And we have ours.

As long as we carry out our plan, the Great King won't have a chance to complete his.

"Let's go," I say.

CHAPTER 22

"What do you know about the four gates?" Dalca asks as we hide out in an abandoned storefront, hammering out a plan to get up to the second ring.

This is what I know: The city has four roads that lead from ring to ring, each controlled by gates. The black gates to the north, the white to the east, the gold to the south, and the crimson to the west. Only the golden gates lead all the way to the first ring; the rest stop in the second. I tell him as much.

"Almost true," Dalca says. "Except the black gates from the third to the second ring were sealed up and constructed over ages ago, to create room for more houses."

I'm not sure what he's getting at. "So we have to take one of the other roads? Wouldn't that make us too visible?"

"No—what I mean is, the black gate station still remains. The black gates are sealed up and ikonlocked, but there's a back way, for maintenance, mostly—"

"Used most often by a handful of second-ringer Wardana apprentices needing a shortcut to the Ven," Cas says. "At least until they earned a cloak."

"You had a shortcut?" I say. "When you're only one ring away?"

"Yes, yes." Cas waves a hand. "Us dastardly high ringers using our advantages to our advantage."

"I never did," Hadria offers. "The extra distance is good exercise." Cas gives her a withering look.

"In any case," Dalca cuts in, "it's our best option."

I'm not sure. "What are our other options?"

Dalca holds up two fingers. "We could go back into the old city, or scale the wall of the second."

I wait a moment to see if he's trying to be funny. "Scale the wall? In full view, completely exposed?"

"It's not the option I'd recommend," Dalca says mildly.

Hadria opens her mouth, probably to offer something horribly heroic, like she'll scale the wall with me on her back. I jump in before she gets a word out: "Where's the gate station?"

I've never had cause to be in this part of the third ring. I serve my curiosity in flashes as we run from one hiding place to the next—a glittering glass-walled shop, a dressmaker's sign carved to look like weeping vines, a fountain large enough to bathe in that's now dried up, a curving street paved with blue diamond-shaped tiles—but none of it truly registers over the fear of running into the lightstruck.

Or the fear that I can't seem to shake, of being watched. Of being seen . . . and followed.

A glimmer of violet light plays at the edges of my vision, something catching on the curved rim of my helm. I turn my head so often I wouldn't be surprised if I sprained my neck. But nothing materializes.

We're nearing the gate station when up ahead, Dalca curses.

The black gates are gone. The ringwall—and the second-ringer houses built upon the black path—are nothing more than a slope of rubble. Lightstruck swarm the mound like dutiful ants, carting away stone and debris.

An orange slant of light shines to and fro. A spectral. At this distance, I can't make out any details of the figure other than the sharp, precise way they march back and forth as they oversee the work.

I retreat with the others into the relative shelter of an abandoned shop. The gate station is gone, and with it our way into the second. What purpose can be behind all this destruction and reconstruction?

"We can turn back," Dalca says. "Take the time to find a better way up to the palace."

"No," I say. "We'll find a way."

"We could climb the rubble," Hadria says.

"Just skirt around the spectral," Cas says dryly. "That'll work."

I catch another glimpse of violet light out of the corner of my eye. I scowl. "If you're here, show yourself."

Dalca, Cas, and Hadria stare at me like I've lost my mind.

A heartbeat. The violet spectral materializes in a cyclone of tiny specks of light.

Cas lets out a shriek—Hadria claps a hand over his mouth and peers out a window to see if anyone heard.

The spectral dips into a bow. "I am yours to command," he says to me.

"Vesper." Dalca's voice, close to my ear and unhappy. "We can't trust him."

I take a breath. "Spectral—"

"Please, call me Dalca," the spectral says, with a coy glance at Dalca.

Dalca bristles like an irritated cat.

"Spectral," I begin again, "if you meant what you said—"

"I did."

"We need to pass that way." I indicate the rubble. "The orange spectral . . ."

"I can distract her for you. Many of the lightstruck should follow; those that are left will be yours to handle."

"For how long?" Hadria asks.

The violet spectral scratches his jaw. "She doesn't like me very much—I can probably give you a good ten minutes."

It'll have to be enough. "Thank you," I say.

The spectral bows. His body melts into a scattering of dancing light that wraps around me like a hug, before it blinks out.

"How long have you been talking to him?" Dalca asks.

Hadria puts her circular blades away.

"Just once since the wilds," I say.

Dalca's expression darkens. "I don't like him."

I bite my tongue. If Dalca doesn't like someone who looks like him, talks like him, has all the same memories . . . that's his own problem. "We don't have another way up. If he does what he promised . . ."

Dalca's jaw is so tense I wouldn't be surprised if he cracks a tooth. "I would have found a way."

We both turn our attention to the rubble below. A violet light falls beside the orange, and they both whisk away. A ripple of attention goes through the lightstruck—no different than if they'd heard the ringing of a bell—and they descend the rubble.

The last of them follows the others, disappearing past the curve of the street. Dalca gestures, and we move.

The wind brushes my neck, kissing the slim gap of exposed skin between my helm and cloak. If the orange spectral swings back—if the

Great King glances our way—there's nothing to hide behind.

Hadria scampers up the rubble, finding suitable footings. Dalca follows right behind me, Cas at our tail. We pick our way past not just the rubble of the ringwall, but the debris of a second-ring mansion. I step over the bust of a dour-looking woman and pick past the shattered remains of a jewel-encrusted basin.

The rocks shift under me. A shout comes from behind—the meaning is lost between the gasps of my breath and the pounding of my heartbeat.

I glance back. Lightstruck—a crew of them, at least four—no, I count six—spot us and break into a run. We've used up whatever time the violet spectral bought.

A hand grabs my upper arm and drags me up the rubble. The back of someone's mirrorcloak comes between me and the lightstruck—a dark lock of hair curls at the nape of his neck—Dalca.

"Move!" Hadria's voice comes from above me—the hand pulling me. I get my feet under me and scamper after her, using my hands and knees to half crawl, half run up the shifting rubble.

"*Down!*" Cas calls, and we drop.

Dun-dun-BOOM. A three-part explosion. A cloud of dust rises in the air.

A dark figure becomes Dalca as he runs to me, grabs my other hand, and together, we run up the mound.

Another explosion comes from behind us.

A high-pitched whine cuts through the air. Above the dust cloud, several lines of white-gold light snap together, forming a thick stream that's so bright it leaves afterimages in my vision. It swings toward us, inching up the rubble.

"Don't stop!" Dalca shouts. My legs pump as we near the top of the rubble.

The scream of the high-pitched light beam grows louder. I glance back. Wherever it passes, clouds of steam and dust rise. The white light cuts stone, jewels, everything in its path. It'll have little problem cutting through flesh and bone.

The orange light—the spectral—reappears, swinging in an arc across the rubble, following—or perhaps guiding—the cutting light.

The ground solidifies under my feet. We've made it up the slope, into the second. We run across flat ground, sprinting through neat side streets and long gardens, stopping in the relative shelter of a covered terrace.

I fold over, catching my breath.

A waterskin is pressed into my hands. "Drink," Cas orders.

My hand shakes; water drips down my chin. Between the spectrals and the cutting lightline, the Great King definitely knows we're coming.

As my body calms, my ears pick up the sounds of the second. It's quieter—less stone-breaking and cart-rumbling than in the third. I peek around the edge of the terrace roof.

A luminous cat's cradle stretches across the sky. Thin streams of light crisscross above us and zigzag through newly widened streets, each lightline changing direction where it runs into a tower.

A thin craft speeds by on one of the lines, its golden sail billowing. I get a better look at the cupped-hands shape of the base; its nose tapers to a needle's point, and as it swings closer, something glints from the very tip. A crystal from the wilds, cut and shaped. The line of light passes through the crystal and comes out fractured—a half dozen shining lines fanning out into the golden sail, powering it.

Four lightstruck perch in the craft, two on either side so the light passes unobstructed through the middle.

"We can go through the Gavells' place," Hadria says, interrupting my thoughts. "There's a servant's entrance. Soriad—she's the youngest—she's a friend of mine. When we were kids . . . Well, her place was the best for playing hunters and seekers."

She leads us through a gate in a low wall, into a prim garden that I can only call small because I've seen the gardens of the first. A squat and gleaming second-ringer house sits with its sides almost touching the wall around it. A line of light passes above the house, and we keep in the shadow of a line of trees heavy with golden fruit as Hadria leads us. Dalca motions to stop as a lightship passes above us.

As it slips out of view, Hadria leads us to a back entrance. She messes with an ikonlock embedded in the center of the door.

"Hurry," Dalca says. "The next one is coming."

"The day her parents were married," Hadria explains as she rotates a brass disc, "and where in the sky the sun was." She moves a metal arm until it clicks into place. She presses the lock, and with a slide of bolts, the door swings open.

We pile into the narrow hallway and shut the door.

A musty smell lingers in the hall and in the wide rooms beyond. Our footfalls are cushioned by thick rugs, but the layer of dust on everything makes it unlikely that anyone is around to hear us.

We make it to the exit door. Hadria calls a halt. "There's a long line of lightships approaching. They'll spot us right away."

Dalca glances over her shoulder. "We'll wait a few minutes, see if they pass."

Minutes stretch. Cas taps his foot impatiently. I look around, take in the dusty, second-ringer splendor.

Trinkets abound on long, low tables. Things that I'm sure are precious—delicate, fanciful, expensive things of the like I'd have never seen if I hadn't left the fifth ring. Things this family hoarded and was forced to leave behind.

"I guess thieves didn't make it this far," Hadria murmurs.

"Thieves?" I say. "Who'd risk their lives for all this? It's just stuff."

"Bezzlers. Borrowers. Divviers. All sorts of little groups with cute names," Cas says. "A case came before the council some time ago. A second-ring family found their heirlooms being sold in the sixth. The seller—a bezzler—claimed he'd come by them honestly. Abandoned property, he said."

"What was the council's judgment?" I ask.

"The council dithered for ages." Cas nods at Dalca. "But Dalca decided it very neatly, I thought."

Dalca brushes it off. "Enough talk about the council."

"Cas," I say, "I thought you hated the council." Wasn't Izamal trying to get him to take his seat?

"I don't *hate* it. It's not emotional. There are too many ditherers and too few with a clear plan."

"Cas," Dalca warns. "Leave it."

"I want to hear about the case," I say. "Don't you, Hadria?"

She watches the window. "If we must."

Dalca sighs, looking at me with half-lowered lids. "The bezzler lost a member of his crew—a fourteen-year-old girl—as they were obtaining the . . . I suppose we'll call them 'goods.' She was lightstruck. She was the most skilled of his people, and without her, he had no way of continuing his work and providing for the five others under him. The family from the second had run out of food and things to sell for food long ago. The parents had turned to the farmers for work and were given jobs clearing cursed land. The father was taken by a beast a few months later. The eldest child was accepted into Wardana training by lying about his age. He was twelve when he joined. They live off his trainee's earnings." Dalca tilts his head and considers me. "Who needed those trinkets more? How would you judge, Vesper?"

"I . . ."

"It's the family's property," Hadria says. "They earned those things. Sometimes with generations of work."

"Who's to say they came by everything honestly?" Cas says. "The second wasn't always a place for the wealthy to live. There are many theories . . ."

Hadria groans, cutting him off.

"Split it between them," I say.

"True, but then what of the next bezzler?" Dalca says in an agonized voice. "Those that risk their lives to get these things—should they give up half their profit to those who don't lift a finger? And now all the second-ringers know that if they can claim ownership of something they find in the markets, they'll be given half its worth. And—what if the bezzlers conclude the cost is now too high, so no one saves these little fragments of the past from the destruction of the Great King?"

I bite my lip, fighting the urge to strangle him. "So what did you do?"

Dalca tilts his head. "What would you have done?"

I scowl at the soft and curious look in his eyes. I'm not sure. I don't like not being sure. "Let me think on it."

"While you think," Hadria says, "we might want to move. There's a gap in the lightships."

We slip out the door, crossing to a part of the outer wall that's all rubble. Hadria leaps across like a graceful goat, Dalca quick on her heels. Neither Cas nor I get credit for grace—but we make it over and into the shelter of a wall before another lightship swings by.

"There are too many lightships," I say. "It'll take too long to keep going like this. Unless you know a string of houses that'll take us to the first."

Hadria shakes her head.

Cas says. "They might not all be empty, either."

I tune them out. How far does the violet spectral's help stretch? Frustration bubbles up in me, sick and oily. I want to get to the King and finish the job. All this scampering, hiding like mice—it all feels cowardly.

"What if we take a lightship?" I ask.

They stare at me.

"We've seen quite a few empty ones. We get in one and ride it to the first."

Dalca crosses his arms. "We don't know anything about them."

"We know not to stand in the middle," I say.

Cas rolls his eyes. "I'm sure that's all the knowledge we need."

"I like it," Hadria says. "It's bold."

"I suppose it will surprise the Great King," Cas says after a pause. "After all, I figure he's expecting us to be clever."

CHAPTER 23

To move through the world the Great King has claimed, we need to understand his rules. Those are the walls of his world, as effective as any of stone. His rules separate those who haven't learnt his secrets from those who the Great King has chosen, who he has struck.

We've watched the movement of the lightships enough to know that about one out of every eight is empty. The lightstruck use long poles with mirrored ends—similar to oars—to reach for lightlines and direct the lightship in a new direction.

"Easy enough," I say.

Cas groans. "Don't say that."

Hadria raises a brow. "Superstitious?"

"He's just tightly wound," says Dalca, smiling, though his gaze is fixed above. "Look sharp now. Our ride's coming."

My thighs tense. From where we are—the roof of the semi-demolished house—it'll take one great, well-timed leap to make it onto a lightship.

One approaches. No different from the rest, except perhaps made of a wood more sun-bleached than typical. A crystal gleams upon its prow, catching a lightline and streaming it into the golden sail behind it.

"Steady now," Dalca says. He counts us down. "Three . . ."

I rise out of a crouch and ready myself.

"Two . . ."

In my peripheral vision, Cas and Hadria line up in position. Dalca's fingers brush my shoulder.

"Jump!"

I leap—for a moment weightless, fingers reaching, ignoring the three-story drop to the stone below—and fall with a thud to the deck. The ship rocks as three more thuds match mine.

The crystal rocks with the ship, swinging wildly across the lightline. The ray fueling the sail flickers, and the ship's momentum stutters.

"Get down!" Dalca presses me into a crouch, his side wedged against mine.

Hadria's knees bang into wood as she and Cas drop to the deck. We come to an intersection, and another ship crosses before us. A lightstruck deftly operates it.

I hold my breath, hoping the lightstruck won't notice the way our ship still wobbles. I meet Hadria's wide-eyed gaze through the fan of lightlines that pass through the center of the ship. Her eyes flick to the lightstruck, tracking him as he passes by. The tension drains from her face and she nods to me and Dalca.

Dalca peeks over the rim. "We're heading toward another crossing."

I peer over the edge, getting my bearings. The streets whiz by at remarkable speed—these ships are maybe even faster than Wardana cloaks. We're running parallel with the edge of the second ring, and our lightline shows no indication of leading to the first.

Ahead, another lightline crosses over ours, nearly perpendicular. I can't tell how far it goes, whether it'll take us all the way to the first—a row of proud, tall buildings shields part of the line from view—but it'll at least take us deeper into the second.

A long mirror-tipped pole is tied to the outside of the lightship. Dalca holds it steady as I undo the ties.

"Hads," he says, rolling it to her. "You're in a better position."

A clank sounds as Hadria clips the side of the ship with the hook. She tests its weight, rolling her shoulders and loosening her grip. There's something beautifully athletic in the way she adjusts her stance—and instantly I trust her to drive a lightship in a way I wouldn't trust myself.

The tip of the hook glimmers in reflected light—it's not a mirror, but a small crystal cut into the shape of a pyramid. A crystal hook to catch the lightline.

Our lightship speeds toward the crossing. Hadria extends the hook, reaching for the lightline like we've seen the lightstruck do.

It touches the golden-white beam.

The lightline bends sharply; the hook diverts a thread of light. Hadria tilts the hook, directing the light to our ship's crystal.

It swings near, a handbreadth away—and misses—the thread snaps back to the main line as Hadria's hook slips, as we pass the crossing. With a grunt of irritation, she swings the hook to the line we've passed, twisting the pole to correct the angle—but we're moving away so fast that the angle she needs keeps widening—she leans over the side, reaching, until she's more out of the ship than in it, and Cas grabs on to her belt, hauling her back.

"I almost had it," she snaps at him.

"It's fine," Dalca says soothingly. "Reset."

I clench my jaw. We're careening toward the third ring—heading backwards, undoing a half-day's progress, just like that.

Dalca asks Hadria, "Can you make the next one?"

I grit my teeth. To just sit here and watch, with nothing I can do to help . . .

Dalca holds Hadria's gaze until she nods. "I can do it."

"Good. Cas, Vesp, get low."

Cas does, though his hands hover as if he expects to need to catch Hadria again.

Dalca gives me a look.

I slouch down.

He peers over the edge. "Next crossing in ten. You know how the light moves now. Trust yourself to catch it. Five."

Hadria presses her lips into a thin, bloodless line.

"Four . . . Three . . ."

I wish I could see more than the sky and Hadria's fierce scowl. How close are we?

"Two . . ."

Hadria leans out—Cas grips her boots—I hold my breath—

The ship shudders. She's done it—a new thread of light shines into the ship's crystal. Hadria blocks the old lightline with the flat of the hook, and the ship swings in an arc, the momentum pinning me flat until we level out, and the ship hums happily along in its new direction.

Cas whoops and Hadria grins.

"Well done," I say, and she ducks her head, embarrassed.

Dalca gestures for us to quiet.

I peek my head over the rim. Through the buildings of the second, the palace shines like a beacon. Other lightlines crisscross the air between us and it. Is the Great King watching?

We speed toward the heart of the second. I keep an eye out for spectrals, but it seems like either luck or the violet spectral has chased them off. The day is warm, and the wind is sweet on my skin. We move so fast—faster even than ramblers. It would've taken me hours to cross this much of the city on foot . . . If everyone in the city had access to these, no ring would feel quite so far away—

"What's that?" Cas asks.

A line of lightships, all packed with people. Our ship is on course to catch up with them.

"Get us away from them, Hads." Dalca surveys our options. "We'll go around the other side. Take the next crossing to the left, and then we'll cross again past the Havelis' place. That'll take us to the first."

Hadria follows orders, directing the ship from lightline to lightline with growing ease. We leave the lightstruck behind without drawing attention.

When Hadria readies herself for the next crossing, I glance down at what must be the home of the Haveli family. Where Cas grew up. It's in a prime location—ringed by gardens, close to the first, but with enough distance to avoid being cast in the palace's perpetual shadow. It glitters like a jewel as the light catches on its diamond-paned, glass-studded windows, on all its gilded railings and ornaments.

It is whole, perfect—untouched by the King's rebuilding. What luck. Once the King is gone, the Havelis can continue on as if nothing happened.

Cas's voice cuts through my thoughts. "We might have a problem."

He's not looking down but behind us. A lightship—a little wider, with a larger sail—follows on our lightline.

It could be a coincidence.

"Make the crossing, Hads," Dalca says, and I follow his thinking: if the lightship follows, we'll know for sure how much trouble we're in.

Hadria hooks the next crossing in one smooth move, and our light-ship swings in an arc, leveling out. I turn back as we career past the Havelis' house.

The rider lowers a hook, and with an expert twist, their lightship makes the same crossing. Its crystal is fat and gleaming, shining a thick ray of light into its golden sail.

It gains on us.

The rider wears a uniform not unlike the Wardana one in cut. But while the Wardana wear red, the rider's is a violet-gray shade that could have once been black. Light catches on the gold trim, and there's no doubt. It's the uniform of the Regia's Guard—the last Regia's Guard, to be exact. But surely that isn't—

Cas sucks in a breath, and Dalca curses.

Ragno Haveli. The light shines upon the severe lines of his face, the pale gray of his eyes. His time in the light faded more than his clothes. His once steel-gray hair is now as pale a white as Casvian's, and honestly, they've never looked more like father and son.

There's something else, too. I can't put my finger on it. Ragno looks softer, somehow. Less perpetually disappointed. His brow is unfurrowed, his mouth unpinched.

"Get down," Dalca says. "At that distance, he'll only have seen Hadria."

Ragno calls in a deep voice as smooth as honey, "You are off pattern, child."

"I have orders," Hadria says.

"No, child. You have not read the light true." A pause. "What is that upon your head?"

Well, he was bound to notice her helm sooner or later. Hadria doesn't respond, but her arms tense. "Hold on," she mutters.

My hands scramble for purchase on the smooth wood. I grip on to the rim.

Hadria swings her hook. The ship rocks violently, nearly pitching us out. I swallow a scream as the horizon rises and my feet swing out—I hold fast, gripping tight even as the ship rights itself. Ragno hooks the same lightline, still gaining on us.

Dalca, crouching, twists a dial on his gauntlet. It shrinks in width as he draws its metal into the shape of a spear.

"Dalca—" Cas starts, fear in his eyes.

Dalca hushes him. "I'm not going to kill your father."

Cas's jaw works. "Aim for the crystal. If that shatters—that'll keep him from following us."

Hadria barks, "Brace!"

She swings the hook—I'm thrown against the side—and again—I grip the rim of the ship to keep from falling into the lightline—the ship's nose rises, and we climb. The lightline angles upward, the lightship rising as if on a ramp. The last few feet of the second ring passes below, then the ringwall, and we continue to rise higher and higher, into the first ring, toward the palace.

"Dalca—" Cas warns. Ragno is three ship lengths away and gaining.

Dalca rises, and aims. The spear flies as Ragno increases his speed. A crack splits the air as the crystal on Ragno's lightship shatters.

The shards scatter in the air, and the ray feeding the sail disappears, but Ragno doesn't so much as blink. His ship speeds toward us, carried by momentum alone. I grit my teeth and brace myself.

The impact shudders through the ship, vibrations ringing through my bones and rattling my teeth.

The ray of light running through our ship flickers. Our crystal loses its glow as we disconnect from the lightline.

We fall.

I reach for the Queen's power as the ground rushes toward me. A puff of stormbarrier is all I get—the ground is slate threaded with gold—I force the Queen's power into it, and the slate becomes thick green vines—arms come around me and turn me in midair—I open my mouth and get a mouthful of hair—

The crunch of impact.

A groan comes from under me, and the arms loosen. I push myself up. Hadria winces up at me, her mirrorshield shattered under her.

I help her to her feet. "Thanks for that."

The edges of her lips quirk in the smallest, shyest smile, and she nods.

Dalca is already standing, and Cas staggers to his feet. The scattered remnants of the ship lie at their feet, and the entire second ring spreads out behind them. We've made it—we've fallen inside the perimeter of the first ring.

The transformed vines are springy underfoot, and they curl and twist in a pattern that mimics how the gold was inlaid into the slate stone path.

A hiss of metal as Dalca unsheathes his sword. "Get back."

Ragno rises from the body of his ship. He has eyes only for Cas.

"Casvian," he says in a voice thick with emotion. "You've come home."

"Father." Cas's voice is thin and soft.

Dalca's blade trembles. "Stay back, Ragno."

Ragno keeps walking. Cas is stunned into stillness—Dalca's poised to fight, but where does it end? Is he prepared to kill Ragno—this lightstruck version of him, who seems softer, kinder than the Ragno who committed so many evils?

And how long before the Great King sends lightstruck, or spectrals, or that awful, cutting light?

Ragno smiles. "Do not presume to fight me," he says to Dalca. He holds a hand out to Cas. "Son—"

The Queen's power rises in me, showing me Ragno. In her grayscale vision, he's a figure of gray cloudsmoke. But deep within him—somewhere between his heart and his gut—a shadow curls. A desire to be invulnerable, to be the strongest. A tremulous confidence—being the strongest has kept him safe, has given him glory. But the world is changing. And under it all is a well of deep fear. For himself, for a son who chooses another path.

I pour her power into the shadow. It resists, but I feed it, drop by drop, until the shadow fills Ragno to the brim.

I blink, and my normal vision is restored.

Ragno's skin shimmers. He's become glass. Delicate. Breakable.

I lower my trembling hands. I've cursed him. It's one thing to take away a curse, to free someone—but to curse him, to make him face what he most fears . . .

Ragno's expression changes. His gaze focuses—and then his eyes widen. Stricken with horror.

He raises hands to his face and his eyes dart to and fro, searching, desperate. "What have you done!"

Cas startles at the sound of his father's voice.

"Casvian! *What have you done?*" He tries to stand, but there's a crunch and crackling—his glass body can't take such movement. "*Please—*"

Bile rises in my throat. The change in him is startling—from the confidence of a moment ago to this. I've done this to him. I've made him suffer.

No. Fury flares in my gut. What else could I have done? This is a smaller evil than letting Dalca maim him. I made this choice. No one could have made it for me. Hadria's athleticism, Dalca's knowledge of the city, Cas's ikonomancy—they all had parts to play. And now I have to face up to mine. "We need to move. He can't come after us like this, but others are surely on their way."

"Then let's go." Cas tilts his head back and pinches the bridge of his nose. "We can't waste time."

We leave him there. I don't know which is worse—the tears in Ragno's eyes that fall with a tinkling of glass on glass. Or the ones Cas blinks away when he thinks we're not looking.

"Come," Dalca says, gaze fixed on the palace. "We're almost there."

CHAPTER 24

The view from the first ring takes my breath away. To stand here, it's as though a pebble's been thrown at my feet, and the city's rings are ripples spreading across the surface of a still pond. All that happens in the first has repercussions that reach as far as the eye can see.

Despite it being night, everything is cast in a soft glow from the brightness of the Great King's lattice of light, even that which is beyond the fifth's ringwall, the gnarled trees and spires of the sixth. The sky stretches on and on, a blanket pinpricked with stars, hovering over the dizzying endlessness of the wilds. What an immense land.

In contrast to the irregular shadows of the wilds, the five rings are a picture of order. The Great King's towers are so perfectly, symmetrically spaced—and the streets that lead to them have been straightened, crooked alleys broadened into smooth arcs—from a bird's perspective, it must look like—

My heart stops.

The others keep on walking; one set of footsteps stops beside me. Dalca's voice is a whisper: "Vesper."

All I can say is, "Look." There, in the curving lines of the streets below, in the intersections of alleys, in the new lines of the city sculpted by the Great King and the lightstruck . . . I thought their destruction senseless. Demolishing parts of buildings, leaving the rest standing and uninhabitable.

But now I see it. It's all part of one idea. A pattern.

Cas and Hadria come close. "Cas," I say. "What do you see?"

He tears his gaze from the small figure of Ragno sitting at the edge of the ringwall. With each blink he comes back to himself. His brows knit, and he draws in a sudden breath. "Is that—"

"No." A slow-moving horror rearranges Dalca's features as he sees it. "No. Impossible."

"Incredible," Cas says. "We never saw it."

Hadria crosses her arms, looking between us. "What is it? What's happening?"

"It's an ikon," I say. "A city-wide ikon. They're carving it into the streets, into houses, across rings . . ."

"Fine," Hadria says. "What does it do?"

It's the obvious question. Pa taught me a little, but I don't know nearly enough to understand all the pieces of this ikon—it's not just the streets, but every courtyard, every fountain indicates some part of the whole. I'd need to be a master ikonomancer to understand this. I look to Cas.

"I can't—I'd have to study it." He points at a section of the third, between the white and black roads. "This structure here means it has something to do with time. But look at the lightships—the pattern of lightlines—it's a moving ikon."

A vision of Pa in his ikonomancer's chambers, showing me the life-ikon in a drop of blood. Longing hits me like a punch to the gut.

"It doesn't matter," I say to quell the breathless, fluttering panic in my chest. "It's not complete."

Hadria nods, sharp and impatient. "We have to get out of the open." She turns toward the palace.

I step after her. The ikon won't be completed if we take care of the Great King here and now. There's silence behind me. Dalca and Cas stare out at the city, frozen.

"Dalca," I say.

He turns his stricken eyes to me. "I never noticed. He built it right out in the open. All I had to do was look."

"This is why he went after the cloaks," I say. "So you wouldn't discover what he was up to. It's not a failing—it's his plan."

Dalca doesn't seem to take this as relief. "I wouldn't have noticed . . . I'd stopped flying . . ."

"Snap out of it." I rap on the armor over his chest with my knuckles. "I need you to focus. You too," I say to Cas.

"We have to move," Hadria urges. "The sky is lightening."

The palace. The gleaming, glittering beacon, the crown upon our city, a symbol of all that never was meant for me and mine. I've changed since I was last here—but so has the palace.

In my memories, it stands like tongues of flame, frozen and gilded. Turrets here and there, beautiful cupolas, towers capped with sinuous domes—a concentration of beauty, to be sure, but also one of eccentricity, of irregularity, of moneyed chaos.

The palace has since been remade. From our angle, the outer palace wall conceals all within it. And gone are the balconies, the archways leading to gardens, the towers studded at irregular intervals—all that has been smoothed over with stone and plaster, as if they never existed at all.

What remains is a curved wall of smooth stone. We circle it, but there's nothing but clean, immaculate wall all the way around. If we still had thousand-and-one-feather cloaks and could see the palace from above, I'm sure it would be a perfect circle, as perfect as any needed for an ikon.

In there is the vessel. Above our heads, lightlines streak over the outer palace wall, heading somewhere inside. They remind me of spokes on a wheel—they come from the towers around the second's ringwall and from other places within the second, and the space between them narrows as they near the palace, until above us is more light than sky.

Wherever the lightlines meet will be the Great King's vessel—the source of the light and the source of his power.

I brush up my courage. We just have to follow the light inside—into what once was a palace, and now looks rather more like a fortress.

"He's changed everything," Dalca says. His wide-eyed fear is visible even through the gleam of his helm.

"Maybe the interior will be as it was," Hadria says without a hint of optimism.

Only one set of doors remains. The main set, immense and gilded.

Hadria says something about scaling the wall; Dalca counters with melting a section of stone.

I tune it all out, reaching for the Great Queen. Maybe I can transform a section of wall . . .

No, the Great Queen whispers in me. *No sneaking, not here, not now. I can feel him. He can feel me. Come now, child. We can face him.*

"—there won't be another way in." Cas's voice breaks through my thoughts. "He would never need one. We'll have to face it, like we faced the Storm."

I take a breath. I ended the Storm. I can face this. My feet move before my mind does, taking me to the threshold of the grand doors.

Even the handles are immense and made of gold. They're warm under my fingers, against my palm.

He will face us, the Great Queen thunders.

I turn the handles and pull.

On well-oiled hinges, the doors swing open silently, invitingly. A bright light shines from within, and I shield my eyes.

The Great Queen rumbles, *Do not fear.*

I take a step.

"Vesper!" Dalca shouts.

Running footsteps. Dalca and the others run after me, their bodies lit brightly, blindingly. The door slams shut, raising a gust of wind that urges us forward.

"Vesper," Dalca says urgently from beside me. "Are you—"

"I'm fine." I meet his eyes—his blue eyes, unobstructed by a mirrorhelm. "Where's your armor?"

He touches his face. "I can feel it. It's there, but I can't see it. I can't see yours, either."

My arms are clothed in black-and-violet leathers—the uniform of my Regia's Guard. Hadria wears the same, but Dalca and Cas are in Wardana reds.

The four of us exchange looks. "A trick of the light," Cas says.

"Let's keep going," I say, squinting down the brightly lit passage.

The light fades, as if a cloud has come between us and the sun. The hall comes into clarity. It's a short, straight hall, some twenty paces deep, with no windows and no other exits, save the way we came and the archway before us.

I take a step.

A great billow of dust rises, as if I've disturbed it—but it's not dust. It's a glittering, gleaming billow of pinpricks of violet light. They float back downward, settling as if on an invisible man, outlining curling hair and broad shoulders, long eyelashes and pleased lips.

The violet spectral sweeps into a regal bow. "The Great King is honored that you would visit. Please, come in."

I smooth away my frown. Of course the Great King knows we're here—we knew it would be so the minute the emerald spectral spotted us. I suppose some part of me was hoping we'd get wildly lucky and still catch the Great King off guard.

I square my shoulders. "Spectral—"

Dalca snarls. "This isn't a social call."

The spectral glances over my shoulder at Dalca. "Is it not?"

I shoot Dalca a quelling look. His hair's almost standing on end, his hands balled into fists, ready to fight a phantom. None of Dalca's princely charms are on display.

Our footsteps ring out on the stone floor as we cross the hall. The light brightens again; from beyond the arch comes the golden glow of the lightlines, tinged with the soft pink of dawn.

My nails bite into my palms. I hold my breath as I step through the arch.

Under an immense glass dome is a little world. In the center is our object: a tall tower.

If we just had a single thousand-and-one-feather cloak, we could fly up to the glass panes of the dome overhead, fly over everything in our way . . . I'd wager that, from above, we'd see a series of concentric circles. Not unlike the rings of the city.

First is the outer ring; a colonnade that curves around the entirety of the circular courtyard. The back wall of the colonnade, which spreads out on either side of the arch we entered through, is covered in a vast and detailed mural that gives an impression of history and of immense, terrible beauty. When I step closer, I find it's not paint—it's a mosaic of tiny stones and tile, made painstakingly.

The archway we stand under appears to be the only way in or out.

"What is this place?" Cas asks.

"There's nothing of the palace left," Dalca says. "Not one inch. All this is the King's work."

A ring of columns separates the outer ring from the next.

The middle ring: a garden. I ache to see it from above. Pathways lead into the garden, but are soon obscured from view by hedges and carefully placed trees. It's a maze.

Rising from the heart of the maze is the inner ring: a tower. It's tall and thin, rising up into the center of the lightlines. The top is too bright to look at directly, even with my helm—I get a vague impression of a ball of light at the top. That'll be where the vessel is.

The tower juts out from a wide base, like an upside-down hammer. Right in the center of the base are a pair of ornately carved black doors, but there are no other windows or openings.

"We make for those black doors," I murmur as low as I can to Dalca.

"Yes," says the violet spectral, his voice so close to my ear that I startle. "In the tower is where you'll find the Great King."

I snap my mouth shut. The King may be expecting us, but even he can't know what we intend. Dalca gives me a small nod, and I square my shoulders and stride forward.

The hedge rustles, as if troubled by an unseen wind. The smooth stone pathway takes us through the hedge wall, through a green arch.

A sweet and heady aroma wraps around me; the air is fragranced with a thousand blooms, but underneath is a harsh note of sunbaked clay and something bitter and medicinal.

The pathway spirals through the low, petite garden. Nothing grows higher than my chest. Each miniature tree has great personality; some look like they're bowing, others like they're gesturing us deeper into the gardens. Many are ornamented with tiny fruit that glimmer like jewels.

Some, a tad taller than their neighbors, have arcing branches that terminate in tiny twinkling ikonlights—to mark the way, perhaps. A squat hedge hems us in, keeping us on the prescribed path.

Out of the corner of my eye, I catch flashes of violet light, but the spectral stays incorporeal. Even when the path branches and forks, he doesn't guide us one way or another. So even if the King is expecting us, he's not expecting us to be fast.

I say as much to the others.

Dalca murmurs, "There's no point going fast, not if he knows we're here. We can take our time. Be smart and careful."

Hadria nods, but her jaw is tense, her gaze locked on the distance. I can guess the nature of her worry. There's been no trace of Toran.

We pick our way through many forks in the path, angling ourselves toward the tower, and only twice meet dead ends.

The lightlines act as guides when the hedges grow so tall that we lose sight of the tower—they gleam overhead, through the glass panes of the domed ceiling. They're strangely beautiful, so constant and so pure a glow—my foot catches on something, and I lose my balance. Hadria steadies me. "Sorry," I say. "I'll keep my eyes on the ground."

She points her chin at what tripped me. A brutish sapling juts from the ground. It's shaped so oddly; a block with a sloping top. Like a house. A tiny, sweet little house.

"There are more," Hadria says.

Plants shaped like buildings are arranged in curving rows, in a pattern that scratches at the back of my mind.

Dalca sucks in a breath. "It's the city."

The buildings, the pathways—the garden is laid out in five

concentric rings. The city but . . . neatened. A model; a prototype.

"This could be the Great King's plan. The complete ikon," I say. "Cas, can you make it out?"

A faraway look comes over him as he walks through the miniature city. We follow him as he goes deeper, as he doubles back and considers. Dalca and Hadria communicate in glances, and they each take up guard on either side of me and Cas.

Violet sparks curl beside me, and the spectral appears.

Cas stands still for several long moments.

Dalca steps close. "Cas."

Cas drags his gaze from the gardens. "A single day. That's what the Great King wants to give them all. A day that repeats—every person has a role, an unchanging part to play. It's a loop—"

"A perfect loop," the violet spectral says. "A perfect day."

A perfect day? What would that even look like? I can almost see it . . . a day on repeat, where only wonderful things happen. Amma loved predictable days, when everyone was well-fed and happy, when she could tuck everyone in at night and count on them still being in their beds come morning. No stormbeast attacks, no new tragedies . . . And yet, to have no choice . . .

"It's a trap," I say. "A cage."

"Paradise," the spectral counters. "All the greatest and noblest desires of our people, fulfilled."

"Vesper." Dalca's eyes glitter, his voice pitched low. "This is more than we prepared for. Perhaps . . . we need to turn back. Before we're caught in a trap of our own."

The tower is right before us. One more turn, and we're there. I'm not immune to his fear. I understand it, I understand not wanting to face the King. To run away with the landtreaders. But I'm more afraid of who I'll become if I give in to it. That, if I run away once, I'll never stop.

"Turn back if you want," I say. "But I'm going ahead."

After a moment's hesitation, their footsteps echo mine. All the way to the squat cylindrical building that encircles the tower, to the set of black doors.

My fingers rest on the doorknobs. A shiver runs up my spine.

Cas's face grows pinched; his hand weighs the pouch at his side. My fingers brush against my own padded bag, where three spheres nestle at my hip. Dalca and Hadria have matching pouches, with five explosives apiece—all we need is for a single one to come into contact with the vessel. I have fewer, as we know the Great King will come for the Great Queen. My job is to keep him occupied long enough so the others . . .

My skin prickles as the Queen's mark rises across my body. I take a deep breath and push them open.

Black everywhere—black stone floor, black stone walls that disappear into shadow. But nothing is dark; all the stone is polished to a mirror shine, and ikonlights gleam from sconces, casting glimmers that are doubled, trebled, so much so that we could be standing in the night sky, surrounded by fiery stars.

There are no defenses, no alarms. Just a thick silence, broken only by the tinny tread of our footsteps. I catch my reflection's gaze in the floor—I glance away and catch her eyes in the wall. The hairs on the back of my neck rise. Someone is watching me, and I fear it's the Great King.

Through the gleaming, starry darkness are two double doors. Black, outlined with the thinnest possible gold inlays. They seem to hover in the dead center of the room—but no. There's another tower within this one. It's barely visible as it's made out of the same black stone.

The tall, thin structure pierces the ceiling. I make a circle around it. There are six sets of doors, all identical. I don't know why there are six—they must lead to the same small space, inside the tower. Hopefully to stairs that will lead us up.

"Once we go through those doors . . ." I draw a breath and let it out. "The vessel will be at the top."

Dalca and Cas pull mirrorshields from their gauntlets. Hadria, having lost her shield in the lightship crash—and with her gauntlet diminished accordingly—draws her circular blades.

Dalca's gaze meets mine. Our hundredfold reflections follow suit. His voice rings in the silence. "Let's get this done."

The door handles are warm to the touch.

I draw in a breath. My heartbeat quickens, echoing the rising pulse of the Queen's power as it fills me to the brim.

With a soft click, the handles turn. The doors rumble open.

Light and heat pours through the crack—a blast like staring into the sun.

There's no turning back now.

I step into the light.

Sparks dance across my vision—I can't see beyond them. I raise my arm to shield my face—*ridiculous, as if that'll protect me*—my muscles taut as a heartbeat passes, and then another. Nothing attacks.

I squint through my fingers. The sparks fade, leaving only a drowsy green veil.

"What is this?" Dalca's voice comes from behind me.

My heart plummets. There should be stairs—the inside of the

tower—a way to the vessel—

But there's no crystal. No Great King.

Just an awfully familiar hall. Gold-latticed stone below, the dia-mond-paned ceiling above. In the distance, an archway haloed in the white-gold glow of lightlines, colored with just a hint of the pink of dawn.

Pinpricks of violet light fall in a spiral; the spectral arrives. "The Great King is honored that you would visit. Please, come in."

What is this? My skin feels too small, and my mouth dries. Dalca was right. *This is no mission—this is a trap.*

My back hits a body—Dalca.

"We have to go back," he says.

He opens the door—I run through after him. Back into the night-sky room with the black stone walls. We run into Casvian and Hadria, both confused, asking questions I have no answer to. I try to find words, but terror clamps my throat shut. Their expressions grow grim, and they keep close.

I run across the polished black floors, retracing our steps to the doors in the other wall. I shove the doors open—the scent of blossoms and sun-kissed earth washes over me. The glass dome, the miniature trees. My legs pump as I make my way through the garden path, back past the columns and the mosaic wall, through the hallway, to the main doors.

Dalca's footsteps echo mine.

The door handles are warm. *Just through these doors will be the city. The city.* I whisper it like a prayer.

I twist the handles and push the doors open.

Polished black stone, twinkling ikonlights. The night-sky room.

Ice runs through my veins, down my throat, down my legs. *This should have let out into the first ring. How can I be in this room again? How can this be possible?*

The doors behind me bang open. Cas, Dalca, Hadria. They stop and stare, their thoughts bare on their faces as the same horrible understanding dawns on them.

"A loop," Cas says. "A loop of space. Just like how he intends to turn the city into a loop of time."

I shut my eyes, cover them with my palms. I can't panic. I can't. After all—what does this really change? We came to stop the King. So be it, if he has the upper hand for now. I drop my hands. "This doesn't change our mission."

"Of course it does," Dalca says. "We don't know anything. Is this even the same room we were in? Or is it another, identical space?" He kneels to make some mark on the floor.

I wrap my arms around myself. "We're not trapped. This is—this is how it should be. Remember: *The only way out is through.* So let's do this."

Dalca grips my shoulder. "Your father wrote that about the Storm, not—"

I jerk my shoulder away. "The Storm was the Queen's trap. This is the King's. She had a thousand years to get hers right, and he had what, three? We can handle this."

Hadria looks to Dalca, but Cas smiles at me. It's a small, quiet smile with no humor in it, just understanding. He says, "As long as I'm able, I'll follow you."

Dalca sighs.

I meet his gaze. Or I try to, but my eyes go to the scar lines running across his skin, arcing across his cheekbones. I find my voice. "If the King wants us to play a game, fine. We'll play it. Because as I see it, we either fight our way out and run home to the landtreaders—and give up on our home and everyone we lost—or we fight our way through. We may yet fail, but I don't intend to quit. Not until we face him."

Dalca's lips are pressed shut, but his eyes ask a question. His eyes and his scars, and the bandages peeking through the collar of his shirt. They all ask, *What if he beats us?*

There's a flicker of doubt in all of their eyes.

They've followed me so far—they've followed Vesper—but that's not enough. Not anymore. They need something else. The hero. The Stormender.

I search for her within me, but there's no such thing. I've never really been the Stormender. The dark, horrible thing I've never been able to admit, not even to myself: there's only ever been me.

CHAPTER 25

My reflection stares back at me from the polished black doors. I step closer. Gilded designs of supreme delicacy curl across the stone; each whorl is made of gold thread that's as thin as a strand of hair, that must've been inlaid into the black stone by the gentlest of hammers.

I follow the golden curls to the top of the doors, where they melt into words: *I must, for none else can.*

I straighten up. This is interesting.

In the Storm, the Great Queen made us walk through our greatest fears. She made us meet ourselves—all the dark, awful parts that we hid from ourselves and everyone else.

The Great King's trap . . . There must be something behind it. And the first clue is these words.

Because otherwise, the structure of the palace is well defined. There's one way in—through the hall, through the garden maze, into the tower. We either choose to go on, or not.

The only real choice is what's before me: the black doors.

There are six pairs of doors, one on each side of the hexagonal tower.

I inspect them. Each set is identical—except for the words set into stone above them. Cas comes to stand by me, and Dalca follows soon after.

All is but an illusion, says one. And another: *Life is something to be overcome.*

The inscriptions . . . "We have to pick the right one," I say. "But which?"

Dalca opens his mouth, but then seems to think better. "Your choice."

We've circled back around to: *I must, for none else can.* There's something about it that rings true.

The golden handle is warm against my palm. I pull it open and step into the blinding light, hearing the others right behind me.

I blink through the sparks dancing in my vision and take in, once again, the palace's entrance hall. Something—some part of the architecture seems a little different—

In my peripheral vision comes a violet shimmering. Flecks of light sweep into a spiral, and the violet spectral arrives.

He sweeps into a bow. "The Great King is honored that you would visit. Please, come in."

Is it my imagination, or is his smile a little wry this time around?

"Keep an eye out," I say to the others. "There must be something— some hint as to how we can defeat this."

Silence answers, and then comes a sniffle. I glance over my shoulder and stop dead.

In place of my towering, intimidating companions—for I'll admit they're all warriors with warriors' builds, even Cas—are instead children of such short stature that their heads come up to my thigh.

A scowling one with a bird's nest of too-long black curls that fall into his blue eyes. That'll be Dalca. He glowers at me, with great red spots in his chubby cheeks.

A serious-looking little girl with mournful eyes. Hadria sniffles. *"Ife rosth Ma."*

"Sorry?" I say, baffled.

Fat tears roll down her cheeks, and she scrubs them away, scowling. *"Ma. I wan' Ma."*

I've lost Ma. I want Ma. My heart breaks. Oh, Hadria.

A tiny hand slips into mine. I startle and jump back. Cas. His white hair tufts up from his head in spikes, like an angry cloud. He inches close and tries for my hand again. I tug it free.

He latches on to my leg instead.

"We have to turn back. Right?" I ask. "Perhaps we need to go through another door . . ."

None of them have answers for me. Of course they wouldn't. They're children. The door we walked through . . . *I must, for none else can.*

It's a test. The King has made it so I must decide alone.

It must be an illusion—but does that mean I must break them out of it? Remind them of being adults? How?

This is a ridiculous test. It's—it's demeaning. I was ready to face monsters, not this.

Not Hadria's tiny, muffled weeping.

"Regias don't cry, you know," comes a voice with Dalca's imperial inflection, in a far higher pitch than normal.

Hadria kicks his shin. Dalca yelps, glowering harder.

This is an illusion. Which means . . . I have to keep moving forward. Just like in the Storm.

"You're going to follow me," I say. "I know where we're going."

Dalca nods seriously and follows along. Hadria takes my hand.

A laugh hangs in the gilded air of the hall, but the violet spectral has disappeared.

I march them through the arch, into the glass-domed space. Something is different—did the columns always depict crowned figures, with dozens of people kneeling before them? I can't remember.

I glance back at the mosaic wall—

Hadria's tiny hand slips out of mine and she takes off.

I bite back a curse and hurry after her, limping along with Cas still clinging to my leg.

Hadria runs through the colonnade—she really shouldn't be so fast on those tiny legs—and disappears past the garden's hedge wall.

"Ma!" she shrieks, her voice coming from the garden maze.

The hedges rustle as I step through the neatly trimmed opening. I call, "Hadria!"

There's no answer.

Dalca soldiers on grimly at my side, and Cas sings a nonsense song to my knee—something familiar, something I remember him humming—as we make our way through the layers of the maze.

I turn the corner and—

A woman in blue, sitting on a stone bench. Sapphire blue light, in large particles that move so very slowly, like ash in a dying breeze. Her face is illuminated almost wholly, save for cracks between the particles, particles that shift as she turns to look at me.

It's a blow to the gut. Those sharp patrician features, so like her son's. The last Regia, Dalca's mother, a spectral.

Dalca gasps and runs into her arms—phantom arms that he passes right through. He recovers and perches up on the bench beside her.

Astonishment has stolen my voice and stilled my limbs. I don't move—I can't move—even as Cas muffles a scream and breaks free, darting past the miniature trees and disappearing into the green. I drag my attention back to the Regia—I'll find Cas and Hadria, but Dalca's now the one in danger.

"I thought you were free, my child," the spectral Regia murmurs to Dalca, her immaterial hands hovering over his curls.

She's younger than when I saw her last, or maybe it just appears that way because she's healthy, without the toll of holding the Great King within her. Her cheekbones are still high and sharp, her eyes still piercing, even without the force of a god behind them.

My feet are rooted to the spot. "Dalca. Come here."

The light of her transparent body engulfs Dalca—he meets my gaze through her.

"You." The spectral Regia rises, her light passing over Dalca. Her eyes are fixed on me.

I reach for him. "Dalca, please."

The Regia smiles at him. "He can stay with me, if he so wishes."

"That's not what he wants."

"Are you so ready to decide for him?"

"If you'd gotten your way," I say, "he would be dead."

"You think me cruel. I meant to spare him from the fate of being a vessel," the Regia counters, with no remorse at all. "I meant to ensure he was spared a life of pain."

Her calm righteousness sends fire burning through my veins. "Spared? He hasn't been spared pain. He tried to put the mark on. Twice. Just about killed himself trying. Everything that he does, he does because he can't see himself as anything other than the last in a long line of Illusoras. You're the problem—"

Tiny fists batter my knees. Dalca. He lets out a wild shriek, punctuated by scattered words. *"Don't—yell—at—Mother!"*

For Storm's sake.

Dalca continues to howl as I pick him up and toss him over my shoulder. His knees thump my sternum, and he yanks at my hair.

"You don't know what's best for him." Dalca's mother reaches out a fragile hand, as if she'd take him.

"I never said I did," I growl, and make for the path. If she follows me, I'll deal with it.

Her voice is sharp. "You don't care for him."

My nails bite into my palms. "We're allies."

The Regia's voice is soft. "He loves you."

"This isn't about anything as small as that, Regia."

"Small? Are you so deluded? Can you not see what is before your very eyes?"

Her words hit their mark. I'm not lightstruck. "I see perfectly. You never stood up to the Great King. You never could. When you finally had a chance to choose for yourself, you chose to abdicate your responsibility."

"You have judged me a failure at something you have not tried. And so you think I have nothing to offer you. And so be it. I will say only this—for my son's sake, not yours—that you have no idea what's happening around you. Every step you take deeper into this place, you let the Great King deeper into your mind."

My rage cools. She's right—she has knowledge that I need. "If you want to help Dalca, tell me how to defeat the King. Tell me the trick to this trap."

"The trick is knowing what you believe. It is knowing who you are. It is seeing clearly."

My mouth goes sour. She's speaking in riddles, even now.

"Dalca," I say to his squirming behind. "I'm putting you down now."

He stills and lets me put him on his feet. I crouch so we're eye level. "You don't remember, but we came here on a mission. We need to keep going. Will you come with me?"

He looks back at his mother. She nods at him. "I'm going to be Regia," Dalca tells me.

He takes my hand.

"Take care of him," the Regia says. She melts into glimmering flecks of blue light, and, like ash rising on an updraft, she vanishes.

Dalca blinks up at me, all innocence. My stomach sinks with guilt.

"Let's go," I say. "Let's find Cas."

We set off in the direction Cas ran. A singsong voice, not exactly in tune, carries on the air. It grows louder as we near a gathering of three trees with pale fruit, their branches braided in a canopy. Cas is tucked underneath, in the hollow made by their roots. He sketches at the ground with a stick, singing his nonsense song. If what's coming from his mouth are words, they're none that I know.

"Cas?" I kneel and reach out a hand as Dalca peers over my shoulder.

Cas looks at me with wide, wet eyes. "You shan't like it."

"What won't I like?"

He throws himself into my arms, his tears wetting my neck. "I want to tell you, but it's a secret."

A chill runs down my spine. "What's a secret?"

"You'll know soon. And you won't like me anymore."

"Cas, you mustn't cry," Dalca says, patting him on the head in a princely manner. In an aside to me, he whispers, "He doesn't want to be a Regia's Guard."

My shoulders relax. If it's about that . . . I pick Cas up, settle him on my waist, and grip Dalca's hand. "We can deal with your childhood miseries later, boys. Let's find Hadria."

Dalca fixes his gaze forward and nods.

"Hadria?" I call.

From far away, in the direction of the black doors at the tower's base, comes Hadria's shout. "Ma!"

I hurry, Dalca's little legs running to keep pace.

We come out of the garden just as the black doors shut. I cross the distance to the tower base, flinging the doors open.

Dalca runs in, nearly tripping me up. My footfalls echo in the night-sky room.

But Hadria is gone. The six doors show no sign of being opened. None are ajar, none bear handprints. Everything is the same, except the inscriptions. The one that felt right last time, the one that began with *I must*, is gone.

Six new inscriptions, six identical doors.

I murmur to myself, "Which one did she go through?"

Cas points with a chubby finger. To a door with a sign that reads *Mine life is but a cross section of the unending.*

"How do you know?" I ask him.

He blinks at me with his big pale eyes.

"Cas is very smart," Dalca informs me.

"Right." I set Cas down to twist the handles. Light pours through the widening crack between the doors. A small hand slips into mine.

Together, we step into it.

I blink through the fading sparks in my vision. The golden walls tell me we're once again in what's becoming my least favorite of all hallways.

I'm still holding a hand. I freeze, too afraid to look at who it belongs to. If Cas and Dalca are still children . . .

The hand squeezes mine. It's not child-sized, at least—and it leads to a Wardana gauntlet, and up to mirrored armor, to a bandaged neck, up to Dalca's face—his usual face, scarred and weary and so welcome a sight I could kiss him.

He exhales, looking me over just as urgently. "Thank the stars."

"Well, that was fun," Cas says, stepping up next to me. "You lot make the worst children."

I glance past him. Where's Hadria?

Dalca takes a few steps down the hall, his brows knitting.

I glance at Cas. "Are you sure you saw Hadria go through this door?"

Cas's eyebrows inch up his forehead. "*You* told me Hadria went through this door."

What Cas said—*you lot make the worst children*—catches up to me. "I wasn't a child. You were children."

Dalca frowns, his gaze growing distant. "We all had different experiences. For me, you three were children. Hadria ran off. And Cas told me she went through this door."

"She could be further ahead," I say.

Dalca glances back at the door. "Or she could be behind another door."

Silence stretches between us, thick with all the fears we're not voicing.

"I agree with Vesper," Cas says. "Hadria might be just up ahead."

"But why wouldn't she wait—" Dalca cuts himself off as Cas takes another step toward the arch at the end of the hall.

I see what Dalca must've seen—a shimmering of violet light. The spectral appears as usual—but something catches my eye, something different about the way his flecks of light move, almost a pattern—and he dips into his usual bow. "The Great King is honored that you would visit. Please, come in."

There's no wry smile this time, but the expression in his eyes is soft. Doubt creeps into me from every side, like a shadow in my peripheral vision. The last loop—that was a test, wasn't it? Did I fail?

"Spectral . . ." I say.

"You won't call me anything else, will you?" he asks.

I ignore that. "Where is the King?"

He gestures. "He's within the heart of the palace. You're nearly there."

Nearly there. My skin prickles. "And one of our number—Hadria—did she come this way?"

He cocks his head, as if listening to something only he can hear. "She's further ahead."

Dalca and Cas meet my gaze. "We should go on," I say. But even I can hear a little tremor of doubt in my voice.

Cas raises his pointy chin at the spectral. "And how much further do we need to go? Can you give us nothing else?"

The spectral takes a step toward him, even as his violet light dissipates, like rain in reverse. "I ask you to put your faith in him. To trust that the King wants a better world, just as you do."

The spectral disappears.

Dalca's gauntlet brushes my arm. "I'm with you."

I bite my lip and take a step. Each step feels like a choice—as though any one of them could be a mistake, as though any one of the tiles under my feet could disappear and plunge us all into horror.

I tear my focus from the floor. Something else feels different. I don't remember the hall being quite this immense. The ceiling is so high it's a blur of distant detailing.

The floors are incredibly detailed. Gold as thin as a strand of hair, in dizzying, overlapping designs, inlaid into marble slab. I hesitate to put my foot down upon it. How long would it have taken to do all this? Could any one person finish this entire floor in a single lifetime? If not . . . how could anyone commit themselves to spending their life crafting one fraction of the floor of this hall? How could anyone commit to something they couldn't see finished?

The palace always seemed a riot of extravagance. Artistry for the sake of it, layers of astounding craftsmanship laid on top of each other until nothing could be appreciated; chaos with no style or meaning other than indulgence. But now . . . the lines of gold mimic the light from the archway, drawing us forward, and it feels as though all this magnificence has been put in an order of some sort. But why? What for?

We follow the dawn light out—and find ourselves in the colonnade. The same exact layout as before—but it's like seeing the original reflected in a rippling pond. The details have all changed. Each door we walk through must show us a slightly different version of this place.

The door that led to the Regia, Dalca's mother . . . It said *I must, for none else can.* And this last one said *Mine life is but a cross section of the unending.*

What are they? Ideas? Thoughts?

The columns are carved with scenes, with different iterations of the city and its rings, each with a band of figures at its base. Figures of men and women bulging with muscle, others of slighter proportions, some of every kind of person—each carved in a pose as if they're holding up the column by sheer might of will.

Each face is rendered so carefully, so beautifully, that I half expect to recognize some of them.

"Vesper." Dalca stands with his back to me, gazing up at the curving mosaic wall that encloses the gardens and the tower. I didn't get a good look at it in the last loop.

It is so detailed, the tile shards so small, that from a few paces away, it looks near as real as life. Dalca taps one of the figures.

A girl asleep. A girl who looks rather a lot like me. Or, to be fair, like Hadria.

But the next scene—the same girl standing atop a watchtower, facing a being haloed in wavy rays of light—makes clear that this is not Hadria's story. It's mine. It begins at the moment I returned, when I awoke, and continues on . . . to her looking at a mosaic of herself. This moment.

Is this a test? Where's the fight?

"Let's keep going," I say.

We enter the garden. The pathway has changed, and so has the miniature version of the city. A set of tiny trees grows in a ring with a single watchtower, like the Ven. Several paces away is the Arvegna arena. Only the third ring is depicted here.

The miniature trees around us have green leaves tinged with yellow, and the deeper we get into the third, the leaves shift from yellow to orange to a dark, burnt red. There's no sign of Hadria.

The path narrows. A straight shot to the black doors.

A flash of light blocks the way. A dusting of yellow-gold light, fine as sand, forming the figure of a petite woman.

She meets me head-on. "Do you know who I am?"

No. She has wide-set eyes that look surprisingly sweet in an otherwise garrulous face. Her hair is thick, falling in orderly curls—half is pulled back in two ropes at her crown, giving her a regal air.

No, I've never seen this woman. I'd remember if I had.

But the Great Queen shifts in me, with something of a guilty demeanor.

"Ah." The yellow spectral gives me a knowing look. "She recognizes me, does she?"

"Who are you?"

"I am the King's chosen vessel. And he whom I loved was the Queen's."

A spark of remembering. In the Ven . . . a dream. The Great Queen showed me a vision of two perfect vessels, the best of all vessels, who gave the city true peace. "I know of you."

The spectral looms closer. "Pray tell, what story did the Queen tell?"

"She said you were what vessels should have been. Should always be. That you brought about paradise."

"Paradise? Perhaps it was so. We had a glorious peace . . . a short peace. He was taken from me. And the war began again."

"That's why I'm here. To end the war."

"You?" Her face twists. "You say you come to end the war—and yet you come with an intent to fight."

She flickers. Every time I blink, she closes the distance between us.

I draw the Queen's power, let stormcloud curl around my fingers.

Her eyes gleam, her face a snarl. "How could the Queen have chosen you? You are nothing like him."

Her words cut into me—I didn't think they would, for who is she to me? But having it confirmed that I don't measure up to the Queen's greatest vessel, her perfect vessel—it hurts, even though I already know it was pure chance that the Queen chose me—

I can't measure up, especially if paradise is two vessels ruling together—two vessels in love—

I throw up a barrier a split second before the spectral flings her arm out, light flying from her fingers like spears. They hit the stormbarrier with hisses of impact, like hot metal submerged in cold water.

I spare a glance for Cas and Dalca—they'd spread out the minute the spectral arrived. Cas has his shield up, and Dalca reaches into the pouch at his waist for one of the ikon explosives.

Not ten paces behind the spectral are the black double doors that lead into the tower's base.

I meet Dalca's eyes, and understanding passes between us—Dalca flings an ikon explosive at the spectral's feet—

A crack splits the air—a gust rushes toward us, and I fling my arms up—a low boom echoes, and the glass panes of the dome above rattle in their frames.

Smoke fills the air. Enough to give us cover. The spectral can't cast her light so easily—the smoke thickens and thins unpredictably, pulling her wide.

We run for it. I fling the tower doors open, and a hand on my back pushes me through, into the night-sky room. Dalca steps in after me, and Cas follows him. They slam the doors shut, Dalca shoving with his shoulder as Cas scrawls a locking ikon across the handles.

I catch my breath. Inside, the tower is the same. Black, gleaming floors. A thin tower in the center. Six doors. I move toward them, my steps echoing, my blood rushing in my ears.

The inscriptions have changed again. One says *There is a plan.*

Another: *There is neither point nor purpose.*

They *are* thoughts. Big thoughts. The kind of thoughts that, once they've wormed their way into your head, give birth to a thousand other smaller thoughts. That shape your mind, that shape your world.

We've been picking thoughts . . . If we pick the right thoughts, will this labyrinth let us through to the King?

A string of thoughts . . . a labyrinth in layers.

My sides warm as Dalca and Cas join me, one on either side.

I share my idea with the others, and add on, "This has to end somewhere."

"If it's a labyrinth," Cas says, "perhaps we had to pick the right door the first time."

Dalca shakes his head. "I fear we've underestimated the King. He's set the rules and picked the battlefield; we cannot win."

Cas bites the pad of his thumb. "Maybe we don't have to win . . ."

A moment of expectant silence. I prompt: "What do you mean?"

He startles. "The vessel . . . We mean to destroy it, but the true plan is for Vesper to meet the King. For the Great Queen to meet him."

An ache starts in the back of my head. I can't quite follow him. "The vessel has to be destroyed. He's too powerful with it. We've got to go ahead."

Cas gives his head a little shake, as if tossing a stray thought. "Yes, yes, you're right."

"There's no point going ahead," Dalca snaps.

Cas and I lock eyes.

Dalca runs a hand through his hair. "I've lived with the King, when he was in my mother's body. And when I tried . . . He was in my mind those few brief moments. His wrath . . . Ikons are all that are keeping me standing. I gave everything I had for the goal of ending the Great King's reign. I want, desperately, to see him defeated." He takes a breath—it costs him something to meet my eyes. "But the other thing that matters to me, very much, is that I protect you. And right now I'm trying to serve both things. If we keep going . . . there's a slim chance we can still defeat the King, but a far greater chance that I won't be able to protect you. That is not a wager I would take."

There's too much pain in his eyes. I don't know what to think about him protecting me. His oathmark has saved me before. But the truth is, I don't want to be rescued. I want to be strong enough to never need to be rescued. That's what the Stormender should be.

Cas interrupts my thoughts. "It'll be a fight either way—forward or back. So why not go forward?"

I nod. It's easy for me to agree. The truth is, going back—finding and fighting our way out of the palace—feels like a much harder decision than to keep moving forward.

"To Dalca's point, perhaps we can choose more carefully," Cas says.

"Thanks," Dalca says flatly.

"We don't need to step through," I say. "We can open each door and decide."

"I don't know—" Dalca says.

I pick a door without looking at Dalca. The writing above it says *Desire has another face.*

I twist and pull the gilded handle. The light shines for a moment, and I shield my eyes until it recedes. Down the hall is the same short hallway, the same archway, and there's a glimmer of green—the gardens—in the far distance. A pinkish haze hangs in the air . . .

"Try this one," Cas calls from around the tower.

I shut the door and circle toward him. Dalca is hunched over, his hand rubbing at his heart. He catches me looking. "I'm fine."

He turns, and I give him the privacy he seems to need. I pass two sets of doors—the first inscription reads *All is even in the end*, and the second reads *Freedom is a choice*.

Cas stares through an open doorway. I glance up. *There is a plan*. It's so very simple compared to some of the others. It's almost . . . comforting.

I reach his side and squint, letting my eyes adjust. The hallway, again. I don't know what I was expecting, but it looks the same. Same short hallway, same archway, same hedge maze at the end. And I'd imagine the same tower and night-sky room beyond it.

"Do you see?" Cas steps back to give me more room.

There's something strangely pleasing about the proportions of the hallway. "What did you see?"

Cas's voice is quiet. "This is it."

The Great Queen lurches beneath my skin. It's unsettling, but I can't tell if she's recoiling, or if she wants to go deeper. Something about the hallway looks so . . . right.

I breathe: "It is."

The Great Queen's mark rises on my skin.

From a distance comes Dalca's gasp of pain. His voice is so hard to hear. "Vesper—the oath—something's wrong—get back!"

I step back into Cas, who's right behind me. His voice is soft in my ear. "This is what he wanted you to see."

A firm push—*Cas pushed me*—*he wouldn't, Cas would never, not unless he were*—

I stagger into the light-drenched hall, falling to the floor.

Cas stands in the doorway, his eyes bright, his smile kind. "I'm sorry, Vesper. But this is all part of the plan."

The door shuts, cutting off an anguished shout. Dalca's shout. The handle jiggles—the lock is jammed.

A glorious warmth sinks into my bones, into my thoughts—I try to hold on to one last thought, about Cas—about the light—

CHAPTER 26

There is a plan.

All else fades. My body is light as air, but I can no longer remember the things that once weighed it down. I'm reborn.

The dust in the air. The dance of light on the tiles, on my armor. The ring of my footsteps. The beat of my heart. Everything is perfect. Everything has a pattern.

I take a deep breath, and a sense of calm washes over me. It's like I'm seeing with new eyes. It's so clear.

Something whispers in the back of my mind, like a fly buzzing around my ear. It says something, I can almost make it out—

I startle as the violet spectral arrives, right before my nose. The motes of light twist and fall in a living pattern. If I look close enough, I know each mote itself will be perfectly symmetrical.

His lips move. "You see it, don't you?"

I do.

I can see it, like writing on the air—and I hear it, a song in every sound.

Everything has an order. There's a place for me in it, a perfect place. A role. The role I have to play—the role I have played, the role I am playing—it has a perfect end. I need not worry if I'm doing the right thing at the right time, if I've made the best choice. Everything has been decided, long before I was born, designed with precision many times more detailed than the most delicate ikonwork—an ancient machinery grinding toward a sublime future.

"Where is the King?" I ask the spectral.

He offers me his arm. "I'll take you to him."

I reach to take his arm without thinking. My fingers meet a wisp of resistance before my hand goes right through him.

"Forgive me," he says. "Sometimes I forget." A flicker of sadness in his eyes. This Dalca, with the circlet on his brow, ghostly pale thousand-and-one-feather cloak on his shoulders, and the confidence of someone sure of his place in the world—I understand this Dalca. I envy him.

We step through the archway. I have a vague impression of passing the colonnade, but my attention is fixed upon the person in the garden.

Not a person. An immense being, who turns as I approach. Eyes of light. It's like seeing a person through broken glass—or a crystal prism.

They're fractured into many beings, just as a cut prism fractures light into many colors. If I tilt my head, the figure before me takes other forms. I focus on the one that looks a little like Pa.

He tosses me a distracted smile and turns back to his work. He has a pair of shears in his hands, and works at pruning a bush. He lets me watch him work. "I could use another pair of hands," he says mildly, "if you wouldn't mind helping."

I take the proffered gloves and shears.

"The pattern will show you the way," he says.

The gardens stretch on as far as the eye can see—I shift a little, and the vision changes, just like looking through a prism—the endless gardens and the glass-domed chamber, laid over each other, both existing in the same space. All so perfectly manicured, so perfectly shaped. "Such hard work," I say.

"Yes. But you'll never taste fruit sweeter."

He plucks a golden sphere from a tree and hands it to me.

Something makes me hesitate, but the thought slips out of my grasp. I take a bite. Oh, so sweet and warm—the sun's warmth is still in it. Wetness drips down my chin, and I wipe it with the back of my hand, though it's already drying sticky. In three bites, the fruit is gone, but I taste it still on my lips.

He looks pleased. "A hundred years it took to perfect that."

I smile back. "It truly is perfect."

"Come," he says, leading me deeper into the gardens. "Trim what needs trimming."

I get to work. It's beautiful, pleasant work, though sweat drips down the back of my neck. I like trimming the trees, choosing which branch should grow and which has grown long enough. I know the pattern, and it's so good to follow it, to not have to choose the best way forward.

The whisper in the back of my mind falls silent. A bleary warmth suffuses my mind, like I've just woken from a long nap under the sun.

In time he returns, and the warmth spreads, as cozy as a blanket.

"You're the Great King," I say.

"I do not call myself that. I am merely one who tidies what has fallen out of order."

"Out of order . . . ?"

"In the time of the Storm, many of my people drank a drink called sundust. You know it."

I nod.

"You drank it in order to invoke the sun, even if only in your heart. To invoke light. Clarity. Order. To drive away the dark." He smiles.

"You asked for me, and I came."

"You came to drive away the dark." A flicker of memory. The Queen. "Am I the dark?"

"No, child. You have done your part, and look at all you have achieved. Without you, this great garden would never have flourished."

The endless garden. The work to keep it beautiful must be equally endless. "What's next for me?"

He puts his shears away and takes mine. "Come along."

I follow him further through the garden. Somehow, between one tree and the next, everything shifts, like looking at the world through a prism of cut crystal—we were in the garden, but now the angle of sight has shifted, and we're in a large clean space, a circular room of vast proportions.

Light falls from a single hole in the ceiling. It casts an immense ikon on the floor. The King's voice rises from all around.

All you children are looking for a place you understand and where you feel safe. A house whose foundations you trust. Whose walls are strong.

You are building a house. You have built most of it without realizing what you were doing. You laid the foundation with stones, each a thing you believe to be true. The walls are ideas that rose up out of those beliefs. The roof, protection from things that would harm the safe structure you have built.

You had built one for yourself. A poor one, for it brought you only suffering. You took the expectations of others and wrote them in gold upon your heart, as if they were true, as if they were worthy of you.

You did a great thing. You ended the Storm. What have you to prove?

Choose another house. This one does not serve you.

"But which?"

If this, the house I am building, if it pleases you—

We're back in the gardens. A double image, a refracted, prismatic image. The gardens, endless and beautiful, manicured in a perfect pattern, and the vast, clean room, where the light casts an ikon.

If it suits you, it is yours.

"What happens when the garden is done?"

The King is again a simple man who looks like Pa. He smiles. "Then I will be free to rest."

"You don't want power?"

"Power? That is of little use to me. Power is for those who fear being usurped. Who do not know their place in the world. They seek power to fill that hole within them. But power cannot fill it. Only purpose can. Only knowing their place in all of time and space; knowing there is a plan, knowing their life has a meaning."

The ikon on the floor . . . there's something about it that reminds me of a flower, albeit one with a thousand interweaving lines crisscrossing over it. The city's new towers mark the points of its petals, and each ring is another layer, in a pattern that makes sense, that could be expanded upon endlessly.

And there are fainter lines, ones that disappear. They follow the thousands of lightstruck in the city, like the trails left by shooting stars.

Everything and everyone has a place.

It reminds me of the ikon Pa showed me—what he called a "life-ikon"—a moving ikon, incredibly complex, where everything leads into everything else. This is destiny. Fate. A perfect design.

"It is in part your doing. All had a common purpose, a common enemy, in the Storm. You have destroyed that which knit them together. Loneliness abounds in their hearts, as now you have put a cruel expectation upon them: they must find within themselves a reason to live. A reason pure enough, good enough, to be worth bearing all the terrible uncertainty they now face.

"And in pursuit of this purpose, they make mistakes, they hurt themselves, they hurt others—they know not what they want, so they fall prey to every idea that comes their way. So many are weak and grasping, wanting a little more for themselves, for their own, always drawing lines in the sand and deciding who stands on either side— those are the vermin in the grain, who seethe with envy and fear, who destroy those few who have found a path worth walking, so all can be as rotten as they are. We must make a better world."

"I . . ."

"You have put that cruel expectation upon yourself. You need not carry the burden of expectations that do not serve you—both theirs, and your own. You may put that burden down.

"I know your place, Vesper. I know what you would need to be happy. I know, of the thousands upon thousands of people of this city, which is worthiest of your love. I see your path to joy, to contentment, to fulfillment. I know where you belong. Come."

He kneels, and gestures.

I follow the angle of his hand, to a tiny person, smaller than an ant. The longer I look, the more my vision expands, until she's life-sized, so close I can see the whites of her eyes. She wears a loose fitting shirt, over which she wears bracers on her wrists. Bracers meant to hold mancer's charcoal. She hurries along, though others call out to her— she smiles, laughingly, throwing greetings back over her shoulder. But she doesn't stop. She's headed somewhere she wants to be, somewhere she's excited to be. What a wide smile she wears.

"Where is she going?" I ask.

"Do you wish to know?"

"Yes."

"Then step onto this path. And no more shall you weep. No more shall you bleed. All will be well. You will see."

And I feel it happening. A warmth rises from somewhere deep inside me. It says, *You will be okay. You will never fall, not when I am here to catch you. Relax. Let me take your burdens from you. You have your place in the world. It is a job only you can do. Not too easy, but you will be good at it. I have seen your path, and it is a good one.*

Come. Take the first step.

I can see it. A path leading to a golden horizon. One step, and it'll be mine. A beautiful journey.

It can't be bad to want this. To be free. To be taken care of. To put down the crippling weight of my own future.

I take a step.

CHAPTER 27

I exhale.

Trees shaped like candelabras arch over my head, dripping with faceted fruit that glitters with inner light. They grow taller, more ornate, their branches twining and looping, symmetrical on both sides of the path. There's a pattern to it, something that I can see only when my eyes lose focus, an expanding kaleidoscopic design, a repeating, unfolding design.

The pattern sinks into me. A warmth wraps around me, as sweet as a hug.

Someone walks beside me, but I pay them no attention.

The candelabras give way to bent trees with pendulous, weeping branchlets. They look like people bowing, welcoming me in. Some are strewn with flowers that perfume the air with a delicate scent—so beautiful and so fleeting that I can't draw enough of it into my lungs, no matter how deep I breathe.

My silent companion plucks a flower and offers it to me. It's pinched between his callused fingertips. I bend to inhale—and I get the scent of another garden—a heady honeysuckle scent that reminds me of a still pool, a boy thrashing through the water—

I raise my eyes to his face. Dalca smiles down at me. "May I join you?"

What do I want? I don't mind having him along. "If you wish."

The path changes again. Flowering vines fall from above; the light is so bright I can't make out their origin. A breeze ruffles the long fingers of the vines, their tips just brushing the white stone ground.

The air grows hazy with heat. A man is up ahead; the light glints off his white hair. He's braiding the vines into thick plaits.

He hears us approach, straightening and turning to us. Pale eyes and a soft smile. Casvian Haveli.

There's something I wanted to ask him—a flicker of unpleasant emotion—something that's been buried deep—

"You know it too, don't you?" he asks me.

What . . . do I know?

"The plan." He hands me a small bag and loosens the drawstring. Inside are seeds that glow like embers.

"We were fighting . . ." I say.

"Do you want to fight?"

The truth spills out of me. "No . . . I never want to fight."

"What do you want?"

"I want . . ." The endless wilds. To go out and see all. And . . . to know there's a home I can return to. A warm place, a safe place, waiting for me.

He nods. Have I spoken out loud? He smiles. "Our home will never be threatened again."

That's what I want, isn't it?

He parts the vines and ushers me through, into a round clearing with a living carpet of clovers. The clovers, the hedge around us, all of it follows the pattern. Cas beckons me to sit beside him.

Cas whispers, as if he's sharing an old secret. "What I want . . . I've always wanted to find someone worth following. The Havelis were made to be the right hands of those who deserved us. My father was Regia's Guard. So was my grandmother, and her father before her. I thought Dalca was that, for me. But . . . then I thought it might be you."

I say nothing, but touch his hand.

He flinches at my touch; something coming over him. His voice changes. "The Great King told me his plan. I had trouble understanding, at first. I believed in you. And when he asked . . . I spared them. None were meant to be hurt . . . I didn't know about her sensitivity. Arvanas . . ."

Mina.

Her name is like a thorn in my mind.

Cas says with quiet urgency, "I would follow you."

I frown at him. Follow me? But where am I going?

He looks at me with tears in his eyes. "Something has gone wrong. My ancestors failed me. There was supposed to be someone worth following. What have I done wrong?"

There is a plan. The pattern rises in my mind, and with it the warmth returns.

"It's all right, Cas."

He weeps.

My hand falls from his, and he relaxes, tears drying. I catch a glimpse of my hands—black patterns dance faintly on my skin. I frown. *They're not part of the pattern.*

They disappear.

Feet stop in front of me, and I lift my head up to their owner. Dalca.

He beckons me back onto the path. I part the vines and step through, permitting myself one glance back.

Cas is back at work braiding the vines, humming a song that's vaguely familiar. A song that follows the pattern: a perfect song, a circular song.

The vines fall, sealing him away.

I walk on, until we come to a fork in the path. Dalca steps in front of me, and my vision blurs—in that prismatic fracturing of light—and there are two of him, two Dalcas, both with their hands outstretched, willing me to take the path to the left or to the right. They speak, but their words get muddled as they talk over each other.

I squeeze my eyes shut and cover my ears. When I open my eyes, there's just one.

I don't take his hand, but I let him walk beside me.

The garden path leads to a fountain. Water bubbles up from a bowl on a plinth, pouring over the edges, into a dark pool. Violet flowers grow in neat tufts.

At the water's edge, a woman unbends, rising to her full height with her back to me. She has a strong build and a long curtain of black hair. Could she be . . . ?

"Of course I am," she says without turning. "Whatever you become, whatever you choose to be, I am your mother. If you make yourself proud, you will make me proud."

"Ma?"

She turns. Light swallows her face—I raise a hand as it dims.

The woman smiles, and my heart falls. Toran Belvas. "Vesper," she says. "Thank you for saving my daughter."

Another figure rises from the water's edge, half-hidden by the violet flowers. Hadria. She smiles, pulling the long curtain of her hair over her shoulder.

Have I . . . saved her?

Hadria comes to me and takes my arms. She kisses my cheeks, my forehead. "You've done it," she says, her dark eyes sparkling with warmth. "Thank you. You gave me what I lost. The time I lost. And now . . . all that I hadn't learnt from my mother, I can. I can learn her stories, her tricks. I don't have to lose her. I don't have to lose anyone else."

Her smile is so sweet, so joyful—I've never seen it before. I embrace her. "I'm glad," I tell her. "I'm glad that you're happy."

I let her go.

They disappear down the path, mother and daughter together. Toran throws me one last smile over her shoulder.

Something aches, somewhere inside me. I press my hand to my chest—my hand is covered in those black pattern-breaking lines.

Something isn't right—

A figure approaches, through a hazy brightness. The air trembles around them. It's Dalca again, but wasn't he behind me?

"Vesper," he says.

"Dalca." My tone is flat, and he notices.

"Of all things, you object to me?"

"I don't object to you."

I meet his eyes. For a heartbeat, they look violet, but I blink and they're vibrant summer's sky blue once more.

He tilts his head. "I wonder who I'd be if I hadn't met you."

"I don't imagine you'd be much different."

"No? Perhaps you're right. I feel different, though, somehow."

We walk on, and he continues:

"I grew up afraid. Terrified, really. Of the future. Of growing up.

Of the legacy that would be mine. You scared me, too. You . . . I was terrified I'd fall in love with you. I couldn't. Not when I knew what was before me. That if you loved me back, you'd end up shackled to a shell. The Storm's curse freed me from my fear, for a time. But you broke my curse and brought it back. The weight of my fear . . . it crushed me.

"When you had my life in your hands . . . I'd hoped you would end it. No one could force me into becoming Regia, or accuse me of being a poor example of the family blood, if I were dead. But something changed when you let me go. When you began to take in the Storm. The only time I've ever felt stronger than my fear . . . was when I fought alongside you. When I fought for you."

My heart thuds in my ears. I don't like it. It's louder than the pattern, than the warmth. "What do you want from me?"

"Vesper," Dalca says, his voice urgent. I turn around.

There he is. But wasn't he just next to—

"Vesper," he says again, in the same desperate and too-loud voice. "Don't you want to see the Great King's vessel?"

Something sparks within me. The vessel. There was . . . a plan. "Yes."

"Come, then. We'll leave the path, just for a moment."

"All right," I say, and follow him.

He sticks his hand in a hedge. That's not right.

I step back. My vision shifts, and a door stands in the same place as the hedge. Dalca's hand is upon the handle.

He opens the door, and I follow him through.

There's a chill in the air here. I rub my arms—my fingers brush something metallic, as if I'm wearing armor. I frown. I am wearing armor, aren't I?

"Vesper." Dalca urges me up the stairs.

Up and up we climb, up steep and spiraling stairs.

"Just a little longer," he says.

We step out onto a landing at the top of a tower, open on all sides, and there it is. An immense crystal, as tall as a person, beautifully cut.

I gaze into it, into the colors, into the dancing light.

"The pouch at your waist." I look down. There *is* a pouch. Inside are tiny ikon-inscribed balls. I've forgotten . . .

A breeze licks at my neck. I turn, and gasp. The city spreads out below me. "Beautiful."

The lightlines are as delicate as lace, weaving a blanket that shields the city.

"Vesper," Dalca says urgently. "Remember your plan."

I can't—the dark lines appear on my skin, coiling like snakes.

"Is your plan better than this?" Dalca says, in a honey-sweet voice.

I look up at Dalca. And at the other Dalca, right next to him.

"You saw his plan," the sweet Dalca says. "He is a god. He knows his plan will go right. It's what we want, isn't it? For the world to be saved, and to stay saved."

The angry Dalca snaps. "He doesn't know all, and he doesn't know better. Remember, Vesper. When the Great King was in charge—when my mother was his vessel—he forgot about the fifth-ringers. And now he's forsaken the high ringers. Who else will he let fall? You cannot put your faith in him."

The sweet Dalca turns on him. "Where should she put it? In the Great Queen? In chaos?"

"In herself." The angry Dalca—though he doesn't seem angry anymore, just scared—he reaches for me.

The sweet Dalca frowns. "She's one girl. How can that compare to a god?"

"He's right," I say.

"He's wrong," the angry one says. "I should know."

He grabs my wrist. My eyes blur and focus—on his armor-clad arm, on a face with blue eyes and wild black hair.

"No." I shake my hand, but he holds tight. "Let me go. This is my path."

He responds, but his lips move with no sound. He doesn't let go.

I turn back to the other Dalca. I reach for him, but my hand passes right through him. His violet eyes narrow. I notice the regal garb. The thousand-and-one-feather cloak. I blink. And I can see right through him, right through the motes of light that make up his body.

He whispers, "You see the King's plan, don't you?"

The light within the crystal brightens, and a warmth spreads through me—the King must be close—

A shout, like an echo. "Vesper!"

It comes from the Dalca who holds my hand. The real Dalca, who won't let me stay in this beautiful dream. He pulls me away, down a stone staircase. My vision flickers—I see double: a gilded set of spiral stairs that end at a garden, a crumbling ruin of a stairwell that continues on.

He'll pull me off the path. Out of the warmth.

I lock eyes with the Dalca of light who stands at the top of the stairs, his thousand-and-one-feather cloak billowing behind him, his violet eyes dark with fury.

I react—I reach for something inside myself—the lines on my skin darken—and something snaps. It's as though I've stepped through rotted wood and fallen into an icy cold river—every last bit of warmth is taken from me.

I'm hollowed out. Empty. All that's left is this: I've failed.

The King beat me.

CHAPTER 28

Once the secret door closes behind us, the darkness eats us whole. Dalca lets go of my hand. A flicker of light, and then comes the soft glow of an ikonlight in his palm. I blink at the tunnels.

My legs shake. My knees give out, and I fall to the ground. I've failed. How I've failed. A crushing, awful coldness runs through me. My hands won't stop shaking.

Bile fills my mouth, and I grow dizzy, the tunnel spinning around me.

"Vesper." Hands grip my shoulders. "Breathe. Yes, like that. Another one. A deep breath."

I do as he says. A small part of my head clears. But that awful coldness is still there, everywhere in me.

Where is the Great Queen? Has she left me?

I squeeze my eyes shut and search for her, for her voice, for that river of power. My nails bite into my palms, but the half-moons of pain don't ground me, don't calm me. There's nothing.

She's gone. I'm hollowed out. A clay pot holding nothing.

I can't wake her power. Her voice is gone.

"Dalca . . . She's gone. I can't feel the Great Queen."

A pause. "Don't worry about that now," he says.

I stare at him, incredulous.

"She hasn't left you." Dalca's certainty makes my stomach drop, because how can I make him understand that she *has*?

"If the council was right—if the Queen has decided I'm not—" I stop, unable to give voice to the word *worthy*. "What if the Storm returns?"

"It won't. You're alive. Your heart is still beating. And the Storm hasn't returned." He hurries on when I open my mouth. "And if it does, we'll figure it out. But we can't stay here—we have to move."

He hauls me to my feet.

"Cas and Hadria—"

"We have to go, Vesper."

I try to get a handle on myself, on the whirlwind of thoughts in my head. "You shouldn't have come for me. You should have saved them."

Dalca's jaw works. "I knew where you were."

It's like being plunged in ice water. Of course. The oathmark. That's the only reason he came for me. I drag a hand across my face. Okay. I need to keep it together. Get to the sixth, to safety. And then figure it all out. But I can't help saying: "I told you that you'd regret it."

"Regret what?"

"The oathmark."

He gives me an inscrutable look and strides off. I drag a slow breath into my lungs and head out after him.

The long monotony of the trek through the tunnel is shattered when Dalca throws his arm out, catching me around my middle and keeping me from moving forward.

The tunnel has come to an end. Dozens of columns of light pour from above, sweeping in careful circles. There are more than before. The King is making sure that there's no refuge from his light, at least not within the bounds of the city.

"There," Dalca whispers. I follow the direction he points, to a bridge ten feet below us. It leads into the cavern wall, into another tunnel.

Shafts of light cross it in an endless stream. If Cas were here to decode the pattern . . . but could he only do so because he was light-struck? When did it happen? When we went up to the third? When we saw Ragno at the high-ringer encampment? It doesn't matter. What matters is that the Great King was a step ahead. He breached the small circle of people I trust.

Dalca and I try to decode the pattern, but we soon give up. "We'll just choose a gap and jump," he says.

He's about to lower me down when the beams of light move, joining together in a far corner of the old city. An emerald glow rises.

"The spectral," I say.

Dalca's brows knit together. "Quickly, then."

He drops me down. My legs buckle and my knees smash into the stone of the bridge. I grit my teeth at the pain that blossoms out.

He drops down beside me in a neat crouch and makes as if to offer me a hand. I scramble to my feet before he can complete the gesture.

The tunnel's darkness is welcome. Dalca lights a tiny ikonlantern, dim enough to illuminate only a few paces before us.

I focus on that bobbing light, forcing all thoughts from my head.

I don't know how long we walk. I don't notice he's stopped until I walk into his back. "Dump everything you don't need. We need to move quickly now."

He divests himself of much of his armor, and I do the same.

He taps the stone at the dead end, working some ikon, and the door opens. We come out into the fourth, not far from the Bazaar.

Lightlines crisscross above our heads, leading to towers at the edge of the fourth ring. I suck in a breath. So the fourth has fallen. Has the fifth? How far can the King now reach?

Some dozen lightstruck walk by. It looks like they just happen to be strolling, but a group of four separates, forming two couples, and within a few paces, those couples break apart, joining up with strangers. It's a dance on an immense scale.

Dalca beckons silently, and we sneak further into the alley, stopping before a simple wooden door. Producing a small stick of mancer's charcoal from the seam of his sleeve, Dalca scrawls a small, neat ikon around the doorknob. He has none of Cas's speed or flair, but nonetheless, it works—the ikon cuts through the wood around the doorknob, separating door from latch. Dalca gives it a push, and silently, the door swings open—leaving the knob and a semicircle of wood attached to the frame.

He exhales as we step into a small shop that, judging by the dust in the air and the grime on the windows, has been empty for some time. "I just need a moment," he says, leaning on the wall, his hands going to the bandages at his throat.

Ikons are all that are keeping me standing. A crush of nauseating guilt. I hover, briefly, but he tenses, his jaw working, his hair shielding his eyes.

I get the hint. I give him privacy to attend to his bandages, and step around the bare display table and go to the window, clearing the grime off a small corner of glass.

Lightstruck pass by in a crowd, moving in that subtle dance, almost like birds in a formation. The crowd thins, and slowly the street empties. I crack the front door open to get a better look.

"Wait another moment," says a feminine voice, so close I nearly scream.

The spectral Regia stands in a dusting of sapphire light, her expression stony.

I circle her, putting myself between her and Dalca. On instinct, I reach for the Queen's power—and grasp at nothing. I'd forgotten. "Run, Dalca," I urge, without taking my eyes off the spectral of his mother.

She gives me a long look. "Enough with the foolish display. In ninety seconds there'll be a gap in the flow. Go to the right. You'll have to double back. There's a wall with three eyes painted on it. Under the middle eye, you'll find an ikonlock. Open it, take the passageway. The left fork goes to the old city, but the right will bring you out near the fifth's ringwall."

Dalca steps up beside me. "I've never heard of that path."

"You think you were the first child your grandfather locked in the old city?"

He meets her eyes, and something passes between them.

The Regia turns to the window. "Go now. But be careful. The other spectrals are hunting for you."

I glance at Dalca, and he nods. We follow her directions as the sound of precise marching comes from a long way away. There's a strange too-crisp unreality to everything—my body aches with tiredness, but terror and guilt are twin alarms blaring in my ears. I jump at a cloth blowing in the wind, and when we make it to the wall with the three painted eyes, a shudder runs through me, a fear that they might be alive and watching.

The sound of marching grows louder. Dalca makes a sound of irritation. "I don't see the ikonlock."

I tear my thoughts from the eyes and run my hands along the wall. Nothing—but a single stone, the size of my palm, moves under my fingers. I grip it with my nails and tug it, millimeter by millimeter, out of the mortar. It comes free. An ikonlock is set into the wall behind it.

Dalca reaches in. His wrist twists to and fro, and a minute later, the outline of an arched door appears. With a shove, it gives way enough for us to slip past, into the dark passage.

A sliver of light cuts through the dark. I add my weight to his, pushing with my shoulder, until the door grinds shut. Dalca ignites his ikonlight, and I follow him through the dark.

Something moves in the corner of my vision. I glance over at it, but all that's there is my shadow. Is it my shadow? I will it to peel itself up from the ground and walk beside me, like it once did in the Storm. At least it would be a sign of the Great Queen.

The silence between Dalca and me stretches taut.

I steal a glance at his face. His jaw is clenched, and his eyes blaze with fury. That crackling anger grows in the air between us, all the way through the fifth ring and out onto the road to the sixth.

We join the dwindling line of people leaving the city, walking the long road to the Queenskeep, carrying their worldly goods in baskets or knapsacks, holding their children and each other. An old woman makes slow progress, leaning on a gnarled cane. I offer her my arm, and she takes it with a small bit of hesitation, an almost visible shaking off of her pride.

I sense Dalca tensing at my slowed pace. He sighs.

When I catch sight of him again, he's with a young boy, no more than twelve, who's trying to herd a group of smaller children. Dalca takes one of the smallest and swings him up onto his shoulders, and picks up another and carries her in his arms. The twelve-year-old smiles up at him, though the smile doesn't quite reach his eyes.

The road curves, and the sixth's watchtower comes into view. Voices rise over the sounds of the shuffling crowd, ones that give directions for families to stay together, to follow the river to the landtreaders.

The woman pats my cheek and lets go of my arm. I watch her hobble off. Dalca hands off the children to a kind-looking couple in their fifties, who offer to look out for them.

For a moment, all I can see is those I did not help: a stooped woman, even older than the one I lent my arm to, a very beautiful boy of seventeen or so with a clubfoot, two little girls holding hands, their faces smeared with tears and dirt. Dozens more, so many more that their faces blend into an endless stream.

Dalca's fingers find my wrist. The warmth of his hand melds with the warmth of my skin, and I don't know if I like it, but the touch draws all of my attention, making my world small and manageable for just this moment.

The sixth's handlike watchtower peeks over the treetops, and a ripple of energy goes through the crowd. For some, it's the first evidence of human workings amongst all the stormtouched chaos of the sixth. It's a comfort to me, too. To walk past silent Wardana, whose eyes widen as they recognize us, who let us pass.

We take the riser. Dalca works the ikon device, and the cage moves. The wind howls through the bars, whipping my hair out of my face. Too much of my hair has left its braid.

The riser creaks higher. The market town is half full; two thirds of the stalls are missing, doors and shutters flap in the wind, giving fleeting glimpses of emptied homes. The line of landtreaders has dwindled. Only a handful are left.

We make our way inside the watchtower. The emptiness has

preceded us here—our footsteps ring flat, as if the air is too thin to contain the full sound.

Out of habit, I make for my rooms, though they were never really mine, these rooms and riches meant for the Stormender. The door swings open.

All that is heavy remains: the great dining table, the chairs, the low divans. All that is gilded and ornamented has been removed with care: the handwoven rugs and tapestries, the carved panels on the walls.

Even the wardrobe is nearly emptied, save for three sets of simpler clothing.

A scratching sound sends a shiver up my spine.

On the too-soft bed, curled up amongst half-shredded sheets, is Izamal's owlcat. It opens an eye, and, as if deigning to do me a favor, it rises and holds out a clawed leg. A scroll is tied to it.

I tug it free and give the creature a brief nod of thanks.

Unrolled, the writing on the scroll is in some kind of code. The air in the room shifts as Dalca nears, and I show it to him.

Dalca scans it. "They've gone ahead. We should be able to meet up with them at the outpost."

He doesn't meet my eyes.

I can't bear it anymore. "Speak your mind, Dalca. I know this is all on me."

A sharp glance. "It's not."

"You're furious."

"What do you want me to say?"

"That it's all my fault. That I'm the reason we lost the city. That the Great Queen made a mistake when she chose me."

He says nothing for a long moment. And then it spills out, as if he's been holding it in for some time. "If anything, it's my fault. If I had done what was expected of me, my mother would have reached the end of her natural life and I'd have taken the mantle of Regia. I need not have dragged you and your father into this. So if you want to blame anyone, blame me."

"I . . ."

"Blame me. I can take it."

My throat closes up and I can't speak.

His voice is soft. Gentle. "You can hate me. It's okay. I can take it."

"I . . ." I want to. But . . . All this awful, churning misery, this oily anger inside—it's a thousand pointing fingers, all directed at me. My vision blurs with tears of hot frustration.

Dalca steps closer, and his voice is barely a whisper. "I understand. I know. But please. Don't let it turn toward you. I couldn't bear that. Hate me instead."

Dalca raises his arms, offering himself up.

I step close, my hands balled into fists. I know what he's offering. I can choose to hate him. To pin all my failure on him. To choose blindness, to choose to feel that I'm all right. That I'm okay. That I'm worthy and it's the rest of the world that's wrong.

My head fits into the crook of his neck. Everything I've been holding in comes out. I weep. On and on. Only when the tears start to slow do I notice his arms around me.

The words come then, repeating in a long and endless stream: "I'm sorry. I wasn't strong enough."

"Neither was I," Dalca says on a whisper to the top of my hair.

CHAPTER 29

I dream of the past. Of the gilded, beautiful past. The palace—an ancient, smaller version of the palace—where a dignified woman with a long face rules from the throne room. I recognize her as the yellow spectral's human form. The sun kisses her golden skin and shines from within her. Beside her is her partner. A man with long dark hair, the vessel of the Great Queen.

It is as the Queen said—they do more than balance each other, they spur each other on to greater heights. The King's vessel gives them structure, order, and the Queen's gives them a yearning for more, a desire for progress. The city flourishes under their guidance: it is they who build the Ven and name it a place of learning. Sigils of power are written down and studied by the first scholars. I recognize them. Cas once had me research them—he called them proto-ikons, precursors to ikons.

These two vessels . . . Their choices changed so much for the better.

Guilt drags me down. This is what a true vessel looks like. What perfection is.

It was done before. So why couldn't I do it?

The dream melts away, into another. Shadows surround me, save for a cone of light. I walk toward it, toward the flat plinth and the woman lying upon it. Ma.

She's asleep as I once was, wearing a peaceful expression.

Her eyes open. They dart from side to side, anxious, trapped.

She can't move.

The light sneaks past my eyelids, no matter how tight I squeeze them shut, and pries me free from the warm, silent comfort of sleep. My body comes back to me all at once, as a map of pain—a throbbing behind my left temple, a rawness in the back of my throat, a soreness across the muscles of my thighs. I'm a leaden weight. Heavy enough to sink right through my bed, to let the feather mattress swallow me up.

Even if I could shut out the light, there's no more sleep to be had.

My eyes open. A pale stone ceiling, mottled all over in the pattern of the vines that once covered it. A little tension seeps out of my shoulders—that's a ceiling of the sixth. We've made it back. I'm safe from the light, at least for now.

It takes effort to move. I inch my legs over the side; my feet fall with a thump. The stone is like ice—the chill goes straight up my spine and to my head. I stand, blinking at the opulence around me. It's startling, still. My memories had softened the grandeur of my rooms, but being here . . . There's no denying that these are rooms made for a hero, a savior.

A heaviness sits upon me, close as my shadow. It walks with me, sways with me, fights my arm as I push open the door to the bathing room.

A washbasin and covered pitcher of water sit on the small table, ready for use. Beside them: a dish holding flakes of soap arranged to look like a flower, a half-dozen glass bottles of fragrant oils, a collection of tiny brass pots containing cosmetic paints and blackest kohl. A comb, a brush, and . . .

A pair of glinting, sharp shears.

I catch my reflection in the blades. The heaviness bows my head. It weighs down my shoulders, curls against the small of my back.

I do it without thinking; with one hand, I take the shears, with the other, I twist the dense length of my hair into a single cord. The shears cut through as easily as if my hair were no more substantial than smoke.

The heaviness falls away. Locks of my hair, thick and long as serpents, coil around my feet. I am so light, dizzyingly light, free from everything but the ringing in my ears.

I wash my face, ignoring the way my hands shake. Dalca and I left most of our armor in the tunnel under the city, but my gauntlet remains. I undo the straps and let it clatter to the floor. My shirt and trousers follow, my underclothes. The skin of my arm bears indentations from the gauntlet, but they will soon fade.

I bathe quickly, sponging away the layer of sweat and misery that coats my skin.

In the wardrobe, I rummage for the simplest, sturdiest clothes I can find. A soft white top, wide-legged pants that narrow at the ankles. I tug on a knee-length coat as a protective layer, but it's more like an ill-fitting cocoon. I'd need Hadria's figure to fill it out.

My hands still over the ties at my waist. Hadria is gone. She followed me, and I left her there.

I shut my thoughts down when they turn to Cas.

It's done. I've failed.

I can't stand the thought of wallowing in this room made for someone I've proved I'm not.

I make my way out to the sitting room. Dalca is curled up on the divan, still as the dead. I hold my breath until his chest moves with a slow inhale. Izamal's owlcat is curled up on his chest. It watches me as I pad across the room, but Dalca doesn't move a hair.

In sleep, Dalca doesn't quite look like himself. His expression is soft and open, untroubled. The Great Queen urged me to forget about him. Said that he's nothing to me. But that's not true. He's the witness of my darkest moments. As I am to his.

The night is far brighter than can be explained by the glimmer of ikon-lanterns alone—the moon is large and full, but most of the credit is due to the distant golden glow of the city's lightlines. The dark of night no longer exists this close to the inner five rings.

I follow the sounds of chaos through the market town, to the landtreader loading area. People hurry to and fro, stepping over the debris and detritus of food, fabric, supplies of all kinds. Even the storm-beasts look rattled.

Two women pass by me, carrying between them a satchel of grain the size of a large child. Another with long braids struggles after them, dragging a satchel by herself.

"Let me help," I say, and grab the other end before she can respond.

"Thanks," she says, panting.

My aching body doesn't thank me, but it feels good to become small, to become nothing more than one foot in front of the other. The weight of the grain pulls at my muscles, and the sparks of pain tether me to myself.

"This is it," she says, as we reach a landtreader. The back is open.

Between the floor and the undercarriage are compartments that are about four feet deep. We shove the satchel of grain into the last bit of space, and they lower a trapdoor to shut it tight.

A child weeps. His mother—or older sister, she looks no older than me—scoops him up. "Shush, now. Things will be better soon." She carries him into the landtreader, where others are preparing to leave.

A touch to my shoulder. The woman with long braids smiles not with her mouth but with her eyes. "If you're willing, we could use more hands."

I nod. There is more work to be done, and I sink into it. No one recognizes me. I give no orders, make no decisions, just do what I'm told. Hours pass in peaceful toil.

This is what it means to be just Vesper, not the vessel of the Great Queen.

I'm startled out of the gray of my thoughts when the woman—I still don't know her name—touches my shoulder. She laughs when I jump, but hides it behind her hand. "Will you ride with us?"

Ride? I blink the last of my stupor away. The landtreaders are ready. Most have departed, leaving behind only tracks in the mud. And something else: an emptiness. It's in the silent streets of the sixth, inside shuttered market stalls, behind the flung-open doors of once proudly-kept homes.

An ache grows in my chest. This is it. We're leaving the city behind.

"It's all right." A voice comes from my side. Dalca smiles at her. "She has a seat in another."

Her eyes widen as she recognizes him, and then, with dawning surprise, she searches my face.

I hold myself steady. If she hates me, if she blames me, I can take it.

But she merely inclines her head in the smallest of bows, her fist to her heart. A sign of respect.

She doesn't know, then, what I've done.

Dalca's fingers brush my shoulder blades, and I turn away from her, letting him show me the way to a landtreader. I reach for the gray nothingness—anything that'll let me step outside of myself—but it doesn't come.

We pass both Wardana and Nosca. They're tense. Half of them ready sprinters while the other half—those who'll be taking the next shift as outriders—finish loading up the landtreader.

Several are already inside. This landtreader has two levels—below, bench seating that runs the length of the space, and above, a half-height space for sleeping.

The wood creaks under my feet. People move out of my way, pausing in their business of hanging up bags and knapsacks of personal items. I pass a few who're settling in with a card game, and find a seat in the corner, near the front and the driver's compartment.

There are three loud bangs, and a handful of others enter the landtreader and lower the main hatch. Dalca sits next to me, leaning toward a Wardana who briefs him on the preparations.

The wood and metal body of the landtreader gives a great groan, and with a lurch, it rolls forward.

Dalca opens a small porthole window. A light still shines from the city, as bright as day.

I watch the sixth drop away, and the wilds rise up around us. As tall as it is, the watchtower soon is obscured from view by immense trees, and then by spires of lightning-struck crystal.

And still a glow comes from where the city must be, shining like a beacon.

Our home. Our city has never needed a name—as far as we and our mothers and our great-grandmothers knew, there was only one city. We only ever called it home.

We should give it a name. Now that we're leaving it behind.

We owe it at least that.

CHAPTER 30

The night has gone peacefully enough. After the shift change—Wardana in the landtreader swapping places with those that manned sprinters—we left the back hatch open. I moved to sit at the edge of the opening, and Dalca moved with me, murmuring something about fresh air when I told him he need not.

We pass through a corridor of thick spires, silvery blue in color, that grow dense and crooked, branching over our heads into a canopy of criss-crossing stone. The wheels of our treader lurch over rock and slate, until the spires give way to monumental trees—many of them blackened by ancient fire, others growing lightning-struck crystals in the hollows of their trunks—and others, though equally scarred by hundreds of years of lightning, are thick with deep green foliage. Soft dawn light dapples through the leaves, warm against my outstretched palm.

The night is over.

Dalca shifts next to me. He flattens his grimace when he catches me looking. "How is the pain?" I ask.

"Fine." Terse, quick, the instinct of a wounded animal. And then something in his eyes softens, opens. "I'm afraid we're at the end of what this ikonwork can do. I'm fine, as long as I don't move. Or breathe, really."

He smiles as if there's humor in it, but it's a slap to the face. He moved with such grace and power through the city that I forgot how hurt he was. "Dalca . . . I thank you for what you've done, but . . . The oathmark—it has done enough. No more."

My hand moves before I can think, and I reach for the medallion, for the chain around his neck, intending to draw it up from under his clothes. My fingers brush the warm skin of his neck.

Dalca's hand closes over mine, his grip so tight it hurts. "Don't."

My voice is a whisper, a plea. "Dalca."

"I know you," he says. "This is your guilt wanting to make something right. But this oath is not wrong." His grip softens, and he brings my hand to his lips. I become aware of the small, stinging scrapes that run across my knuckles.

His kiss lands featherlight.

"If you knew me," I say, "you wouldn't have made such an oath."

His dark curls fall into his eyes as he looks up at me. "Then ask me why."

My breath catches as Dalca interlaces our fingers, sweetly and carefully, so loosely I could pull away. My hand feels no longer wholly my own.

Dalca's voice is warm, a fire burnt low. "Ask me why I made the oathmark."

"I know why," I say. "To protect the Great Queen."

He shakes his head. "That was merely a fortunate side effect."

"Then . . . to keep the Storm from returning."

"That is the same reasoning, just in different words."

"There's no other reason." There can be no other reason. Nothing that should exist after the harms we've committed against each other.

His eyelashes are so long and dark, his eyes liquid. "Vesper," he says. "If there were no city, no Great Queen, no gods at all—I would still make an oath to you."

"Dalca—"

"You owe me nothing. You owe me no thought, no guilt. What I do, I do freely."

I blink carefully, willing the wetness obscuring my vision to clear. "But, Dalca. I'm not worth it."

The pad of his thumb brushes across my knuckles. Soft but sure. "How can you believe that to be true?"

I force a smile and pull away. "So, it turns out that I'm right. You don't know me."

"Vesper." Dalca's gaze bores into the side of my face. "You are worth it. What will it take for you to believe?"

The rambler slows, and I hop out through the open hatch before it's stopped.

A squat fortress rises from the black earth, sheltered by a grove of immense trees. A hodgepodge of building styles, with towers added seemingly at random, half in ruin and reclaimed by the vines of the wilds. The outpost.

Like slumbering beasts, landtreaders nestle at its base. But the people are awake—everywhere I turn, there's motion and preparation. This is what's left of my home.

Gravel crunches as Dalca reaches my side. Some part of me feels that I owe him an answer. I speak quietly. "If I'd saved everyone . . . If I'd been the hero they deserved . . ."

"Do you require all the world's love as proof of your worth? Must they all honor you before you can honor yourself?"

A fire, clean and furious, rises up through my chest, my throat—*how dare he make it all sound so small, so selfish*—my hands grab his jacket and heave him close. Heat rolls off him, carrying the scent of leather and something honeyed, heady.

Dalca's eyes are dark, all the blue eaten away by the black of his pupils. "Do you need them all?" he whispers. "Or will one man do?"

The outline of his oathmark medallion is faintly visible through his shirt. I trace it with the tips of my fingers. His lips part.

There's a pit inside me, dark and devouring. Would he be enough to fill it, to satisfy the miserable, aching hunger inside me? Would anything be enough?

He doesn't know what he's asking for. I can't give him this. I can't let him be swallowed up by this thing in me. I've already lost Cas and Hadria to it. Toran, and who knows how many others.

Maybe I couldn't save them, but I can save him.

"I know you," he whispers. "I know what you're doing. But we have lost so much." His voice falters. "Whatever more we have to face—are we not stronger together?"

Are we? A flash of pain crosses his expression—his injuries. "You need to get to a healer," I say.

"Vesper—" Dalca grunts as I swing his arm over my shoulder and force him to keep walking.

A man runs toward us, blue Nosca jacket slung over his shoulders and dark hair blowing in the wind. His long-legged, catlike gait announces him well before I can make out his features. "Izamal!" I call.

His golden eyes drink us in, the hope in them dying down.

With our sides pressed together, I can't miss the way Dalca tenses. I find my voice. "Dalca's hurt."

"The healers are ready, first floor." Izamal points his thumb in the direction of a door at the base of the outpost tower, but his gaze goes over my shoulder, to the rambler. Searching.

"It's just us," I say. My mouth goes dry. "I couldn't—"

Dalca squeezes my side. "We walked into a trap," he says softly. "The Great King saw it all. Every plan, every preparation. His light-struck . . . Cas was his long before we went in."

"Cas?" Izamal's eyes widen. "It can't—*Cas?*"

He rears back and tilts his head up, blinking hard. When he speaks, his voice is gruff. "And Hadria?"

"She's the King's now." Dalca grips Izamal's shoulder.

Izamal takes a single shuddering breath, holding himself so tightly that the veins in his neck and arms stand out, and then a mask falls over his expression, one that shields his heart from view. "It's done," he says. "All we can do is move forward. Healers first."

Izamal slings Dalca's other arm over his shoulders, hoisting him aloft. Dalca doesn't complain, which tells me the pain must be far worse than he's admitted.

We gather the weight of dozens of stares as we cross the distance to the tower. Nosca standing guard open the doors for us, and Iz mutters a quick word to them, too low to make out.

Our footsteps ring on the stone floor. The air inside is still and heavy, though dozens of people move through the wide foyer into rooms beyond. Dalca trips, his weight dropping onto me, till he catches his balance. His breath puffs against my ear. "Sorry."

I catch Izamal's worried gaze over Dalca's bowed neck. Izamal points his chin to an archway at our right, which opens up into a wide, long space that may have once been the mess hall. The healers have set up in one corner of the room.

Among them is a familiar helmet of hair. Aysel Marzel. His sleeves are rolled up to his elbows and there's a smudge of something dark on his cheek. He grows serious as we approach.

"Bring him here," he says, directing us through a small door, into a room lined with stone shelves. A pantry. A cot is already laid out in one corner.

Dalca lets us lower him to the bed. He sucks in a breath when his head hits the pillow, but his eyes stay closed, his brows pinched.

Without hesitation, Aysel gets to work undressing him.

"Iz," Dalca says. "The advance teams—have they returned?"

Aysel interjects. "Can you sit up? Or shall I cut this jacket off you?"

Dalca frowns. "I'll sit."

Izamal helps him. "The northern team returned a few hours ago. We're waiting on the east now. The northern team found the remains of a village, about two weeks' ride. Unless the other teams find anything more promising . . ."

Bandages crisscross Dalca's chest, a complicated ikon written across them. Blood has seeped into the gauze, severing the ikon in places. He's so hurt. The oathmark rests askew, right over his heart.

"I'm going to change your bandages. But this ikon—I can't in good conscience put it back on you. Not until your body has had a chance to heal some of this damage."

"No. I can't rest yet."

"Dalca," I say. "You can rest. There's nothing more to fight. Not now."

He holds my gaze for a long moment. "A day," he says. "That's all."

Aysel blinks. "I meant, more like a month—"

Dalca glowers. "A day or a minute. Your choice."

"A day it is. In any case, Casvian will want to have a look at you—"
Aysel reads our expressions. His face loses color. "I see. I'll do my best."

"When the scouts return," Izamal says, retreating to the door, "I'll come by."

Dalca nods and lets his head fall back.

Izamal holds my gaze, jerking his head to the side. "Outside," he mouths.

The door closes behind Iz, and Dalca turns to me. "Vesper. Will you wait, until I wake?"

"Wait for what?"

His eyes lose focus as Aysel unwraps more of his bandages. "Don't go where I can't reach you."

"I won't."

His eyes flutter closed. Dalca looks so at peace. It reminds me of when I saw him in the underworld. When he knew he was dead, he felt not fury, but peace. How much has he carried alone?

"How bad is it?" I ask.

Aysel speaks quietly, without meeting my eyes. "If it were anyone else, I'd say he was dying."

My breath catches. "What do you mean?"

He gives me a hesitant smile, as if he thinks I'm joking. "You and Dalca, even Cas and Iz—I'd say no one knows the extent of what you can do."

"You're wrong." I clench my jaw. "We're ordinary people. We hurt, we bleed, and we die."

Izamal waits with another Nosca, whose back is to me. He catches my gaze and says something to her. She startles, turns, and flashes her dimples at me.

"Gamara?" I ask.

She blinks rapidly, and her smile trembles. But all she says is, "What have you done to your hair?"

I owe her an explanation of what happened in the city. I take a breath. "When we went up—it went wrong—"

She holds up a hand. "Izamal told me. Give me half an hour, and I'll gather the rest—we all took odd jobs when they let us go—"

"No," I say. "It's okay. Nosca blue suits you."

She tosses her hair. "Yes, true. But I look just as good in black and violet."

"I don't need a Regia's Guard. Not anymore."

She gives me a long look. "Hmph." She turns on a heel and strides away.

Izamal watches her go. "Are you sure?"

I'm sure I don't need to waste their time. But some part of me aches for the strange camaraderie we briefly had—and for what could have been, if I were a true Regia and they were still my guard. I settle for giving him a shrug.

Izamal lets it go. "That's not what I'm here for, actually. The council is meeting in an hour's time."

"Dalca won't be awake," I say.

"I didn't tell Dalca the whole of it. The river forks in three about a half day's ride from here. We sent a team down each of the three paths. One path ends quickly, no more than two days' ride. One path ends a little further."

"What about the third?"

"They haven't reached the end just yet. We got word back from them a few days ago that they're still following the river." He takes a breath. "The council is taking a vote. To stay here and keep sending scouts out, until we know the best way forward . . . or to head out. Hope for the best, that the third path is what we're looking for."

My chest hollows out. I crave the Great King's warmth, the certainty of his vision. To never make the wrong choice.

But another part of me—a far smaller part—wonders. What is out there?

"Izamal," I say, "I still have a vote, right?"

"Yes. As does Dalca." He takes a breath. "I told them you were taking a reinforced rambler and making your way slowly, safely. That you were going to keep your head down and meet us at some point."

"Iz . . ." I'm touched.

He flashes me a smile. "So stick to the story, or they'll have my head too."

I blink hard. "You're a gem amongst men, Iz."

"Yes," he says. "I know."

I smile at my feet—and a thought sparks. "Iz, before you go—this is the outpost where they found a mancer's library, isn't it?"

The library is in a far tower of the fortress; Izamal returns, having borrowed the key that fits into the new ikonlock set into an ancient door. "Precautions," he says at my look. "I hear there are some dangerous little books in here." He shrugs with the casual disregard of a warrior.

The library is small but tall, lined with diamond-shaped shelves meant to house scrolls in protective cylinders. The lower levels are for pages bound into books. Much is missing—streaks through the thick layer of dust reveal all that was removed.

Izamal explains. "Cas . . . the mancers took away the most promising tomes to study, and ordered it sealed . . . They always thought they'd have more time to look it over. The mancers may have the collection with them—they're bringing several miniaturized tomes. Much was lost in the Ven—the lightstruck came for the libraries the same time they came for the cloaks."

How many more little rooms like this exist here, and back in the city? In the other watchtowers of the seventh? Places that bear the mark of those who lived and thought within them? All this history—soon to be lost.

"Remember the council meeting," Izamal warns before he leaves.

The silence is palpable, a thick shroud that hangs in the air between this room and the rest of the world. A retreat, a place of the mind, a place of learning. A place lost so long ago that I'm sure Pa never even dreamt of its existence. The details—the carved wood edging the bookshelves, the three small burn marks on the table, the gouges in the wooden floor from furniture that's no longer here . . .

A groove in the floor, half-hidden by dust.

Curious, I follow it.

An ikonlock, faded by the passage of time or the touch of many hands. I twist it.

A passageway opens. A little domed room, a private workspace. A large, old-fashioned ikonlantern hangs from the ceiling, but there are no windows.

Left as if someone just got up to make food and never came back. A cup of tea.

A loose sheaf of fine paper—finer than what we use now. I blow on the page and a cloud of dust rises up. One little scrap of paper flies up, and I catch it.

On it are bundles of tally marks. Under them are words in a spindly script, of so old-fashioned a spelling that it takes me a moment to translate: *Let it be known that Haverin lost three games of gilgarney and owes Rovon and Lanira twelve each, and Porina fifteen. Haverin has refused the wise counsel of his betters—me—and insists on playing every round. I don't know how much more he owes Aenon.*

The paper crumbles in my hand, but I've read enough to know it's nothing more than a note amongst friends, a lighthearted admission of debt.

The larger papers are covered in neater handwriting. A record of some sort: *It's been three weeks since the last storm-crossing. Fewer and fewer do so, now that the rumors have spread of some who enter being afflicted with peculiar ailments. But Regia Ivonen says it's no loss; the far cities are cruel, backwards places with no ikonomancy—and we have all the means to grow whatever we need ourselves.*

The Regia is right, of course, but I can't help but wonder . . .

Far cities? Storm-crossings? How long ago was this written?

I don't dare lift the paper to read the next page, not with how easily the scrap fell to pieces.

The only other thing that's open is a map on the edge of the table.

Drawn upon it is a crescent-shaped city, but the name is blurred.

Hundreds of years ago, another world existed beyond ours.

There is hope.

Izamal holds open the door of the landtreader where the council is holding their meeting. I duck my head and enter.

My eyes adjust to the darkness.

Someone draws in a breath. A wide-set woman with a burn scar and a wooden arm. I search for her name. Tharmida. Tharmida Sel. "Well, well. The Stormender returns."

"And where have you been?" Imbas glowers.

"She took her own path, as discussed," Izamal says.

Imbas eyes him. I blink. This is the first time I've seen them at odds.

"And it doesn't matter, as she's here now." Izamal steps up to the table. "You were waiting for my vote. Vesper has her vote, and will stand in for Dalca."

I flatten my expression and nod.

"Then let's take a vote," Rosander says.

"We're missing the ikonomancer vote."

Izamal speaks. "Aysel sends his vote—he's with me."

Mother Yul raises a brow. "Casvian?"

Izamal swallows. "Casvian Haveli is gone."

A silence falls.

"We can stay here," says Tharmida. "The outpost has the kind of infrastructure we haven't seen anywhere else. My smiths could be far more useful here than on the road."

Imbas shakes her head. "It's not far enough away from the threat. We're only a day's ride from the sixth. Remember—the Storm took half the sixth in a single day."

Izamal clasps his hands. "I'd like to put it to a vote. Who votes to stay in the outpost?"

Tharmida raises a hand. No others join her. She curses.

"And who votes to follow the scouts to the northern path?"

There are no smiles at seizing the slimmest of hopes. But they all vote—Rosander, Imbas, Izamal, Mother Yul.

They all look to me. I think of the maps, of the far cities, of all that we don't know.

Of the slimmest of hopes, that there may be a land where my people might be safe.

I vote. For myself, for Dalca. I vote to protect everyone I still can, the way I couldn't protect Cas.

"All right," Izamal says. "We leave at sundown."

CHAPTER 31

The day is on its last legs; the sky has grown violet in mourning. Only glimpses of the outside world reach me through the landtreader's porthole window. The spires jut like fingers, casting long, grasping shadows. We could be trespassing on the graves of thousands of giant beings, who, with their dying breath, reach through the earth and to the sky.

And no matter how far we get, how dense and immense the spires behind us grow, I can't shake what feels like a whisper on my neck, a warning of a gaze from afar, from the gleaming, illuminated city at our backs.

Our progress has slowed. The advance team cleared much of the way—demolishing spires and marking a path through the wilds—but the way is narrow, and the going is tedious.

I let the curtain fall back as the landtreader rumbles on. At once, I wish I hadn't. The landtreader feels claustrophobically small. The main hatch in the back is shut—too dangerous to have it open on this stretch, we've been told—so the air is still, save for what little makes its way through the vents between the landtreader's armored plating. Some dozen or so Wardana rest up for their next shift out protecting the caravan; half are asleep. Of those who aren't, four play a card game with grim determination and forced cheer, one reads a book of poetry—he offers the lines that delight him to the indifferent ears of those nearby—and another mends a tear in the red leather of her jacket. There are fewer people in this landtreader than in others—but the Wardana just seem to take up a lot of space.

On the bench beside me, Dalca pores over a hand-drawn map of the greater wilds. I've been strange around him. Watching how people come to him, asking for direction and leadership. They need him. Even without being a vessel, he has a purpose and a power.

The Great Queen was the only power I've ever known. I examine my hands, willing her lines to rise. But nothing happens. I meet my reflection's eyes in the mirrored surface of my gauntlet.

Dalca shifts, and something changes in the air. A curl falls into his eyes—eyes that see a little too much. His lips part, and I tense—I don't want to be consoled, I don't want him to even mention the Queen—

The landtreader shudders to a stop. Momentum throws me back, and I catch myself on the side. The Wardana come alert as one—the asleep snap awake, the awake grow sharp.

Dalca rises to his feet, his attention on the forward hatch that separates us from the drivers. It bangs open, and a Wardana with short-cropped hair pops her head in. She looks us over before zeroing in on Dalca.

"Word from the Nosca," she says. "There's a creature incoming. The Nosca haven't been able to herd it away like the others—they'll have to make a stand. They're asking for reinforcements."

"All right," Dalca says as he pulls on his jacket. "Niven, Perrin, Isha—take your teams to meet them. Rou, Madri, get the landtreaders in defensive formation. You know what to do."

They all spring into motion, flinging the back hatch wide open and leaping out.

"Dalca," the Wardana messenger calls.

Dalca tugs tight the last strap of his gauntlet and gestures for her to speak.

"Iz is asking for—" Her eyes land on me. "The Stormender."

I get to my feet. My heart thuds against my ribs, the speed rising, deepening. I haven't told Iz about the Queen's power, that it's gone.

I meet Dalca's shadowed eyes. "Let's go."

"Vesper—"

I hop out of the landtreader before he can finish. The Wardana have already begun to carry out Dalca's orders, guiding the landtreaders.

Wordlessly, Dalca approaches my side. A Nosca comes running and bids us follow her.

The spires grow thick and twisted, like little dancers gathering around their mother: a massive black tree, tall as ten men and as wide as a landtreader. Its twisted branches blot out the sky.

The branches creak and groan, leaves tinkling like glass. The wind wails, louder than a whisper and not yet a howl.

Globe-shaped ikonlanterns have been rolled to the base of the trunk, casting a small bit of light up onto the tree.

Izamal stands apart, his eyes trained on the branches. I follow the path of his gaze, squinting up. Nothing. But then a branch creaks, bending as if something heavy sat upon it.

"It's been following us some time now," Iz says quietly. "It's old, whatever it is. And clever."

"It's invisible?" I ask.

Iz answers, "Some kind of camouflage. Watch for the path it takes as it moves—look for where things aren't."

The branch moves, rising as the weight is lifted from it, and a neighboring one bows. It's moving from branch to branch—but what is it?

Dalca murmurs, "Can we go around it?"

"It attacked two riders who tried to make their way past it. It's fast. It won't let anyone else pass—maybe we could find another way around it, but we could lose a week trying to find the edge of its territory. Maybe we could power through—but I fear it's strong enough to overturn a landtreader. Vesper"—Iz turns to me—"can you calm it the way you did before?"

I bite my lip. I didn't calm it—the Queen did. But I nod and close my eyes.

A buzzing under my skin. Nerves—or perhaps something else. I breathe in and out, evenly, slowly, searching inside myself for a drop of her power, the dregs of anything in the clay pot inside me.

Please. I beg. *Wake up. Help me.*

My insides are cavernous, hollow, empty. I gaze into the dark inside, hoping, yearning. Something, a small shadow, shifts inside me. I reach for it, but it slips through my fingers. A figment of my imagination.

"Vesper?"

I open my eyes and meet Iz's. He raises a questioning eyebrow. I shake my head.

"I can't—" I stop. Ice runs down my spine—the awareness of something malevolent. Coming from the tree above.

A massive serpent, coiled through dozens of branches and wrapped around the trunk. The branches rise and lower as it shifts its weight.

Izamal curses at my side, and a shudder goes through the warriors as they clap eyes on it.

You, the beast whispers in a skittering voice, inhuman and ancient.

"Can you hear that?" I ask. I'm met with blank gazes.

"Hear what?" Dalca asks.

Mother, the beast says, *you've returned*.

A thrill goes through me. If I can hear the beast, if it still recognizes the Great Queen within me, then perhaps she's truly still there. Perhaps I'm still her vessel.

A flicker of its emotions—hunger, anger, fear—cuts through me, even as it disappears from sight, camouflaged once more.

"It's coming!" I say the same moment Izamal yells, "Archers!"

The Nosca fire. Nets embroidered with ikons blaze as they're launched, activating as they make contact with the serpent.

Of the dozen nets, five hit, pinning the beast to the tree. The beast writhes. In places, its skin shimmers, growing briefly visible.

A ripple of terror goes through the Wardana as they see just how large it is. Goose bumps rise across my skin. Half of me is in awe of its majesty, the other half petrified of its anger.

I reach for the Queen's power, but it doesn't come. I try to speak to it—*Beast, worry not, I am here*—but it's just my voice shouting in my mind. I can't reach it.

The nets tense as the serpent twists and coils. Its tail is free, and it swings it wildly, clobbering the two Nosca that get too close.

"Steady," Izamal calls. "Ready yourselves—"

With one great twist, the beast breaks free of the nets. It becomes fully visible, eyes glinting, long fangs dripping acid that bubbles and sparks where it hits earth. Its fury reaches fever pitch.

It speeds toward us, carving a path in the earth.

Dalca shouts, "Shields!"

The Wardana step into a line, snapping dials on their gauntlets.

In a flare of ikonomancy, a line of man-height shields materializes. A Wardana's shield goes up in front of me, and he half kneels to brace it.

"Brace!" Dalca calls.

A heartbeat. A crash like glass on steel, loud as a thunderclap. The serpent twists, smashing along the line—a wave goes through the Wardana as they brace against it.

"Spears!" Dalca pulls his spear from his gauntlet, maneuvering it into a notch in the Wardana's shield before me.

The serpent bashes itself against the line again, but this time the spears pierce its skin, tearing scales from its body.

It retreats a good ten feet, spitting acid. It rears up.

"Nets!" Izamal shouts.

The Nosca fire a volley, ikon-nets blossoming in the air and catching the beast. This time, all of them land.

"Over!" Iz calls, leaping over the line of shields. His eyes blaze with purpose; as he runs he draws several short daggers, flicking them into the creature's body.

His Nosca follow, leaping over the line of Wardana. None of them flinch, none of them hesitate.

Their daggers do something to the creature—where they touch scales, the beast stills, as if paralyzed.

The Wardana close in, but it doesn't look like the beast will break free. I make my way past the line of shields.

Izamal presses a hand between its eyes.

It screams in my mind—a wordless cry, all terror and fury, wanting to lunge and kill us all. There's no pacifying it.

I don't know the exact nature of Izamal's gift, but he must sense something similar. "It's not like the others," he says. "It won't be tamed." He shoots me a glance full of fear—fear for the beast.

The beast thrashes. The wilds have gone silent, and the weight of a thousand inhuman eyes settles on my shoulders, judging, condemning.

Please, hear me. I speak to it, to the Queen I hope is still with me. *Please.* I step closer.

Fear chokes me—fear that she won't come, that my time as a vessel is over—that I can do nothing here—

A hand grabs me—Izamal's, he drags me back—a shield drops over us just in time—fangs pierce the metal of the shield, dripping acid on the dirt below.

Dalca shoves us both back, releasing the shield. The acid smokes and sizzles as it dissolves the metal of the shield. The serpent shakes its head, dislodging the metal remains.

It broke through the ikon-net that trapped its head. The serpent twists and bucks—it's only a matter of time before the others fail.

A shout from behind. "Connect the ikon-nets!"

The Wardana slink in from behind, timing their movements to the serpent's writhing. They link the ikon-nets together, strengthening them.

I catch Izamal's elbow. "I can't reach it, Iz. I can't help."

"Get back!" Dalca yells.

A link of the ikon-net fails at the serpent's tail.

"If we can't calm it, if we can't contain it," Dalca says, "there's only one option."

Izamal grits his teeth. "Vesper?"

The hope in his eyes hurts to take in. "I can't save it."

The hope dies. He nods.

"Nosca!" he calls, and they go to him.

Izamal flings something at the creature's fangs. A tar-like substance that encases them and part of its mouth. He breaks into a run as he twists a dial on his gauntlet, materializing a spear. The Nosca pin the beast down, keeping it still.

Izamal leaps, and with one quick, sure motion, stabs down through the serpent's head. It lashes, once, twice, then stills.

The stillness is awful. All the writhing hate—all the aliveness—quashed at once. My stomach turns. A cheer rises from the Wardana, then fades.

Blood pours from the serpent. Far more than there should be from such a wound. Black blood, pooling and sinking into the earth. Everyone draws back.

I move forward. With the Queen's power, I could have saved this beast.

This was a needless death.

My foot slips as the ground under my feet slides: a scale, smooth as glass, shimmering with color. I kneel and pick it up. Tilted one way, it's visible—tilted another, it becomes nearly invisible.

A trill rises from above. A mournful tune, a lament.

I search the branches, the clearing. Perched on a spire is a massive bird, tall as three men. Its black feathers catch the light, revealing iridescent patterns that curl like oil on water. I know those feathers; I've worn them. A kinnari. Alive and majestic. Its graceful, long neck is bowed as it sings for the serpent. As it weeps for it. Its call rings through the gnarled branches, through the shards of the spires.

Stormbeasts of the wild answer its call. The ground trembles.

"Shields!" Dalca yells.

A distant roar. A stampede—dozens of creatures, all shapes and sizes, crawling insects, long-legged sprinting beasts, heavy-bodied armored creatures—antlered, horned, scaled, furred—all have come for vengeance—

I throw myself out of the way—pressing myself against a tree trunk.

Blood rushes in my ears, drowning all else out—

Time stands still—

My shadow rises.

This is your fault, it says in the Great Queen's voice.

"Help me," I ask.

You turned me away. You chose the King.

"I didn't—"

He offered you a cage, and you walked right in.

"Forgive me."

How can I?

I scream—great talons grab me by the arms—my feet leave the ground—I rise, caught in the grasp of a great bird—

It takes me higher, above the tops of the spires, above the great tree—my mouth fills with sharp, coppery taste—it's the taste of fear, for myself, for the others still fighting—

A great light blinds me. The sun—no—it's the city.

The city radiates light. So bright I have to block it with my hand. So bright it's as though the sun itself sits upon the horizon.

The light is growing. How far does it now extend? At least to the fourth—perhaps to the fifth. We'll never be able to outrun it.

How does it grow so fast? It grows faster than the Storm ever did.

Understanding dawns, cold and brittle: the Regia and the Great King held the Storm back. There's nothing holding back the light.

There's no one left to fight it.

Look, my shadow says. *His cage is coming for you.*

I scream again as talons dig into my skin. My fingertips brush the ikondial on my gauntlet—I twist and draw the head of a spear—my fingers slip, and the spearhead comes out uneven, but still sharp—I slice the bird's leg.

It drops me.

I plummet.

Breath leaves me—everything leaves me—

My shadow wraps itself around me as I plunge into water. The force of impact rattles my bones.

I sink, deep into the endless cold.

A voice comes. My shadow, now so immense I can but fit on her palm. It speaks: *Who are you?*

I'm Vesper Vale.

Who are you?

"I'm—I—" I don't know what to say. A thousand answers, none of them right. I'm more than my parents' daughter. I'm more than the vessel of the Queen. I—I'm not quite the savior they think I am. I don't know. Am I what I've done? Am I who I'm becoming?

Who am I?

Am I floating? Or am I sinking still? I can't tell. I can tell nothing about my body.

She comes to me. Her face ripples like water. Her hair melts into serpents, into vines. Her skin goes from bronze to moonlight to sapphire, and her body lengthens and shrinks, plumps and withers.

She nears until I put my hands on her to keep her from taking me over.

You think you can hold me?

Her hands grip mine.

Her mouth widens, her teeth lengthening into points, her jaw into a snout. And then she's twisting into a gnarled tree, into a wisp of smoke, into fire that licks at my cheeks and singes my eyelashes.

I can't let go. My hands burn, they freeze. Vines work their way under my fingernails.

Nothing is anything.

I'm being changed.

No—

Who are you?

I tell her without words—all my fears, all my hopes, all that I hold dear, all that I do not know about myself, all that mystery that I hope to discover—

And she says, *I know.*

Her voice echoes, but it is soft.

She continues: *You thought it was by chance that I chose you. You came to me by chance, it is true. I had chosen many before you, and if you had not come, I would have chosen many after you. But you, and only you, chose me in return. Only you accepted this bond, this burden.*

Hold me if you can.

It burns. It's a serpent, a ball of fire, a hundred thousand wasps—but I hold on. I hold until I'm nothing but pain, until even the pain fades, and there's perfect, roaring quiet.

CHAPTER 32

My eyes open. Blue-black spires reach toward the dark sky. Earth cradles me; I sit up and find myself on a bed of clovers at the edge of a small, still lake.

The wilds are full of rustling, of the song of beasts and birds, of the scratching of smaller creatures. There are no sounds of fighting, no familiar voices, no voices at all.

But I am not alone: the Queen is within me. Her presence should be a comfort, a balm. But somehow, her power feels like an ill-fitting coat. I don't understand—her power changed everything. It changed my life, it changed the world. If what she said is true . . . If some part of me still longs for the King's vision—his cage, she called it—then I have to cut that part out of me.

Something draws my attention—a sour note in the song of the wilds. A thin keening—all sorrow and pain. I get to my feet and follow the sound to its source.

A kinnari bird. An immense one—its leg alone is as tall as I am. It snaps its beak at me, and I flinch.

It favors its right leg. The other bears a gash that leaks dark blood.

"You're the one who carried me off," I say.

It spreads its wings. Its feathers are beautiful; black but for the blue-green where they catch the light. An iridescent pattern. Almost an ikon, but wilder, less structured. It's what ancient Wardana studied to make our cloaks. No other bird so large has flight.

There's an intelligence in its eyes.

"I'm sorry," I say. "Can we call it a misunderstanding?"

It beats its wings. A gust of wind nearly sends me flying.

I raise my hands in supplication. "Let me help. You can murder me after, if I don't."

It ruffles its feathers and then, with a suspicious look, settles down.

I inch closer to its leg, kneeling beside it. The spearhead I pulled would impress no Wardana, but it did a fair amount of damage. I reach within me for the Queen's power, hoping that this at least is something I can set to rights. Her power rises through me, dark and familiar, and I pour it, drop by drop, into the wound, willing it to change, to return to unharmed flesh.

The kinnari trills. Its flesh knits back together, leaving a thin scar.

Look, I tell the part of me that is uneasy at the Queen's presence, *could you have done this alone?*

I get to my feet, light with elation. The kinnari lowers its beak in something like a nod. As regally as I can manage, I nod back.

But my heart sinks as I take in my surroundings. None of it is familiar. I have no idea how to get back to the landtreaders and to the others. Please let them all be unhurt.

A shadow falls over me; the kinnari steps close.

I freeze. It considers me. I consider how sharp its beak is.

It offers me its good leg. *All right*, it seems to say, *I'll help you in return.*

Its taloned foot is firm under mine. I wrap my arm around its leg and hold on tight.

It rises into the air. My breath catches. This is nothing like flying with a cloak—each beat of the kinnari's wings sends my stomach plummeting, and I never feared a cloak changing its mind. All the same, it's glorious to rise above the tree line, to see the horizon.

From behind comes the ever-bright glow of the city. Has it grown even in these few hours?

We fly on, over wilds teeming with life, some cruel, all wondrous.

The kinnari banks right. It's spotted the landtreaders, parked in a series of defensive circles. It dives.

The ground rises to meet us.

It lets me down, nipping at my hair. "You'll stay nearby, won't you?" I ask.

It trills. I understand it to mean *perhaps*. It takes to the air, disappearing into the trees.

"Vesper!" Something barrels into me, and I'm lifted into the air— but this time only a foot. Izamal whoops, swinging me around as if I were a child, surprising a laugh out of me.

Izamal sets me on my feet and reaches as if he would ruffle my hair. I smack his hand away—that's a step too far.

He grins and lets me look him over. There's not a scratch on him.

There's a commotion at the edge of the landtreaders. Dalca leaps off a sprinter, his long legs eating up the distance between us.

"He went out to search—" Izamal explains in a whisper that cuts off as Dalca nears.

Dalca stops in front of me. His eyes are ringed with dark circles; the hollow of his neck shines with sweat.

"I'm here," I say, for lack of something intelligent.

Dalca's throat works, and I think he might reach for me, but instead he runs a hand through his hair. He nods.

I'm told that once I was carried away, the creatures disappeared back into the woods. My abduction was the only real loss, and my return is marked by a lessening of grimness. I might even call it joy.

Instead of another meal of dried rations, Mother Yul's priestesses set about making a hot supper. Anyone with any sense of cooking has pitched in, and the aroma of spices and grain wafts on the air. Imbas and her people, and others from the council, keep things organized, all working together in surprising harmony.

The clearing in the circle of landtreaders has filled with people sitting on blankets, with makeshift tables, with logs for chairs. Several small fires burn away—amongst the ordinary orange fires burn ones of blue and green, in a gleeful use of ikonomancy. So many strangers, all come together. Unbidden, thoughts of Carver come to mind. She could be any one of these people. We blamed her for Cas's deeds, but perhaps she wasn't lightstruck. There's no evidence that she was. Perhaps she found that being my guard was too difficult, too dangerous. Perhaps she just wanted a different life. Perhaps I'll see her again, and perhaps I won't . . .

And there are familiar faces:

Gamara, Jhuno, and Zerin follow me around like lost ducklings, while Ozra watches from a graceful distance.

Izamal tries to steal a ladle from a priestess, who promptly smacks him with it.

Dalca sits a little distance away on a folding table, poring over a map. A small curly haired child peers at him. When Dalca meets her eyes, she shrieks and runs away. He hides his smile.

An expanding sense of warmth fills me up. For all of them, even the folks I haven't met yet. To go on this adventure, to find a new world—to be so brave . . .

The map fragment, the crescent city, the worlds we may or may not yet discover . . . I haven't had such a sense of hope. Not since I've returned from the land of the dead.

But the Great King is growing his domain. His cage. Nothing can hold him back . . . nothing but the Great Queen.

My pulse quickens, heart beating in double time. I breathe in and out, counting the seconds, willing myself to calm.

I exhale. The drumbeat speeds on

I press a finger to the pulse point in my neck.

It's not my heart. It's the Great Queen. She's with me. She knows what I mean to do, and she is prepared. Every part of her was made for it, honed over the centuries.

There's one last thing I must do before we go. I borrow some paper from a mancer and write a few short notes. One for my guard, thanking them. One for Izamal, an inadequate one, for I don't know how to tell him what his friendship has meant to me.

And one to Dalca.

I wait till Dalca retires, till many have gone to sleep.

I find him in the Wardana landtreader, curled on his side. Slumber has taken him, softened his sharp features. He'll be a good leader. I can only hope he takes his place on the council—they'll need him.

I tuck the note by his pillow.

I'm sorry that we were so bound by our history. I meant what I said, that I've forgiven you. I hope you will forgive me for what I go to do. I've realized what it means to be a vessel, what it means to be a Regia. The King won't stop. But I can hold him back. I can give you all a chance.

I reach for him. Dalca shifts in his sleep. I hold my breath and silently raise my dagger.

Under the collar of his shirt is the leather cord that he hangs the oathmark on. I pinch the cord between my fingers and slice it. As slowly as I dare, I pull the medallion from around his neck.

I back away, holding it. His breath is steady, even—he hasn't woken.

I'm not sure what'll happen if I destroy it, if there'll be some kind of backlash against Dalca. It must need to be on him to work, otherwise there would be no reason for him to wear it. I take it with me.

Outside the landtreader, dust rises with the beat of the kinnari's wings, as the great bird descends. Did the Queen call for it, or did I? It's no matter.

The kinnari bird lowers its beak, as if it's bowing. It offers me its leg.

I climb on.

I will contain the Great King. I'll draw a storm, one that'll ring the city. An impenetrable wall. The King may have made his domain, but its borders will end there. I will protect everyone I can from him.

My arms are covered in the dark iridescent lines of her mark. I sense them dancing across my body, across my face.

There's an electric taste in the air. A storm is coming.

CHAPTER 33

The kinnari's wings cut through the air. The wind tears my hair from its cord and whips it into my face. I hold on tight to its outstretched leg as the muscles of its clawed foot shift ever so slightly under my feet. Oh, what I would give for the smooth flight of a cloak—I cut my thoughts off, glancing up at the kinnari. It seems in poor taste to wish to wear its feathers while it holds my life in its claws.

We plummet; my heart skips a beat. We soar low over a bridge that leads to the Queenskeep. Only the wind lives here now; it moans through narrow streets and whistles through gaps in wood and stone. Little breezes dance in corners, wearing like jewelry bits of grain and earth and things left behind: dried herbs, torn paper, and a lone scrap of violet fabric.

The kinnari soars higher, over rooftops and over the square, skimming the statue that was never truly of me. The watchtower looms large, filling my vision, and then we bank right—so close I could touch the vine-covered rock if I reached out—and we're past it.

We follow the road as it curves—and there it is. Five rings, stacked one on top of the other. My city, my home.

It glows, like a kingdom from an old tale, strewn with lightlines thin as spun sugar. It's as I feared—even the fifth is now caught in the cat's cradle of light. The King has claimed it all.

New towers sprout from atop the immense ringwall separating the fifth from the sixth ring. Every other one catches lightlines from within the city, but the other half are unlit. Waiting, I realize, to refract lightlines into the sixth, to yet unbuilt towers. It's only a matter of time before the King spreads his cage over the sixth.

I can't wrap my head around the pace of the Great King's expansion. It might be days before he's claimed all the land between the fifth and the river. Days more before he comes upon the sixth's market town.

My body is a string pulled taut. The Great King has the upper hand in all ways. All I can do is hope to contain him.

I whistle to the kinnari, and it descends to the river's edge. Its claws sink into the earth, sending a jolt through my body. The ground is hard underfoot, and after so long flying, braced on the ever-shifting surface of the kinnari's foot, it takes me a few steps to trust the earth to stay still. The muscles of my stomach unclench, sore from the effort it took to stay balanced in the air.

The river is dark; its surface undisturbed. I toe off my shoes and step in. The cold bites; a shiver runs up my legs to my spine, raising goose bumps in its wake. I grit my teeth to stop them rattling.

And now we begin, I tell the Queen.

Her power is a trickle, just the dregs, the last drop of grainy tea in a near-empty cup.

You wanted things to be how they once were, I say to the Queen. *You wanted the King to acknowledge you as his equal. To rule together, even being as opposite as you are. That's not what you got. But he doesn't get more than what he's taken. We will make a storm, a cage just for him.*

The Queen unfolds within me, her presence like a ghost within my body. Her mark rises across my skin, dark and bold.

Yes, she says in her ancient, thousandfold voice. *Let us make war.*

The Queen's power comes in a flood, bitter and crushing—I gasp, it'll drown me—but no, it melds with my blood; it threatens to change me, to make me not her vessel but her puppet—

I grit my teeth and push back. She relents, but her power fills me up to the brim.

I let my awareness sink into the river around me.

The river: a thick ribbon that splits in two, eyelids that surround the iris of the city. It courses through man-made channels, through the aqueduct, where the river is slivered off into streams that run through ancient pipes, into every ring, into the faucets of well-appointed homes and the fountains and pump-wells of the lower rings.

Water is changeable by nature. It laps at my ankles, eating happily the drops I feed it of the Great Queen's power.

Riding on her power is my command: *Quicken.*

The river heeds it.

A mist rises. Thin, like a gossamer veil, but it thickens and darkens, until a heavy fog hangs above the river, curving with the water and enclosing the city. A thick, churning wall.

Thick enough to make lightlines visible.

An extra-bright lightline shines from the city, probing at the fog. It's weakened by the mist as its light is dispersed. But the fog is not enough—even a full stormbarrier might not be enough, not with the King's power amplified by the crystals. With the lightlines, he'll pick at such a barrier until it falls.

I clench my fists. Without the crystals, I could have built a stormbarrier from the river to seal the city away. It would have been enough. But not now. I have to bring the storm to him—have it rage through every street, disrupt every lightline.

Obeying my command, the wall of fog moves inward, even as mist continues to rise from the river.

I whistle and am answered by a gust from the kinnari's wings. "To the city." It stretches out a leg, and I balance myself on its foot once more. With a beat of its immense wings, we take to the sky.

We stay within the shelter of the growing mist. It keeps the King blind to our approach, but it blinds me to our surroundings. I sink into the Great Queen's power—into an awareness of distant emotions, of shadow images of people, like layers of ink in water. They grow dense below as we cross the fifth's ringwall, into the fifth proper.

A sound like water bubbling—or oil sizzling—I open my eyes as a golden lightline slices through the fog.

My stomach lurches as we bank sharply left to avoid it.

Another sizzling beam—from below—the kinnari soars high and right, wind whipping into my eyes. I grip the kinnari's leg tight, trusting its instincts, even as we spin in a barrel roll.

It flattens out, and we soar. It screeches in triumph—a long, bloodcurdling call—and that's something no cloak has ever done—

Two lightlines scissor through the fog, and the kinnari drops into a nosedive. I lose my grip on its leg.

Time slows.

Black wings far above—growing smaller. The wind hisses through my ears—the air feels thick as a blanket, but it does nothing to slow me—

I fold myself tight, wrapping my arms around my middle—and something else wraps around me—my shadow, immense and tangible, cradling me in its arms. I brace.

Impact. All the wind gets knocked out of me. An awful gasping noise comes from my lips—I can't breathe.

My lungs expand—I suck in air—glorious, sweet air—and I brace for the pain that's sure to come—

My hands scrabble on something soft and springy, and I open my eyes.

All around me is a perfect circle, a bed of moss, nearly two feet thick. My shadow—it transformed the stone. I get to my feet, marveling. I'm alive. And unhurt.

Do not dally here, the Great Queen hisses. *He seeks you.*

I suppose the circle of moss is hard to miss. The more distance I put between it and me, the better.

A screech comes from above. The kinnari circles, evading the light, trying to get to me. There are too many lightlines—it'll only get itself killed.

"Go!" I shout, waving my arms.

It gives a mournful hoot, but rises, streaking into the air. Lightlines chase it—my line of sight ends as a building blocks the way between us. I pray that it got away.

With the kinnari goes the small bit of peace I'd carved out for myself. My heart thuds, and my stomach churns, all acid and oil. The walls loom large over me—everything is more daunting here than from the kinnari's vantage—and I miss the sense of security that came with flight. I get my bearings, taking in a handful of market stalls, wide, straight pathways, neat wood shutters. Not the crowded chaos of the fifth; no, I'm somewhere in the fourth ring.

Focus, Vesper. The mist has stilled, and I urge it to move. If I can get to the palace, the Great Queen can take over. They'll have their endless fight. And my people will be protected.

It's funny. When I think of *my people*, it's really only a few faces that rise in my mind's eye. And of all of them, it's Dalca I think of now. He was willing to be Regia like his mother was Regia, a mind trapped in a body, a puppet for another being. He'll understand why I've chosen to come back.

Footsteps near, and I draw myself back, into the relative shelter of an alley.

The mist parts for a girl of fifteen or so years, with a basket tucked into the crook of her arm. She hums as she walks, a faint smile on her face. The mist might not even be there, for all she notices it.

I press myself to the wall, but she pays me no mind. She looks down, digging for something in her basket, just as a door swings open and a boy steps out, calling something over his shoulder.

She bumps into him, her basket tipping. He grabs her elbows and straightens her out, and in a supreme show of reflexes, he catches the trinket that went flying from her basket. She tucks a lock of hair behind her ear, and they share a look—a first-love sort of look, all promise and sudden enchantment.

The scene has the familiarity of a story, of a child's tale, of a play. Unreal and beautiful.

A memory comes unbidden, of the Great King's voice: *I know your place, Vesper. I know what you would need to be happy. I know, of the thousands upon thousands of people of this city, which is worthiest of your love.*

His city-wide ikon—his plan—he's put it into action. The shape of it, a flower with layers of petals, rises in my mind's eye. Each ring of petals can be completed independently. He'll keep adding more to it. There will never be an end to his ambitions.

A lightline swings by, and the boy and girl pay it no attention. But just as it brushes past them, as if it's the most natural thing, they part ways, throwing shy looks over their shoulders.

Keeping track of the lightlines, I hurry my way deeper into the city.

Everywhere are lightstruck, going about their perfect day. The streets are full of surprised second glances, of lovers clasping hands, of tearful apologies and forgiving hugs.

Sitting on the edge of a fountain, a young man exclaims—a poet, I figure, from the billowy outfit and the zither at his hip. He scrawls down a line in his book, his face bright with inspiration and focus. Will he write that same line each day till the end of time?

My toe catches a loose stone as I twist to follow a head of white hair—an elderly woman, not Casvian Haveli. Hope flickers dimly in my chest, but after I nearly trip twice more, I force myself to put Cas and Hadria out of mind.

A stall keeper organizes what, at this distance, seems to be an assortment of rubbish. She greets a customer, who stops in his tracks and, with shaking hands, picks up a pendant. They're too far for me to hear their exchange, but I can read the awed expression on one's face, and the smiling way the stall keeper waves away their payment.

It's a reoccurring theme in his grand play. Revealed in each tiny, monumental moment. This is the culmination of the Great King's plan?

There are no arguments. No friction.

A perfect day. A plan for everyone. A deep dark doubt settles into me. Is this so bad?

A glimmering brightness out of the corner of my eye. I jump—but it's too late. A faint lightline passes over me, bathing me in faint warmth. I'm thankful it's not the sizzling kind that cuts and sears flesh, but all the same, the King now knows where I am.

The fountain. I rush to it, forcing the water up and high, thickening it into fog. A brief shield. I feed it more as I take off at a sprint.

The Great Queen whispers a warning. *If his light cannot reach you . . .*

The hair on the back of my neck stands tall. Something's changed. The mist is thickening still—it's not that. I duck into an alley, catching my breath and shutting my eyes, dipping into the Queen's power, into the awareness she grants me. Into the vision of shadows.

The lightstruck. Their movements have changed. No longer do they move in a pattern so vast as to seem random—now they march in neat lines, scouring the streets, the alleys.

They're coming for me.

They loom out of the mist, hands reaching, eyes scanning. Their expressions are fixed in puzzled half smiles—the kind Amma might've worn if a stray cat made its way into the house.

I raise my hands and the Queen's power spills out of me, turning stone into vines that grow in a thicket, blocking the alley's mouth. I run down to the other end.

If they kill me, I say to the Queen, *you'll be unbound. Fight the King as you will, but keep the fight contained to the city.*

She bristles. *Do not presume you have power over me.*

I grit my teeth. *Please.*

She doesn't answer.

My lungs burn, but fear keeps my legs moving from alley to alley. The crimson road is a few streets away—I might be able to take that to the third ring. The curved façade of the Ven peeks through the gaps between rooftops, looming over the fourth.

I turn the corner, and the way is blocked. Lightstruck stand in a row, silent and waiting, blocking the way. One has white hair—but no, it's an old man.

Focus, Vesper.

Footsteps sound behind me.

To the side is a narrow alleyway—I run down it—skidding to a stop before a door. I push it open. A storeroom, bare but for a table set for tea, one cup overturned. A layer of dust covers everything. On the far wall is a door—I push it open, running through a tidy pantry, to another door. A shopkeeper's house and home, from brief glimpses—

Footsteps echo, following me.

I dash down a hallway, reaching for the door at the end. The knob is locked—with a drop of the Queen's power, it crumbles in my hand—the door gives way and I dart through, slamming it shut—

A hand catches the door. A strong hand—even with me shoving with all my might, it pushes the door open.

I back away.

A flash of white hair and a wry voice. "Thank you for the exercise, but that's quite enough."

My heart leaps into my throat. "Cas?"

CHAPTER 34

The man framed in the doorway has long, pale white hair. His eyes are Cas's eyes, the wry twist to his lips one that Cas often sports. But this man wears his years as lines around his eyes and between his brows, and—though it's perhaps not charitable to Cas to mention—he's twice Cas's size, all brawn and intimidation.

"Ragno Haveli," I say. I'd feel safer with a rabid stormbeast.

"Vesper Vale," he returns. Light glides across his unearthly smooth skin, glints from every strand of his hair.

His curse. A shiver runs up my spine. His skin, his hair—every visible part of him is glass. Save for his Regia's Guard leathers, once black on gold, now a sun-bleached white-gray.

There's a window at my back. I could—

"We need to move."

He turns on his heel in a showy way—a move, I realize, designed for a thousand-and-one-feather cloak, to have it billow impressively—and strides into the hallway.

I poke my head through the door. He's a few steps down the hall, at a door cracked open. He frowns at whatever he sees. I swallow around the dryness in my mouth. "You're—are you lightstruck?"

Ragno gives me a withering look. "That is a poorly designed

question. Surely no one would answer yes, lightstruck or not."

My thoughts skid to a stop. Hearing Cas's sarcasm from Ragno's mouth—

"Come."

I flinch when he reaches for me.

He exhales, quick and irritated. "The lightstruck are back on pattern—a gap will come in five seconds." He scowls, as if it's my fault he has to explain himself.

I probe him with the Queen's power, seeing with her eyes. There's no denying that her curse is in him. It's there in the hollow of his heart, a shadow shaped like a shard of glass.

A tingle of familiarity, of premonition—

Ragno snaps his fingers. "Now."

I scowl at his back. What winning personalities, these Havelis.

He darts into the alley. No sign of the lightstruck. I hesitate. It doesn't make sense. If he's lightstruck, why is he helping me avoid the others?

But something urges me after him. If he's not lightstruck—then he's the first to ever come back from it. I have to know how. If I could seal the Great King away but save the lightstruck . . . A flicker of hope burns in my chest.

And besides, even if I'm wrong and he's lightstruck, I have the Queen's power. He's no match for me.

I steel myself and follow. "If you're helping me, I need to get as deep into the city as possible."

"All right. Keep moving." He takes off with distance-eating strides. I match his pace through the twisting streets of the fourth, sidestepping rubble from the Great King's reconstruction. His speed slows and quickens at a rhythm only he knows. When I catch up to him—a feat that occurs only every fifteen minutes or so—I make out a few notes of a song he hums under his breath. It's a different song to the one Cas was singing in the palace, but it reminds me of him all the same.

We make our way like that for over an hour, perhaps for over two. Until Ragno calls a halt. "We have just under twenty minutes. There's a wedding procession. Blocks the street for a half hour each day. Once they pass, we'll cross."

I nod and peer over a tower of crates that block the view of the street. They seem a happy bunch—drummers, dancers, flower-throwers— all escorting what seems to be the groom, judging by his hat, to the wedding hall.

I turn to Ragno. "What's that song you've been singing?"

He drags his attention from some dark corner of his mind, fixing his eyes on me. "Your mother never would have followed me."

The air leaves my lungs. A blow I didn't expect.

"She hated asking for help." Ragno pulls back. "Pardon me. That was overly familiar of me. Though I saw you as an infant, once." He holds his hands a few inches apart, demonstrating not the size of an infant, but a shalaj root. Unless I was an unfortunately small baby.

I cross my arms. It's possible, I guess.

His gaze darts to the lines rising on my skin. "There was a voice. It told me all was well. It told me how I fit into the beautiful plan. I loved that voice in a way I have never loved anything before. Perhaps I should be ashamed. It was such an easy, overwhelming devotion. And you came. Whatever you did to me . . . A war broke out within me. I prayed for the voice to triumph. But it could no longer drown out everything. My fears, the ones I had left behind, of being too weak to save those who mattered to me—I could not shake them.

"I was useless. Like a wounded dog. I barely moved at first. It felt like I broke apart with even the slightest motion." He looks at his hand, flesh colored but gleaming, as if he wears a glass glove. "I can control it. Change from glass to flesh at will. Glass shatters, but can be mended. In a sense, a body of glass is stronger than a body made only of skin and bones."

My mind reels. Being cursed saved him from the light. "Do you miss it?" I ask. "Being lightstruck?"

A long pause. "No."

"So many of them seem happy," I admit. "It's enough to make me wonder . . . if I'm making a mistake."

"A mistake? I cannot say. I will say that my son would not have been at your side if he hadn't believed in you. And he is far more brilliant than I could ever hope to be."

"You don't understand. Cas was lightstruck."

"He followed you before that. Do you not know? No . . . perhaps you wouldn't. He became of the light at the same time as Toran Belvas."

That means . . . I lost Cas when the third fell.

He throws me a glance. "He likely still believes in you, somewhere under the influence of the King."

I bite my cheek. "But if he's happy . . . If people are happier being lightstruck . . ."

"These people are not happy. They're asleep. All this?" He gestures at the procession, at everything. "It is an avoidance of suffering. Of choice, of agency. They would be as good as dead."

I shake my head, neither disagreeing nor willing to believe.

"I could show you," Ragno says. "All you need to do is look long enough. Every day, it's the same pantomime. A single perfect day. Repeated forevermore. You asked about the song. Any song of the right tempo will do. Watch carefully, and you'll see evidence of a single mind behind it all. A single point of view."

Is that so wrong?

His gaze goes over my head, and he tenses. "Time to move."

We cross the street, skirting past homes, to a narrow stairwell that zigzags up to the third ring. But when we come out onto the wide boulevard of the third—just a few blocks from the Ven—we stop dead.

A line of lightstruck stand in our way. Their expressions are flat, but their eyes watch us.

"Ragno—" I start.

Ragno nods, his hair falling into his face with the tinkle of glass on glass. "Keep going."

I take a step to one side, and the lightstruck follow, mirroring me.

"Well, now. This is different," Ragno says. "Where did you need to get to?"

I'd hoped to reach the palace . . . "The Ven will do."

"Then we shall go. I'll clear a path."

He can't mean to take them on alone. "There's too many."

Ragno gives me a roguish grin—and for a second, I see the boy he must have been once, an arrogant, reckless troublemaker. He turns the ikondial on his gauntlet and, in a flash, draws out a long handle topped off with a curved blade. His scythe. "You children are always underestimating your elders."

My feet won't move. "You'll kill them?"

"If I must."

They're just people. "You make it sound easy."

"Everything is easier with practice. Your father should've taught you that."

"I can't condone—"

"Vesper. The burden of bravery is that of the young. The matter of weighing lives against a future, bloodying our hands . . . that's a burden better borne by those who've already dirtied their hands."

I don't like this.

"I have made my vows, child. I am a Regia's Guard." Ragno holds my gaze until he sees I understand. With a smile, he sweeps into a precise bow, a low bow, with all the respect due a Regia. When he unfolds, there's no levity in his expression—just perfect focus. "Keep close."

Ragno swings his scythe and clears the way. I follow in his wake. Two blocks to the Ven. But more and more lightstruck show up.

I draw mist from faucets, from fountains, from the moisture in the air. The Great Queen's power pulses in time with my heartbeat—out of the corner of my eye, my shadow rises behind me, a swirling creature of transformation. One block to the Ven.

A tinkling of glass. A lightstruck lands a blow to Ragno's arm, shattering it. I take a step, but with a vicious expression, Ragno flicks his arm and the shards fly into the lightstruck's side. The lightstruck crumples—Ragno lowers his scythe, stepping over their body instead of delivering a greater blow. I exhale. He's not going in for the kill indiscriminately. Not even—as another attacks—when it would be an easier shot.

The hair on my skin rises, and a metallic taste coats my teeth. The air becomes electric.

A beam of light—so focused it makes a sound, like oil sizzling—cuts through the fog, heating and dissipating the mist, leaving a trail of clear air behind.

"Vesper!" Ragno calls from the archway into the Ven, a trail of bodies leading to his feet.

I tear my gaze from the swinging lightline and race into the Ven.

The mist is thick; the fog immense. It's time to churn it into a

Storm, to give it greater life. To do more than run. Yes, the Ven will work for what I need to do.

The archway into the Ven is carved with the stories of the heroes of the past. The dust of the courtyard rises into the air, and I glance up at the second-story walkway that surrounds the yard. There's a way onto the roof that Iz showed me, back when I was powerless, when I was just Vesper. That's where I'll go. That's where we'll make our stand.

I sprint up the stairs, pausing at the railing as Ragno holds off the lightstruck below. "Ragno," I call. "If it's true. If being cursed saved you from the light—I can save Cas."

A spark lights in his eyes. "Good. I might owe him an apology."

I make for the roof as sounds of fighting follow me. I scramble up a ladder and onto the sloping slate tiles, catching my balance.

A layer of fog has penetrated the city, but the first ring is clear. Lightlines sweep through the fog, and their heat will slowly but surely disperse the mist.

It's not enough.

The Queen hisses in my ear. *Give me more control.*

I hesitate for a fraction of a second. The more I give, the more she takes. Must I let her take me over, turn me into a puppet, like how the King used the Regia?

I ease open our connection, just the barest amount. It's like opening the door to a flood—she pours in, taking and taking, until I wrench the door shut. Half of me is mine; half of me is hers.

Darkness slips over my vision; all shadows seem to grow more intense. I close my eyes and focus.

The entirety of the mist quickens, thickens, moves. With aching slowness, it spirals around the city. It grows dark and electric—a crack of lightning and a low rumble of thunder that rattles through my bones.

Glass shatters. The sound breaks through my concentration. In the courtyard below, Ragno locks weapons with a man with long, pale hair, clad in shattered mirror armor. My stomach plummets, even before they circle, before the man turns and I make out his features.

Casvian.

Focus on the Storm, the Great Queen admonishes.

Help me, I say to her. It's my fault Cas is lightstruck. If being cursed is a shield from the full brunt of the light—that means I took away his protection when I undid his curse. I can make this right.

A clang of metal against metal—Ragno and Cas fight, blows landing almost too fast to follow—

I reach for Cas with the Great Queen's power. She fights me—my vision flickers—shadows bleeding into color, bleeding into shadows—

Ragno's scythe lowers to Cas's neck. It stays for one second, for two. Agony twists Ragno's face—he will lower his scythe no further.

Cas takes the opening, darting forward. His sword cuts through not glass but flesh.

My heart stops.

Ragno falls to his knees, hand clutching his side, his bloody fingers grasping for purchase on the hilt. It's too deep—*please, Ragno, stand up*—but there's no one to hear my prayers.

Cas raises his head. He wears an expression I've never seen on him, a soft, bland smile. He steps closer to Ragno, his toes brushing Ragno's knees. He picks up Ragno's scythe.

Ragno tilts his face up. He says something I can't hear. And before Cas can land another blow, Ragno grabs him around the waist.

Not a fighter grappling, but a father embracing a son.

CHAPTER 35

Ragno falls at Cas's feet.

My chest hollows out, and a tingling sense of emptiness runs through my veins. Everything tears itself out of my throat—in a great gasping sob—and I scrub away the hot wetness that runs down my face—

These tears . . . I can't believe they're for Ragno. I hated him so, so much when I learned what he had done all those years ago. If, in the days after he burned Amma's down, I'd had a chance to kill him . . . there's not a doubt in my mind that I would have. With my bare hands—with my teeth, even, if that's all I had. And in time, I probably would have come to regret that choice, but that's what it would've been.

A choice.

My tears are for Cas, who will never weep for himself, not with the Great King in control. He'll never be allowed to know what he's done, never be allowed to mourn.

I was wrong. No perfect plan can be worth the price the Great King demands. No perfect day, not even a perfect lifetime. Nothing is worth what Cas has been made to do. What anyone can be made to do, at the Great King's whim.

The Great Queen simmers under my skin. *Yes. We have come for war.*

Her power courses through me, a deep and endless river. I wipe my palms on my trousers and ignore the acid churning in my stomach. Ragno . . . he was many things, but he was also the last ally I'll ever have. The last I'll ever fail.

I take hold of the Queen's power, submerge myself in the flow of it. She's right. This is a fight.

From the rooftop, I have a magnificent view. The fog has thickened beautifully down in the fifth ring, but it grows thinner, until it's but a faint chalkiness in the air around me. It should be thicker than this.

Cutting through the fog like spears are thousands of lightlines, each no thicker than a strand of hair. They move in small increments, side to side and up and down, like they're mapping the city.

I take shelter in the slope of the roof. The lightlines can't reach me from their angle. But it doesn't look like they're searching, not exactly. More like . . . fingers grasping at the fog.

I follow one lightline, watch it pierce a patch of fog. I squint. The lightline leaves behind a trail, almost like . . . like the fog's been thinned out in its wake. The Great King is making a move. He's warming up the air, to force the mist to clear and the clouds of the storm to disperse.

To break apart the barrier, to remove all that cloaks me from his view. He's fighting back.

Cas tilts his head up, scanning the rooftops for me. I crouch low. "Vesper," he calls. "You agreed with the Great King's plans. Why do you now interfere?"

He climbs up the stairs. It won't be long before he's climbed the ladder to the roof.

I close my eyes and reach out with the Queen's power. She doesn't fight me, not this time.

Cas's emotions are a still lake, placid, mirrorlike. There's not a trace of his old curse within him. I force myself deeper, into the lake. Memories are buried here, painted in shadows, in layers of dark smoke. A small boy amongst larger children, watching quietly, carefully. Scenes of a hulking figure I recognize as a warped portrait of Ragno. Fearful images: of finding Dalca in a pool of blood. Of reading day after day to a sleeping girl, terrified she'll never wake.

I taste each of his fears. The Queen's power would make them rise, turn them into present horrors, ones he must face. If the King's light offers a chance to put down the burden of one's own life, the Queen's touch forces one to confront what has been buried deep. One is a forced forgetting, one is a forced remembering.

I hesitate. Which is merciful? Which is right?

Is there such a thing as a choice that is so right, it remains unquestionable in every circumstance? Or does everything become a mistake, sooner or later? Is there any way to know?

The crack of slate tiles shocks me out of my thoughts. Cas treads over the roof tiles, his eyes on me. Blood is splattered across the lower half of his mirrored armor. He carries Ragno's scythe.

The Queen's mark curls across my skin. I reach for him.

Cas raises his scythe.

My shadow rises to meet him, a figure of dark curling smoke. His scythe goes through its heart—but as the curved blade touches shadow, it is transformed into sand. Cas lets go of the long handle, and it clatters to the rooftop.

I step forward, moving through my fading shadow, and my fingers brush the warm skin of his cheek.

The Queen's power runs through me, and a drop flows into him. A curse.

I hold my breath as it sinks into him. Will it free him from the King's light?

Cas's pupils dilate. He staggers back, and a strangled scream tears itself from his throat.

"Cas," I say. "Casvian?"

He doesn't hear me. He falls to his knees, hands clawing through his hair. My limbs are frozen.

Move! the Great Queen shouts. *The King is coming.*

I kneel beside him. *Please, Cas.* I clench my fists, willing him to move, to rise. A shudder goes through him, and he crumples.

I catch him and slap his cheeks. "Casvian Haveli—can you hear me? You need to get up—"

He's so still.

"Cas, please," I whisper.

The Queen's cutting voice echoes through my mind. *You can do no more.*

A crack of focused light. White light. It grows louder—a sizzling hiss—it separates into several lines of color. The spectrals.

I drag Cas a few feet down the slope of the roof. His cheek is cold to the touch, but his pale eyelashes flutter. I whisper in his ear, "I have to go now. I'll draw them away. Just—wake up, all right? And for Storm's sake, don't get yourself killed."

The King's minions are here, the Queen warns. *Leave him.*

With one last look at Cas's slumbering figure, I escape into the halls of the Ven. Footsteps ring out—the lightstruck. I make no effort to mute the sound of my feet pounding against the stone floors—better the lightstruck come after me than find Cas.

I run, forcing water out of fountains, out of groundwork pipes, out of a jug someone left behind—each drop adding to the might of the Storm.

The sizzling, crackling light draws near and swings past. I need to get somewhere I can see it all.

Over the rooftops, a tower juts toward the sky. A lightline shines from it; a solitary lightship speeding away to another tower.

It'll do. I make for it as fast as I can—doubling back at the sight of lightstruck—and pausing as I reach the edge of the courtyard that circles the tower.

I hum Ragno's song, timing the lightstruck crossing the courtyard. On cue, a gap appears.

My feet pound on stone, carrying me to the base of the tower. A simple wooden door is the only way in or out. It's locked, but a single drop of the Queen's power turns the knob into a fluttering of violet flowers.

Steps spiral upward, and I take them by twos until I reach the top.

A great crystal sits in the center of the space. It's been cut carefully, and a ball of light glows from within it. I step closer. It's dimmer than I'd expected—perhaps it hasn't been filled to the brim with the Great King's power.

I turn my back to it. From the edge of the tower, the city spreads before me. My stomach falls. The fog is thinning, and the spectrals are on the hunt. The red spectral flits across rooftops—in an image of the Regia Dalcanin running, each step a great leap, blinking in and out as his lightline is interrupted by buildings that block the line of sight between him and the palace.

A thin emerald lightline moves through the streets. I can't make out the emerald spectral at the end of it, but as he rises from a pile of rubble, I understand: he's searching the old city. They draw near, just a few streets away.

My hand shakes as I scrub my face.

Have you come to cry? the Queen asks. *Or to make war?*

I draw a breath and spread my arms. A thick mist forms around me. She's right. The Great King won't stop. I can give Iz and Dalca a chance, a real chance at establishing a better future.

"Why, Vesper?" A low, crackling voice speaks.

I jump out of my bones. The violet spectral stands behind me, beside the crystal.

"What do you want?" I ask, scanning the tower, but it appears he's come alone.

"Why are you doing this?" he asks. "All this . . . Isn't this what you wanted? Look how much smaller the world is now that he's destroying the barriers that separated the rings. Look at the lightships—at how much easier it is for a fifth-ringer to access the third—or even the palace. That which divided us is all falling away, now that our people have a greater purpose. They have found meaning; they have found peace."

His words echo thoughts I once had. There was a time when I'd never dreamt of setting foot in the palace—even the third ring was a world beyond my reach. But there's one thing I do not doubt. "Does Cas know peace?" I ask. "With his father's blood on his hands? He'll never hear what Ragno wanted to say."

The violet spectral stills.

"I don't have a grand plan," I say. "I'm just trying to protect those who don't want this."

He looks at me for a long moment, the violet specks of light settling into a slow, gentle churning. "You've always frightened me."

The pinpricks of violet light dance quicker. I tense, steeling myself for his next move.

He looks down at the dancing motes of his hands. "Things come undone around you. I used to know who I was meant to be. I used to have a place in the world. I used to know what was right . . . Because of you, I knew doubt. I knew fear so immense it choked me—I can feel its hands still, wrapped around my throat." He demonstrates, touching his neck. "The Great King ordered us to strike you down. I understand why."

I brace, drawing a barrier around my body.

"Long ago, I made the wrong choice," he says. "This time, I won't." He puts his hand to the crystal, and it brightens, glowing with violet light. He meets my eyes.

Between one blink and the next, he's gone. A line of violet light runs from the crystal down to the street below. And there he is, drawing other lightlines toward him. What does he intend?

The emerald spectral goes to meet him.

Call the Storm, the Great Queen urges. She bristles within me, like a creature caged.

From every source of water in the city—from the clouds above—from the river, from the air—I become aware of it all. The Queen's power rushes out of me, and it's her will, not mine, that draws the Storm.

I am just a conduit. A vessel. It's her power that matters. And, like any clay pot, when I shatter, I'll have outlived my use.

Sparks of light come from below. The violet spectral battles the emerald—both raise their arms, commanding an array of the King's lightlines. Hope rises in my throat, fragile and aching.

I focus on the Storm—another flash of light—

A quake rattles my bones—its source is the fight below, where a violet lightline connects with one of emerald. Where they meet is a ball of crackling light, of surging energy—it glows violet then emerald, switching back and forth a dozen times in a violent tug-of-war.

He's granting me the gift of time, to build the Storm.

I sink back into the Queen's power—thick clouds spiral, knitting together—

A blinding flash—the crystal brightens at my back—as below, the violet spectral rises to his feet. He's a vision of Dalca, triumphant, his cloak billowing in the wind. The emerald spectral is gone. But something's changed—the violet spectral has darkened, like he's absorbed the emerald spectral's light.

He staggers, and the vision fades—he's just the image of a boy in a too-grand costume, exhausted. His head jerks toward the palace—I follow his gaze, seeing nothing—and then he's gone.

From the direction of a palace comes a rhythmic thumping. The march of a hundred boots, in inhumanly perfect unison.

Pebbles by my feet vibrate in time, quivering their way to the platform's edge. They fall, one by one, rattling down the side of the tower.

They land at the feet of an army of lightstruck. The lightstruck spill into the courtyard from every street, rounding every corner. They halt in a circle around where the emerald spectral fell.

They stand in silence. A soft sound grows, like wind rising and falling.

A tingle of electric shock runs down my spine. The sound is the lightstruck breathing in perfect unison.

They wait.

A screech like a knife down a sitar string heralds the coming of a red beam of light. It cuts through the mist and lands in the center of the gathered lightstruck. The red spectral paces, then squats down and examines the place the emerald spectral fell.

A crackling hiss echoes through the stone tower, shaking my bones and grinding my teeth. A yellow beam of light shines over the crowd. The ancient Regia bathed in yellow light lands with a gentle step beside the red spectral.

An urgent whisper comes from behind me. "Get down!"

The violet spectral materializes at my elbow. I duck back behind the tower wall as a line of orange light streaks past the tower and lands between the yellow and red spectrals. Together they pace the circle, exchanging words I'm too far away to hear.

The violet spectral staggers backwards. His eyes are shadowed, mouth drawn, the motes of light moving sluggishly. Who would have imagined spectrals could get hurt?

As if he heard my thoughts, he straightens, flashing a swaggering grin. A deflection. "I had no idea I could do that." He shows me his hand. Emerald specks of light swirl between the violet motes that make up his fingers. His grin softens. "I suppose you bring out the best in me."

I just resist rolling my eyes. "I need more time."

He winces as he leans forward over the edge, taking the measure of the three spectrals, surrounded by an army of lightstruck. "A full audience."

I clench my fist as blue sky appears through the clouds above, forcing them to knit tighter. "Can you hold them off?" I ask.

He looks at me with a weary smile, like I said something funny without knowing it.

"What?"

"It's nothing."

He gathers himself, standing tall, the flecks of light within him quickening. He cracks his neck and brushes some light particles off his arms. "When I was a child, I anticipated the moment when my people would look up to me as their Regia. Their hero."

He steps to the edge of the platform and leans over as if gauging a jump. He takes a deep breath and meets my eyes. "Lately, I've been dreaming that it might be enough . . ." He shakes his head, an embarrassed twist to his lips.

I prod. "Enough?"

He meets my eyes. "Enough to be just one person's hero."

He's gone. The crystal brightens, and a violet stream shoots from it, slicing through the air. The violet spectral puts on a show, separating into thin beams of light that scatter amongst the lightstruck.

The three spectrals meet him head-on. Sparks fly—I catch a vague impression of a tug-of-war—before the light grows blinding. All I can tell for sure is that the violet spectral is giving me time.

I sink back into the Queen's power—thick clouds spiral, knitting together—

The Queen hisses. *More.* She trembles with anger, aching to pour herself out into the city.

I reach with her power through the streets, yanking the water from the falling mist back up, up toward the palace, pulling it together into denser and denser air.

More!

The Storm crackles, a dome forming overhead. I strain, willing the clouds to turn—for all the softness of clouds, it feels like pushing a thousand boulders—and with great reluctance, the clouds move, gaining momentum.

A flash.

Down below in the street, the violet spectral is on his knees. The yellow spectral is behind him, her arm around his throat, pinning him.

He can only fight so long. I push the clouds with all my might; they roll and rumble, turning round and round the city.

The orange and red spectrals reach for the violet—he screams as they tear him apart.

The light from the crystal behind me dims.

In a thousand voices, the Queen screams, *MORE!*

I heave our power into the clouds and the churning air crackles with the first rumbles of thunder.

It echoes through the street, and the three spectrals tilt their faces toward the sky.

The violet spectral looks up at me with Dalca's eyes. The yellow spectral sees, follows his line of sight to my tower. She makes a quick movement—his eyes widen—

He fades, and the crystal behind me falls dark. He's gone.

No. Thunder roars through the city as my voice.

The yellow spectral points to my tower, and the others turn to me. They approach in flickers of light, crossing huge lengths in seconds.

In an instant, I draw my awareness down from the churning storm, throwing up a stormbarrier to block them from my body.

They cut through with crackling beams of concentrated light.

I'm knocked backward. My hands scrabble on rubble as I'm tossed into the stairwell, tumbling down a flight of steps.

My back hits stone, and I gather my breath in the darkness of the stairwell. Lights flicker from the top of the stairs.

I have a brief reprieve—they can't refract themselves into the bit of shadow where I lie. They pace the opening, the multicolor glow of their light cast on the stone wall.

The red spectral's gaze is fixed on me. His face is a twisted mask of hate, of fury. The air trembles as if in a haze, and just visible are the great prismatic hands of the King, guiding them.

His voice crackles. "Enough of this. The fight is over. All you do now is risk the lives of those you claim to protect. What is this madness that you've brought to our city?"

I get to my feet, pressing myself against the wall. How long can I stay here?

The yellow spectral calls. "Enough, child. You disgrace the legacy of the vessels that came before you. Bring no more shame upon them."

My nails bite into my palms. To fight three of them . . .

The light intensifies—a great crash. A sizzling lightline blasts open the roof of the tower. Dust and debris rain down on me. I shield my head, but the cold kiss of wind tells me there's only sky above me. My reprieve is over.

The spectrals descend.

And there is perfect silence in my mind. A single thought, tremulous and awful and true, rings through my ears:

I am not enough.

I can't fight them. I'm no warrior. I'm no great vessel, skilled in using the Queen's power. And it is her power that matters.

Take over, I tell the Queen. *My body is yours. Have the fight you want, but—please—protect my people.*

A heartbeat of silence.

Her answer comes in a rush, in a choking, howling flood of power.

I am devoured. Bowled over and carried deep into a half-drowned part of myself. She seals me in, locks me there.

And I let her.

CHAPTER 36

My hands rise, but not of my volition. The Queen takes a step with my feet, my lips twist with her triumph.

The spectrals fall back, for good reason—they're more powerful with direct line of sight to the palace.

The Queen doesn't care. She doesn't stop; she puts one foot in front of the other until she's standing at the top of the tower—now more like a platform open to the air—her hair blowing in the wind.

The red spectral leads the pack. He draws smaller lightlines to him and grows larger and brighter with their light. He rises before the tower, pointing an accusing finger. "Warmonger. I separated the gods and ended the war. And now you, you call them to battle?"

The Great Queen gives him no answer—and I can't move my mouth. I'm riding along in my own body.

With another flick of my hand, the Queen creates a wave of black shadows—they appear between one blink and the next, effortlessly—and makes them rise over the spectral. I expect them to go right through him, but they latch on to him, dimming his light. He flickers like a candle in the wind—and when he reappears, he's further away. A retreat.

Good, I say. *You can make the stormwall to trap the King.*

If the Queen heard me, she makes no sign of it. She raises her hands—my hands—and with a flick of her fingers, shadows rise from every corner. They chase down the spectrals.

Hands of shadow rise up and cup the orange spectral—the same way a child's hands might cage a lightning bug. They squeeze tight.

A muffled crackle. The hands open; the orange spectral is gone.

The emerald spectral fights back, sending columns of light that pierce the shadows, splitting them into dozens of smaller ones. The Queen's shadows slither like snakes, wrapping around him, tighter and tighter, until he too is snuffed out.

The Regia Dalcanin—the red spectral—commands a dozen light-lines to meld together. The immense lightline lets out a high-pitched wail as it swings forth, cutting through everything it touches.

The Queen raises several walls of shadow—but the lightline cuts through them with ease. She raises more and more, and then she creates a dozen figures made of shadows—each that take the form of a running girl, each leaping down onto different rooftops. In the same moment, the Queen draws shadows over our body, so we blend into the tower wall.

The shadow girls draw the lightline away from us, and it splits to follow them.

The red spectral swings his head, following each girl, sending lightlines to cut each shadow in half. He's distracted.

The Queen raises a wave of shadowy stormcloud that rises over the spectral, falling like a blanket over him. He screams as he's crushed into nothingness.

A dim glittering of sapphire blue light dances across the remains of the battle. It forms into the spectral body of the last Regia, Nayeli Azerad Illusora. Dalca's mother. She makes no move to fight; she only stands with her hands behind her back.

She disappears from below—and reappears at our side. She touches a hand to the crystal.

"My son gave all he had . . . And for what? So you could give your power to her?" She turns to me with lips curled downward. Her disdain is clear, her contempt unmistakable.

I can give her no answer; the Queen pays her little attention.

"I understand," she says. "The only thing more terrifying than being trapped with the King was having to lead my own life."

She's speaking to me, not the Queen. I shout, *That's not what I'm doing,* but the words only echo in my mind. My voice is forbidden from passing through my lips.

The Regia shakes her head. "I thought you weren't like me."

I'm not. I'm nothing like her. I'm giving myself up so those who are still free can choose for themselves—I'm understanding that the Queen is stronger than me, that only she can fight the King.

The Regia snaps, "It's your body to do with what you will."

Shadows encircle the Regia. Her gaze is fixed on me, even as the shadows rise into a cage, as they grow thick, as they seal her away, as they snuff her out.

All is calm. My heartbeat echoes in my ears.

A great light shines from the palace like a shooting star. It makes for us. A being of immense proportions, a being whose shape is altered by the angle at which he is beheld. The Great King himself has come.

My body takes a step back as the Great Queen readies herself. I sense her thoughts like a vague echo, a stream of images and emotions. She fears his strength, fears that it still surpasses hers, with all the crystals of the city amplifying his power.

And she comes to a decision: she needs everything.

My blood chills with dark foreboding.

She draws on the stormwall. Drawing it back to her.

No, I shout at her. *We have to keep him contained.*

But the Queen pays me no mind. She cares only for the King, for the war she has waited long to wage.

She raises a sea of darkness. Churning waves of cloudsmoke, spilling through streets, rising over buildings, a surge swelling high into the sky.

A great light rises. Afterimages blossom across my vision—an immense face, ancient, burning, cruel.

A sword of light meeting a shield of darkness. My veins run cold and electric with the Queen's power—my face twists with her smile—

Light and shadow battle, spreading wide. Beams of cutting light shatter buildings—people are underneath, watching, but the Great King's attention is focused on the Queen—he doesn't spare a thought to command them to run, to save themselves—and they wait, placid, unthinking, his forgotten puppets, his forgotten toys—

Save them! I shout at the Queen, but she pays me no mind.

She has her war. She has the full attention of the King. She has all she wants.

The Great Queen loves the fight more than she cares for me. More than she can care for any being smaller than herself.

Only through their vessels could they see humanity. Only humbled could they love us.

Unfettered, they comprehend only the thrill of war, the joy of testing themselves on the battleground, of understanding themselves through the measure of each inflicted wound, each inch of ground gained. This is their great, godly love story.

And in their wake, we suffer.

I fight against the Queen, against her flood of power, for dominion of my body. It's like banging my fists against a stone wall.

My body. My hands. The ability to shutter my eyelids. All of it was once mine. *Why did I think she could better wield my power than I could?*

Why did I think the King should decide for us all?

Pain. My body is on fire. I scream—my scream bleeds into the Queen's.

The Great King's light touches us, bathing us in scalding heat—

We're outmatched—we're losing. With his many crystals, the King is still stronger.

The scent of burning stone—burning hair—I hold myself tight—

An explosion rends the air—a shock wave rumbles through me. The Great King lets go. The pain cuts out—the light disappears.

I gasp, catching my breath. The Queen's power cools and soothes my skin, healing me. *What happened?*

A plume of gray smoke rises from the palace.

The King's light dims. He's formed himself into a giant man of light, and he staggers. From towers, lightlines run like chains to his arms, his wrists, his legs, his neck. He's being pulled in a dozen directions by his crystals—what were the safeguards of his power have become his tethers.

My pulse quickens. The lightlines in the first ring are gone. The smoke from the palace . . . Could it be his crystal vessel?

From a tower in the second, a great bird takes to the sky. The kinnari. A warmth fills my chest, watching it rise into the air. It came back. But how did it destroy—

It bears a rider. A man with dark curls. Dalca. He lets out a howl—a war cry. My heart skips a beat.

A rattling *boom*—an explosion—a billow of glittering dust rises from the tower's opening. The lightline disappears, as if it were a thread cut by immense shears.

The kinnari screeches, and another answers. My heart leaps—another kinnari, another rider—in the blue of the Nosca—Izamal, who was ready to leave this city behind—

From a different tower comes a *boom*—

They're destroying the crystals.

The Queen moves my body. She clothes us in great swaths of shadow, raising us to the level of the King. With each angle, his face changes, like looking through a prism. But all his faces are sneering.

She sends her shadows to devour him, taking advantage of the unexpected aid. Dark creatures lap at his legs, tendrils of cloudsmoke reaching across his body. The Great King thrashes, but he is fixed in place.

One by one, the crystals are destroyed and the lightlines are cut. With each, the Great King is incrementally freed—but he also dims as the store of his power is destroyed.

Destruction rains down on the lightstruck, on the people of the city, who are enslaved by a vision of what should be. I am no different. That vision seduced me.

When? When did I fall for his plan? Was it when the King showed me the garden, the vision of my happy self? Was it when I saw the statue of the Stormender? When I woke up and saw the beautified, sanitized story on those mosaic walls? When did I start—when did I choose the life I felt I ought to live instead of trusting myself to find my way? I put shields up out of fear—shields that made me blind.

Did I come back to the world of the living to spend this precious time trying to measure up to a statue? Did freedom frighten me so much that I chose submission instead?

A kinnari bird hovers above, over the blasted-open roof. A dark-haired rider disembarks and leaps down, landing between me and the crystal.

Dalca rises from a crouch and offers me a small smile. His chest heaves with exertion. "Vesper. Are you all right?"

A touch of soot on his cheekbone. Crystal dust glitters from his hair.

I'm not all right.

A shout. Dalca glances over his shoulder. Izamal and his kinnari take off from the roof of the Ven. Clutched in the kinnari's claws is a man with white hair. Cas. He wields a mirror shield, deflecting light-lines. They fly to us.

The kinnari perches on the half-destroyed wall as Cas and Izamal drop down. "Half the crystals are destroyed," Iz says. "And look, I've picked up a stray. Seems he's gotten rid of his old master."

I can't turn my head to see them clearly—is Cas himself?

"Vesper," Dalca says. "The vessel is destroyed. Can you do it? Convince the King to take a human vessel?" Dalca pauses as the Queen pays him no mind. "Vesper. Look at me, please."

The Queen's attention is on the King, at the lightstruck crowding around the base of the tower. I catch glimpses of Dalca from my peripheral vision—picking out their voices, though they're muffled by the howling wind and the sizzling light.

Dalca sucks in a shaky breath. "Vesper . . . are you still in there?" And to Cas and Iz: "The Queen's taken her over."

"Vesper was in control only a little while ago," Cas says in a shaking, quiet voice. "She saved me. She spoke to me."

Iz: "If the Great King won't choose a human vessel—even if he already has chosen someone, we have no way of knowing who—"

"He might not have," Cas says. "If he had chosen someone, surely they would have accepted already."

Dalca says, "Not if they were afraid. If we had time, we could find them, help them, convince them . . . We have no time. We have no choice. We have to use the Regia's mark."

I grow cold. No. After all this, to return to the Regia's mark . . . Cas will talk sense into him. But he says nothing.

Dalca undoes the ties of his armor. "My scars follow the lines of the mark, for the most part. Help me fill in the places where my body healed over."

Cas moves to his side. "All I've got is mancer's charcoal. Won't be pretty."

Dalca barks a humorless laugh. "What a pity."

The tip of Cas's charcoal hovers over Dalca's collarbone. It wavers. No one knows better than Cas the consequences of his next move. Connecting the mark—trapping the King inside Dalca—he'll lose his friend. He'll be condemning him to the same fate Dalca's mother couldn't bear, to the fate he himself just woke from, to being a puppet of the Great King. To my fate.

Dalca meets his eyes. "Do it."

"*Stop*." A faint voice. It comes from the crystal. The violet spectral. I can't believe it. He's alive. So faint I can hardly make him out, but he's there. "Don't . . . You don't need it."

Dalca bristles. "What do you want?"

"You were chosen, Dalca. That's why I exist. Have you not wondered what the spectrals are? We're the King's chosen vessels."

"What trickery is this?" Dalca says.

"Regia Nayeli and Regia Memnon were not chosen," Cas says, naming Dalca's mother and grandfather.

"They were," the spectral says in a voice faint as air. "He chose your mother and grandfather after they had put on the mark, after he was trapped in their bodies. He meant it as a compromise. They could undo the Regia's mark and accept the King in the way of the vessels of old. But they never understood. You . . . When you held him off to let Vesper take in the Storm . . . he chose you in truth . . . in the old way, in the way of vessels from legend, in the way Vesper was chosen by the Great Queen. All you have to do is accept the bond, and he's yours."

Dalca looks at his hands. Something sharp glimmers in his eyes. He wore that same look in the underworld—relief that he could put down his burdens. But no, there's something a little different . . . His shoulders loosen, and he raises his head, meeting the spectral's gaze. "Why help us?" Dalca says. "When you have fought us at every step?"

"I know you," the spectral says. "You are the better me."

Dalca holds his gaze for a long moment. He nods.

To Iz and Cas, he says: "Go now. Finish the crystals."

He waits till they've each called a kinnari and taken to the sky.

In a graceful movement, he rises to his feet. "Great King," Dalca bellows. "You once chose me. And now I accept you."

All is silent.

A beam of light engulfs him, sinks into him. His eyes open wide. The light shines through his skin—a red-gold glow like sunlight through closed eyelids—it glows from within him as though he's swallowed the sun. The veins and bones of his face and hands grow starkly visible against his skin; through his clothes and armor, light shines from the seams at his sides, down his legs, across the broad angle of his shoulders.

Dalca lets out a muffled scream. The last flicker of violet light disappears; the crystal dims out.

A thrill goes through the Great Queen, her blood—our blood—hot with triumph. Two human vessels, ruling together, in the ways of old. *This is it.* Her dream.

But a sneaking ambition worms through her heart—my heart—delicious and dark—

The old ways are not enough. A greater victory is at hand.

A true victory. A final victory.

The King cannot fight as he is being drawn into his vessel—

The cold, sweet ambition fills us up. *The King will end.*

She draws her army of shadows into her arms, focusing it, aiming it, readying herself—

In a single heartbeat, I understand what will happen: the Queen sees only the King, hungers for his destruction, barely registering the insignificant man who would be his vessel.

Dalca's jaw is clenched as he's consumed by light, his hands grasping at air—agony and determination warring across his features—

The Queen will kill him. She cares nothing for him.

But I do.

I'd been afraid. That without the Queen, I'm nothing. That the Stormender is more important than Vesper.

She moves my body, and she doesn't spare a thought for me. Vesper is gone.

This is what it feels like to be nothing.

The Queen speaks in my mind. *Do not complain. You accepted me. You chose me.*

I've given up my own power. A power I didn't know I had. I had it long before the Queen, and I'll have it long after she's gone.

I find my voice. *Your power . . . blinded me to my own.*

She shoves me deeper into a small corner of my body and leaves me to wither here while she wages her war with the King.

But do I not know my own body?

My tongue knows every ridge in the cavern of my mouth. My feet know every mile I've ever walked, every step of every dance, every trip and fall. My lungs know my every breath, my lips know my every word—those I spoke and those I swallowed—

I know my scars—the sitar-string burn on my palm, the dark starburst on my knee from when I was eight and enamored with running, the pale faded scars on my left pointer finger marking every time the kitchen knife slipped out of my grip, the splinter that bored its way under my skin and masquerades as a birthmark—I know my body's oddities, my minuscule peculiarities—the way my veins run blue at my wrists and violet at my elbows, that I can leap further if I lead with my right foot, the way that when I stretch, my back pops in three rising notes, always the same crescendo—

Each of the secrets of my body is a way back to myself—each scar, each memory a door—

The Queen rages. She fights me with cold and thunder, with bone-splitting pain, with pounding-heart terror—

A numb prickling rises across my skin from my toes up to the roots of my hair—my arms are leaden—my little finger moves—

I take my body back inch by inch—

The Queen's power rises in a wave, a crushing wave—it crashes against my chest, and it aims to drown my heart, my will.

But I raise my hands. I smile with my own lips. My body is mine.

Dalca meets my eyes.

Dalca braces himself, feet set wide in a warrior's stance. Light streams into him—more and more—as each lightline snaps, as each crystal is destroyed and more of the captured light is released—all of it is drawn into Dalca's body.

The light grows soft as it sinks into him, taking a new form, like a star that's fallen from the sky. Perhaps it is the Great King's truest form, unlike the hard lightlines and the fractured spectrals.

Dalca draws it in as I once drew the unbound storm. Blood splatters to the ground as his skin splits along his scars.

Our places are reversed, and it is worse on this side. It's brutal to see him torn apart. To know it's his fight, that I can do little.

I reach his side. His eyelashes are wet, and the light inside him shines through the tiny droplets, casting prisms.

Lightlines snap one by one as more towers fall. The kinnari birds have given the Wardana might in the air.

A whoop of joy. Izamal. Even from this distance his wide grin is visible, as he hangs from a kinnari's leg, tossing another explosive into a tower.

The light is searing Dalca from the inside out. The Storm killed me, just about. Will the light kill him?

He breathes. "Vesper . . ."

"I'm here."

"He won't be bound."

"He will. You can do it."

"If he takes me over, will you—"

"He won't. Leave him no quarter. You're not afraid of anything. You saved our people."

"That's not—"

"If you can't trust yourself, trust me."

He searches my eyes. Written in them so clearly is a plea, a flicker of hope. A fierce desire rises in me—I want him to see himself the way I see him, to know his idea of himself isn't the truth.

"Trust me," I say. I grab his hand and lean my forehead against his. "What do you feel?"

His eyes flicker shut and his voice comes soft. "The light . . . it was an antidote . . . born from all the hopelessness of all those who live here. All their terror of what the future holds, all their shock and amazement at how big the world became once the storm was lifted—how small they became when the world grew so much larger—how their questions grew, even as their understanding shrank . . . When the Storm ended, their dreams and their fears expanded to the infinities of the great beyond, to the horizon and past it—they feared that they did not matter, for how could they? Everything became inconsequential, their families, their homes, their dominion . . . The light . . . it showed them a way through it all. A way to matter."

His eyes open. Light shines through them; they're no longer blue, but suffused with white light.

"This is how it begins," he rasps. "Us as Regias, as powerful as gods. And they'll look to us as their saviors. To give them a sense of meaning."

We could do it again. We could parade as saviors, bask in their applause and praise, soak in their worship. And when we die, we'll be replaced by the next vessels. We would continue this cycle, risking leaving the fate of future generations to the whims of individual vessels. This system was broken by the sin of a single madman, who stabbed a lover and doomed his city to centuries of despair.

Dalca gasps. "And that light . . . pinpricks of it are in all of them. The lightstruck. I can see them, little flickers. In everyone that he's touched . . . in Cas, in Izamal . . ."

Izamal? How could Izamal be lightstruck?

Another explosion comes from a tower in the fourth. The kinnari flies freely, with Iz on its back. He's not lightstruck—with the Queen's power, I search for him, find him—his curse is visible as a shadow that twines with his heart.

Of all the stormtouched, only Izamal conquered his curse—I'd never heard of anyone controlling his curse the way he does. No one . . . except for—

Ragno. Ragno could become glass at will; he could control the shards of his body—and Ragno was both lightstruck and cursed.

Izamal said there was a moment where he saw his path, his purpose. He saw how to turn his curse into something that served him—into a blessing. Is that part of the light?

The King saw what I wanted. What I desired. Not just little petty desires, but the great desire for meaning. For purpose.

The Queen shows us our deepest fears, what we must overcome— and perhaps the King can show us what means most to us, what we can strive toward.

"I can give everyone a drop of the Queen," I say. "Divide her great power, that great river, into all these people."

A little voice whispers inside my head—I've gotten so used to hearing the Great Queen's voice, but it's not hers, it's mine—and it says, *If you give up this power, if you give up being a perfect vessel, you give up being a hero.*

"Yes," Dalca says. "I can divert the light. Disperse it into thousands of glimmers. Just as he struck the light into them. I can split the King amongst them all. The King would no longer be concentrated. He would no longer bend them to his command."

His other hand reaches for mine. I take it, hold both close to my heart. "They'll be cursed. Stormtouched."

He nods. "And struck by the light. All of them . . ."

For centuries our people lived under the vessel of a god, fearing the power that they didn't understand and would never wield, hopeless to do anything to change the course of history on their own.

I look into Dalca's eyes. And the Great King and Great Queen see each other.

Maybe we could rule as those ancient Regias did, and create a paradise. But it would only last as long as we do. The city would fall prey to anyone seeking to abuse power, and the cycle would repeat. The war would begin once more.

Even now—the Queen within me and the King in him—they claw at us, aching to resume their endless war. If we let them do what they willed, they would never stop. Not for a human life, not for hundreds, not even if they razed the entire city down to stone and ruin. These gods are so immense, so ageless, that they do not see us as their equals; they're blind to our worth, and careless of the suffering they leave in their wake. Everyone has suffered, from the smallest child living in fear, to the vessels of the gods themselves. Vessels carry too much. Too much power, too much pain, too many of our people's hopes, too many of their fears. It's a weight no one should bear alone. Not the Regia. Not me. Not Dalca.

We must deny our gods their ruthless instincts. We must deny them dominion. We must split them. Shatter them amongst our people. Let their powers sink into the blood of every last person, let them be passed from parent to child forevermore. Let every person carry within them a fragment of the Queen, and one of the King. Let our gods wage their war on a battlefield the size of a human heart. Let every person decide for themselves the victor.

"Let them all be gods," I whisper to him.

The power comes easily. My power.

I call a rain. The first drops of it fall on my cheekbones, on my lips. I pour the Queen's power into each droplet. All whom the rain touches will gain her power.

Light beams from Dalca—he's at the heart of a thousand-pointed star. He lets the King's power go.

The light pierces the raindrops—casting hundreds of thousands of prisms.

The enchanted rain falls on all of our people, reaching every person in the city, every person in the caravan, those who race to our aid in sprinters and ramblers, and those who've stayed behind. It falls on the wilds. It falls as far as the eye can see.

The Queen leaves me drop by drop.

I hold on to Dalca, and he holds on to me. His eyes fill with wonder as he takes in the glimmering, glittering rain. Rain like jewels, sparks of falling color, reflecting on rooftops, on streets, on spires of the wilds, on the upturned faces of our people. Reflecting on my clothes, my hands, his skin, his eyes.

I rise to my feet, and he joins me. My heart is calm and steady, and I am sure of one thing: I know who I am.

And maybe they won't call us heroes. Heroes are for fighting a war. What we've done is end it.

EPILOGUE

I've chased the horizon. I've seen a black mountain wearing crowns of white-blue ice—and, when the wind blew, all the black rose up in a cloud, as thousands of leathery-winged creatures took to the sky.

I've seen a lake as large as the third ring, guarded by serpentine creatures, where strange things were submerged, where jutted the spires of a sunken fortress.

I've walked through meadows of clovers and mottled flowers that glowed at night like stars of a thousand colors.

I've filled a journal with drawings, with maps, with memories. My bags have grown heavy with samples: a pressing of glowing flowers; a cutting of the shed skin of an unknown creature, that never cools, providing the heat of a fire even on a cold night; a half dozen silvery blue scales that blunted every sword and axe we took to them.

The horizon still beckons. But lately . . . my longing has grown quiet. Another hunger grows. A wondering, for what we left behind . . .

I look down again at the letter in my hands and tuck it into my pocket.

"Vesp," Cas says, bringing me out of my thoughts. "Will you do the honors?" He holds out a chisel, gesturing to the crystal beside him.

I engrave the last of the ikon onto the surface—he's left me a fairly easy part—and it takes but a minute to finish and to blow away the crystal dust that's settled into the lines.

Jhuno and Gamara heave the crystal up and set it upon the stone plinth. They give it a twist, and it falls into place.

I hold my breath.

A light flickers in the heart of the crystal—it ignites, flaring bright, and a lightline beams into it. Courtesy of Cas's ikon, this one is powered not by the King, but by the sun's rays.

Cas whoops. He lifts Gamara into the air and tries the same with Jhuno, who merely stares him down. Somewhere around the fourth month of our travels, the shadows haunting Cas's eyes lightened. And though he still won't tell me what he sees when he looks in the mirror, he no longer flinches from it. Whatever may come from the war within him—the one between his curse and the light—he's prepared to meet it.

And just like that, the last station is operational. In six months, we've set up six stations.

Jhuno and Gamara set a lightship on the line—one that was made using parts from the many that fell and shattered when the King's lightlines disappeared.

The lightship's sail unfurls, and it settles into the lightline. It holds steady.

"That'll do," Cas says.

They look to me. They know what I've been feeling, and my own yearning is reflected in their eyes.

I hop into the lightship. "Let's go home."

The world speeds past. We make the exchange at the next five stations, interrupting a game of cards at one and stopping for a meal at the third. We're soon sailing over the sixth ring.

"There." Gamara points.

The tip of the palace. More and more of the city comes into view. My heart rises.

Familiar faces meet us at the second to last station, the last before the city. Hadria leaps to greet us, beaming. She stayed back to watch over Toran as she healed. "Where have you gone? What have you seen? Tell me everything."

"They've only just arrived, Hadria," Zerin says. She reaches for her twin, and she and Jhuno clasp hands.

Carver offers me a small smile and I return it.

"Go on," Gamara says, when she catches me looking to the city. "We'll follow."

Cas and I take the lightship to the end of the line. As the city comes into view, butterflies flutter under my skin, and I can't quite remember how to breathe.

We approach the city's tower station, jutting high over the fifth ring. The lightship slows, and with a little maneuvering toward a free dock, it slides to a stop.

"Vesper!" Izamal reaches for my arm, hauling me out onto the tower platform. Behind him is the rest of the council. I guess word of our arrival has preceded us.

Izamal thrusts pastries into my arms—burnt ones. "I've been practicing," he says, with such boyish pride that I haven't the heart to turn one down.

Imbas smiles, taking my hand and pulling me close. "Don't eat it," she murmurs in my ear. "Even his owlcat won't."

Cas plucks the untouched pastry from my hand and bites it.

Imbas sighs.

He chews. His expression flickers—his lips press together for the briefest of heartbeats, an expression only someone who spent the last year traveling with him would be able to tell was Cas's version of revulsion. Cas swallows. "It's quite good."

"Really?" Izamal says hesitantly, suspiciously.

Cas takes another bite. "Why would I lie?"

Izamal ducks his head, his cheeks pinking.

I hide my smile, and move to greet the other council members.

We're high above the fifth ring, and the streets are full. A few upturned faces peer at the dock, but most folks are going about their lives. All are both cursed and lightstruck—some battle secret wars, some have brokered peace within themselves and found new abilities, strange and wondrous. The letter in my pocket told me about them, about their powers, about how the people had given them a name: the blessed.

The last of the council moves to greet me. A man with dark hair and summer-sky blue eyes. A man who once refused his position, but who now stands among the councilors with the assured calm of one who's found his place.

Dalca. He's filled out; his skin glows. Each line and curve of his face is as familiar to me as my own. A sense of warmth rises in me at the look in his eyes. An ephemeral, electric joy. Between us, a promise hangs in the air, a possibility, one that we could reach out and grab. A new beginning.

He smiles. "Welcome home."

ACKNOWLEDGMENTS

Once more, a toast—

To you, who, by reading, have made this dream your own.

To those readers who wrote in and, kindly, bravely, shared what Vesper's story meant to them. Thank you for sharing a piece of your heart with me. I'll treasure it always.

To the stewards and the shepherds who turned this story into a book: editors and champions Emilia Rhodes and Elizabeth Agyemang; designer Joel Tippie; artist Peter Strain; marketing and publicity experts Michael D'Angelo, Anna Ravenelle, and Grace Fell; those behind the scenes, Mary Wilcox, Erika West, Heather Tamarkin, Emily Andrukaitis, Ana Deboo; and all the rest of the wonderful team at Clarion and HarperCollins.

To the incredible Molly Powell and all those in the kingdom across the ocean: Kate Keehan, Callie Robertson, Sarah Clay, Natasha Qureshi, Sophie Judge; cover artist Andrew Davis; those who made the audiobook come alive, especially Ellie Wheeldon and Rachel Petladwala; and all the rest of the extraordinary team at Hodderscape and Hodder and Stoughton.

To Tracey and Josh of Adams Literary for taking such good care of this story and finding it such wonderful homes.

To Anissa, Michael, and the marvelous folks at FairyLoot, who have shared Vesper's story with so many.

To my family and especially my parents, who have taught me much more than they could ever know.

To my friends, who have tried to teach me many things. I appreciate your efforts.

Most of all, to the light of my life.

WANT MORE?

If you enjoyed this
and would like to
find out about similar
books we publish,
we'd love you to
join our online Sci-Fi,
Fantasy and Horror
community, Hodderscape.

Visit hodderscape.co.uk for
exclusive content from our authors, news, competitions
and general musings, and feel free to comment, contribute
or just keep an eye on what we are up to.

See you there!

H🐦DDERSCAPE
NEVER AFRAID TO BE OUT OF THIS WORLD